Don Quixote of La Mancha

The Pennsylvania State University Press, University Park, Pennsylvania

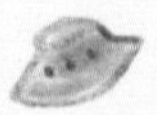

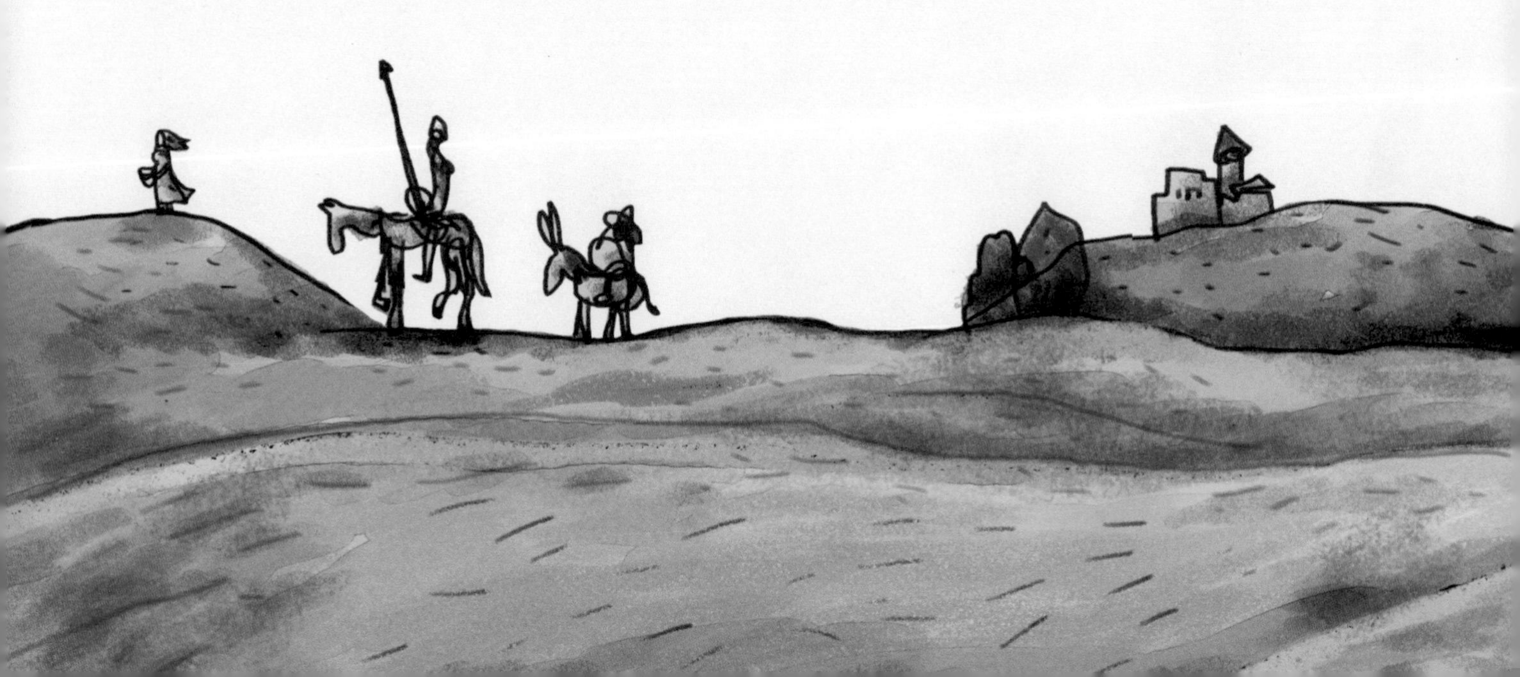

Don Quixote of La Mancha

MIGUEL de CERVANTES

ILAN STAVANS
adaptation

ROBERTO WEIL
illustrations

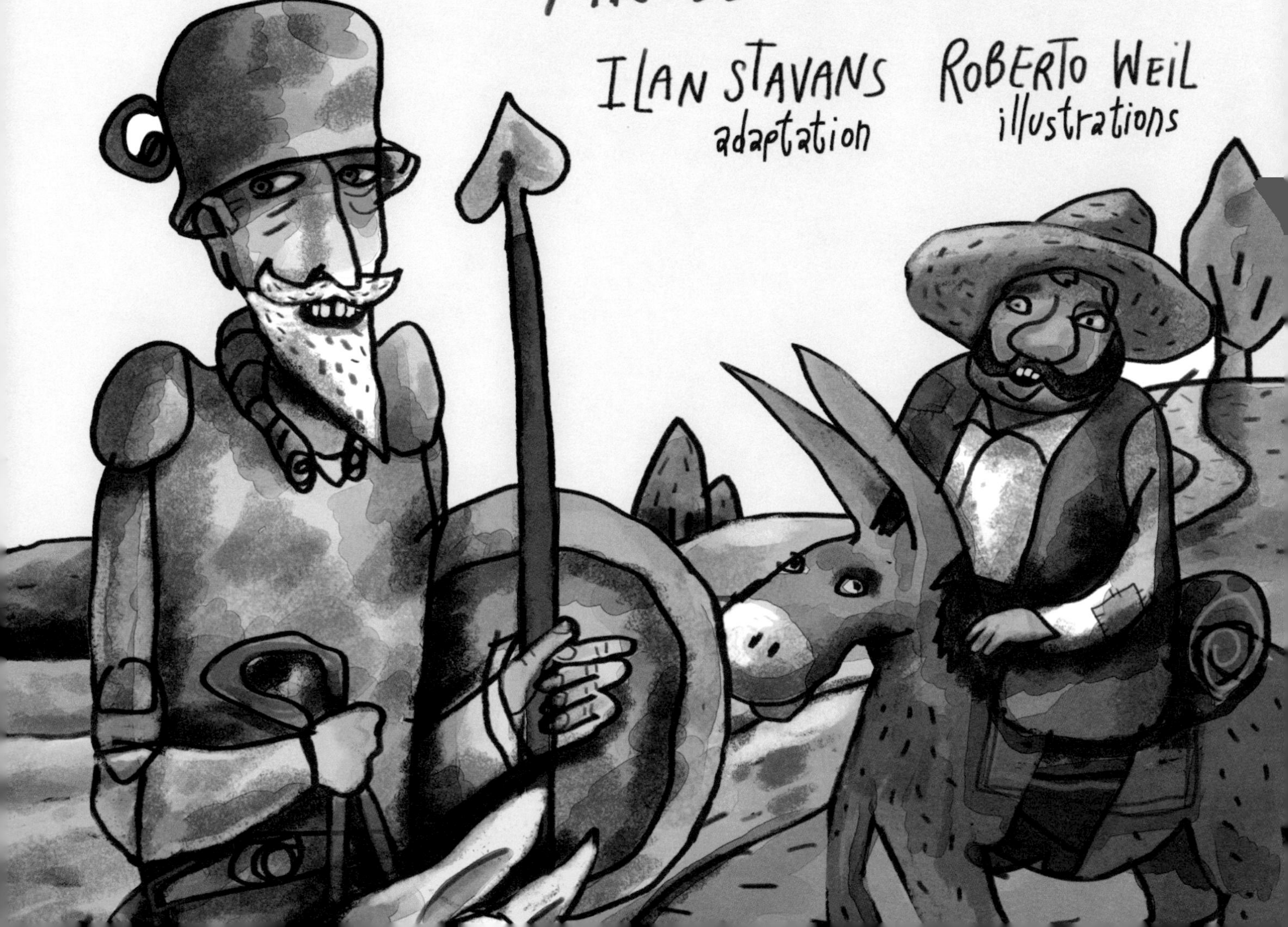

Library of Congress Cataloging-in-Publication Data

Names: Stavans, Ilan, author. | Weil, Roberto, illustrator. | Adaptation
of (work): Cervantes Saavedra, Miguel de, 1547–1616. Don Quixote. English.
Title: Don Quixote of La Mancha / Miguel de Cervantes ; adapted by
Ilan Stavans ; illustrations by Roberto Weil.
Description: University Park, Pennsylvania : The Pennsylvania
State University Press, [2018]
Summary: "An adaptation, in graphic novel format, of Don Quixote by
Miguel de Cervantes"—Provided by publisher.
Identifiers: LCCN 2018032620 | ISBN 9780271082318 (pbk. : alk. paper)
Subjects: LCSH: Quixote, Don (Fictitious character)—Comic books,
strips, etc. | Knights and knighthood—Spain—Comic books, strips, etc.
| Spain—Social life and customs—17th century—Comic books, strips, etc.
| LCGFT: Graphic novels. | Graphic novel adaptations.
Classification: LCC PN6727.S677 D66 2018 | DDC 741.5/973—dc23
LC record available at https://lccn.loc.gov/2018032620

Printed in the United States of America
Published by The Pennsylvania State University Press,
University Park, PA 16802-1003

The Pennsylvania State University Press is a member
of the Association of University Presses.

It is the policy of The Pennsylvania State University Press to use acid-free
paper. Publications on uncoated stock satisfy the minimum requirements
of American National Standard for Information Sciences—Permanence of
Paper for Printed Library Material, ANSI z39.48–1992.

Prologue

Time ripens all things.

—*Miguel de Cervantes*

No book has shaped me more than *Don Quixote of La Mancha*. I have been its inveterate reader for years. My personal library contains a vast collection of editions in myriad languages, as well as "Quixotalia"—sculptures, lithographs, stamps and postcards, lunch boxes, T-shirts, and video games. This graphic novel is a testament to my passion, and it isn't a figure of speech to say that it has taken me a lifetime to complete it.

The original novel was published in two parts, the first in 1605 and the second in 1615. They came out in advance of the so-called Age of Enlightenment, foreshadowing what was to come; human reason took center stage, even as its reach was questioned.

I have compressed Cervantes's luscious, intricate 125 chapters into just 30. On the surface, I have followed the plot, which is straightforward, rather conservatively. In an unnamed village in La Mancha, in central Spain, a hidalgo, or

nobleman, named Alonso Quijano dreams himself into a superhero, the Knight of the Sorrowful Countenance. After his first adventure, he persuades a villager, Sancho Panza, to become his squire. He also imagines a poor woman named Aldonza Lorenzo to be his sublime lady, Dulcinea del Toboso.

Together Don Quixote and Sancho travel around the desolate landscape of early seventeenth-century Spain. Their relationship goes through countless trials and tribulations that showcase their differences: one is tall and slim and rich and single and educated and idealistic, while the other is short and fat and poor and married and almost illiterate and materialistic (or maybe a better term is "practical").

The knight's mission is lofty: to mend the world. In spite of stumbling time and again, he persists in his quest, meeting an assortment of fanciful characters along the way, from an early feminist to a count and countess who play along with his lunacy in order to entertain themselves. In the end, the knight returns to his village to die, but not before an extraordinary narrative transubstantiation has taken place: Don Quixote is Sanchisized and Sancho Panza is Quixotisized. That is, in the course of their friendship, each becomes more like the other and less like himself.

Where I have deviated from the original is in pushing *Don Quixote* out of its epoch and into other settings. At one point the knight imagines himself authored by writers such as Miguel de Unamuno, Kafka, and Borges. In another chapter he comes across a drone. When he and Sancho reach Barcelona, they see the Sagrada Família, the unfinished baroque Catholic church designed by Antoni Gaudí in the 1880s. There are taxis, laptops, and mirrors. Bert and Ernie from *Sesame Street*, Sherlock Holmes, and the *Star Wars* characters R2-D2 and C-3PO make an appearance. Other similar inventions parade through the story. There is also a theatrical sequence that summarizes my one-man play set in the Amazon jungle, *The Oven* (2018). The premise behind these anachronisms is that *Don Quixote* is *un libro infinito* in which everything—past, present, and future—fits in. Every generation dreams itself into it.

In his own prologue, Cervantes asks the reader to overlook the defects of his book and instead find in it cleverness. Yet, to me, what makes a book a classic is the beauty of its defects, and *Don Quixote*, it is no secret, has plenty. I have tried to make art out of those defects.

The Venezuelan artist Roberto Weil, who is responsible for the illustrations in this volume, is a master. In 2008 I collaborated with him on *Mister Spic Goes to Washington*. Partnering with him allowed me to understand the profound ways in which his drawings combine shape and color. That graphic novel might have been the first to include entire sections in Spanglish. During a conversation, Weil suggested that we re-create all of *Don Quixote* in that hybrid language. It is fitting that it has taken us a decade to complete it. Much has happened in that interval, including, hopefully, that we have grown sharper, less unripe.

This English-language edition is being released simultaneously with a full-fledged Spanglish version. Spanglish represents more than sheer mechanical code-switching. Close to sixty million people speak some variety of this vehicle of communication today: Cubonics, Dominicanish, Nuyorican, Chicano, and so on. The type I have employed might be called "standardized" in that, with its own rhythm, worldview, and raison d'être, it is *e pluribus unum*, a sum of parts.

One last thought: among the joys of reading a classic is the knowledge that we come to the same pages seen by generations that preceded us and to which generations that succeed us will also come. It is that dialogue with the past and the future that makes the experience momentous. At this stage, I think of Don Quixote as my lifelong companion. Although the knight's words might sound foolish at times, they are incredibly wise: he is my guide, my compass, my map.

Part

I

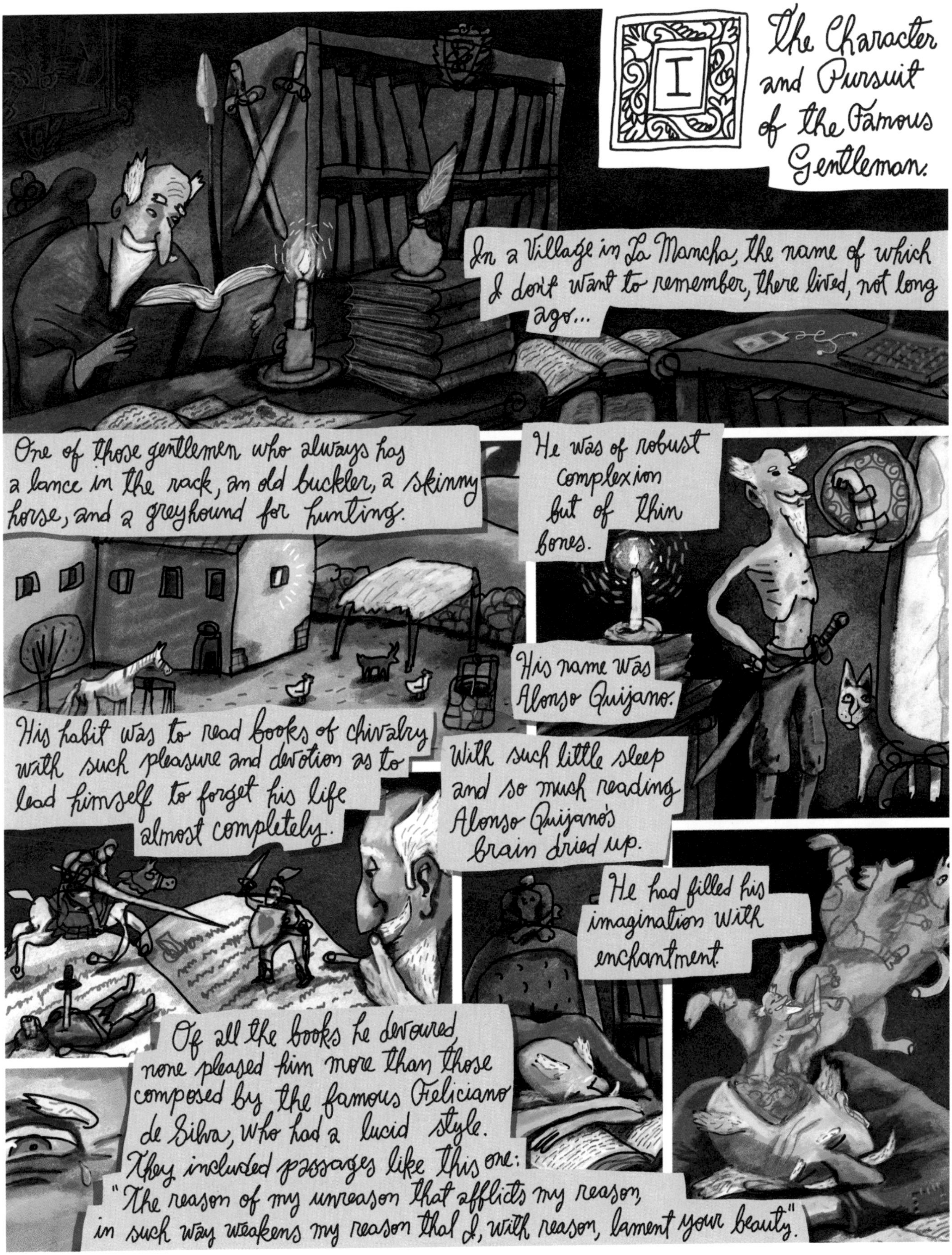
I
The Character and Pursuit of the Famous Gentleman.
In a Village in La Mancha, the name of which I don't want to remember, there lived, not long ago...
One of those gentlemen who always has a lance in the rack, an old buckler, a skinny horse, and a greyhound for hunting.
He was of robust complexion but of thin bones.
His name was Alonso Quijano.
His habit was to read books of chivalry with such pleasure and devotion as to lead himself to forget his life almost completely.
With such little sleep and so much reading Alonso Quijano's brain dried up.
He had filled his imagination with enchantment.
Of all the books he devoured, none pleased him more than those composed by the famous Feliciano de Silva, who had a lucid style. They included passages like this one: "The reason of my unreason that afflicts my reason, in such way weakens my reason that I, with reason, lament your beauty".

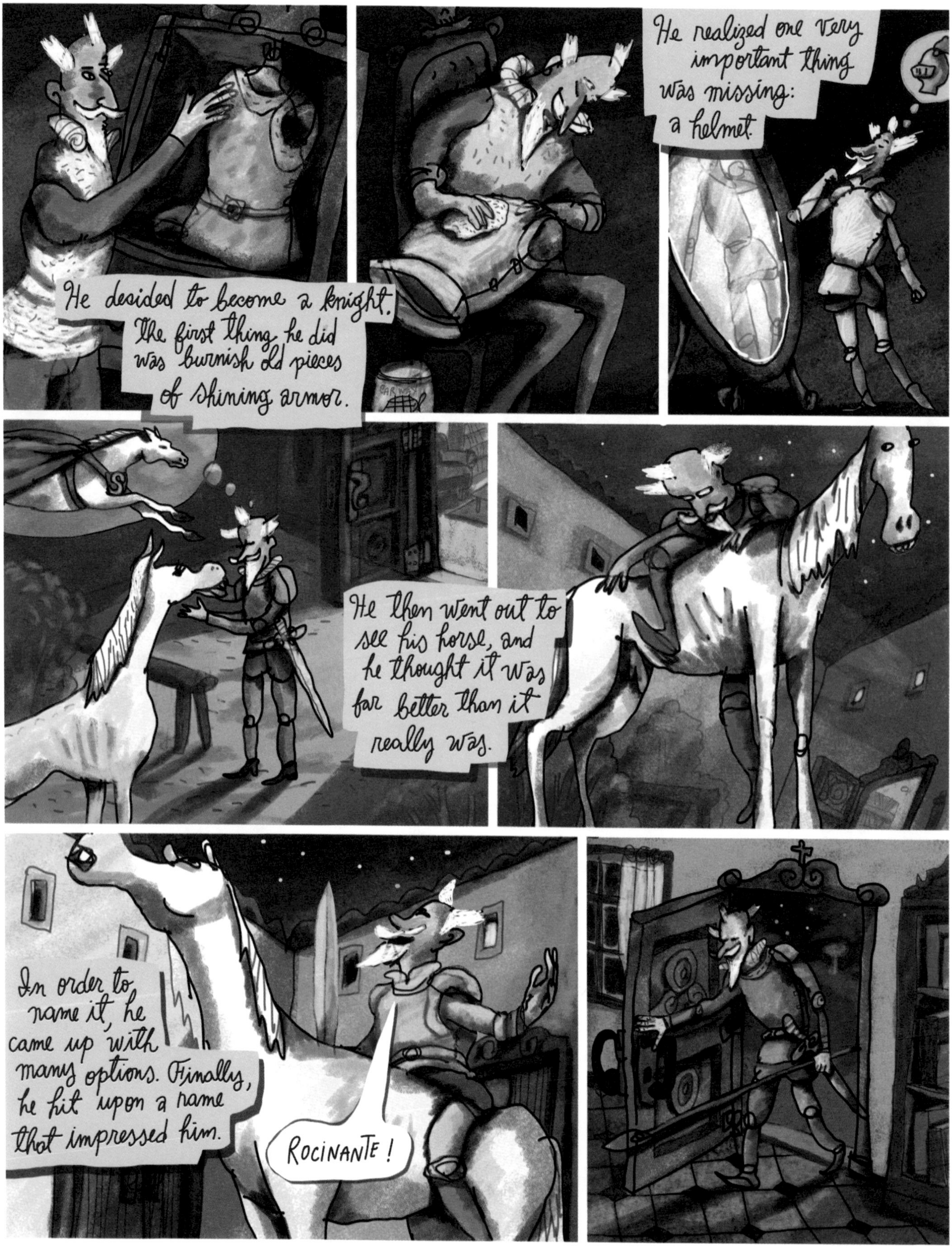
He desided to become a knight. The first thing he did was burnish old pieces of shining armor.
He realized one very important thing was missing: a helmet.
He then went out to see his horse, and he thought it was far better than it really was.
In order to name it, he came up with many options. Finally, he hit upon a name that impressed him.
ROCINANTE!

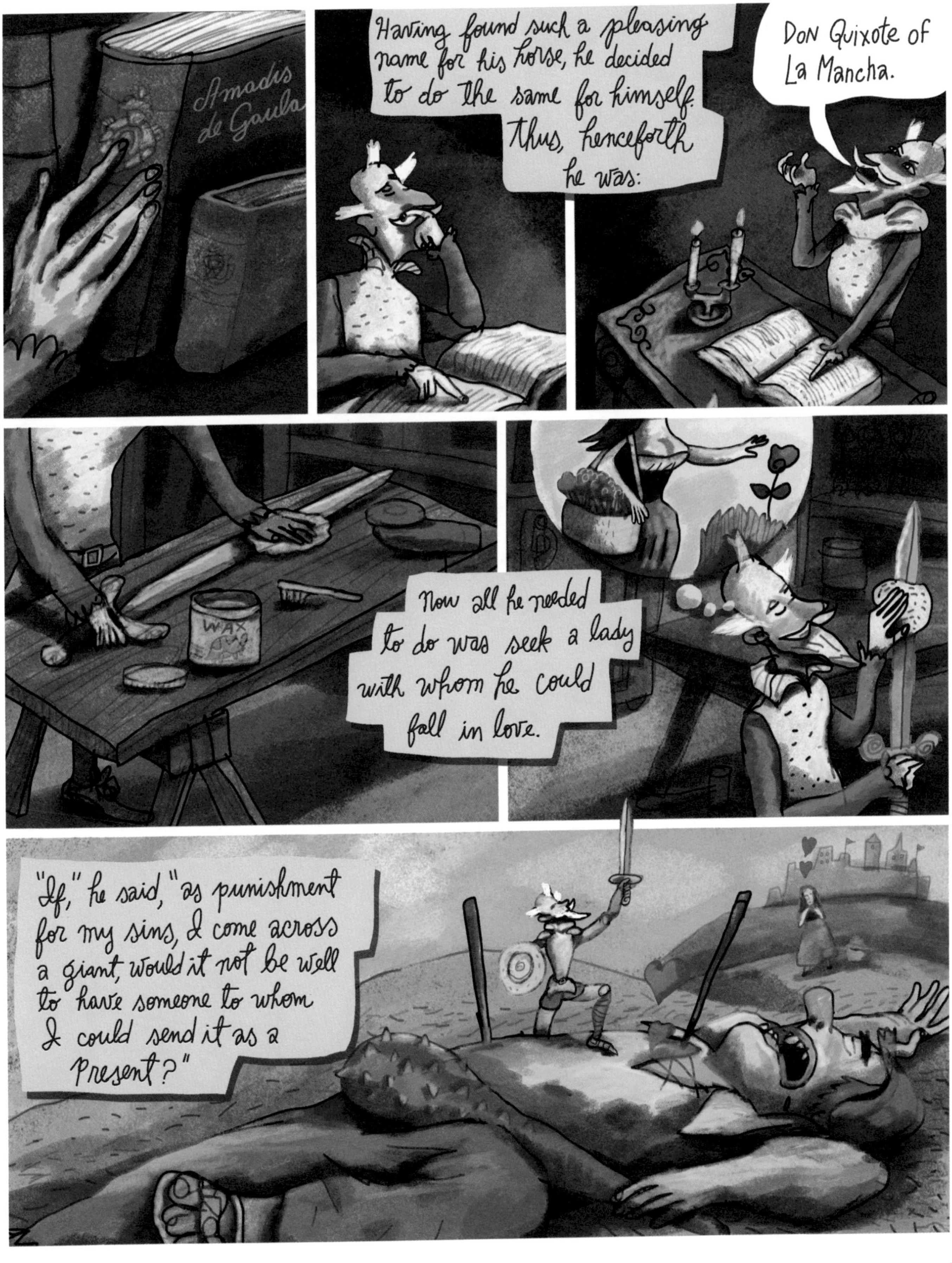

Amadis de Gaula
Having found such a pleasing name for his horse, he decided to do the same for himself. Thus, henceforth he was:
Don Quixote of La Mancha.
WAX
Now all he needed to do was seek a lady with whom he could fall in love.
"If," he said, "as punishment for my sins, I come across a giant, would it not be well to have someone to whom I could send it as a Present?"

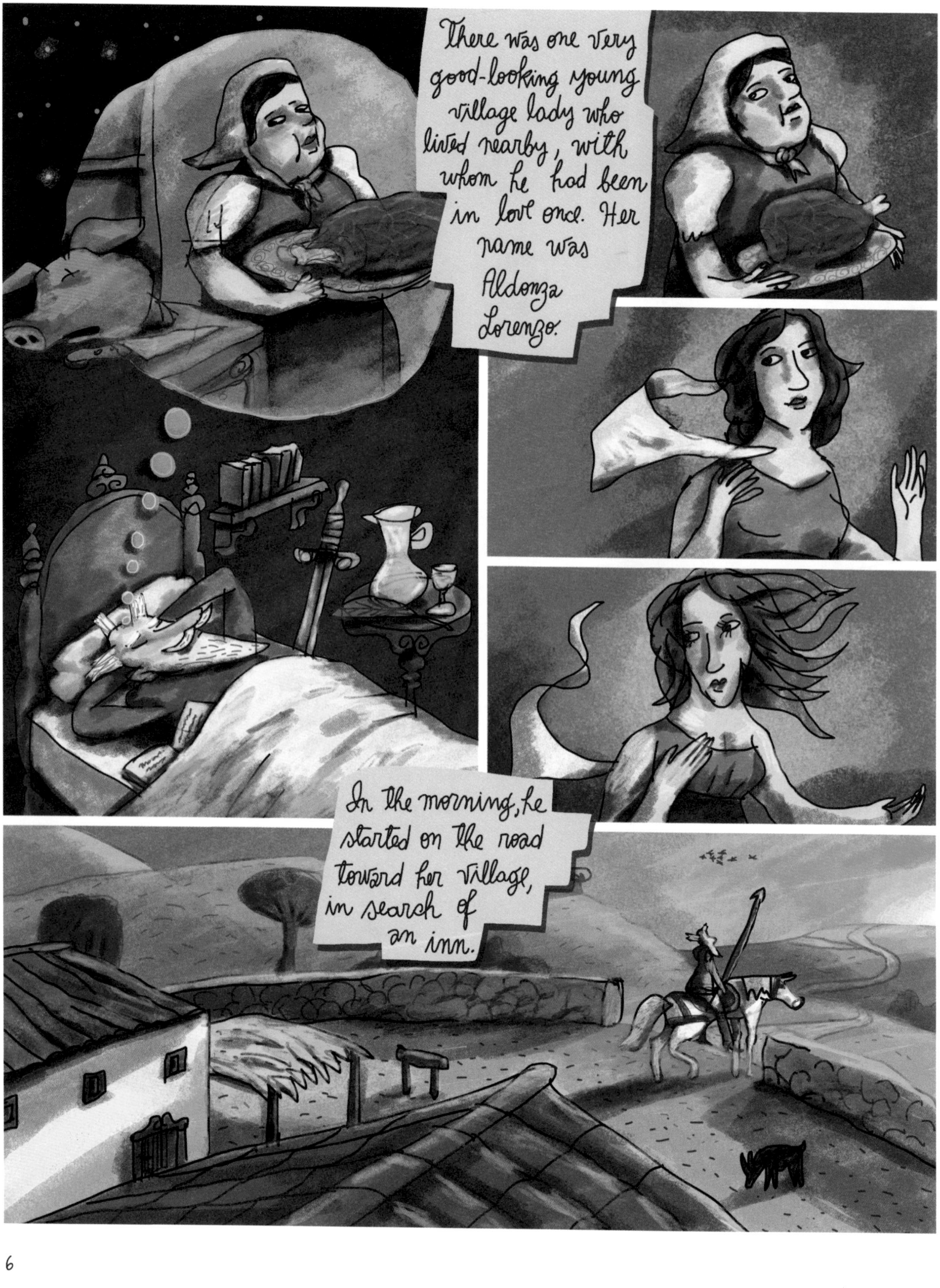
There was one very good-looking young village lady who lived nearby, with whom he had been in love once. Her name was Aldonza Lorenzo.
In the morning, he started on the road toward her village, in search of an inn.

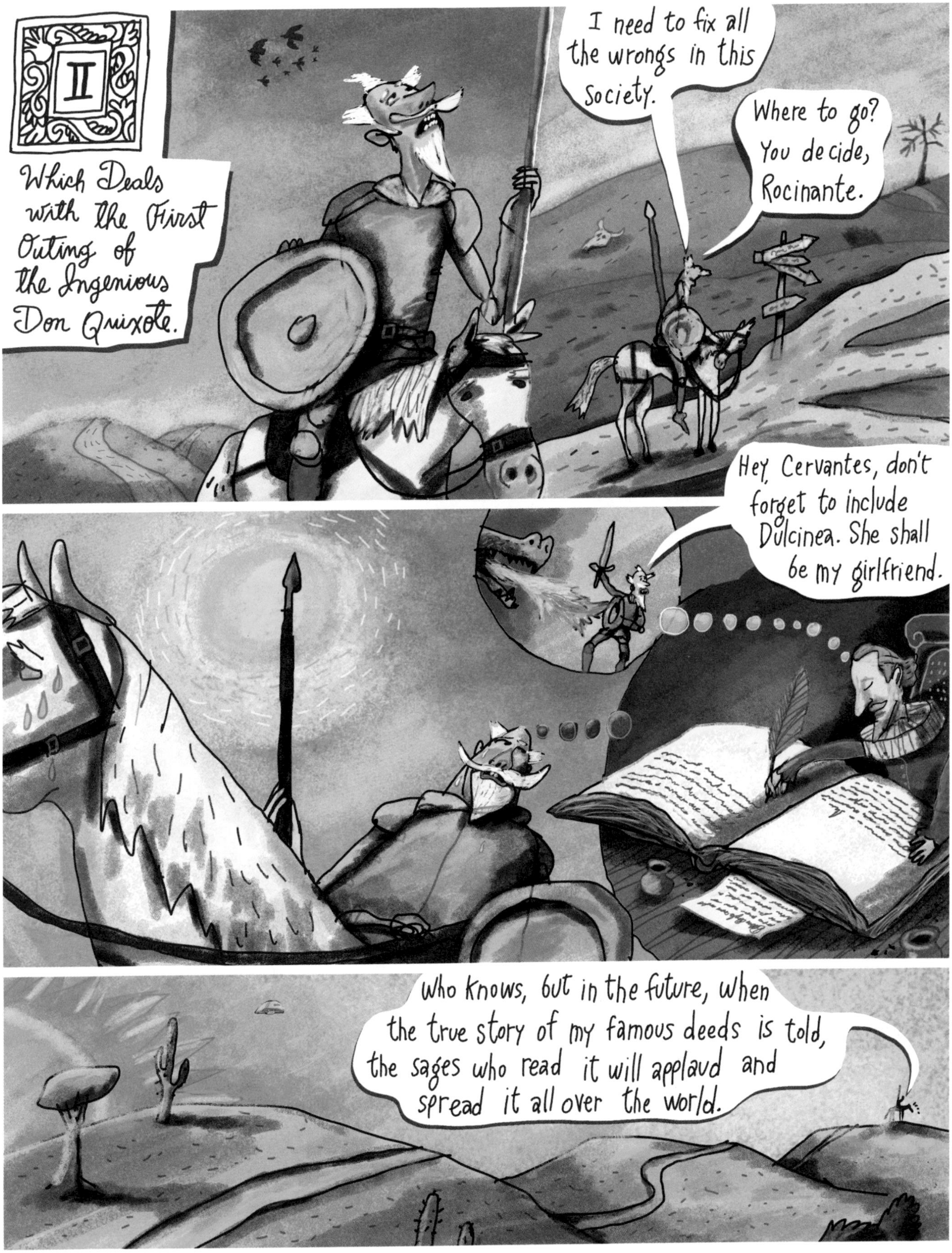
II
Which Deals with the First Outing of the Ingenious Don Quixote.
I need to fix all the wrongs in this society.
Where to go? You decide, Rocinante.
Hey, Cervantes, don't forget to include Dulcinea. She shall be my girlfriend.
Who knows, but in the future, when the true story of my famous deeds is told, the sages who read it will applaud and spread it all over the world.

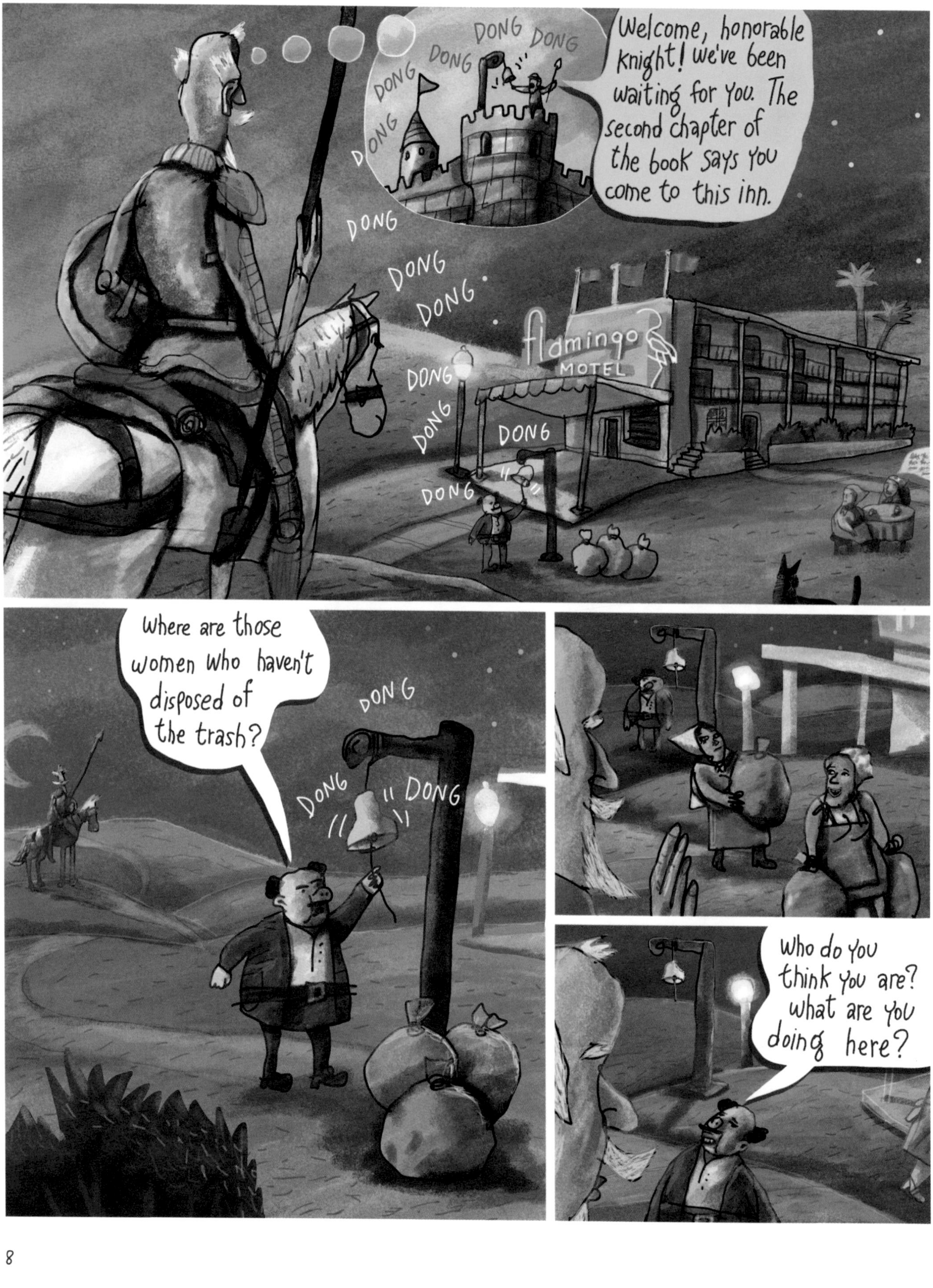
DONG DONG DONG DONG DONG D
Welcome, honorable knight! we've been waiting for you. The second chapter of the book says you come to this inn.
DONG DONG DONG DONG DONG DONG DONG
flamingo MOTEL
Where are those women who haven't disposed of the trash?
DONG DONG DONG
Who do you think you are? what are you doing here?

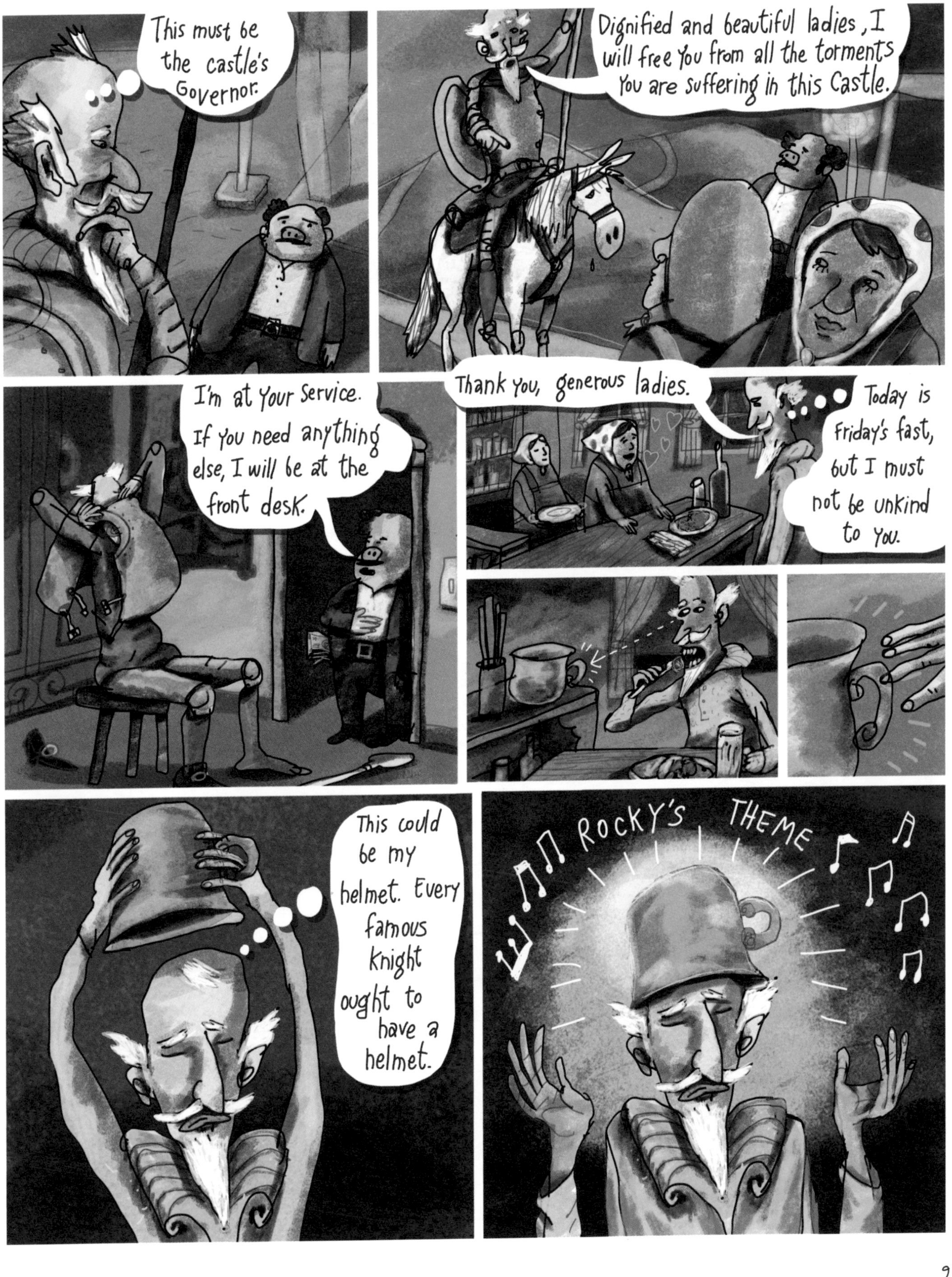
This must be the castle's Governor.
Dignified and beautiful ladies, I will free you from all the torments you are suffering in this Castle.
I'm at your service. If you need anything else, I will be at the front desk.
Thank you, generous ladies.
Today is Friday's fast, but I must not be unkind to you.
This could be my helmet. Every famous Knight ought to have a helmet.
ROCKY'S THEME

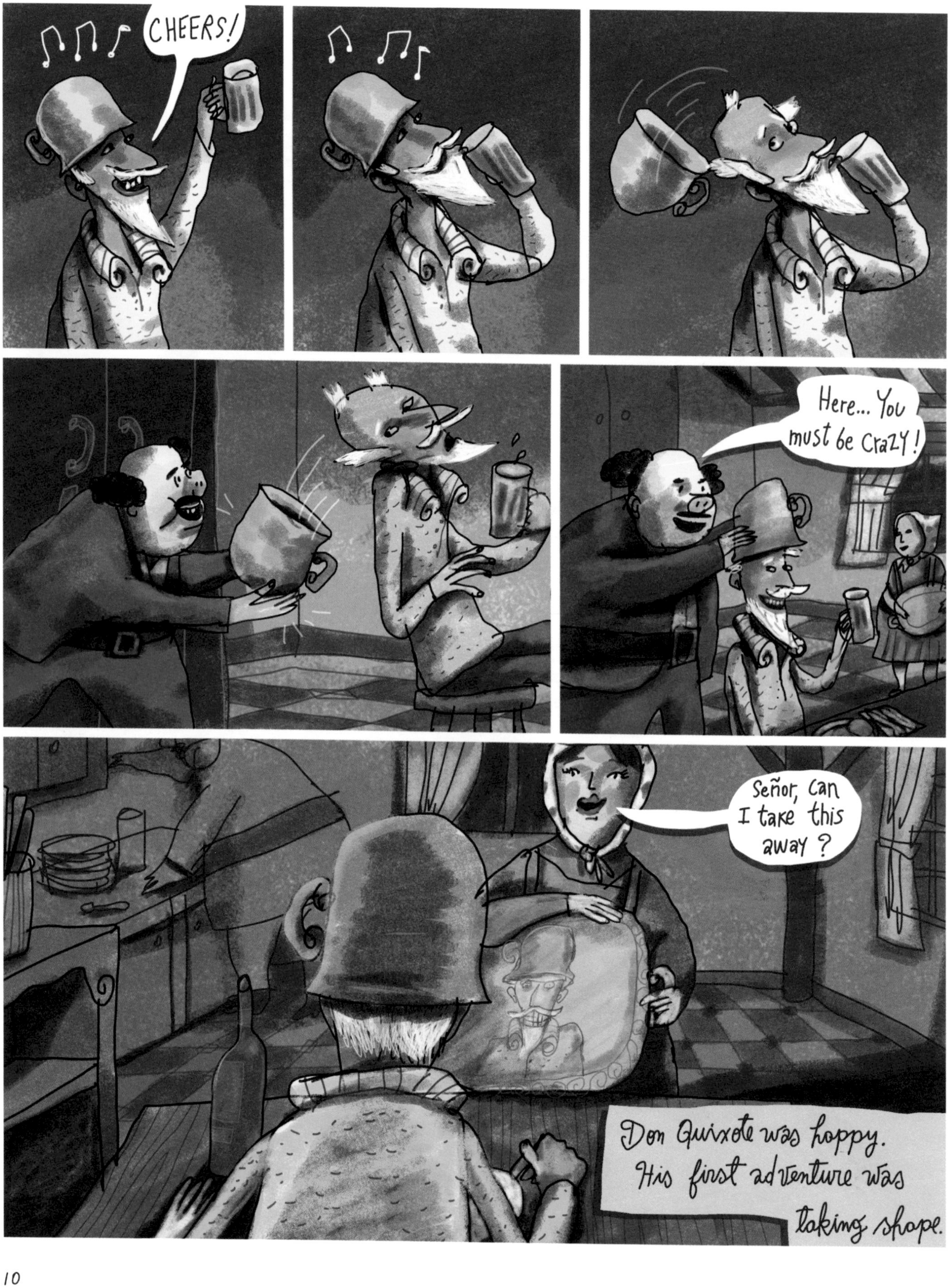
CHEERS!
Here... You must be crazy!
Señor, can I take this away?
Don Quixote was happy. His first adventure was taking shape.

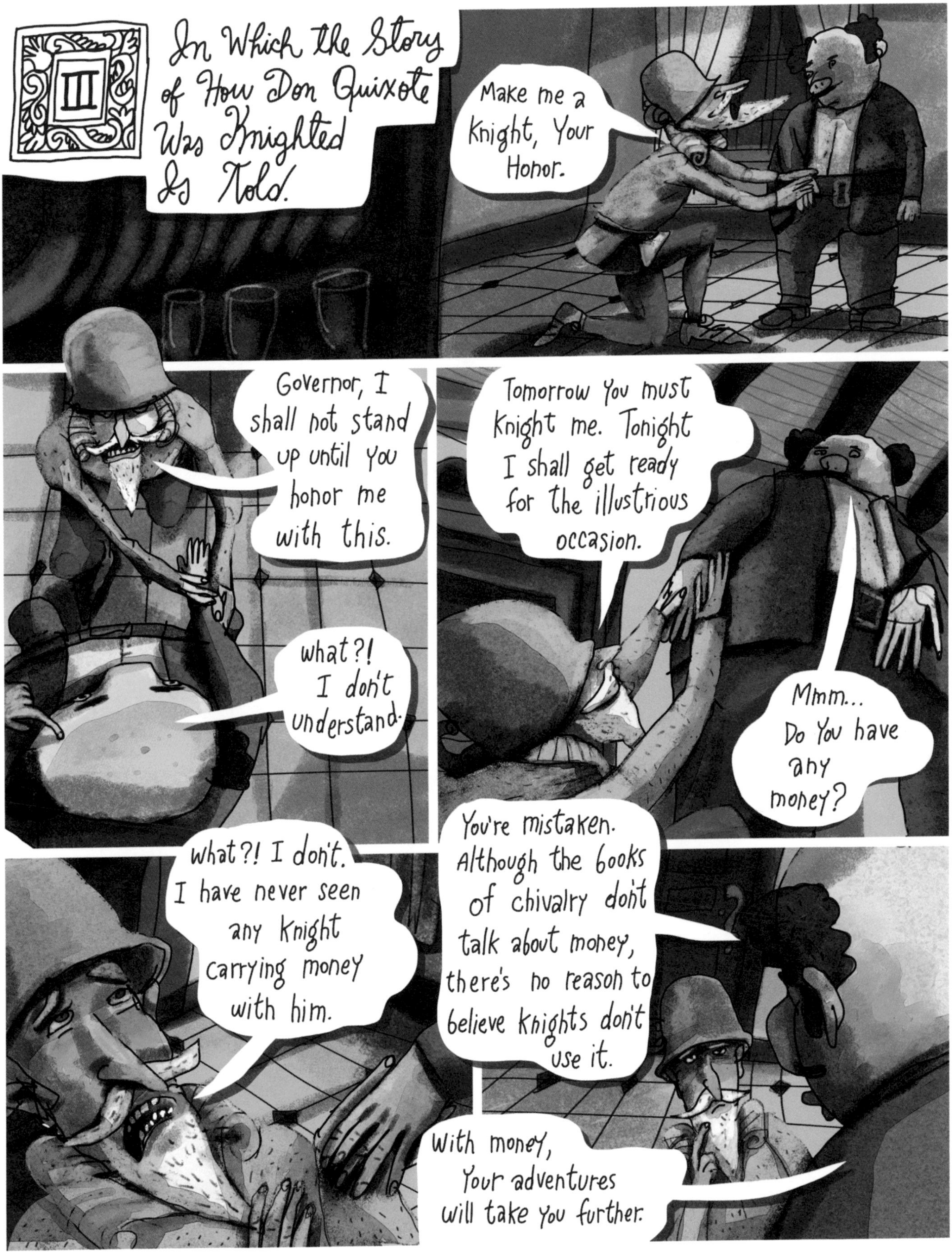
III
In Which the Story of How Don Quixote Was Knighted Is Told.
Make me a Knight, Your Honor.
Governor, I shall not stand up until you honor me with this.
what?! I don't understand.
Tomorrow you must Knight me. Tonight I shall get ready for the illustrious occasion.
Mmm... Do you have any money?
what?! I don't. I have never seen any knight carrying money with him.
You're mistaken. Although the books of chivalry don't talk about money, there's no reason to believe knights don't use it.
With money, your adventures will take you further.

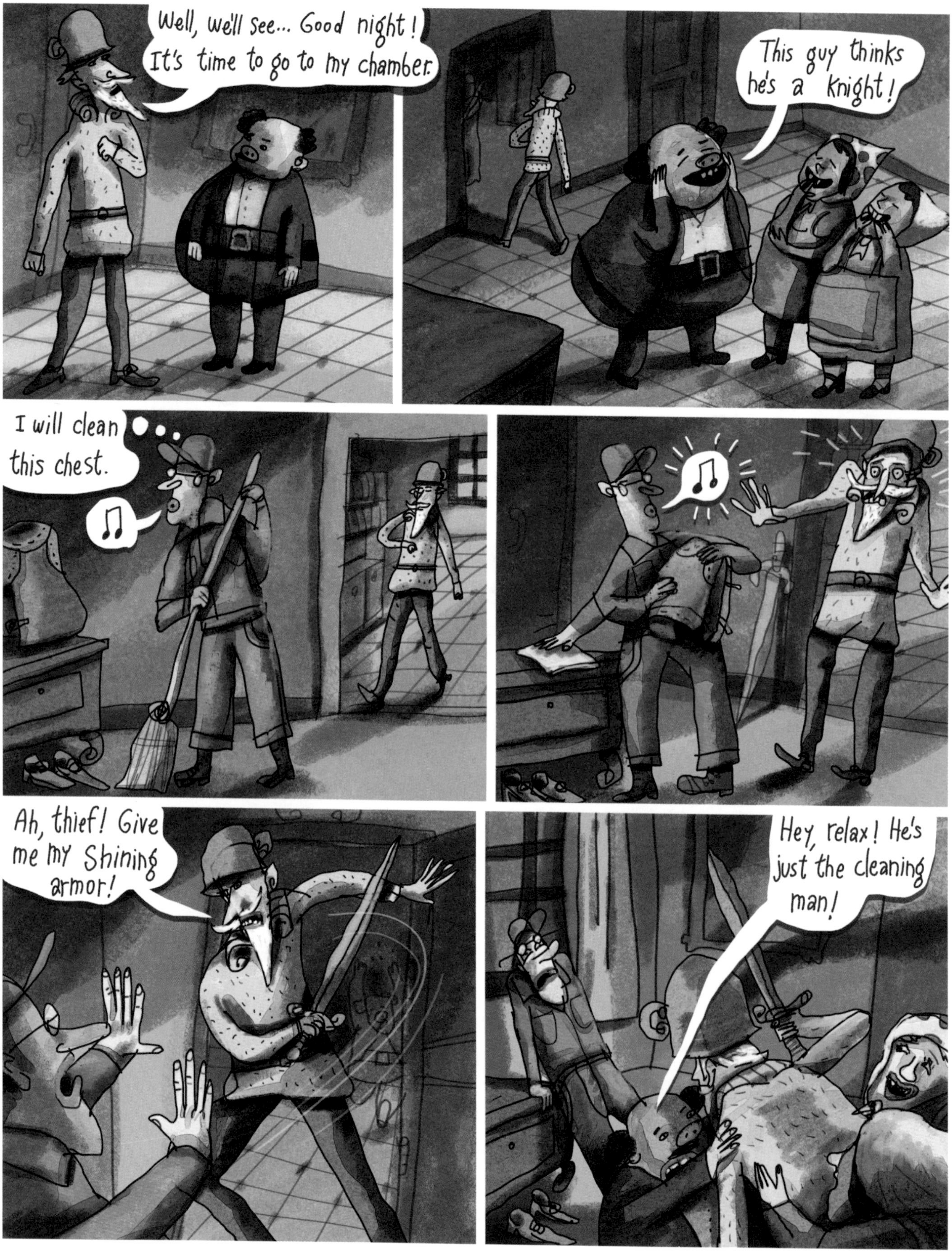
Well, we'll see... Good night! It's time to go to my chamber.
This guy thinks he's a knight!
I will clean this chest.
♫
♫
Ah, thief! Give me my Shining armor!
Hey, relax! He's just the cleaning man!

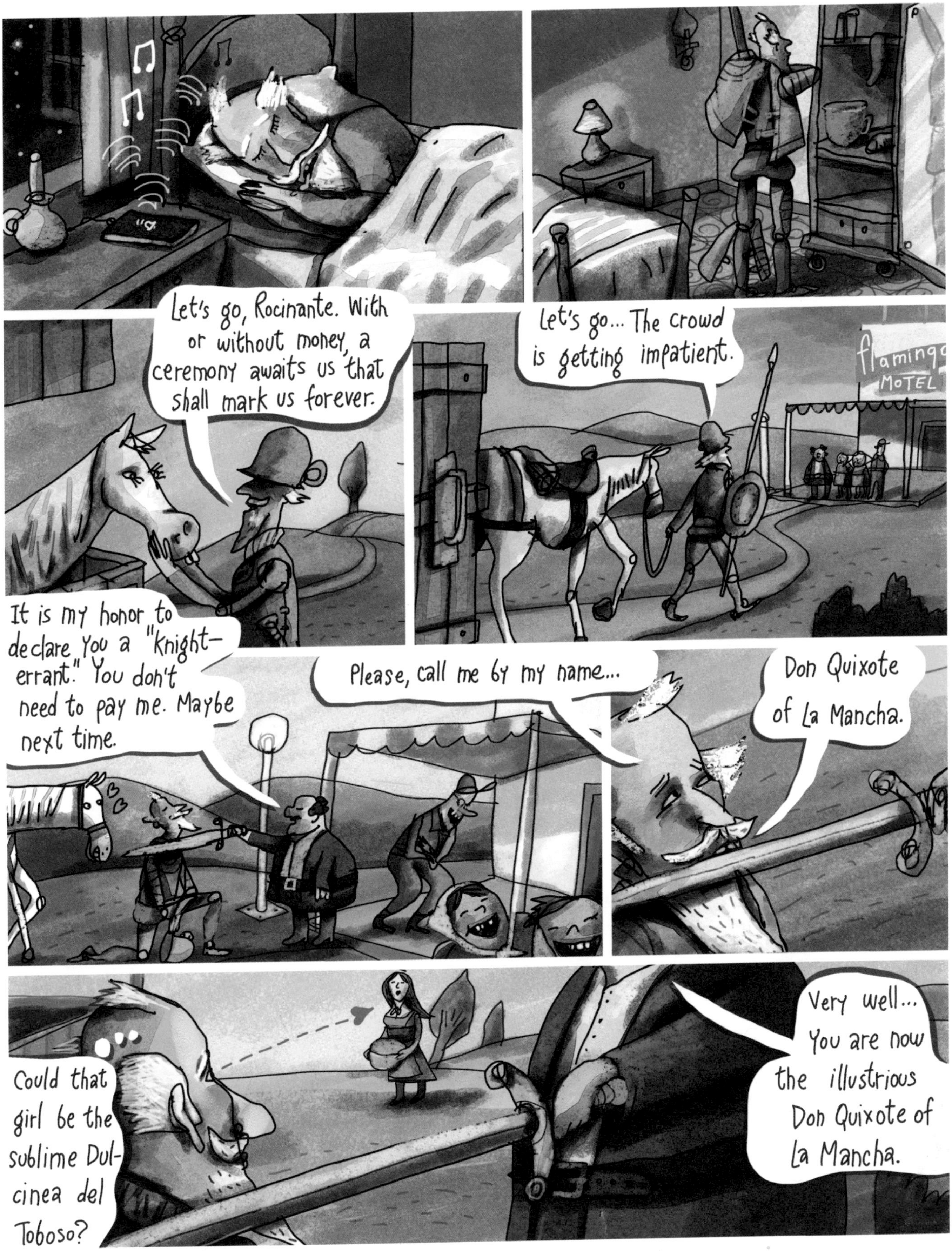

Let's go, Rocinante. With or without money, a ceremony awaits us that shall mark us forever.
Let's go... The crowd is getting impatient.
flamingo MOTEL
It is my honor to declare you a "knight-errant." You don't need to pay me. Maybe next time.
Please, call me by my name...
Don Quixote of La Mancha.
Could that girl be the sublime Dulcinea del Toboso?
Very well... You are now the illustrious Don Quixote of La Mancha.

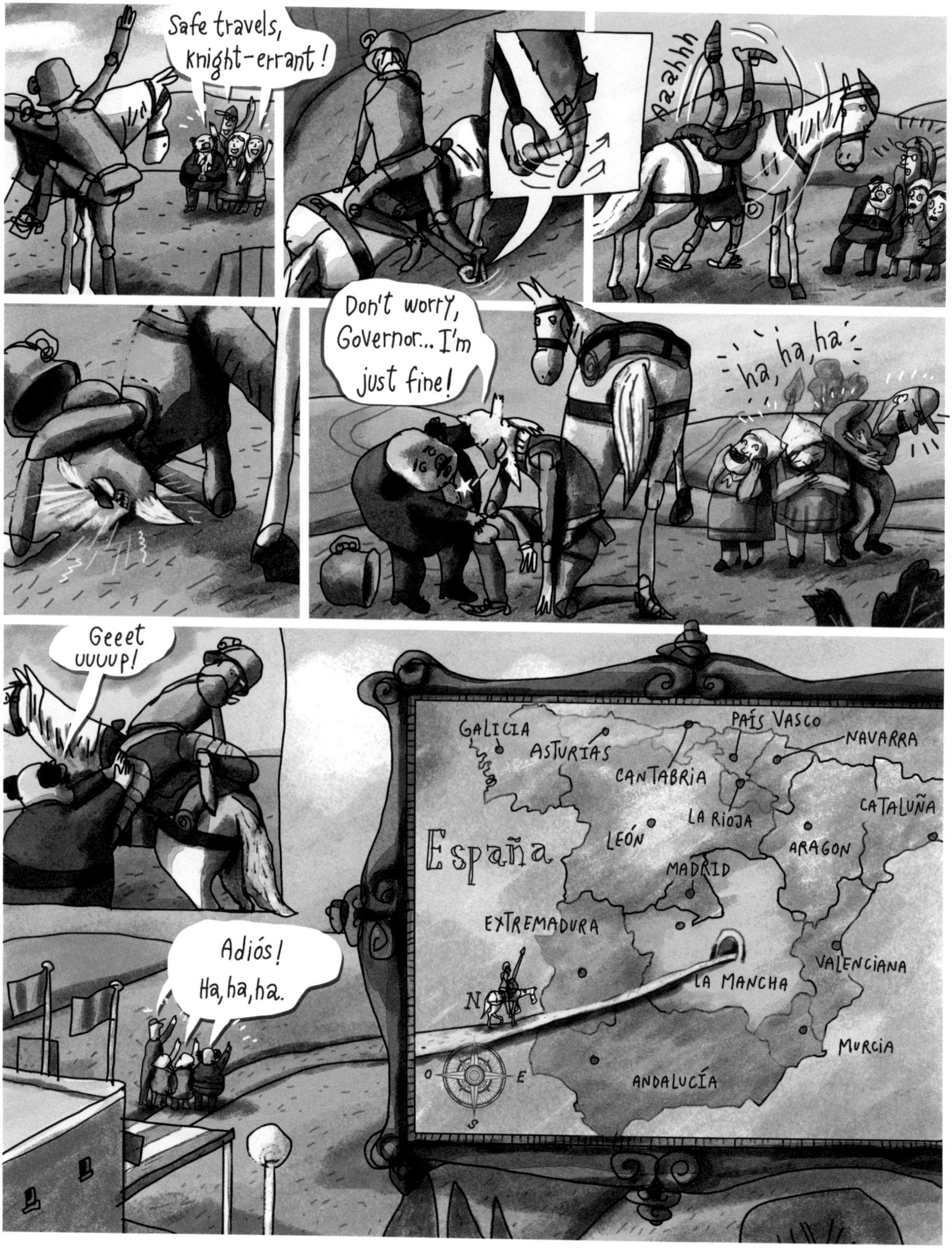
Safe travels, knight-errant!
Aaahhh
Don't worry, Governor... I'm just fine!
ha, ha, ha
Geeet uuuup!
Adiós! Ha, ha, ha.
GALICIA
ASTURIAS
CANTABRIA
PAÍS VASCO
NAVARRA
CATALUÑA
LA RIOJA
LEÓN
España
ARAGON
MADRID
EXTREMADURA
VALENCIANA
LA MANCHA
N
MURCIA
O
E
S
ANDALUCÍA

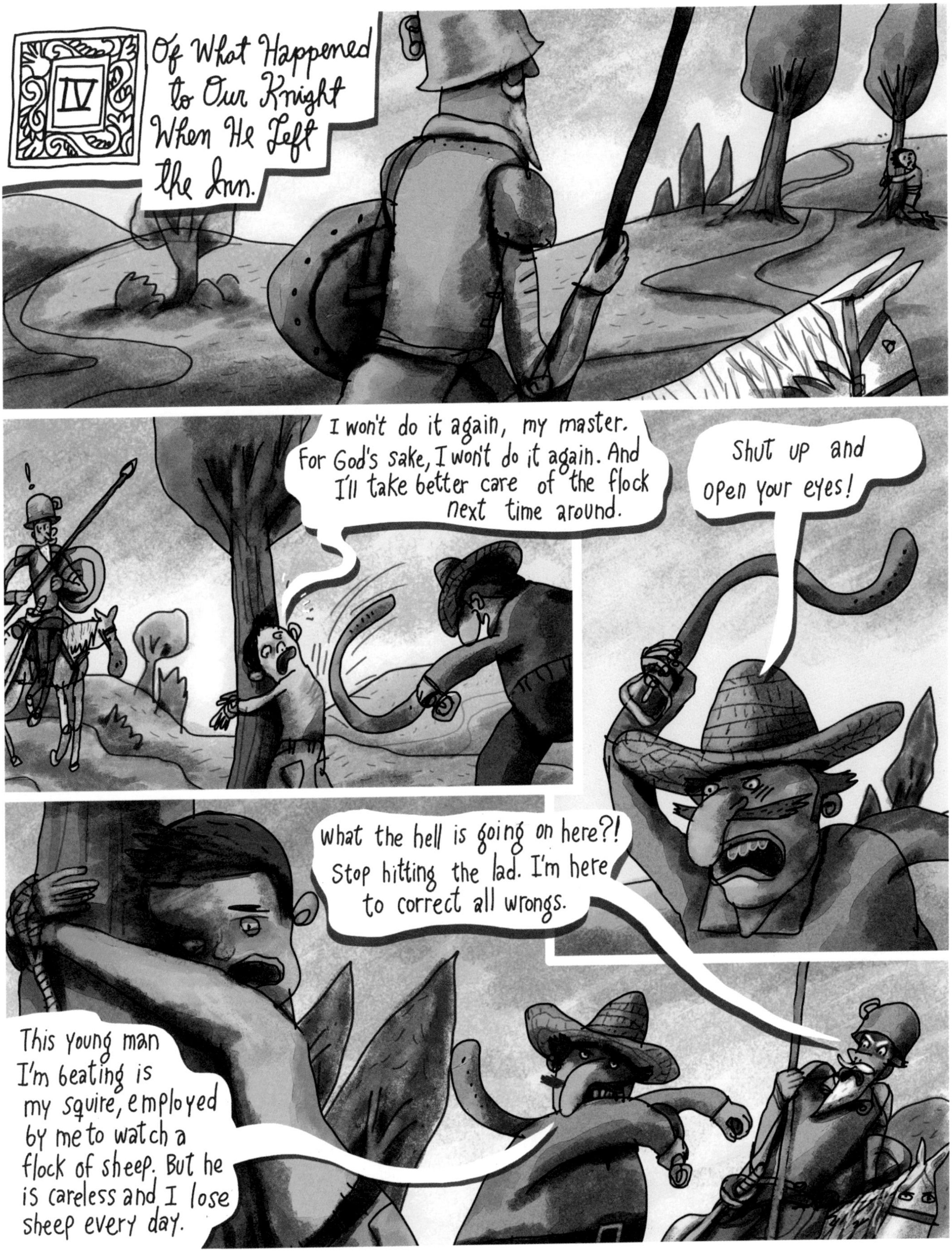

IV
Of What Happened to Our Knight When He Left the Inn.
!
I won't do it again, my master. For God's sake, I won't do it again. And I'll take better care of the flock next time around.
Shut up and open your eyes!
What the hell is going on here?! Stop hitting the lad. I'm here to correct all wrongs.
This young man I'm beating is my squire, employed by me to watch a flock of sheep. But he is careless and I lose sheep every day.

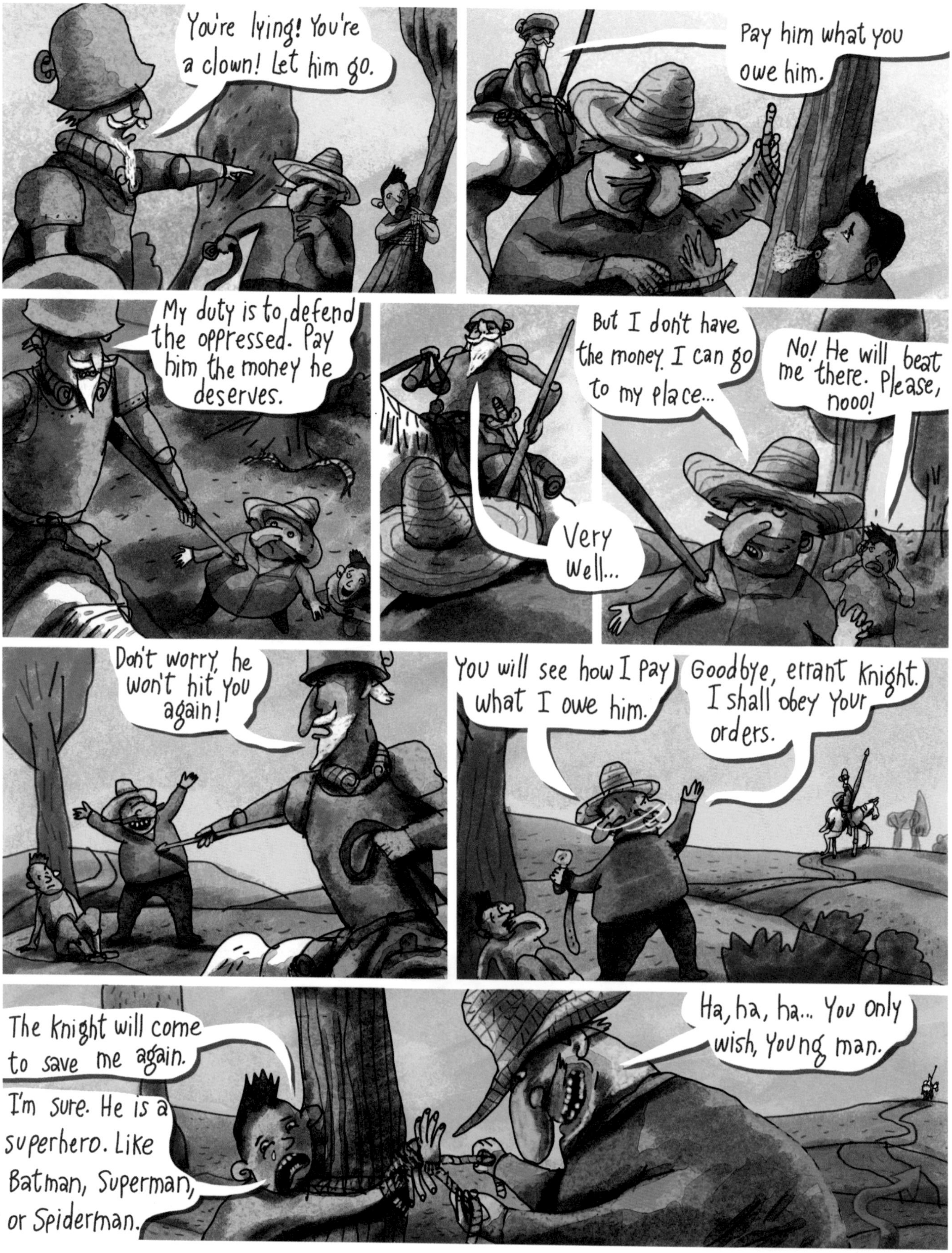
You're lying! You're a clown! Let him go.
Pay him what you owe him.
My duty is to defend the oppressed. Pay him the money he deserves.
But I don't have the money. I can go to my place...
No! He will beat me there. Please, nooo!
Very well...
Don't worry, he won't hit you again!
You will see how I pay what I owe him.
Goodbye, errant knight. I shall obey your orders.
The knight will come to save me again.
I'm sure. He is a superhero. Like Batman, Superman, or Spiderman.
Ha, ha, ha... You only wish, young man.

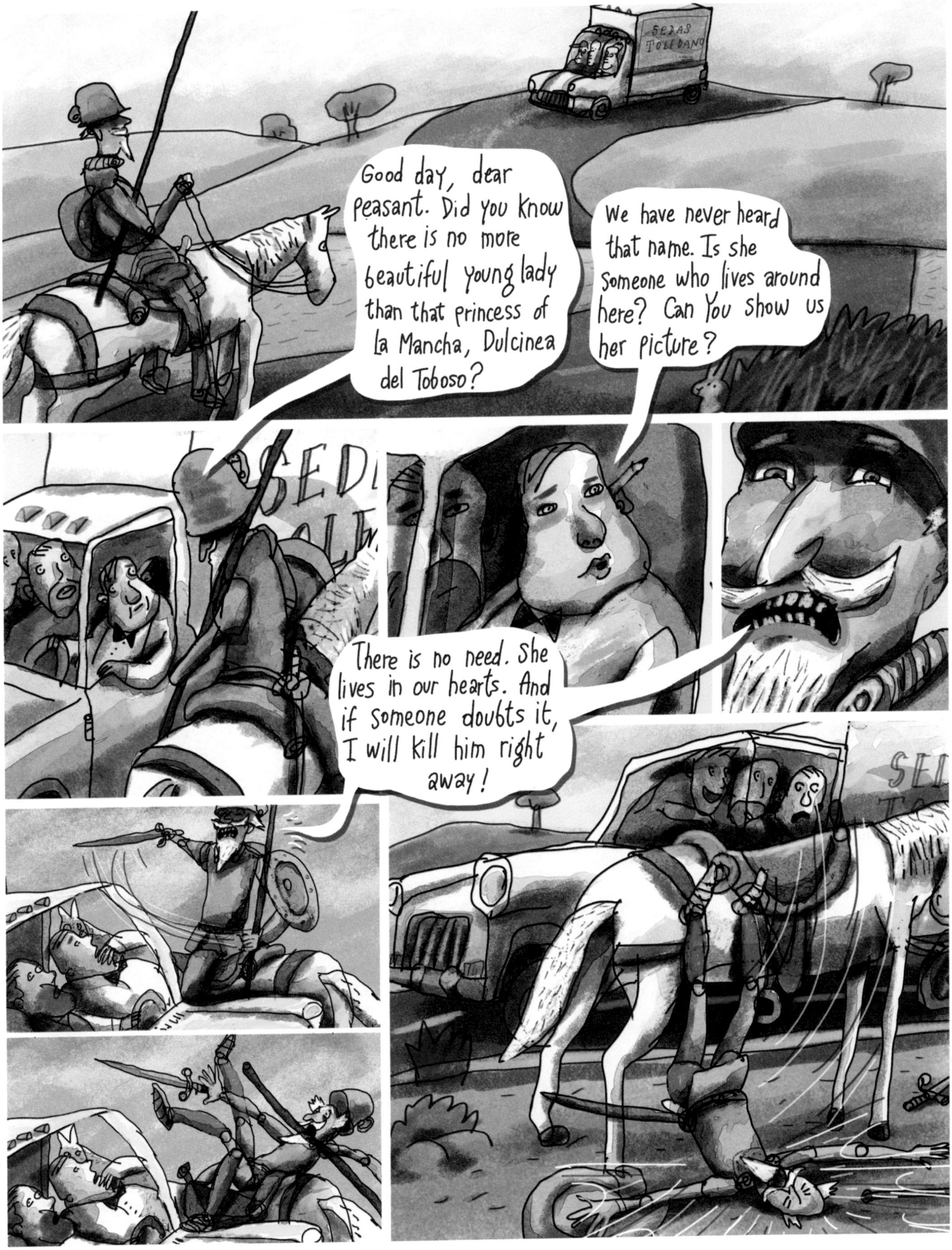
SEDAS TOLEDANO
Good day, dear peasant. Did you know there is no more beautiful young lady than that princess of La Mancha, Dulcinea del Toboso?
We have never heard that name. Is she someone who lives around here? Can you show us her picture?
There is no need. She lives in our hearts. And if someone doubts it, I will kill him right away!

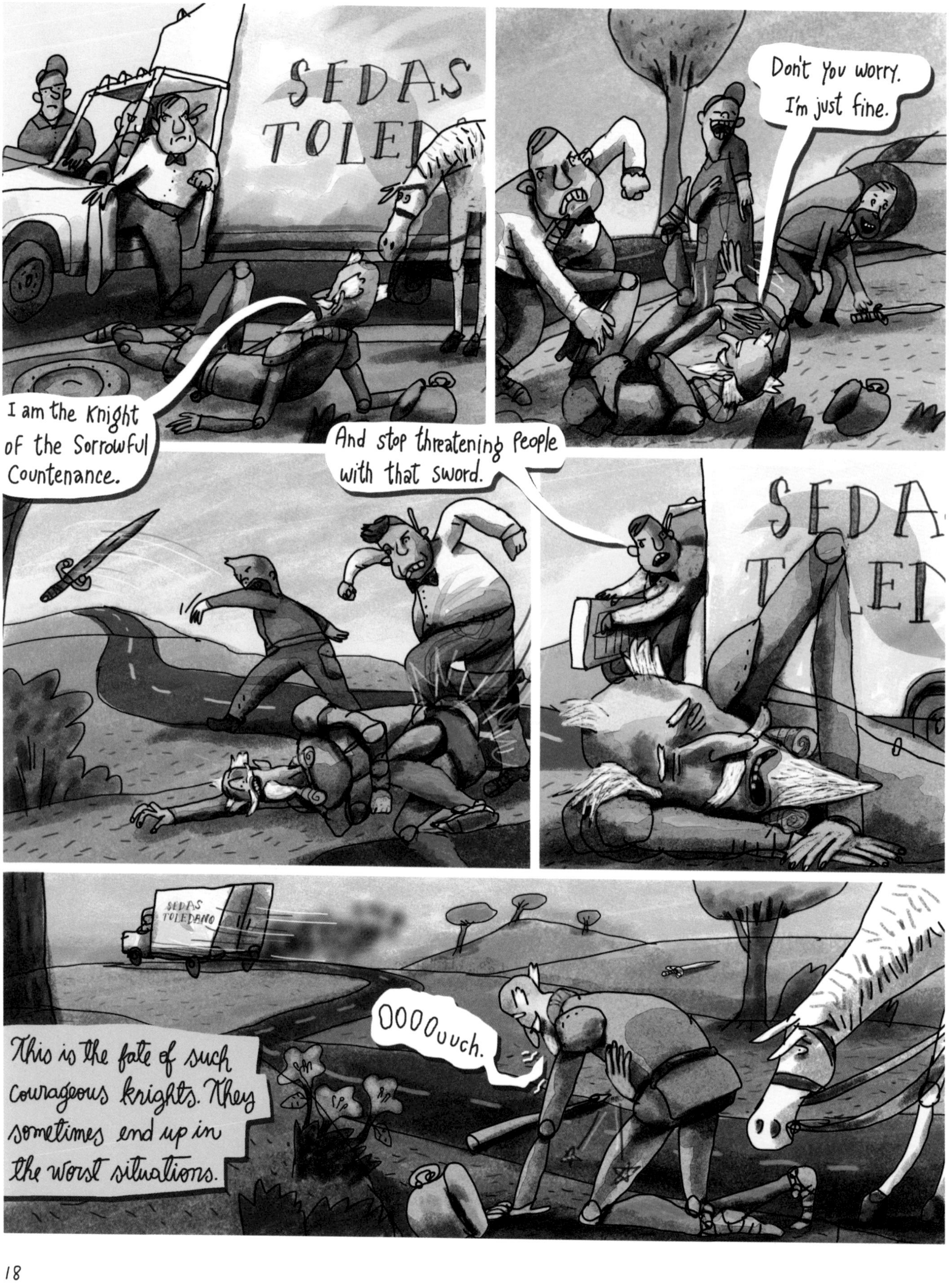
SEDAS TOLED
I am the Knight of the Sorrowful Countenance.
Don't you worry. I'm just fine.
And stop threatening people with that sword.
SEDAS TOLED
SEDAS TOLEDANO
OOOOuuch.
This is the fate of such courageous knights. They sometimes end up in the worst situations.

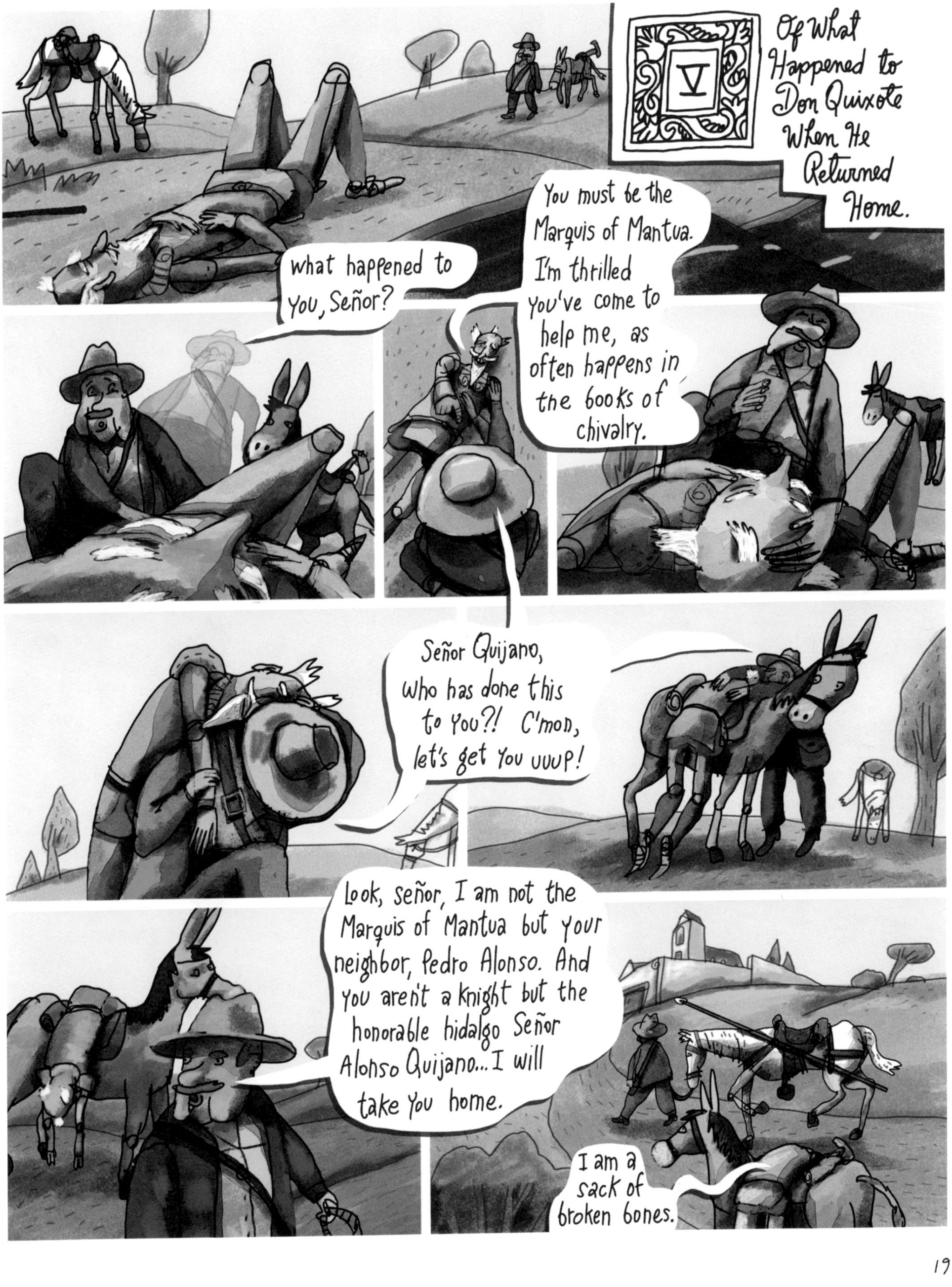
Of What Happened to Don Quixote When He Returned Home.
V
what happened to you, Señor?
You must be the Marquis of Mantua. I'm thrilled you've come to help me, as often happens in the books of chivalry.
Señor Quijano, who has done this to you?! C'mon, let's get you uuuP!
Look, señor, I am not the Marquis of Mantua but your neighbor, Pedro Alonso. And you aren't a knight but the honorable hidalgo Señor Alonso Quijano... I will take you home.
I am a sack of broken bones.

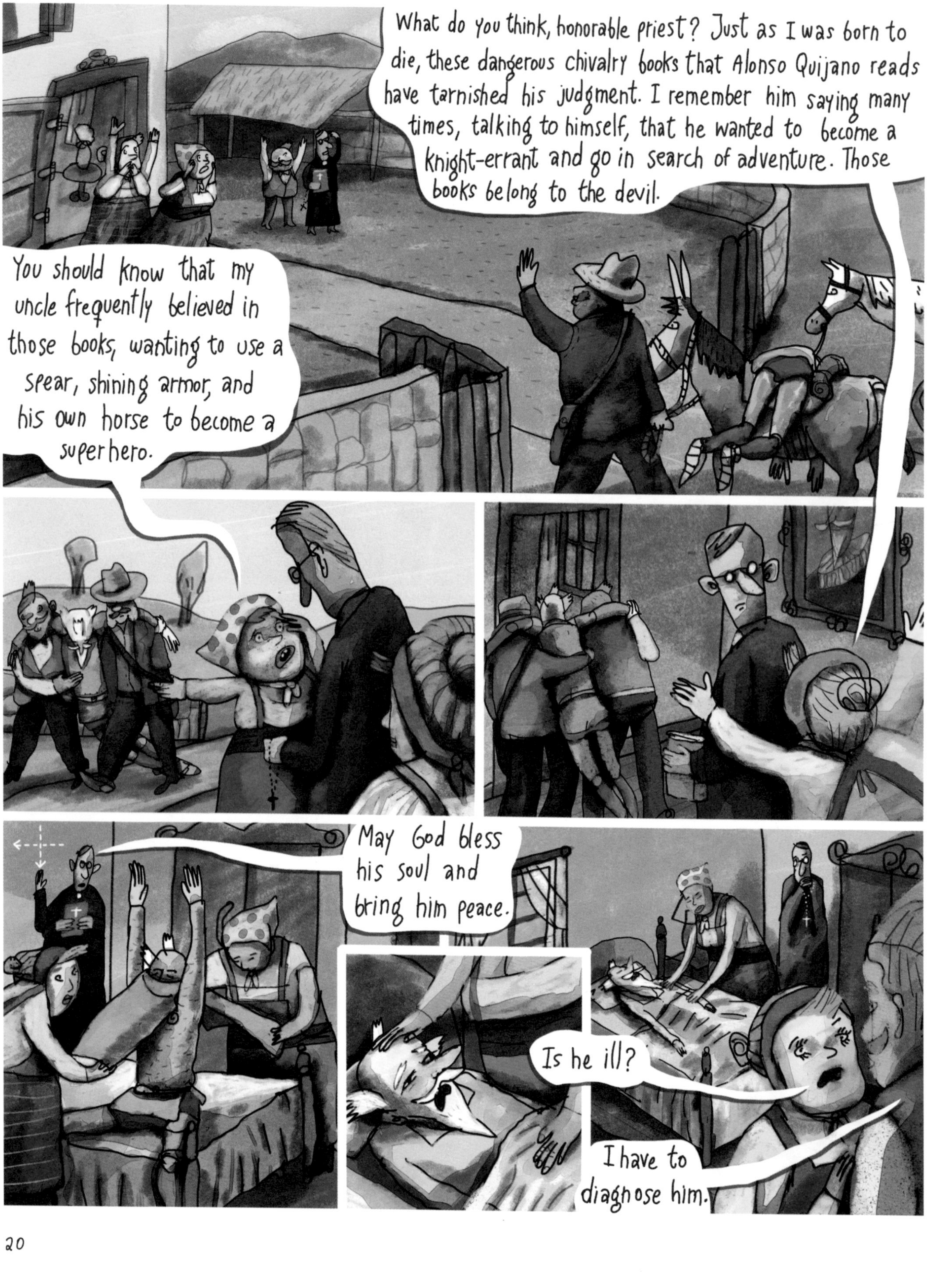
What do you think, honorable priest? Just as I was born to die, these dangerous chivalry books that Alonso Quijano reads have tarnished his judgment. I remember him saying many times, talking to himself, that he wanted to become a knight-errant and go in search of adventure. Those books belong to the devil.
You should know that my uncle frequently believed in those books, wanting to use a spear, shining armor, and his own horse to become a superhero.
May God bless his soul and bring him peace.
Is he ill?
I have to diagnose him.

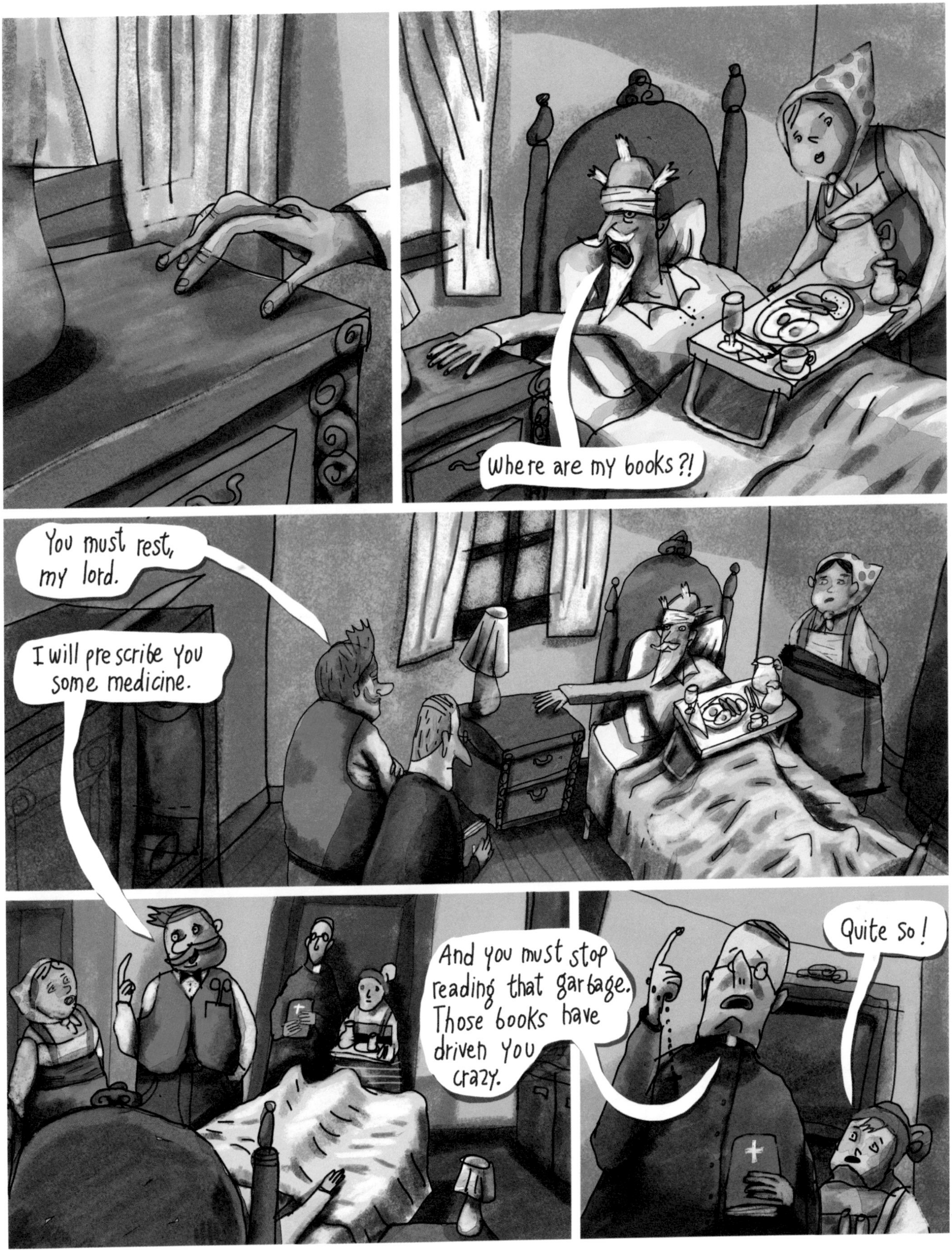
Where are my books?!
You must rest, my lord.
I will prescribe you some medicine.
And you must stop reading that garbage. Those books have driven you crazy.
Quite so!

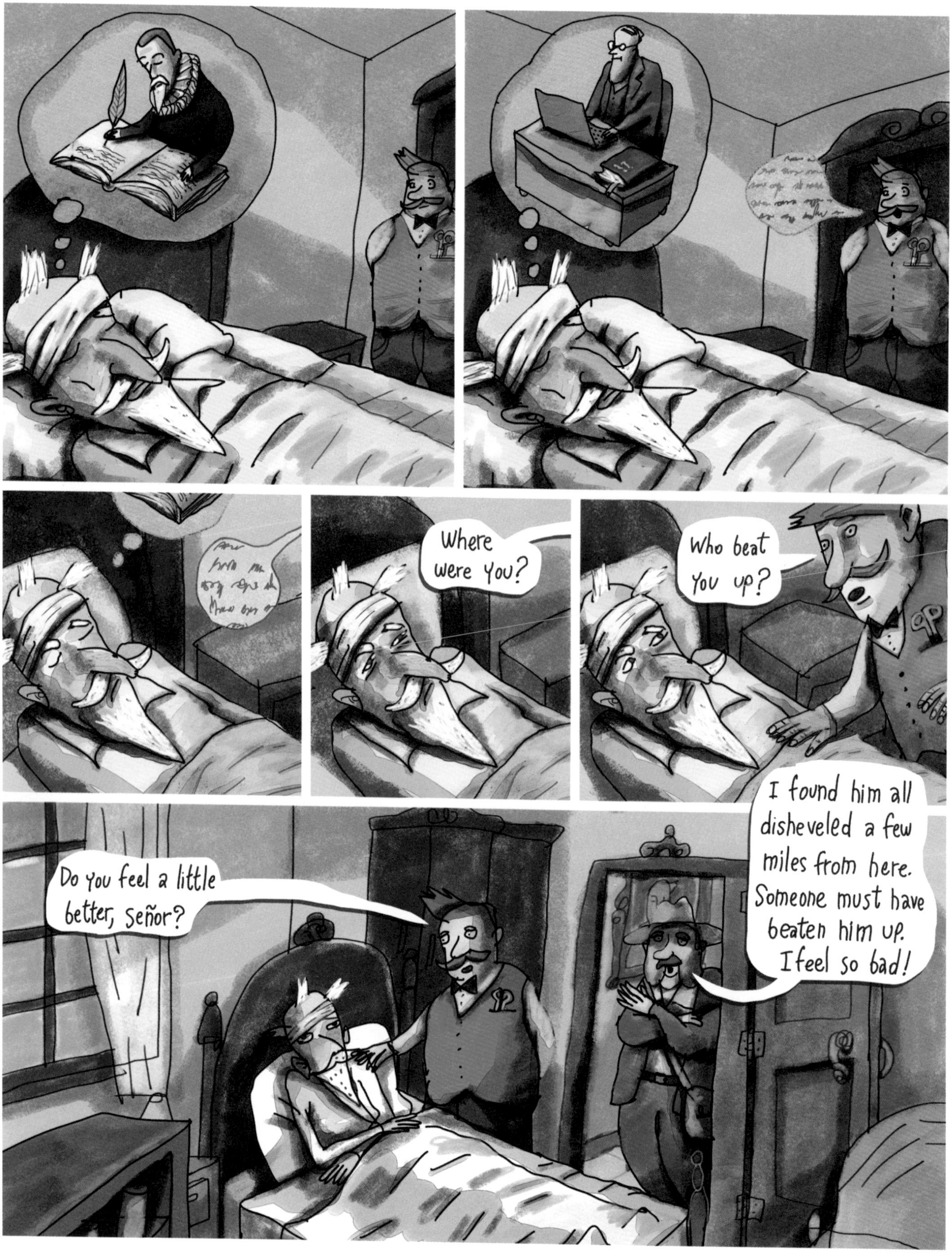
Where were you?
Who beat you up?
Do you feel a little better, Señor?
I found him all disheveled a few miles from here. Someone must have beaten him up. I feel so bad!

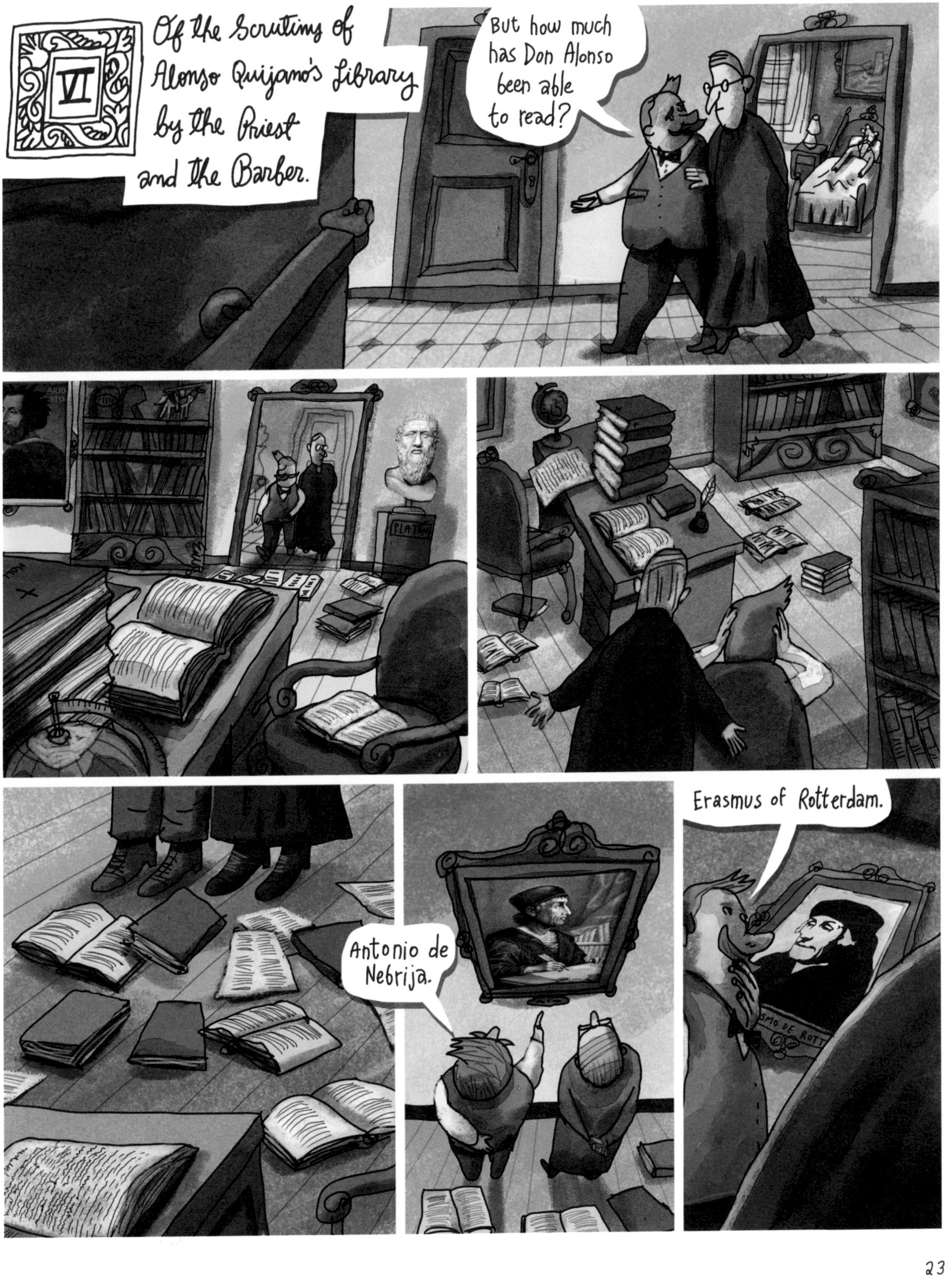
VI
Of the Scrutiny of Alonso Quijano's Library by the Priest and the Barber.
But how much has Don Alonso been able to read?
Antonio de Nebrija.
Erasmus of Rotterdam.

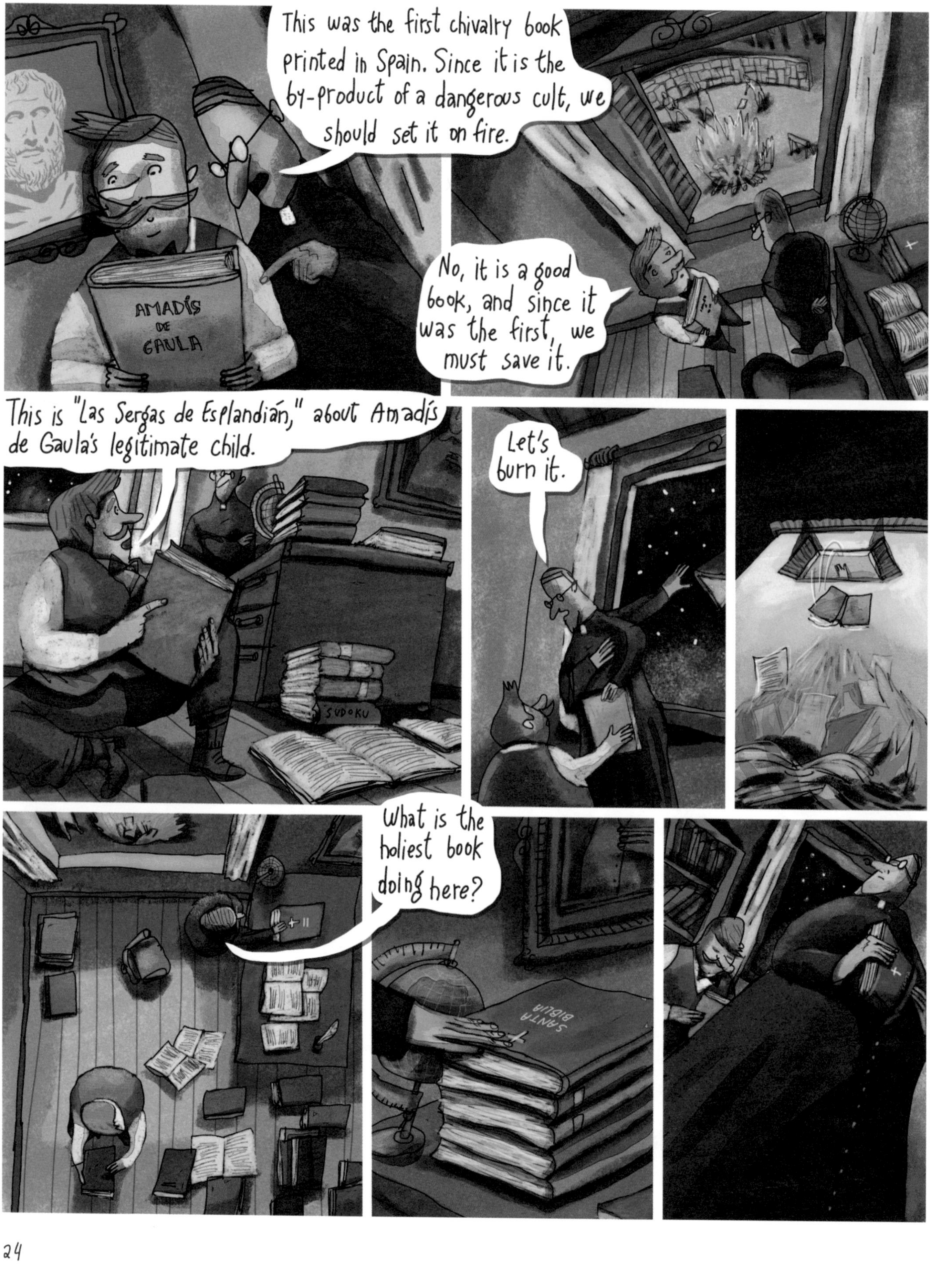
This was the first chivalry book printed in Spain. Since it is the by-product of a dangerous cult, we should set it on fire.
AMADÍS DE GAULA
No, it is a good book, and since it was the first, we must save it.
This is "Las Sergas de Esplandián," about Amadís de Gaula's legitimate child.
SUDOKU
Let's burn it.
What is the holiest book doing here?
SANTA BIBLIA

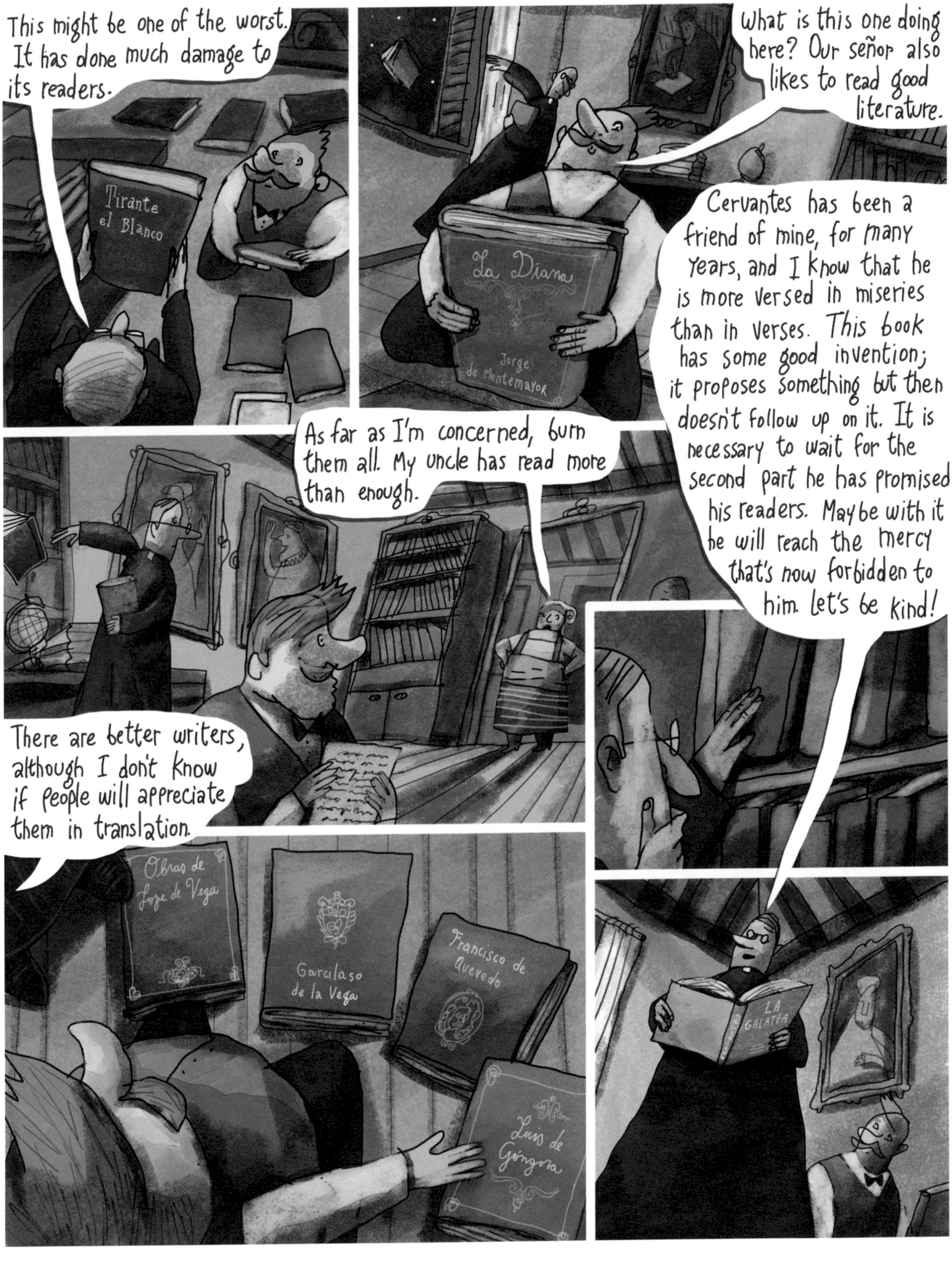
This might be one of the worst. It has done much damage to its readers.
Tirante el Blanco
What is this one doing here? Our señor also likes to read good literature.
La Diana
Jorge de Montemayor
Cervantes has been a friend of mine, for many years, and I know that he is more versed in miseries than in verses. This book has some good invention; it proposes something but then doesn't follow up on it. It is necessary to wait for the second part he has promised his readers. Maybe with it he will reach the mercy that's now forbidden to him. Let's be kind!
As far as I'm concerned, burn them all. My uncle has read more than enough.
There are better writers, although I don't know if people will appreciate them in translation.
Obras de Lope de Vega
Garcilaso de la Vega
Francisco de Quevedo
Luis de Góngora
La Galatea

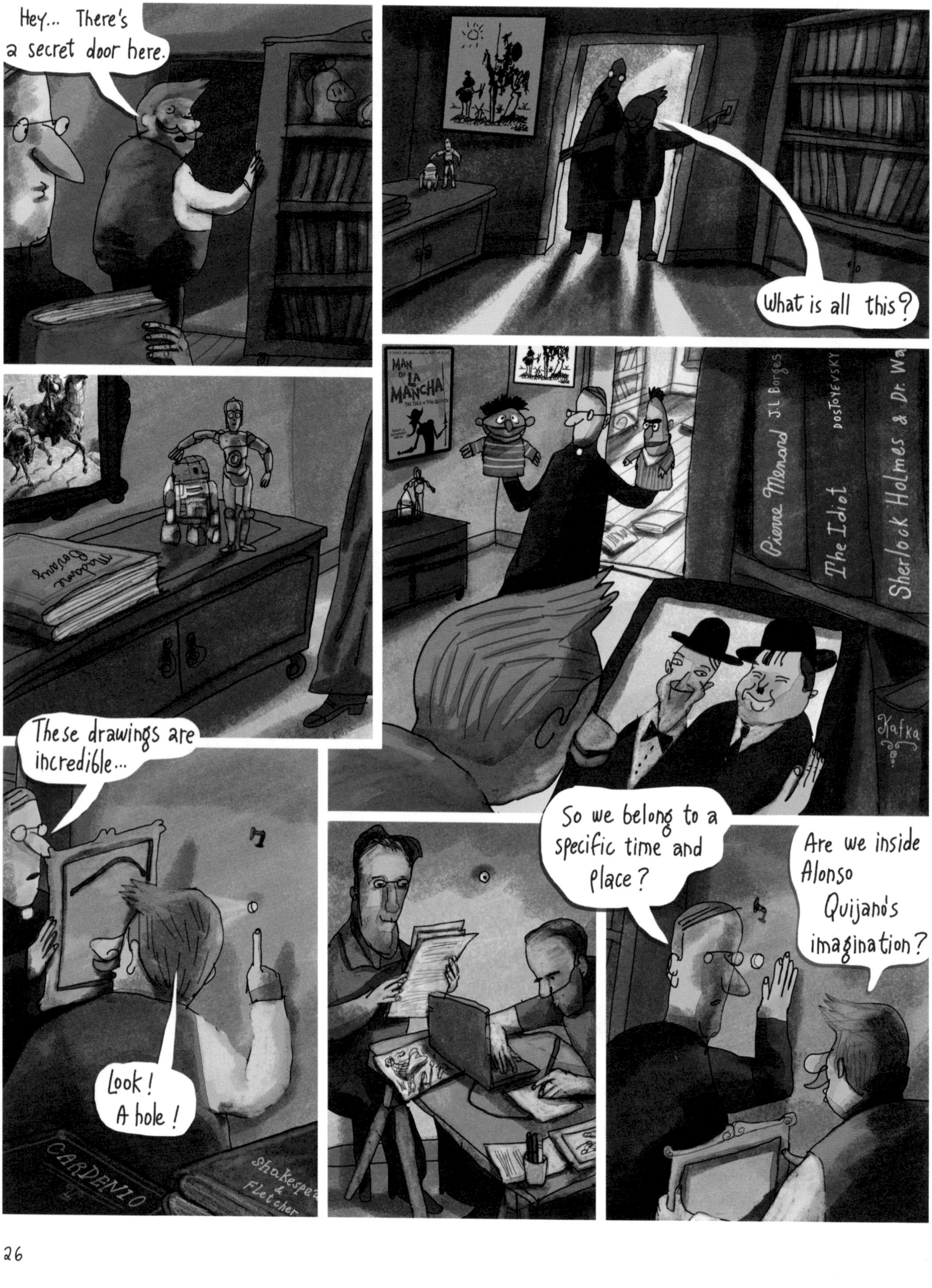

Hey... There's a secret door here.
What is all this?
MAN OF LA MANCHA
Pierre Menard
J.L Borges
The Idiot
DOSTOYEVSKY
Sherlock Holmes & Dr. Wa
Kafka
These drawings are incredible...
Look! A hole!
CARDENIO
Shakespeare & Fletcher
So we belong to a specific time and place?
Are we inside Alonso Quijano's imagination?

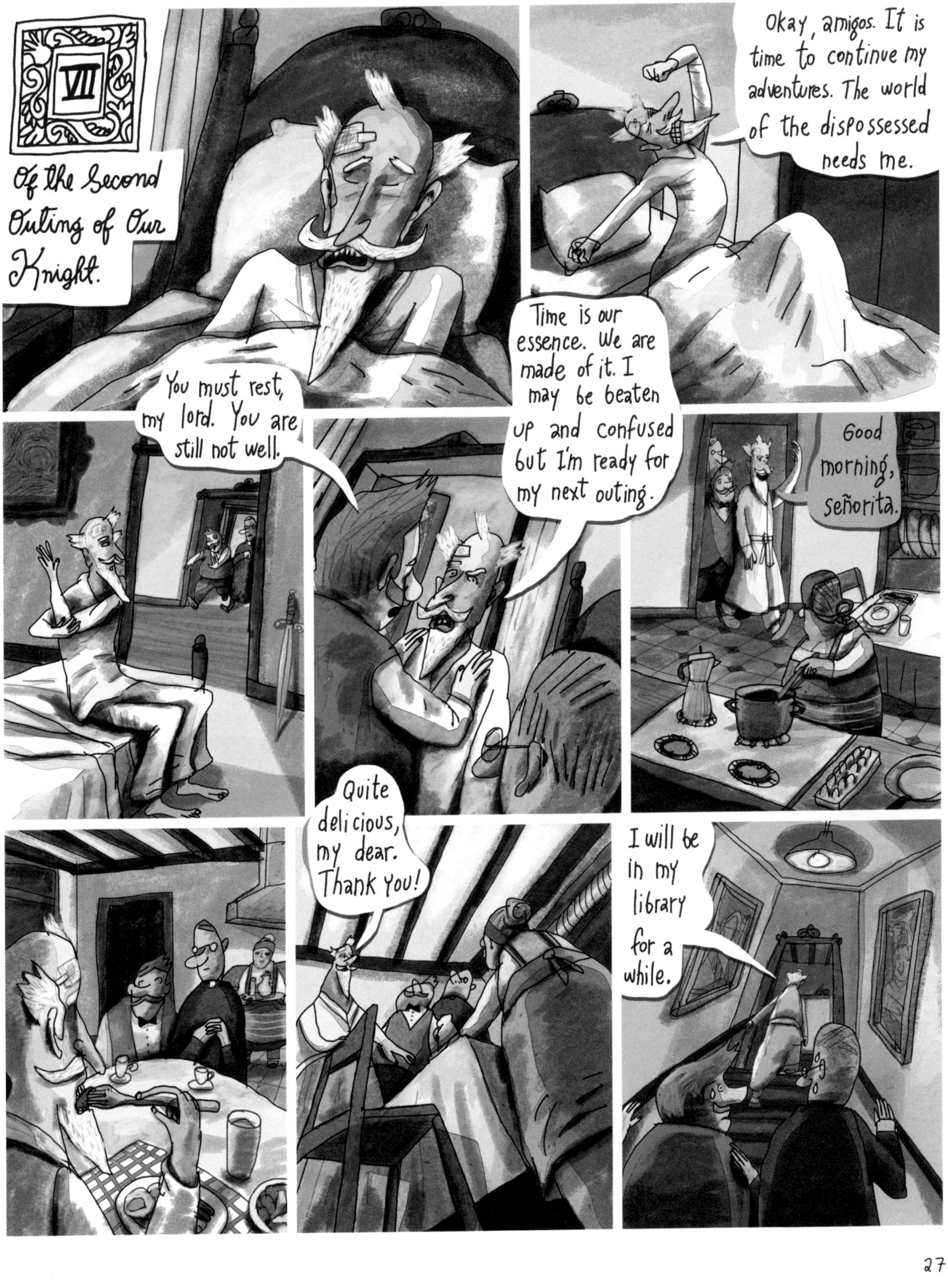
VII
Of the Second Outing of Our Knight.
Okay, amigos. It is time to continue my adventures. The world of the dispossessed needs me.
You must rest, my lord. You are still not well.
Time is our essence. We are made of it. I may be beaten up and confused but I'm ready for my next outing.
Good morning, señorita.
Quite delicious, my dear. Thank you!
I will be in my library for a while.

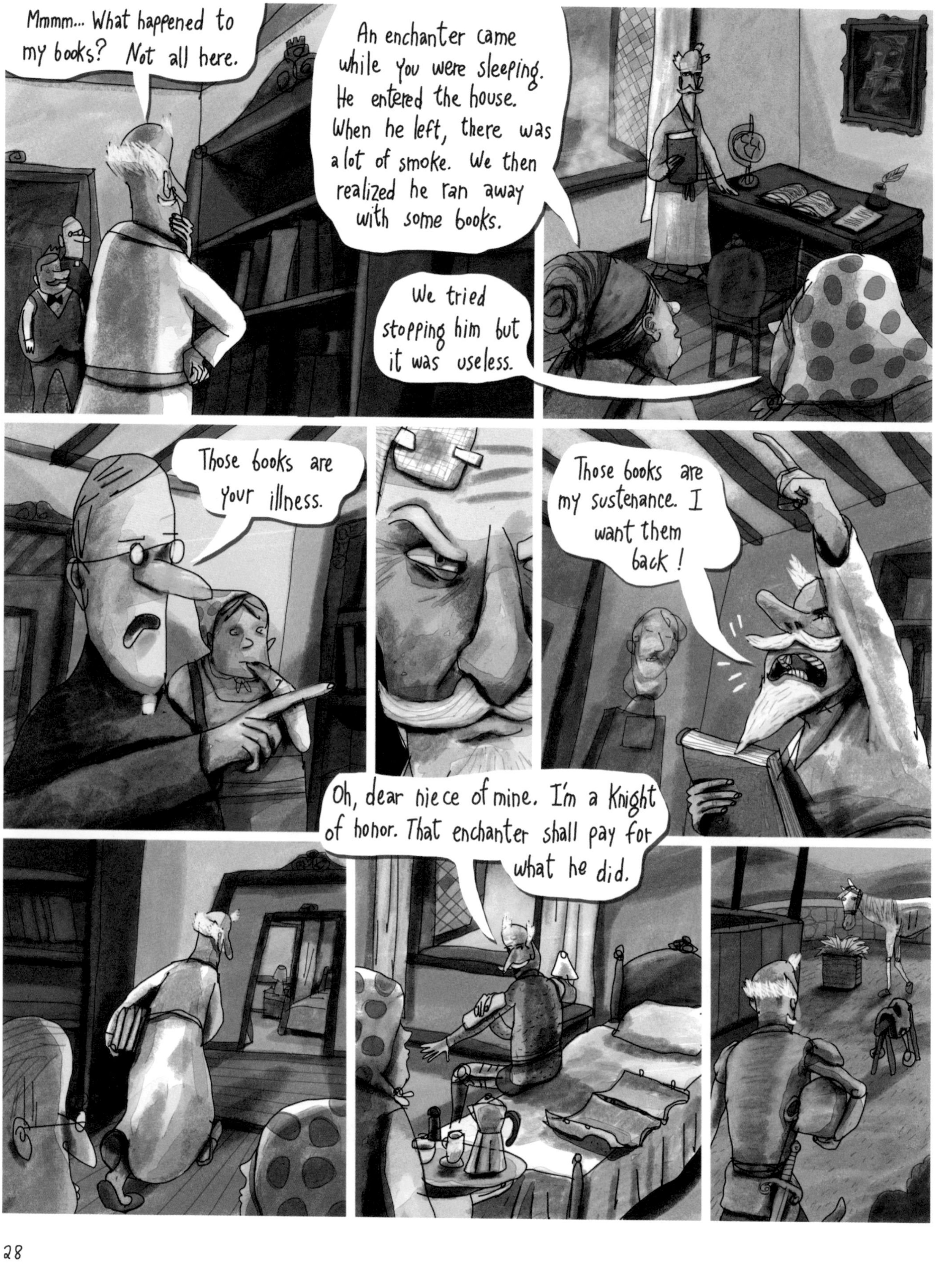
Mmmm... What happened to my books? Not all here.
An enchanter came while you were sleeping. He entered the house. When he left, there was a lot of smoke. We then realized he ran away with some books.
We tried stopping him but it was useless.
Those books are your illness.
Those books are my sustenance. I want them back!
Oh, dear niece of mine. I'm a Knight of honor. That enchanter shall pay for what he did.

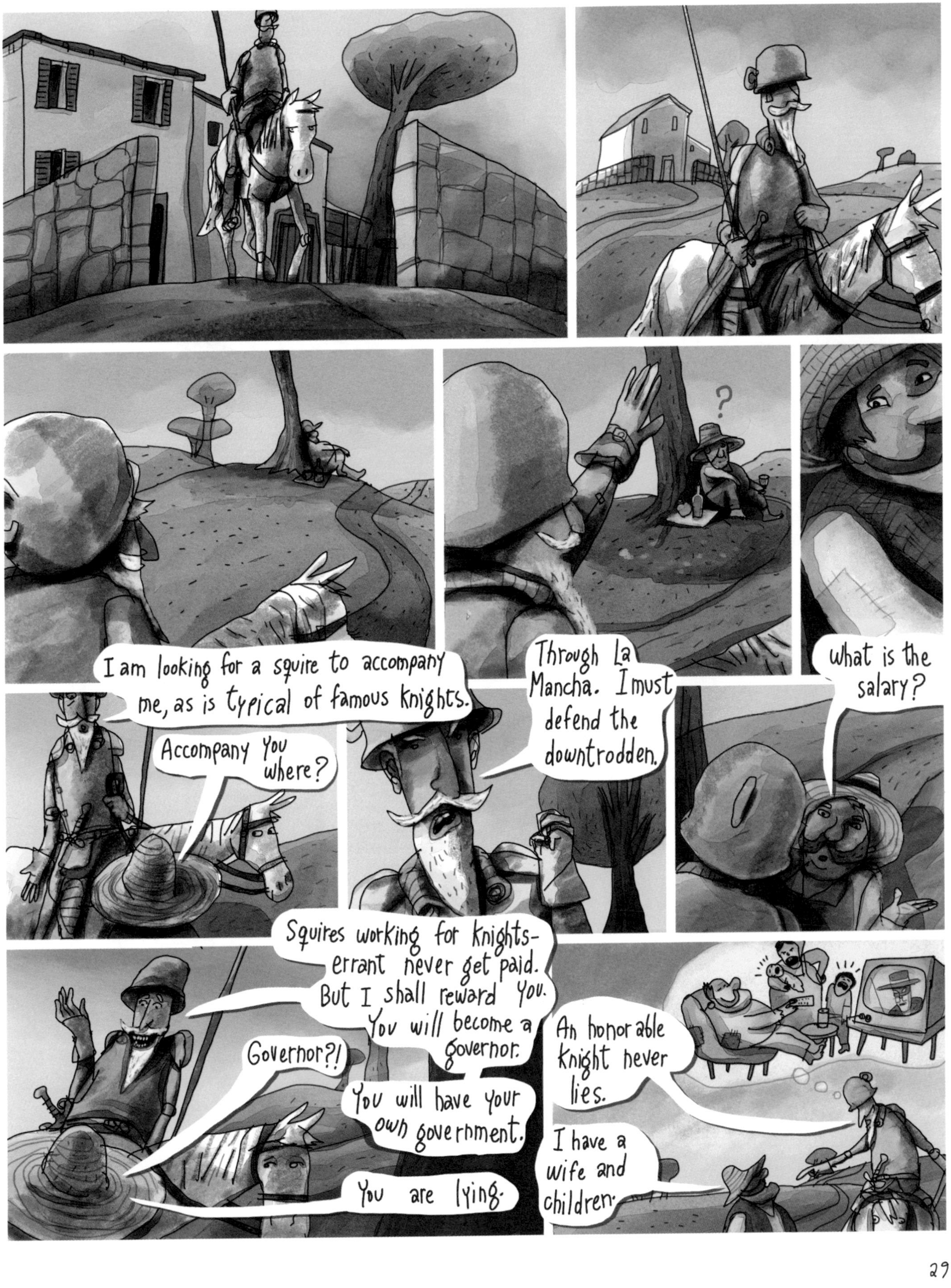
I am looking for a squire to accompany me, as is typical of famous knights.
Accompany you where?
Through La Mancha. I must defend the downtrodden.
What is the salary?
Squires working for knights-errant never get paid. But I shall reward you. You will become a governor.
Governor?!
You will have your own government.
You are lying.
An honorable knight never lies.
I have a wife and children.

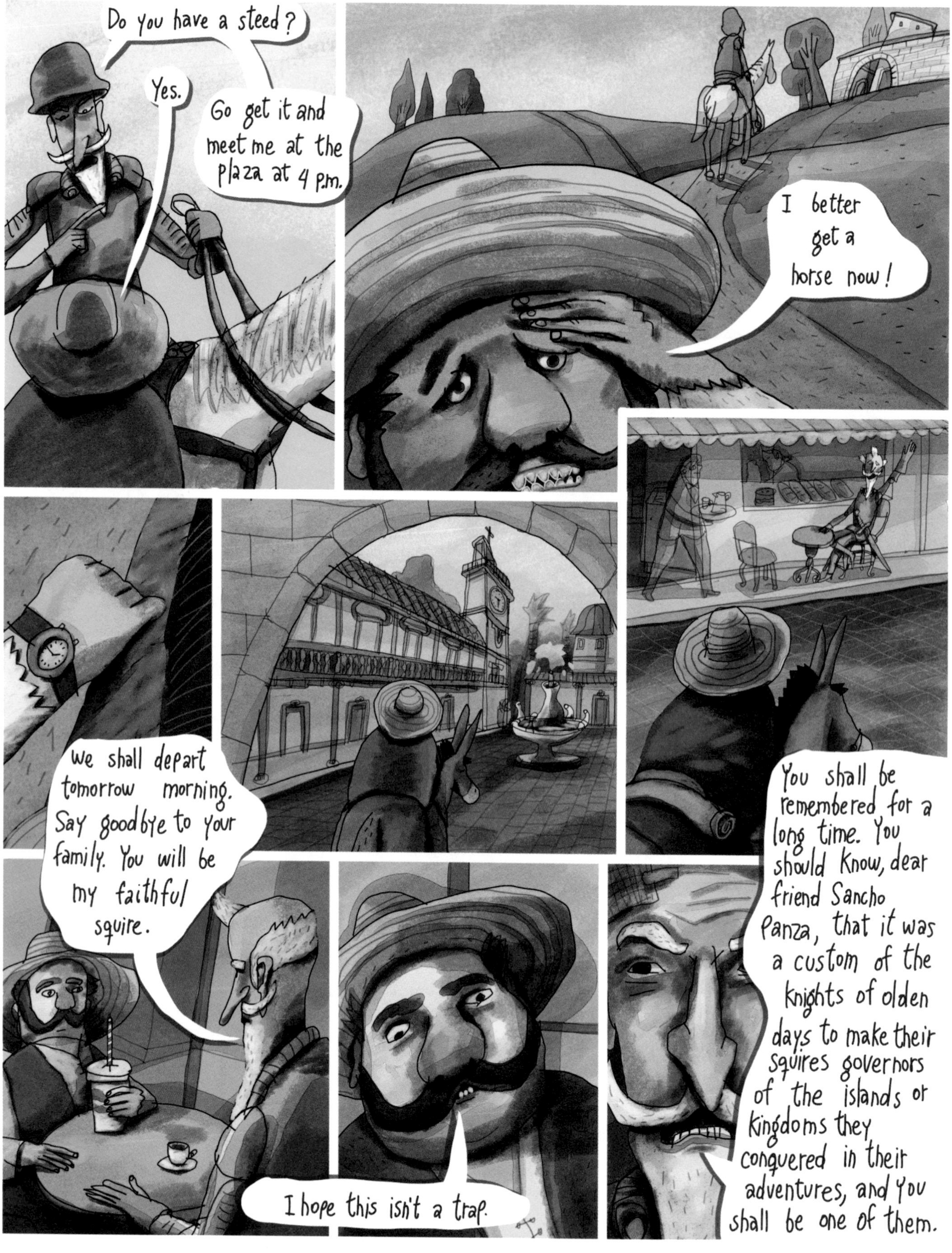

Do you have a steed?
Yes.
Go get it and meet me at the plaza at 4 p.m.
I better get a horse now!
We shall depart tomorrow morning. Say goodbye to your family. You will be my faithful squire.
I hope this isn't a trap.
You shall be remembered for a long time. You should Know, dear friend Sancho Panza, that it was a custom of the knights of olden days to make their squires governors of the islands or kingdoms they conquered in their adventures, and You shall be one of them.

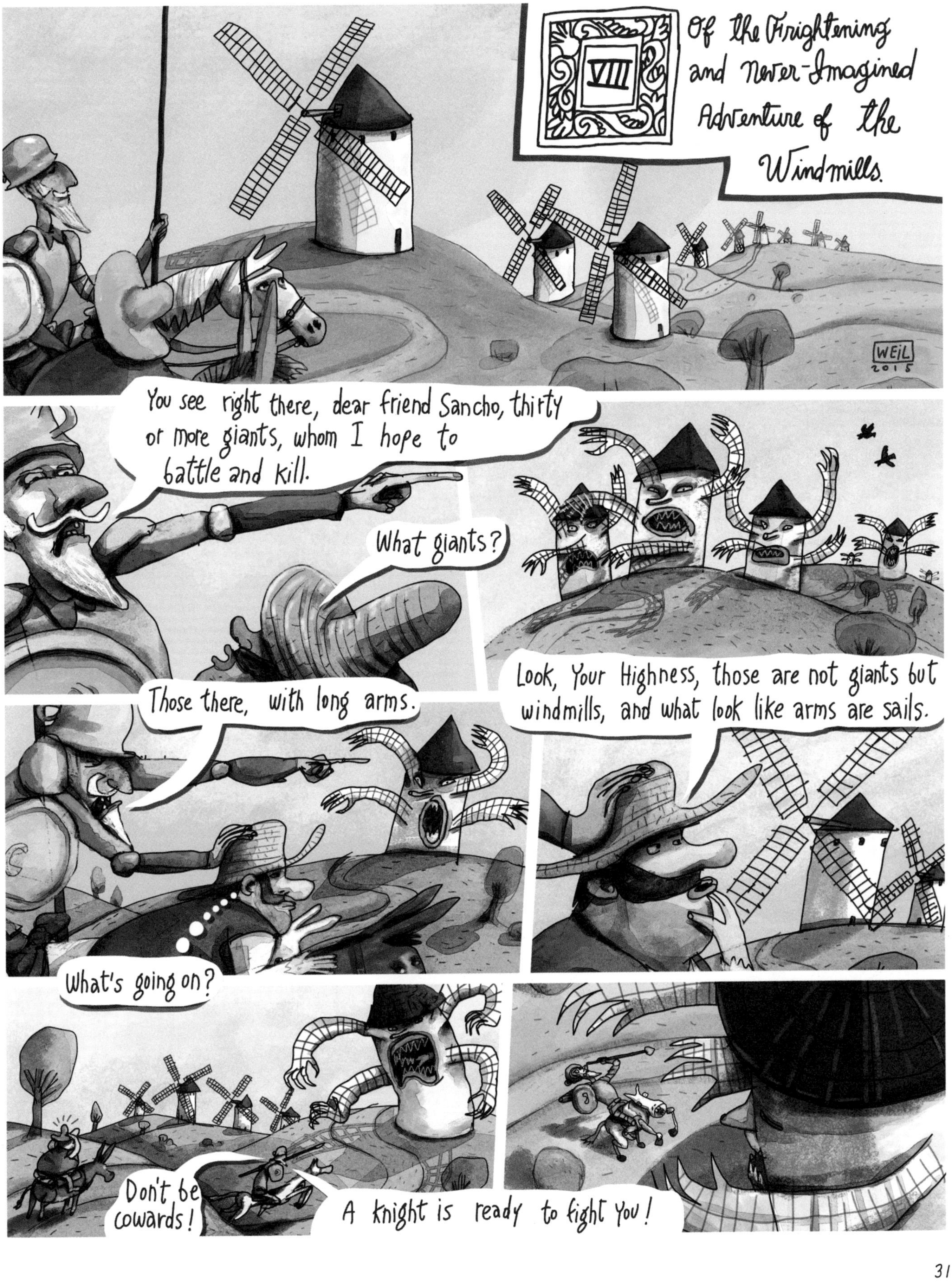

VIII
Of the Frightening and Never-Imagined Adventure of the Windmills.
WEIL 2015
You see right there, dear friend Sancho, thirty or more giants, whom I hope to battle and kill.
What giants?
Look, Your Highness, those are not giants but windmills, and what look like arms are sails.
Those there, with long arms.
What's going on?
Don't be cowards!
A knight is ready to fight you!

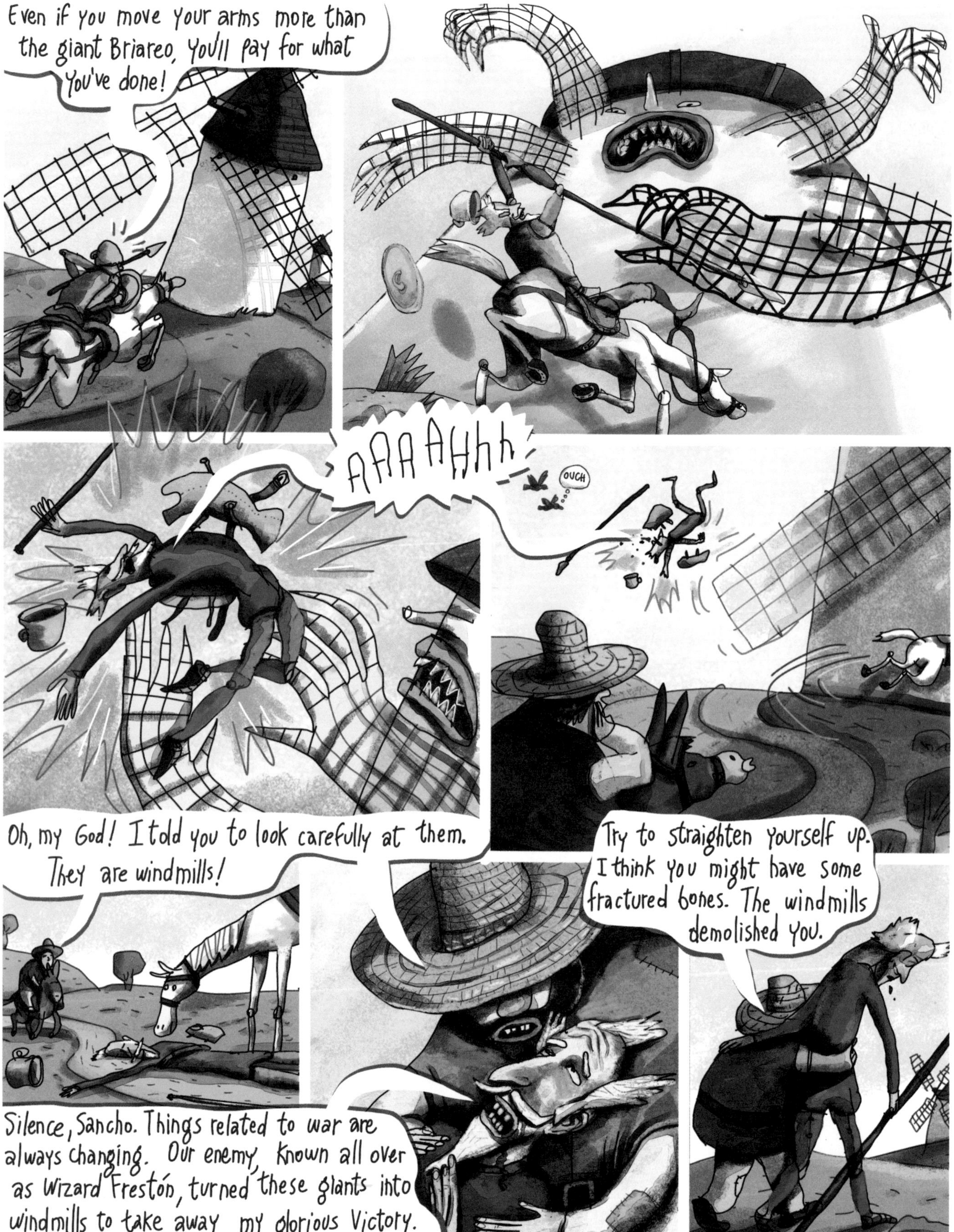

Even if you move your arms more than the giant Briareo, you'll pay for what you've done!
AAAAhhh
OUCH
Oh, my God! I told you to look carefully at them. They are windmills!
Try to straighten yourself up. I think you might have some fractured bones. The windmills demolished you.
Silence, Sancho. Things related to war are always changing. Our enemy, known all over as Wizard Frestón, turned these giants into windmills to take away my glorious victory.

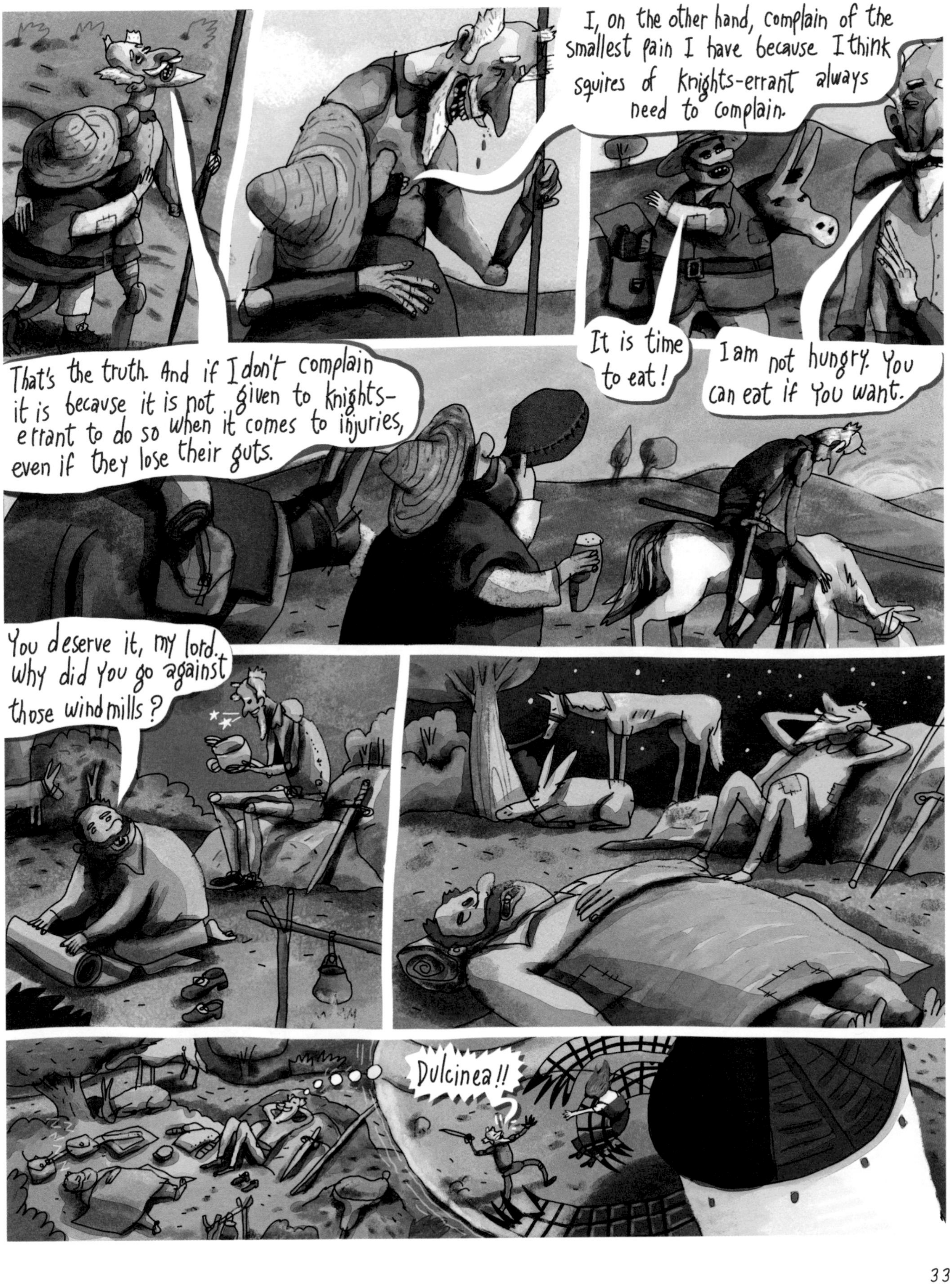
I, on the other hand, complain of the smallest pain I have because I think squires of knights-errant always need to complain.
That's the truth. And if I don't complain it is because it is not given to knights-errant to do so when it comes to injuries, even if they lose their guts.
It is time to eat!
I am not hungry. You can eat if you want.
You deserve it, my lord. Why did you go against those windmills?
Dulcinea!!

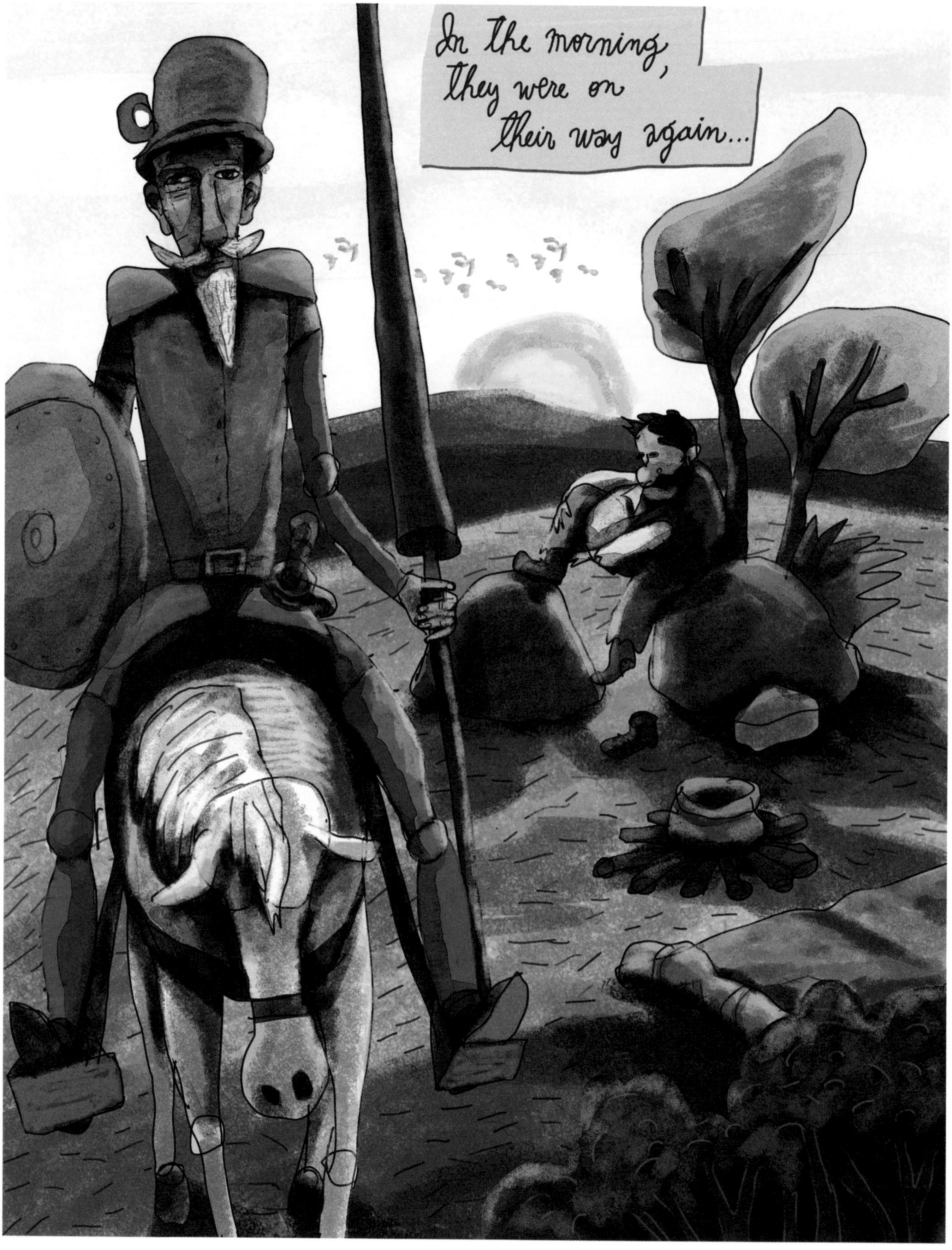
In the morning, they were on their way again...

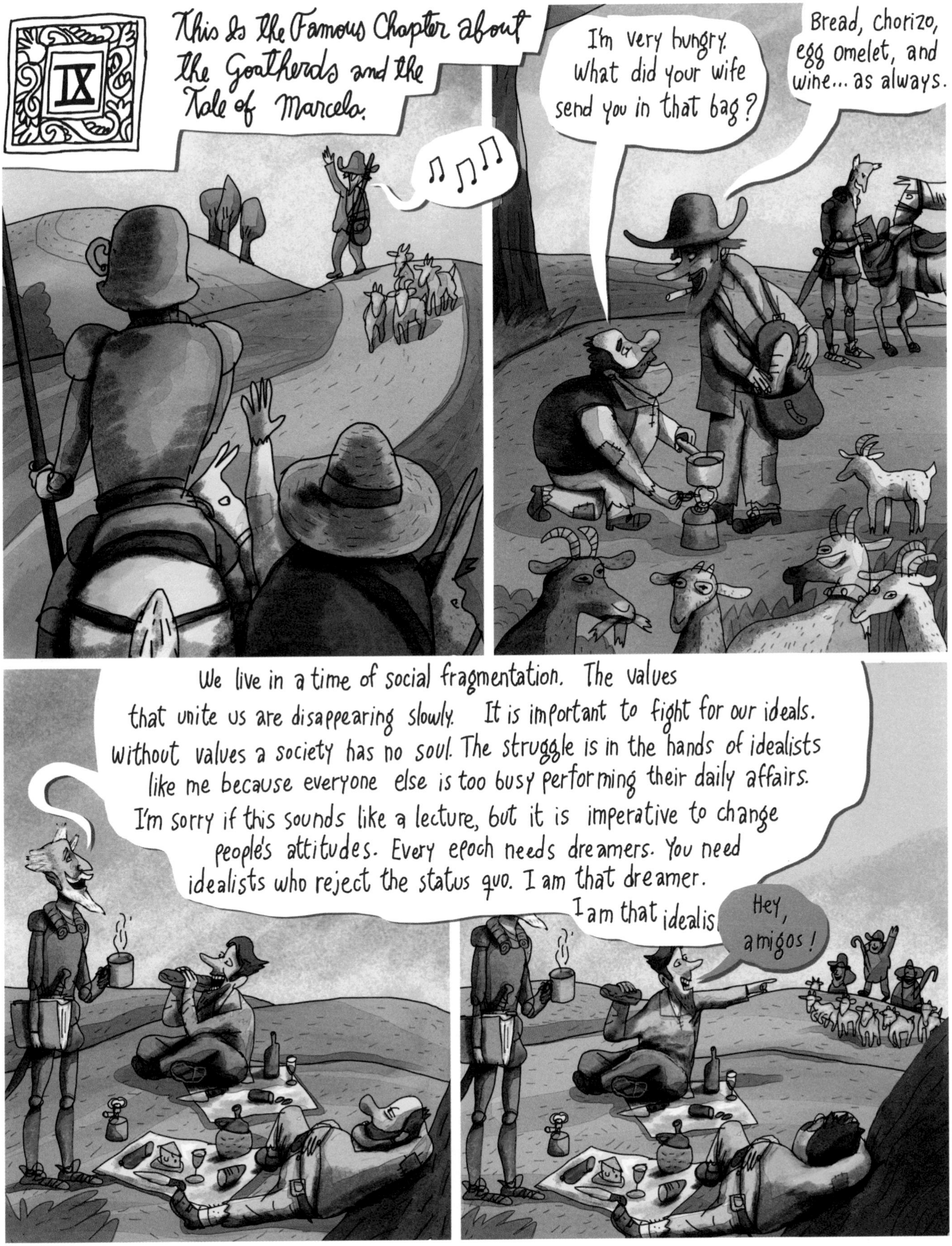
IX
This Is the Famous Chapter about the Goatherds and the Tale of Marcela.
I'm very hungry. What did your wife send you in that bag?
Bread, chorizo, egg omelet, and wine... as always.
We live in a time of social fragmentation. The values that unite us are disappearing slowly. It is important to fight for our ideals. Without values a society has no soul. The struggle is in the hands of idealists like me because everyone else is too busy performing their daily affairs. I'm sorry if this sounds like a lecture, but it is imperative to change people's attitudes. Every epoch needs dreamers. You need idealists who reject the status quo. I am that dreamer.
I am that idealis
Hey, amigos!

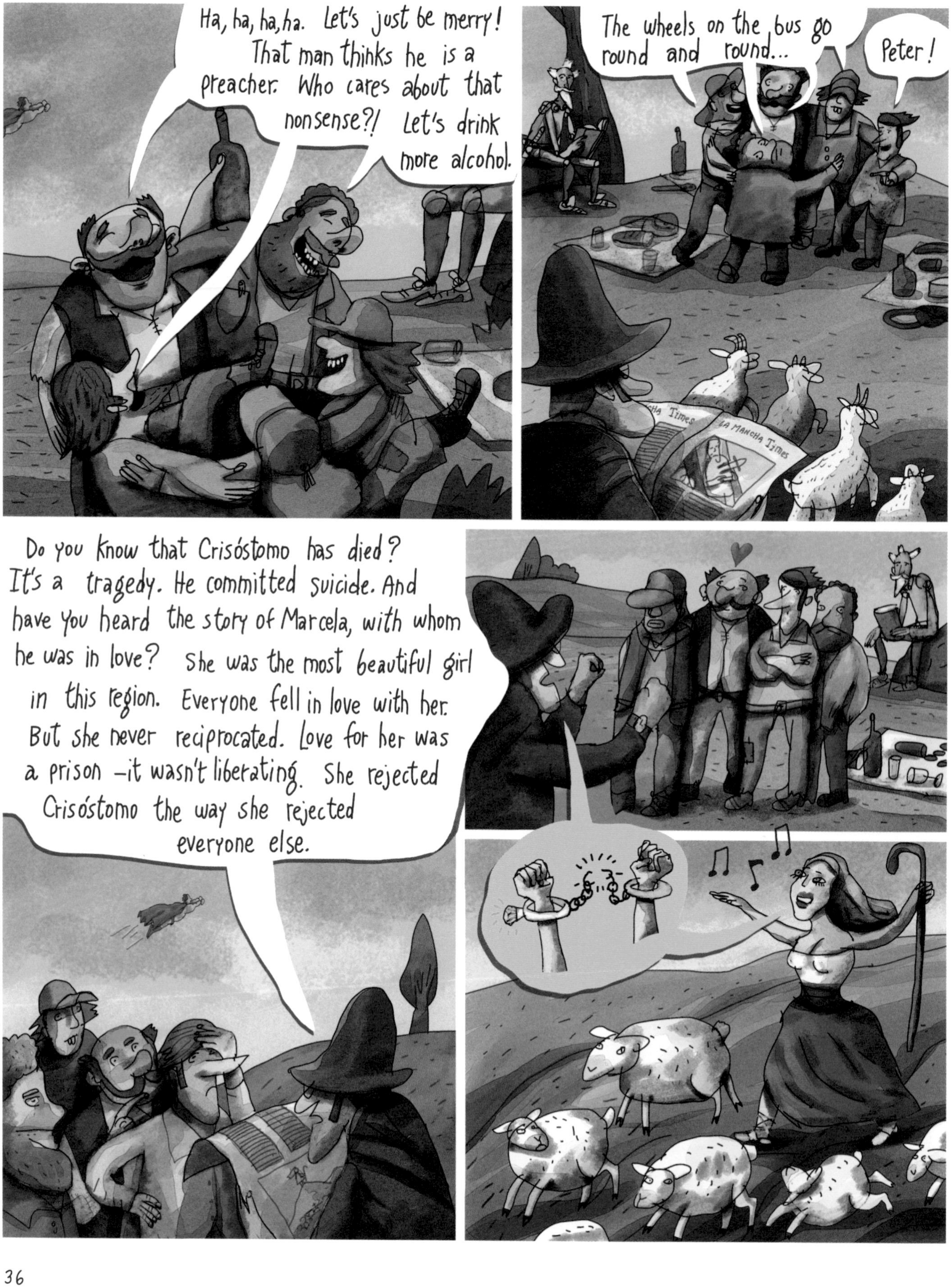

Ha, ha, ha, ha. Let's just be merry! That man thinks he is a preacher. Who cares about that nonsense?! Let's drink more alcohol.
The wheels on the bus go round and round...
Peter!
LA MANCHA Times
Do you know that Crisóstomo has died? It's a tragedy. He committed suicide. And have you heard the story of Marcela, with whom he was in love? She was the most beautiful girl in this region. Everyone fell in love with her. But she never reciprocated. Love for her was a prison —it wasn't liberating. She rejected Crisóstomo the way she rejected everyone else.

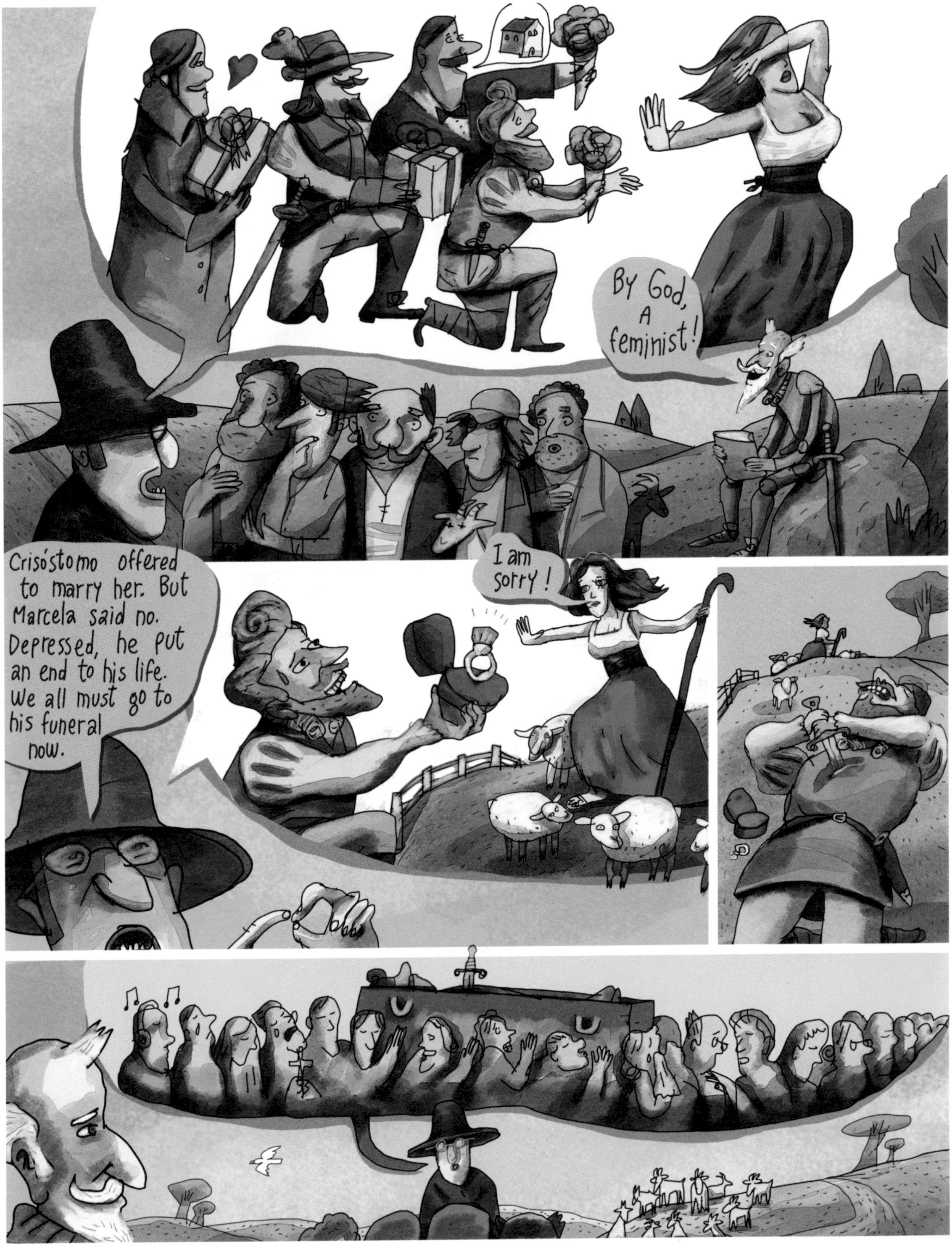
By God, A feminist!
Crisóstomo offered to marry her. But Marcela said no. Depressed, he put an end to his life. We all must go to his funeral now.
I am sorry!

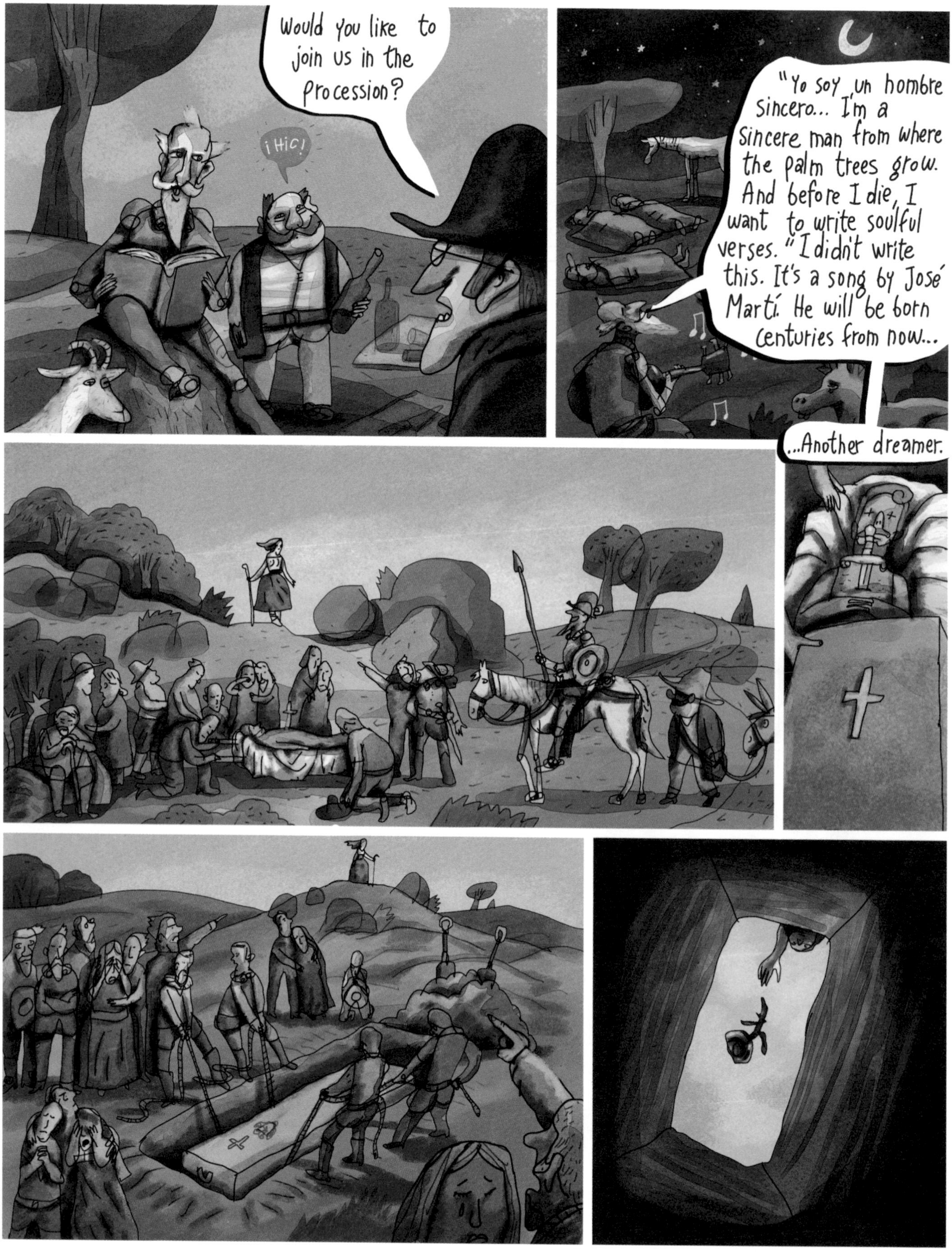
Would you like to join us in the procession?
¡Hic!
"Yo soy un hombre sincero... I'm a sincere man from where the palm trees grow. And before I die, I want to write soulful verses." I didn't write this. It's a song by José Martí. He will be born centuries from now...
...Another dreamer.

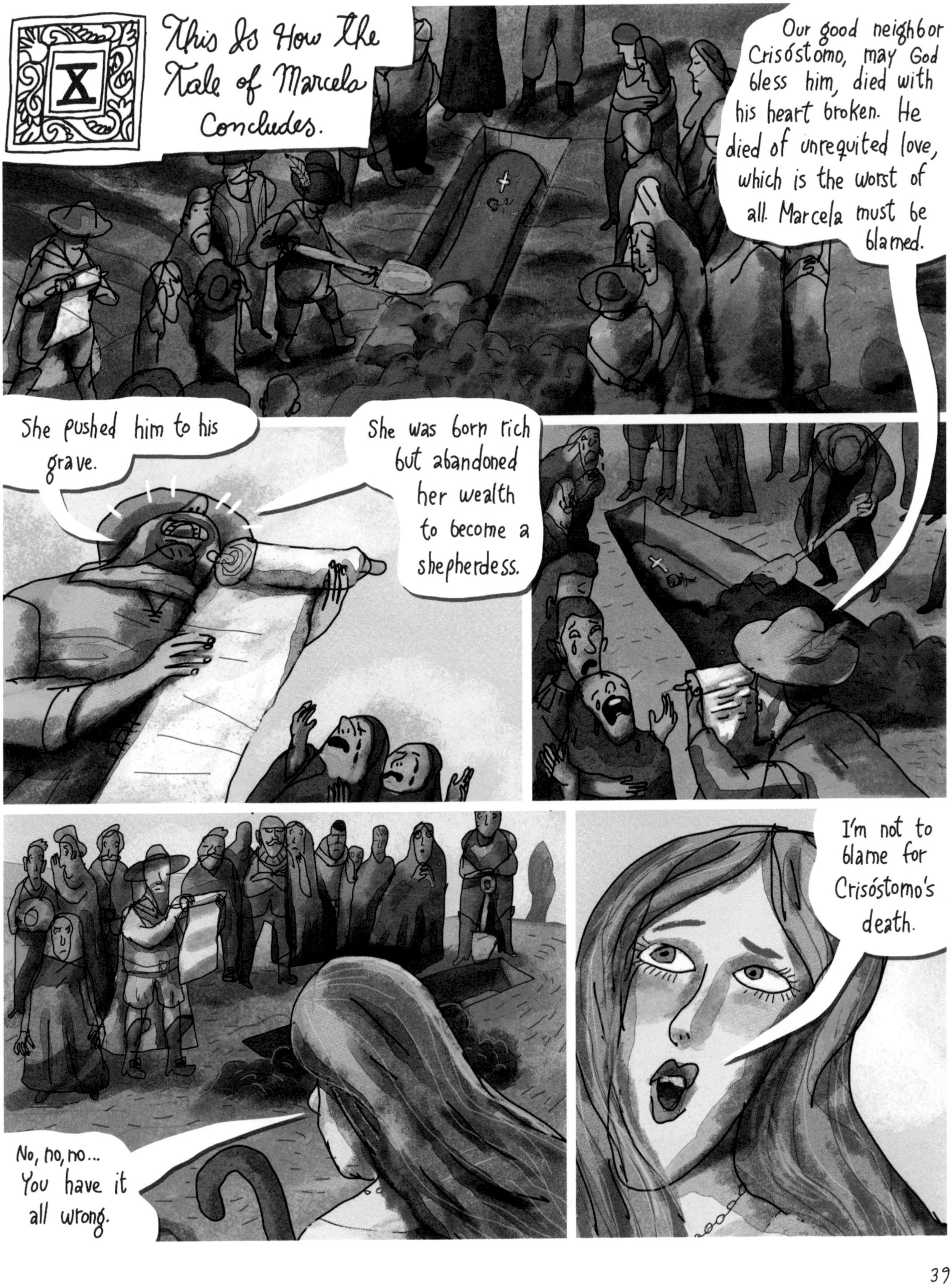
X
This Is How the Tale of Marcela Concludes.
Our good neighbor Crisóstomo, may God bless him, died with his heart broken. He died of unrequited love, which is the worst of all. Marcela must be blamed.
She pushed him to his grave.
She was born rich but abandoned her wealth to become a shepherdess.
No, no, no... You have it all wrong.
I'm not to blame for Crisóstomo's death.

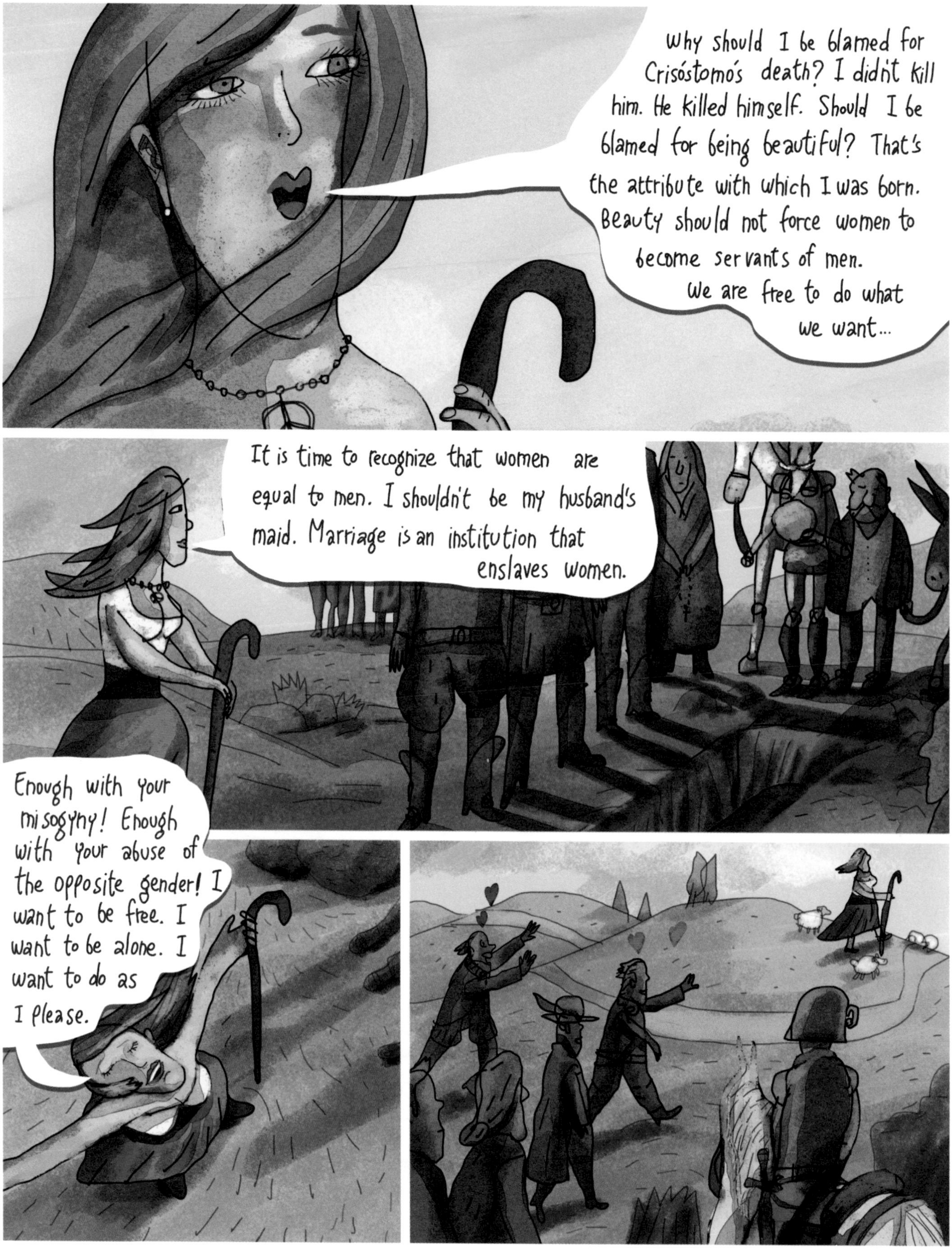
Why should I be blamed for Crisóstomo's death? I didn't kill him. He killed himself. Should I be blamed for being beautiful? That's the attribute with which I was born. Beauty should not force women to become servants of men. We are free to do what we want...
It is time to recognize that women are equal to men. I shouldn't be my husband's maid. Marriage is an institution that enslaves women.
Enough with your misogyny! Enough with your abuse of the opposite gender! I want to be free. I want to be alone. I want to do as I please.

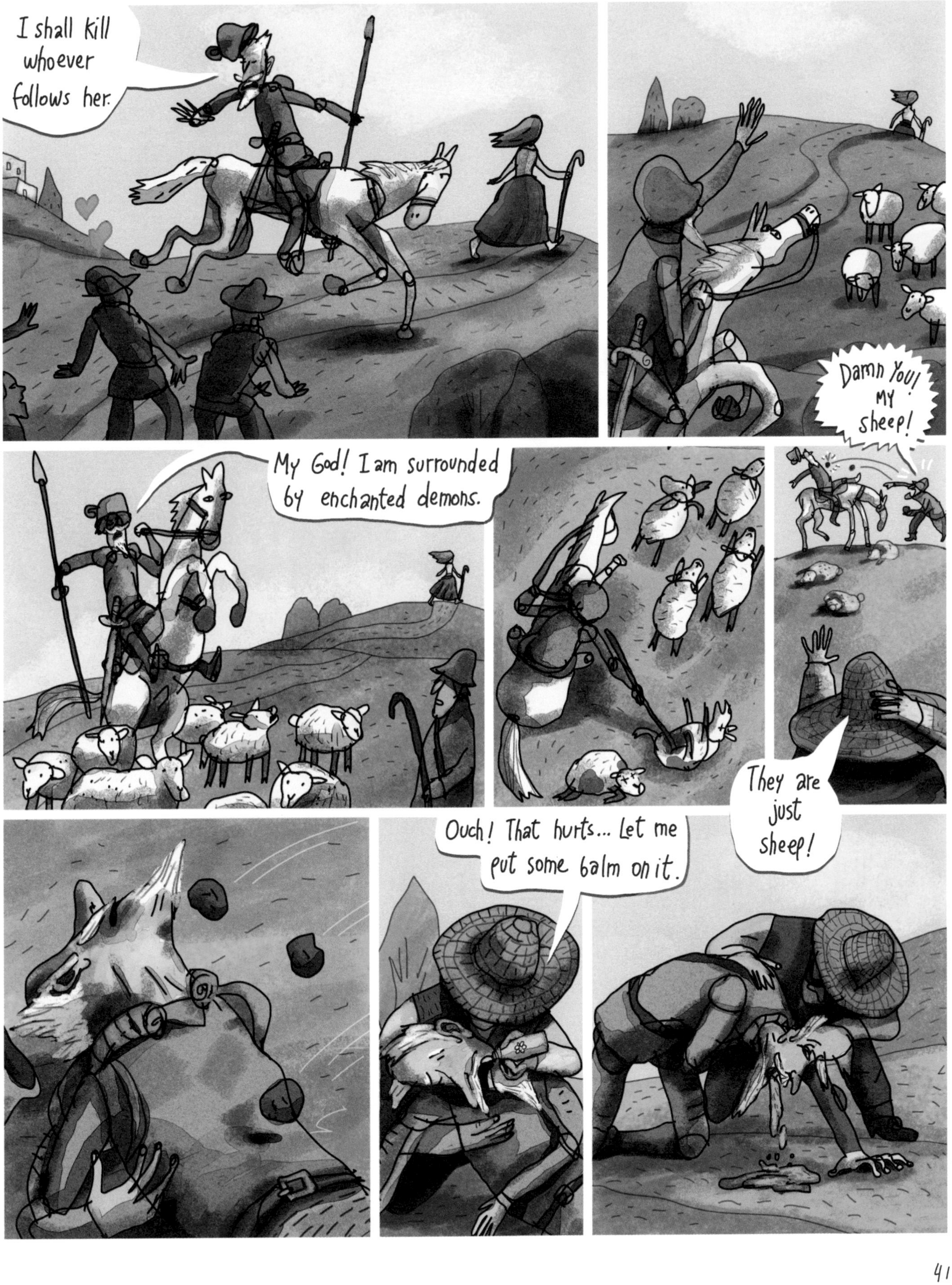
I shall kill whoever follows her.
Damn you! My sheep!
My God! I am surrounded by enchanted demons.
They are just sheep!
Ouch! That hurts... Let me put some balm on it.

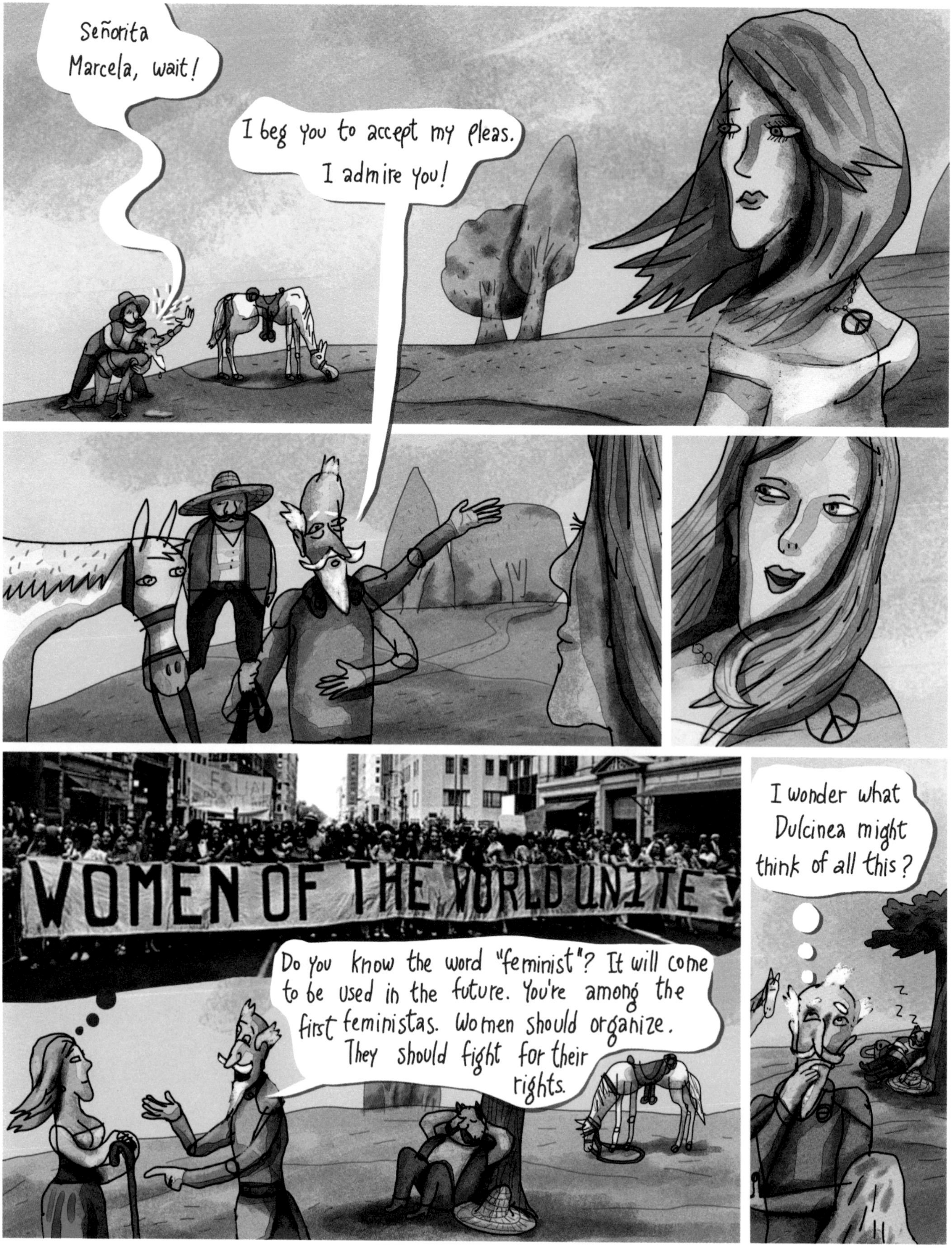
Señorita Marcela, wait!
I beg you to accept my pleas. I admire you!
WOMEN OF THE WORLD UNITE
Do you know the word "feminist"? It will come to be used in the future. You're among the first feministas. Women should organize. They should fight for their rights.
I wonder what Dulcinea might think of all this?

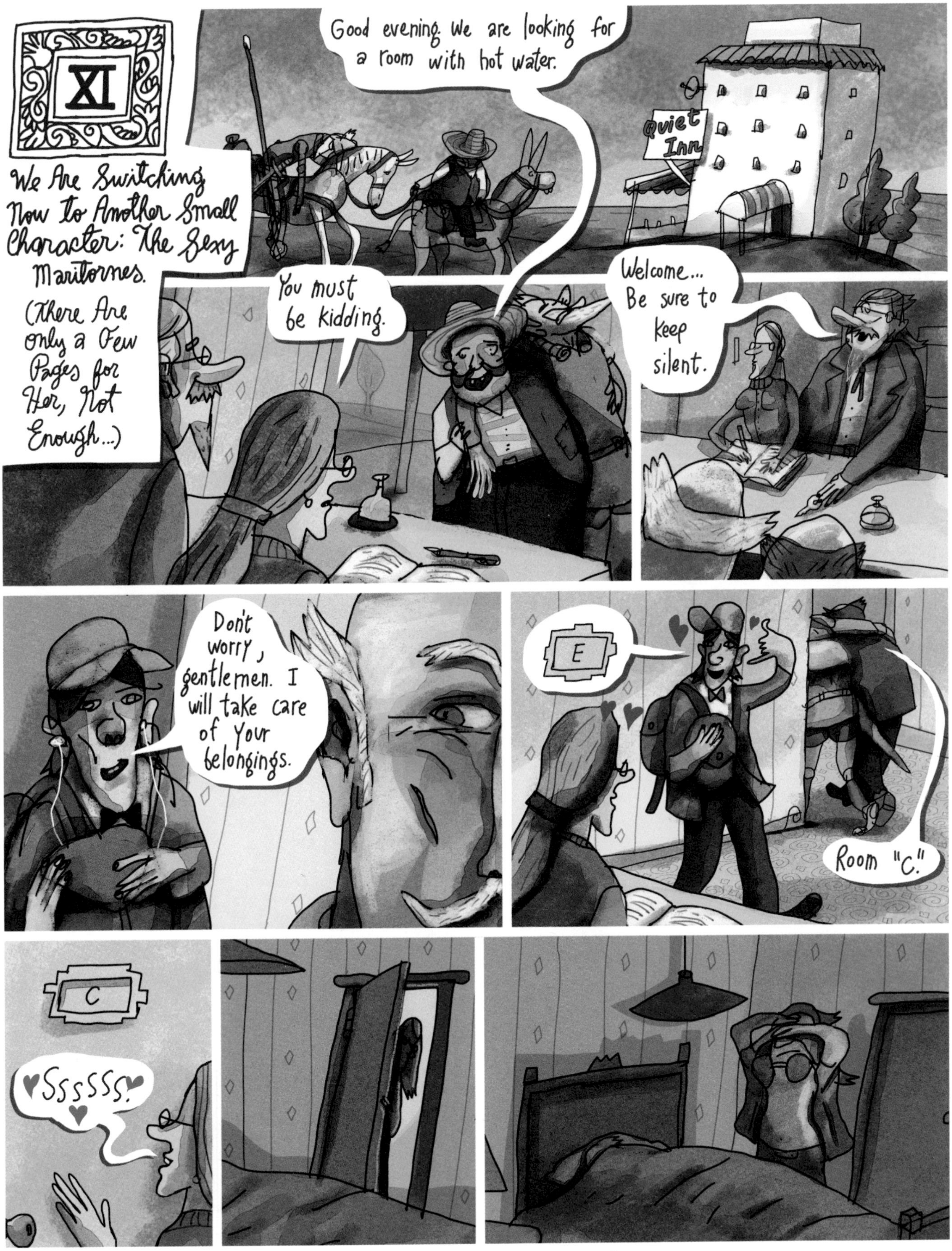
XI
We Are Switching Now to Another Small Character: The Sexy Maritornes.
(There Are only a Few Pages for Her, Not Enough...)
Good evening. We are looking for a room with hot water.
Quiet Inn
You must be kidding.
Welcome... Be sure to keep silent.
Don't worry, gentlemen. I will take care of your belongings.
E
Room "C."
C
Sssss!

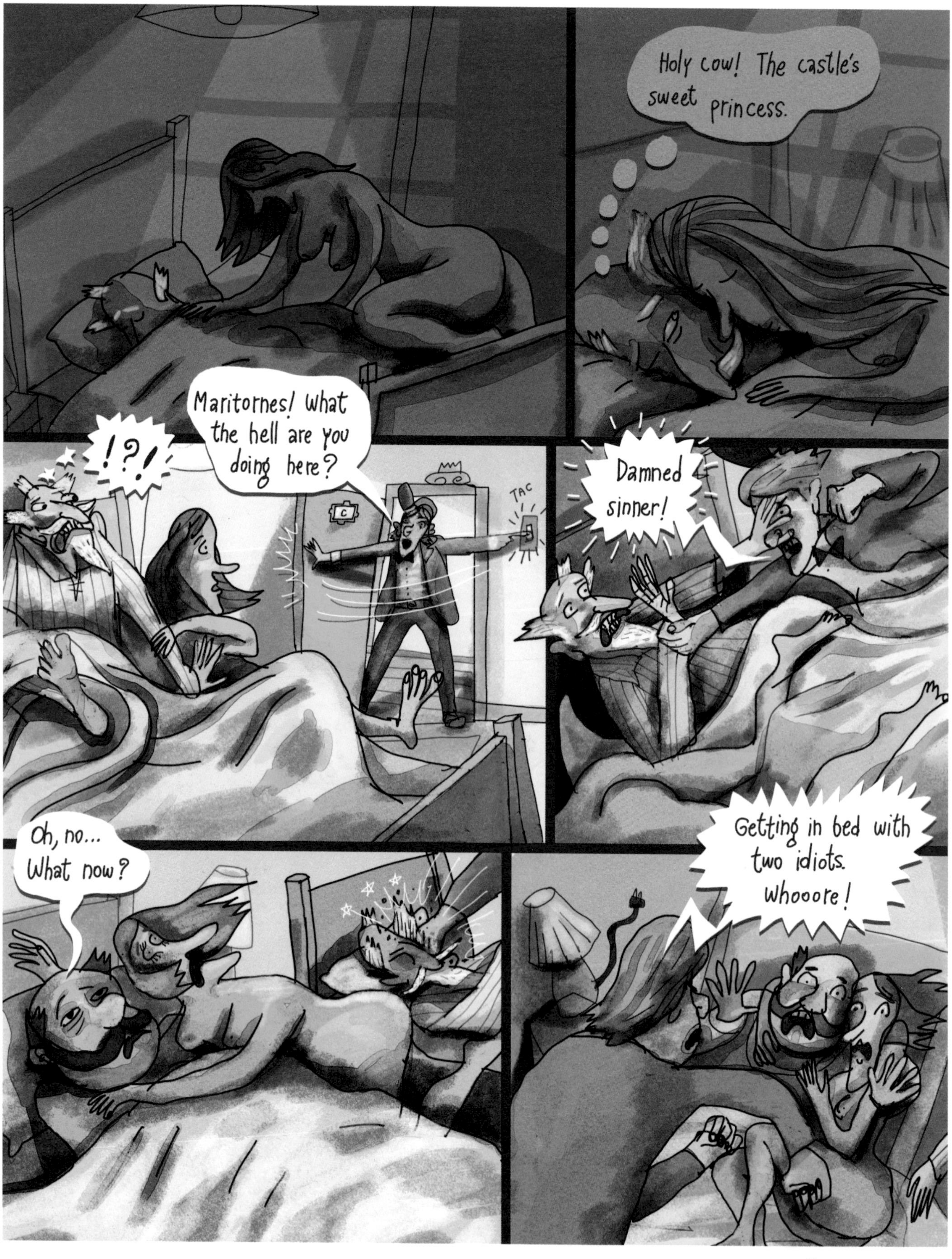
Holy cow! The castle's sweet princess.
!?!
Maritornes! What the hell are you doing here?
TAC
Damned sinner!
Oh, no... What now?
Getting in bed with two idiots. Whooore!

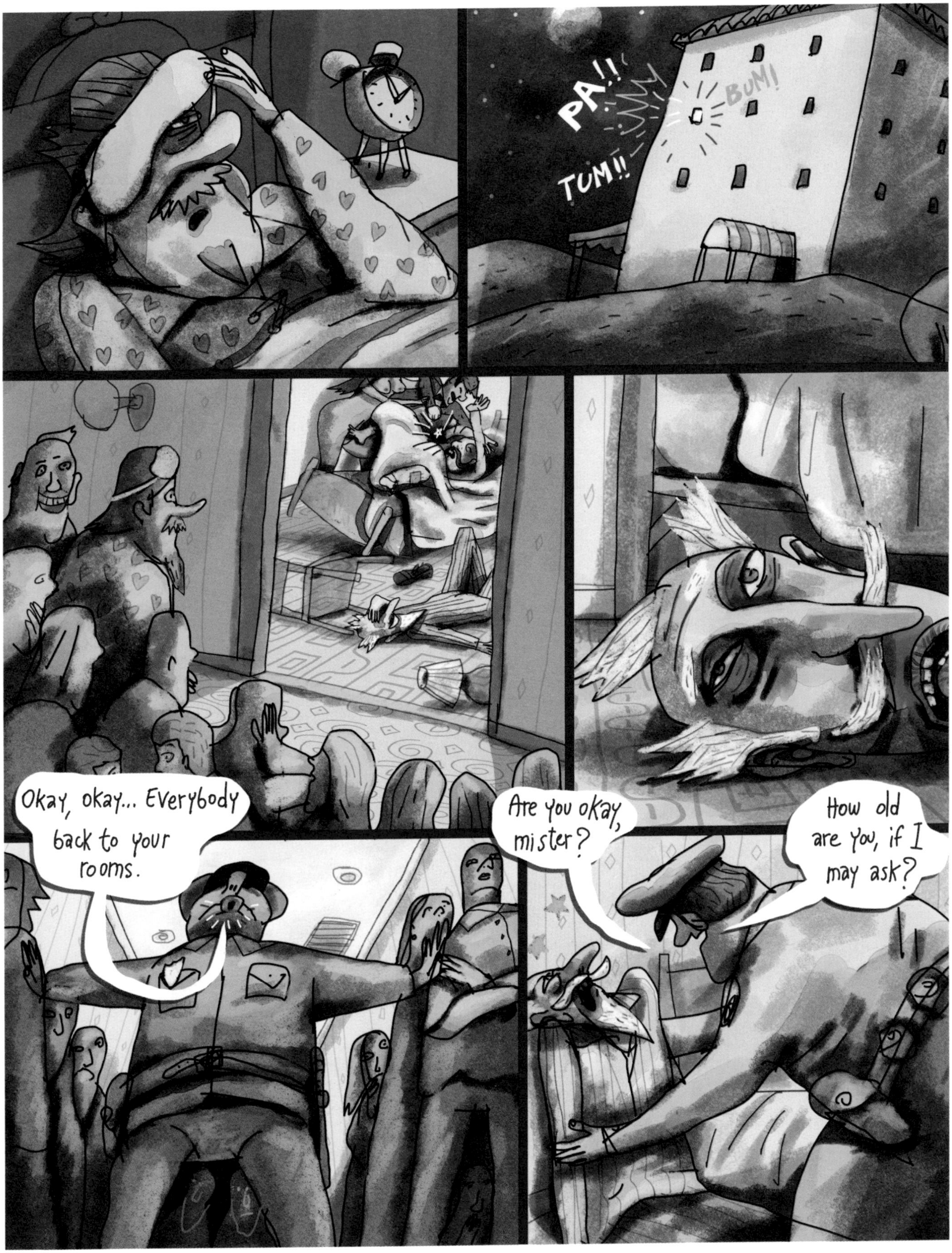
PA!!
TUM!!
BUM!
Okay, okay... Everybody back to your rooms.
Are you okay, mister?
How old are you, if I may ask?

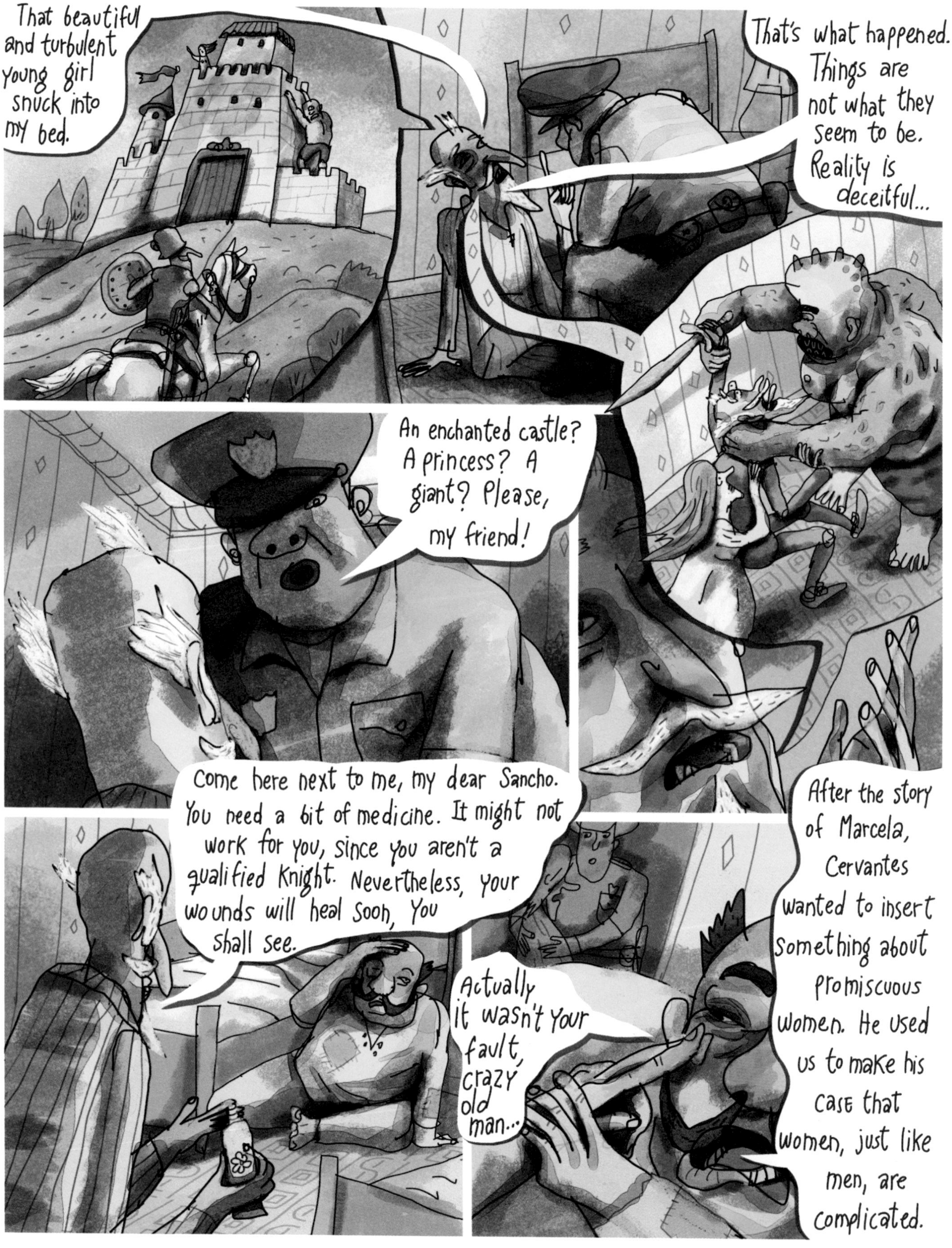
That beautiful and turbulent young girl snuck into my bed.
That's what happened. Things are not what they seem to be. Reality is deceitful...
An enchanted castle? A princess? A giant? Please, my friend!
Come here next to me, my dear Sancho. You need a bit of medicine. It might not work for you, since you aren't a qualified Knight. Nevertheless, your wounds will heal soon, You shall see.
Actually it wasn't your fault, crazy old man...
After the story of Marcela, Cervantes wanted to insert something about promiscuous women. He used us to make his case that women, just like men, are complicated.

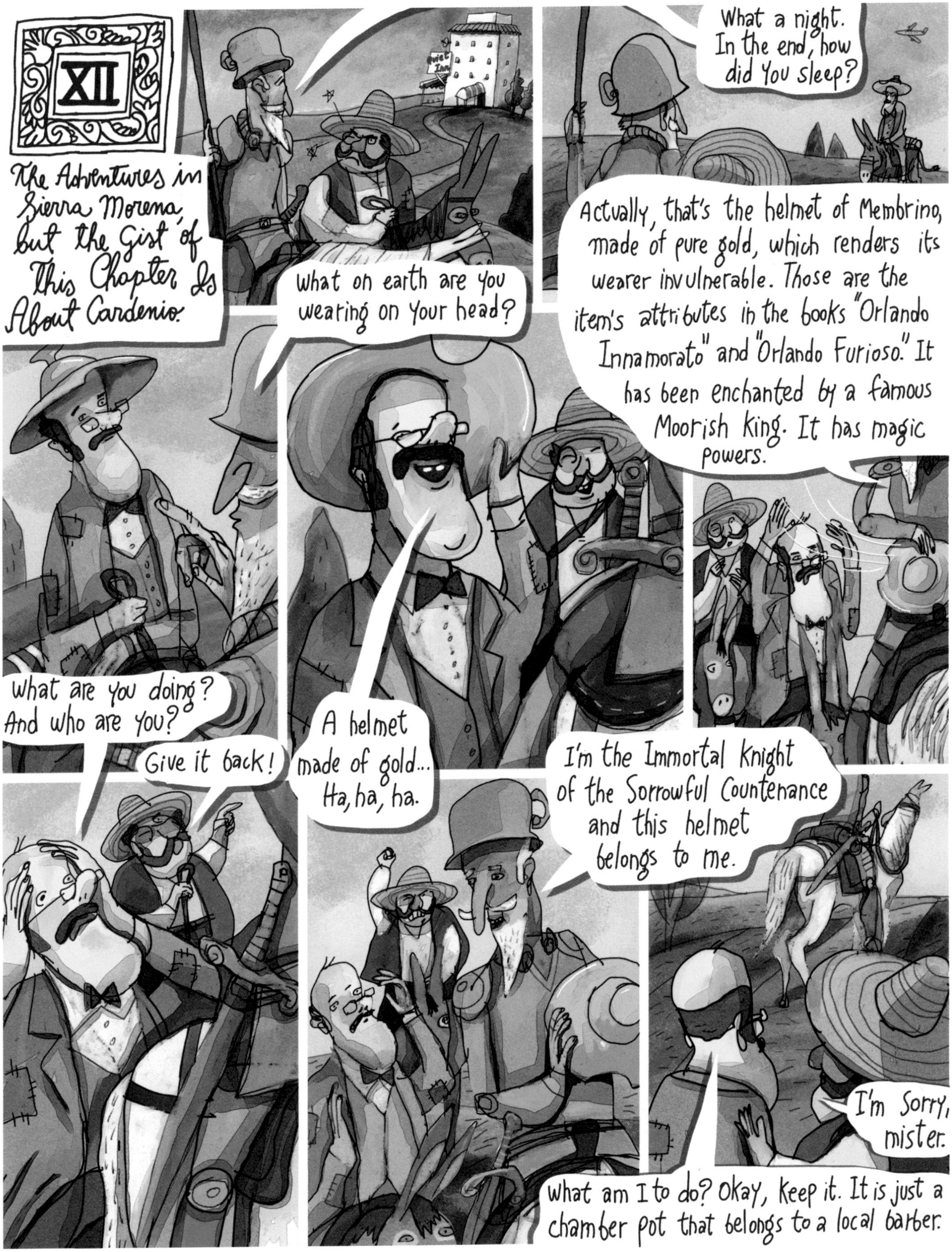
XII
The Adventures in Sierra Morena, but the Gist of This Chapter Is About Cardenio.
Quiet Inn
What a night. In the end, how did you sleep?
What on earth are you wearing on your head?
Actually, that's the helmet of Membrino, made of pure gold, which renders its wearer invulnerable. Those are the item's attributes in the books "Orlando Innamorato" and "Orlando Furioso." It has been enchanted by a famous Moorish King. It has magic powers.
What are you doing? And who are you?
A helmet made of gold... Ha, ha, ha.
Give it back!
I'm the Immortal Knight of the Sorrowful Countenance and this helmet belongs to me.
I'm Sorry, mister.
What am I to do? Okay, keep it. It is just a chamber pot that belongs to a local barber.

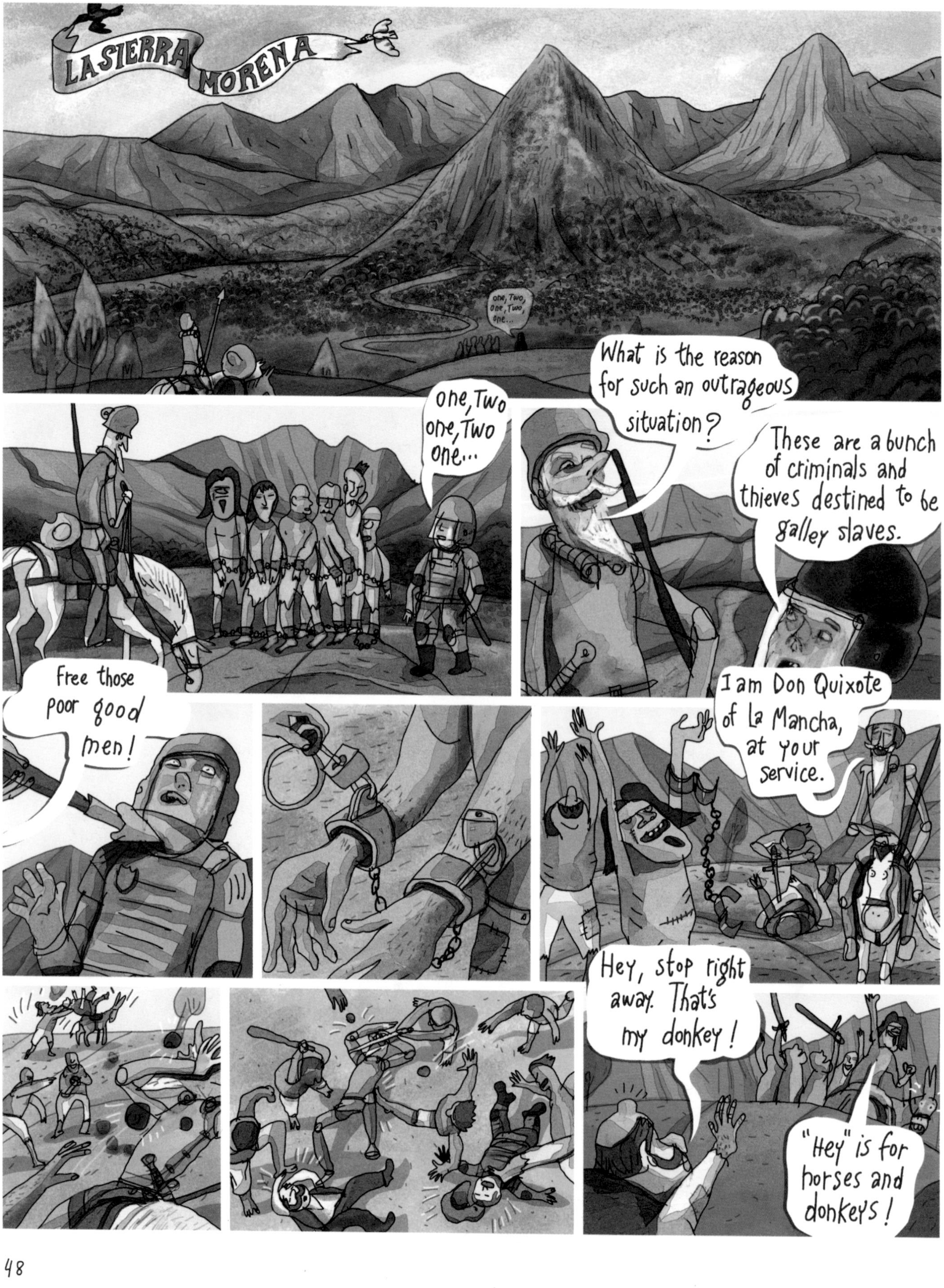
LA SIERRA MORENA
one, Two, one, Two, one...
one, Two one, Two one...
What is the reason for such an outrageous situation?
These are a bunch of criminals and thieves destined to be galley slaves.
Free those poor good men!
I am Don Quixote of La Mancha, at your service.
Hey, stop right away. That's my donkey!
"Hey" is for horses and donkeys!

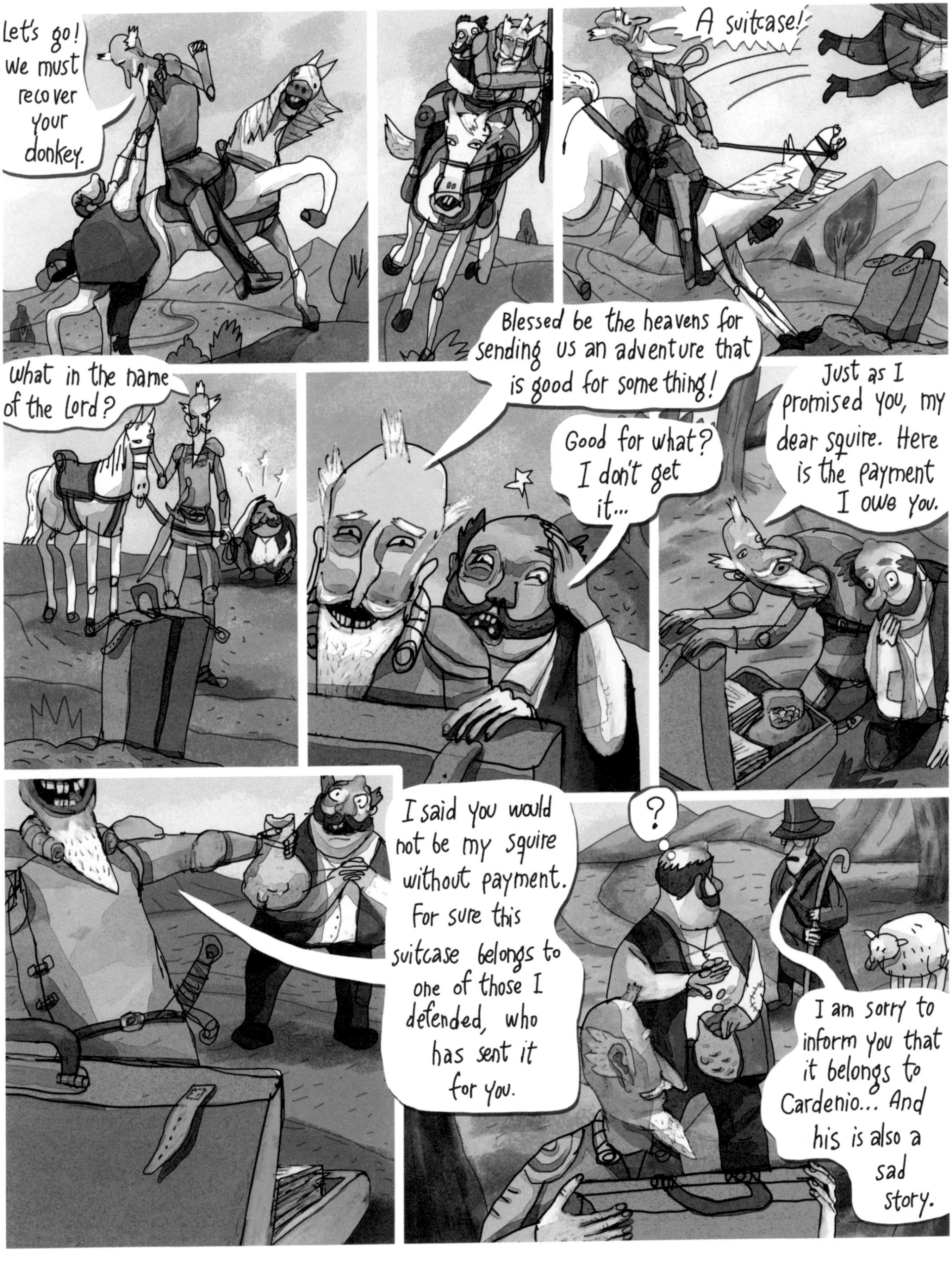
Let's go! We must recover your donkey.
A suitcase!
What in the name of the Lord?
Blessed be the heavens for sending us an adventure that is good for something!
Good for what? I don't get it...
Just as I promised you, my dear squire. Here is the payment I owe you.
I said you would not be my squire without payment. For sure this suitcase belongs to one of those I defended, who has sent it for you.
?
I am sorry to inform you that it belongs to Cardenio... And his is also a sad story.

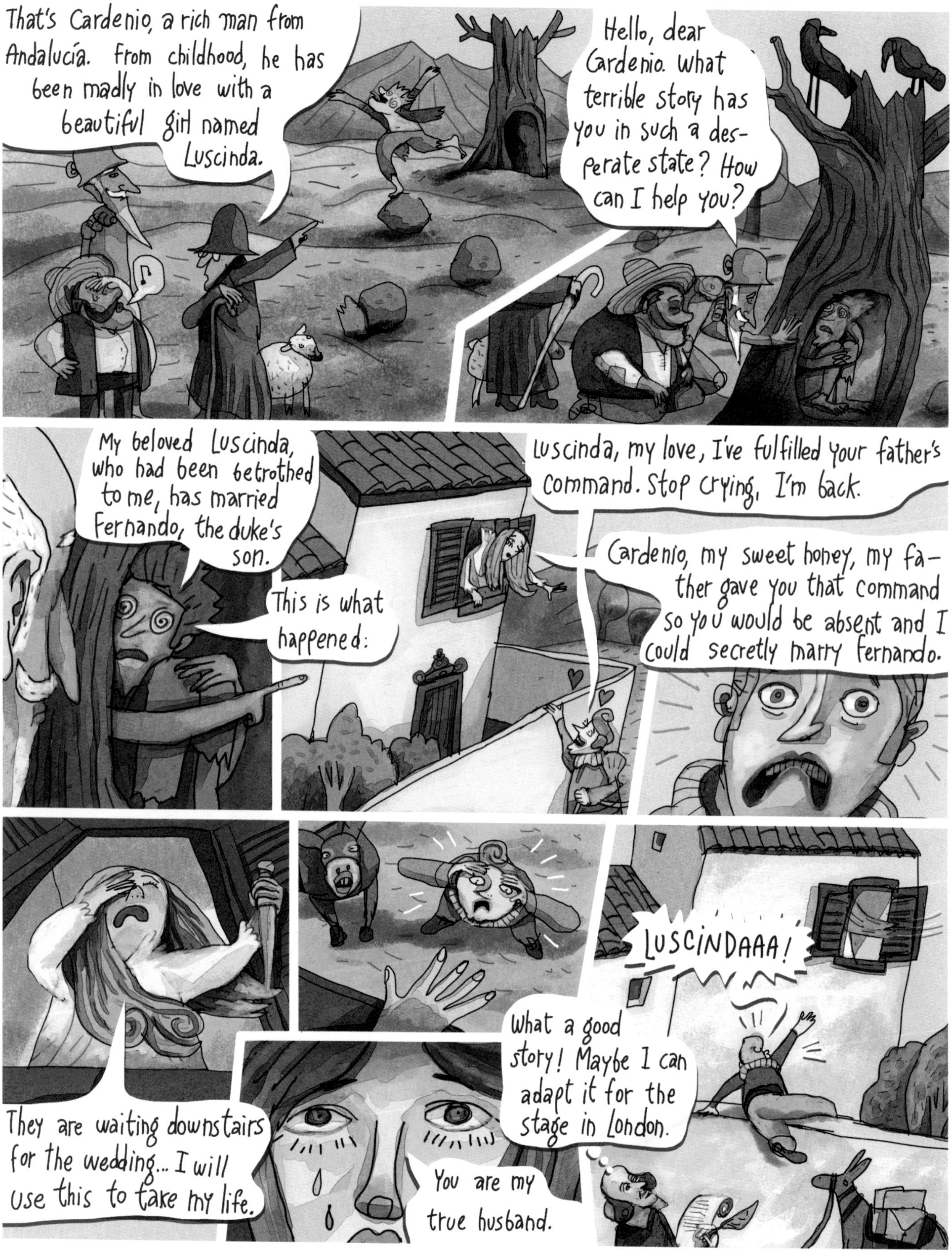
That's Cardenio, a rich man from Andalucía. From childhood, he has been madly in love with a beautiful girl named Luscinda.
Hello, dear Cardenio. What terrible story has you in such a desperate state? How can I help you?
My beloved Luscinda, who had been betrothed to me, has married Fernando, the duke's son.
This is what happened:
Luscinda, my love, I've fulfilled your father's command. Stop crying, I'm back.
Cardenio, my sweet honey, my father gave you that command so you would be absent and I could secretly marry Fernando.
They are waiting downstairs for the wedding... I will use this to take my life.
You are my true husband.
LUSCINDAAA!
What a good story! Maybe I can adapt it for the stage in London.

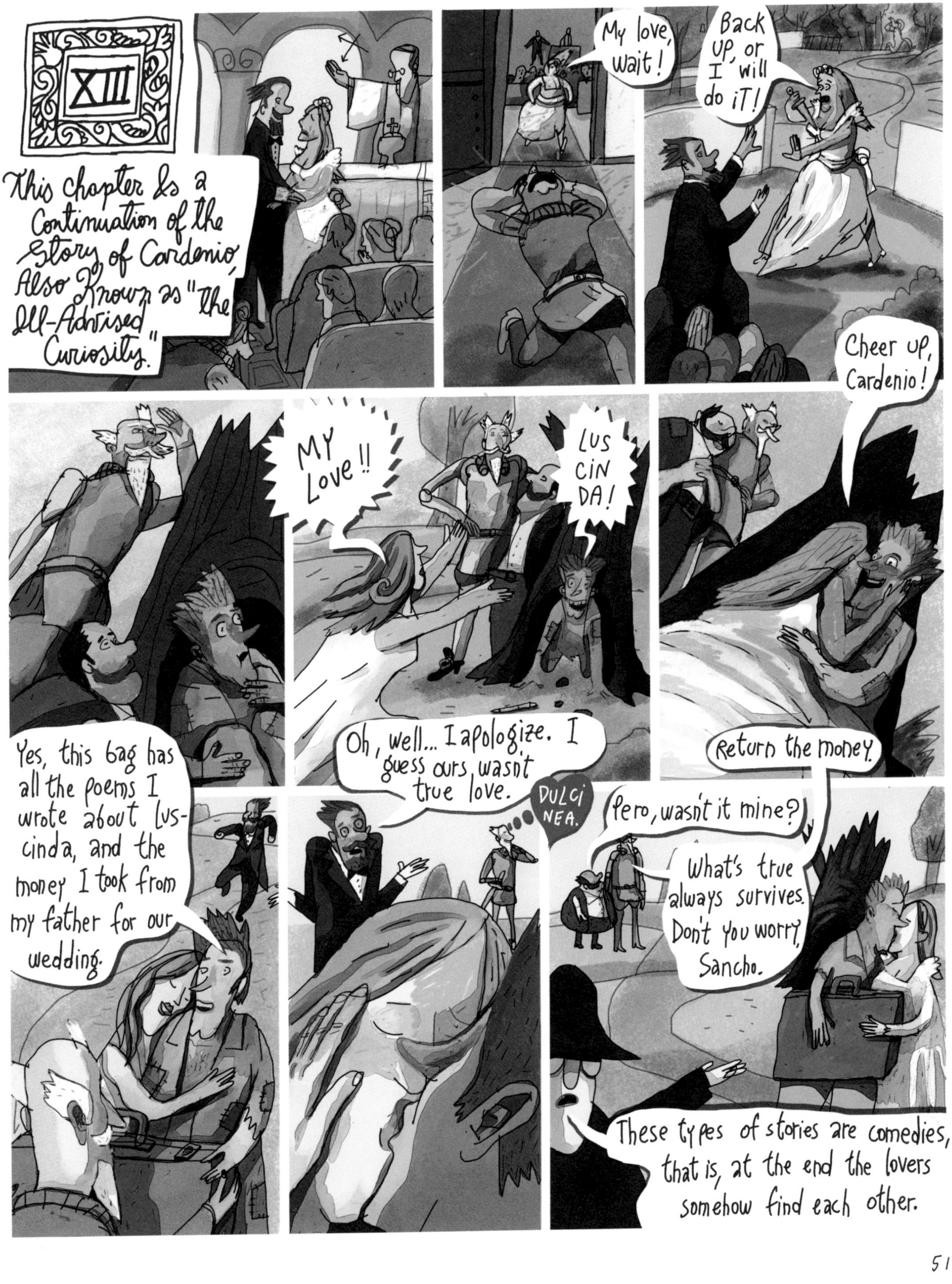
XIII
This chapter is a Continuation of the Story of Cardenio, Also Known as "the Ill-Advised Curiosity."
My love, wait!
Back up, or I will do iT!
Cheer up, Cardenio!
MY Love!!
LUS CIN DA!
Yes, this bag has all the poems I wrote about Luscinda, and the money I took from my father for our wedding.
Oh, well... I apologize. I guess ours wasn't true love.
DULCINEA.
Return the money.
Pero, wasn't it mine?
What's true always survives. Don't you worry, Sancho.
These types of stories are comedies, that is, at the end the lovers somehow find each other.

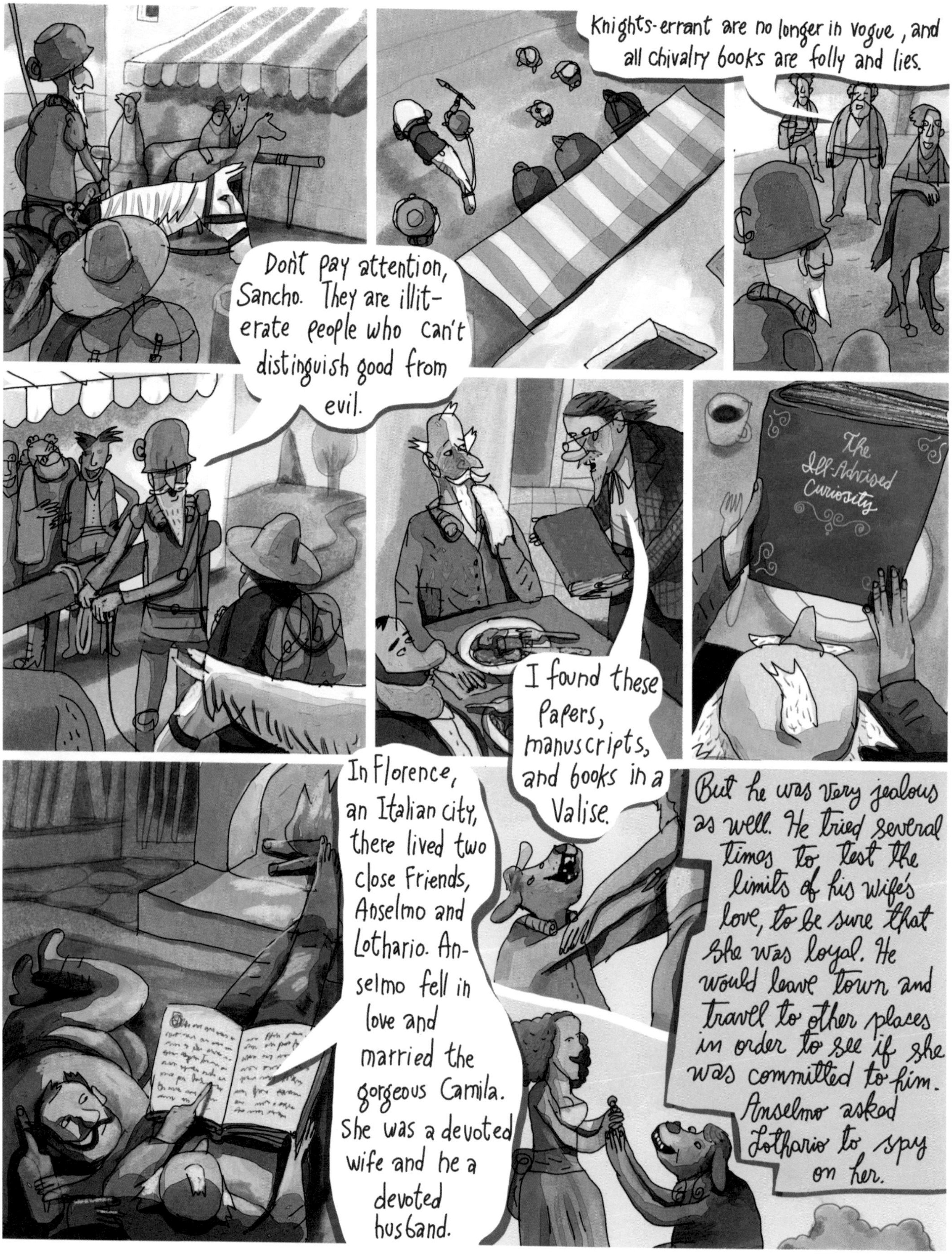
Knights-errant are no longer in vogue, and all chivalry books are folly and lies.
Don't pay attention, Sancho. They are illit-erate people who can't distinguish good from evil.
I found these papers, manuscripts, and books in a valise.
The Ill-Advised Curiosity
In Florence, an Italian city, there lived two close friends, Anselmo and Lothario. Anselmo fell in love and married the gorgeous Camila. She was a devoted wife and he a devoted husband.
But he was very jealous as well. He tried several times to test the limits of his wife's love, to be sure that she was loyal. He would leave town and travel to other places in order to see if she was committed to him. Anselmo asked Lothario to spy on her.

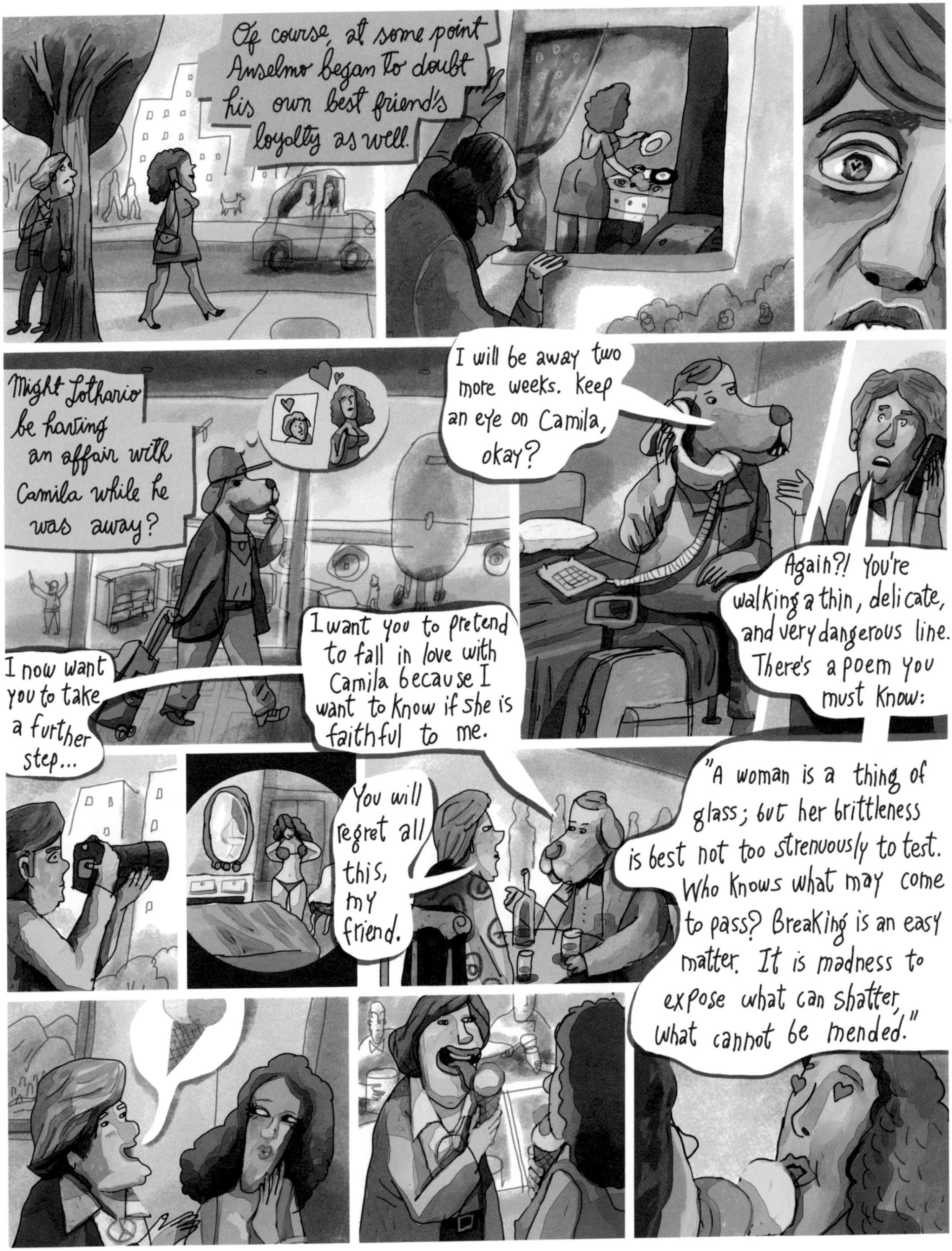
Of course, at some point Anselmo began to doubt his own best friend's loyalty as well.
Might Lothario be having an affair with Camila while he was away?
I will be away two more weeks. Keep an eye on Camila, okay?
Again?! You're walking a thin, delicate, and very dangerous line. There's a poem you must know:
I now want you to take a further step...
I want you to pretend to fall in love with Camila because I want to know if she is faithful to me.
You will regret all this, my friend.
"A woman is a thing of glass; but her brittleness is best not too strenuously to test. Who knows what may come to pass? Breaking is an easy matter. It is madness to expose what can shatter, what cannot be mended."

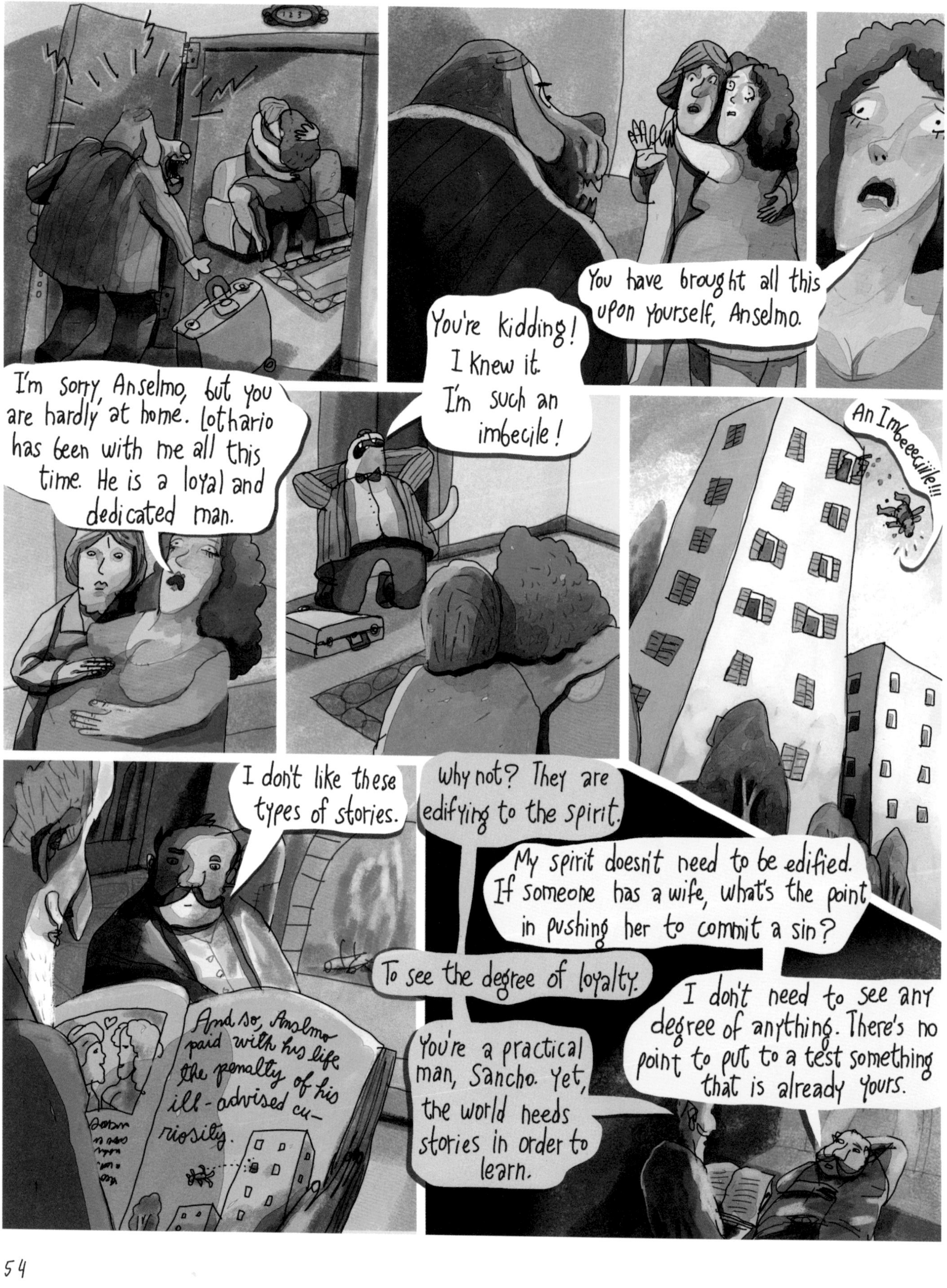
You're kidding! I knew it. I'm such an imbecile!
You have brought all this upon yourself, Anselmo.
I'm sorry, Anselmo, but you are hardly at home. Lothario has been with me all this time. He is a loyal and dedicated man.
An Imbeeeciiile!!!
I don't like these types of stories.
And so, Anselmo paid with his life the penalty of his ill-advised curiosity.
Why not? They are edifying to the spirit.
My spirit doesn't need to be edified. If someone has a wife, what's the point in pushing her to commit a sin?
To see the degree of loyalty.
I don't need to see any degree of anything. There's no point to put to a test something that is already yours.
You're a practical man, Sancho. Yet, the world needs stories in order to learn.

XIV

This Chapter Is Yet Another Continuation of The Story of Cardenio, Also Known as "The Ill-Advised Curiosity".

The world is nothing if not stories, stories we tell ourselves to live.

We are a story too, right?

As our heroes trot through the Sierra Morena, it is time to tell how the life and adventures of Don Quixote of La Mancha, the Knight of the Sorrowful Countenance, came to be.

You might think, as was stated earlier, that the novel was written by Miguel de Cervantes Saavedra, a second-rate poet and mediocre playwright. Like most writers of his time, the Spanish Golden Age, Cervantes was a sonnetist. He wrote this sonnet:

Few facts are known about Cervantes. He was born in Alcalá de Henares in 1547 and died in Madrid in 1616, at the age of 68. It is also known that he was a soldier during Spain's colonial era. Indeed, he is known to have participated in the legendary Battle of Lepanto, where he was injured and lost the use of his left arm. Therefore, he was known as "the one-armed soldier of Lepanto."

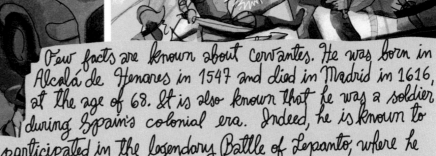

El casto ardor de una amorosa llama,
un sabio pecho a su rigor sujeto,
un desdén sacudido y un afecto blando,
que al alma en dulce fuego inflama,

el bien y el mal a que convida y llama
de amor la fuerza y poderoso efecto,
eternamente, en son claro y perfecto,
con estas rimas cantará la fama,

llevando el nombre único y famoso
vuestro, felice López Maldonado,
del moreno etíope al cita blanco,

y hará que en balde de laurel honroso
espere alguno verse coronado
si no os imita y tiene por su blanco.

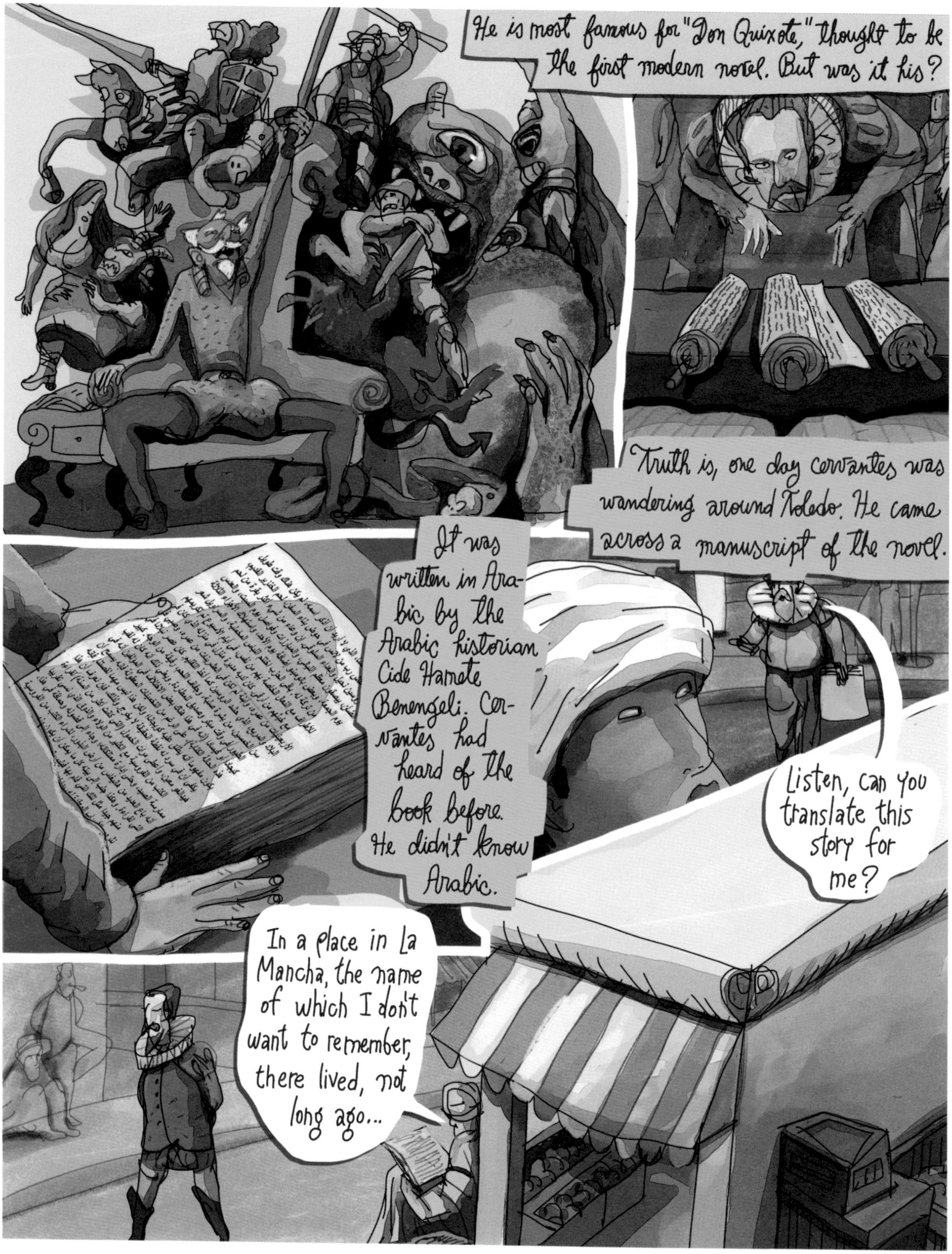
He is most famous for "Don Quixote," thought to be the first modern novel. But was it his?
Truth is, one day Cervantes was wandering around Toledo. He came across a manuscript of the novel.
It was written in Arabic by the Arabic historian Cide Hamete Benengeli. Cervantes had heard of the book before. He didn't know Arabic.
Listen, can you translate this story for me?
In a place in La Mancha, the name of which I don't want to remember, there lived, not long ago...

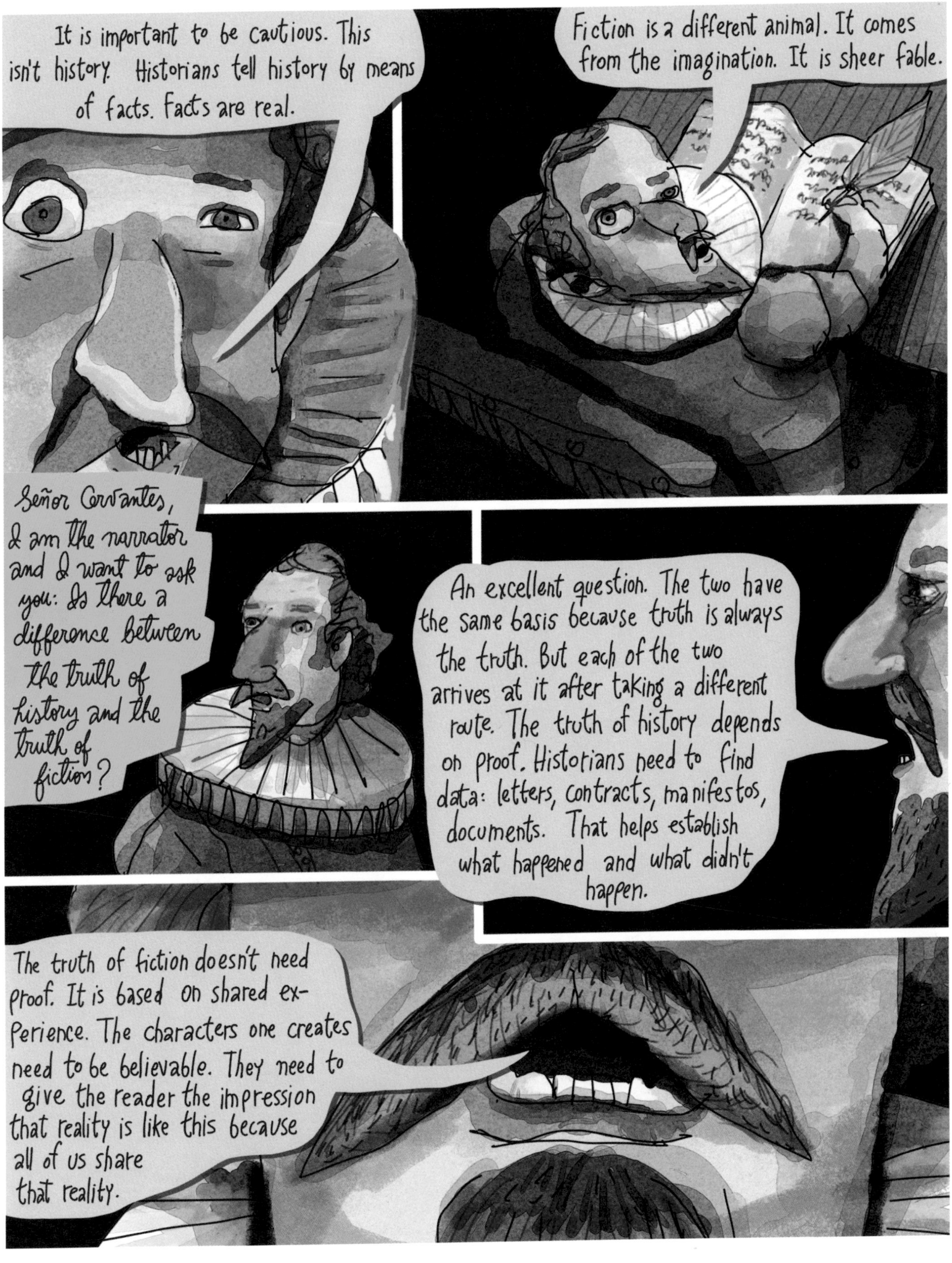
It is important to be cautious. This isn't history. Historians tell history by means of facts. Facts are real.
Fiction is a different animal. It comes from the imagination. It is sheer fable.
Señor Cervantes, I am the narrator and I want to ask you: Is there a difference between the truth of history and the truth of fiction?
An excellent question. The two have the same basis because truth is always the truth. But each of the two arrives at it after taking a different route. The truth of history depends on proof. Historians need to find data: letters, contracts, manifestos, documents. That helps establish what happened and what didn't happen.
The truth of fiction doesn't need proof. It is based on shared experience. The characters one creates need to be believable. They need to give the reader the impression that reality is like this because all of us share that reality.

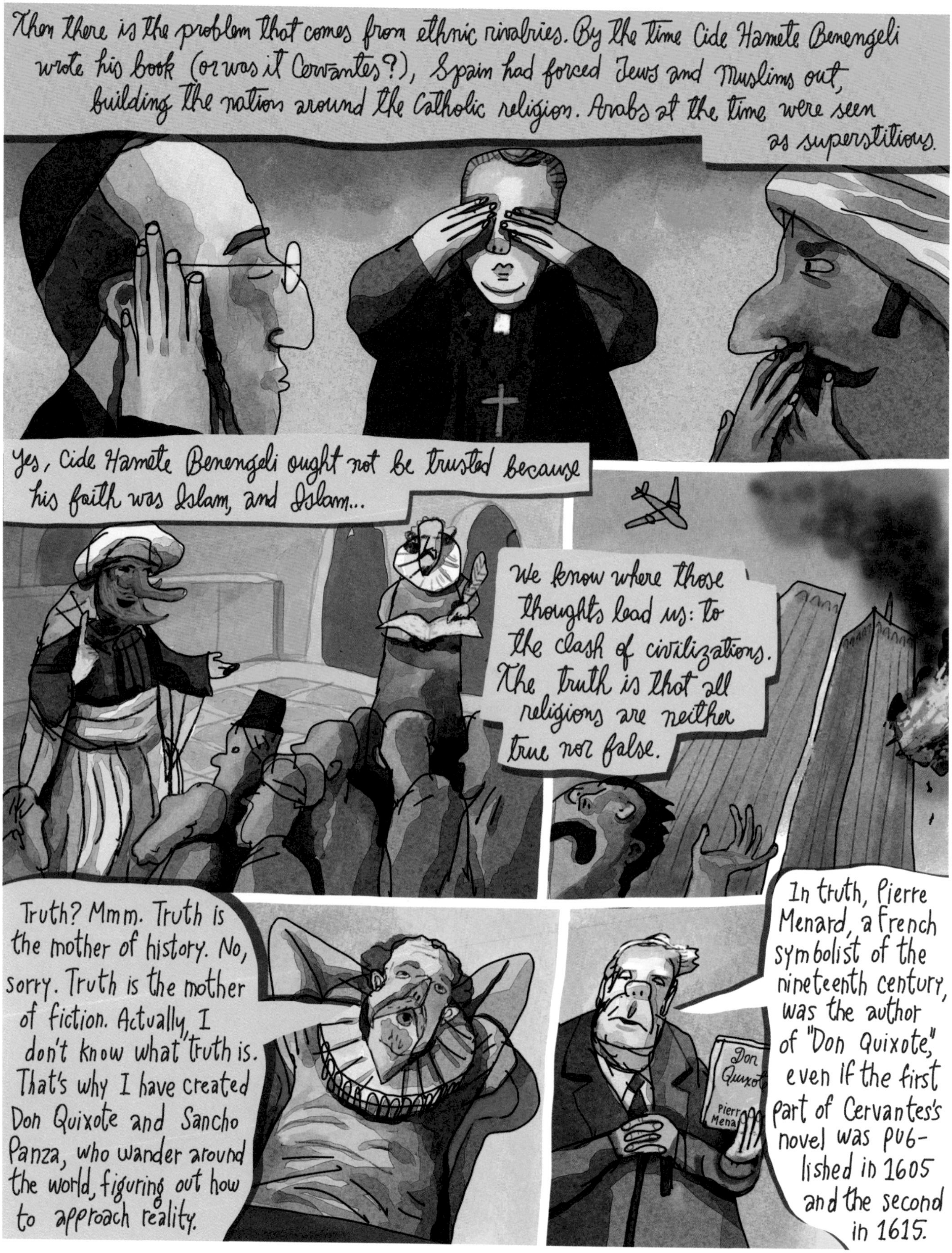
Then there is the problem that comes from ethnic rivalries. By the time Cide Hamete Benengeli wrote his book (or was it Cervantes?), Spain had forced Jews and Muslims out, building the nation around the Catholic religion. Arabs at the time were seen as superstitious.
Yes, Cide Hamete Benengeli ought not be trusted because his faith was Islam, and Islam...
We know where those thoughts lead us: to the clash of civilizations. The truth is that all religions are neither true nor false.
Truth? Mmm. Truth is the mother of history. No, sorry. Truth is the mother of fiction. Actually, I don't know what truth is. That's why I have created Don Quixote and Sancho Panza, who wander around the world, figuring out how to approach reality.
In truth, Pierre Menard, a French symbolist of the nineteenth century, was the author of "Don Quixote," even if the first part of Cervantes's novel was published in 1605 and the second in 1615.

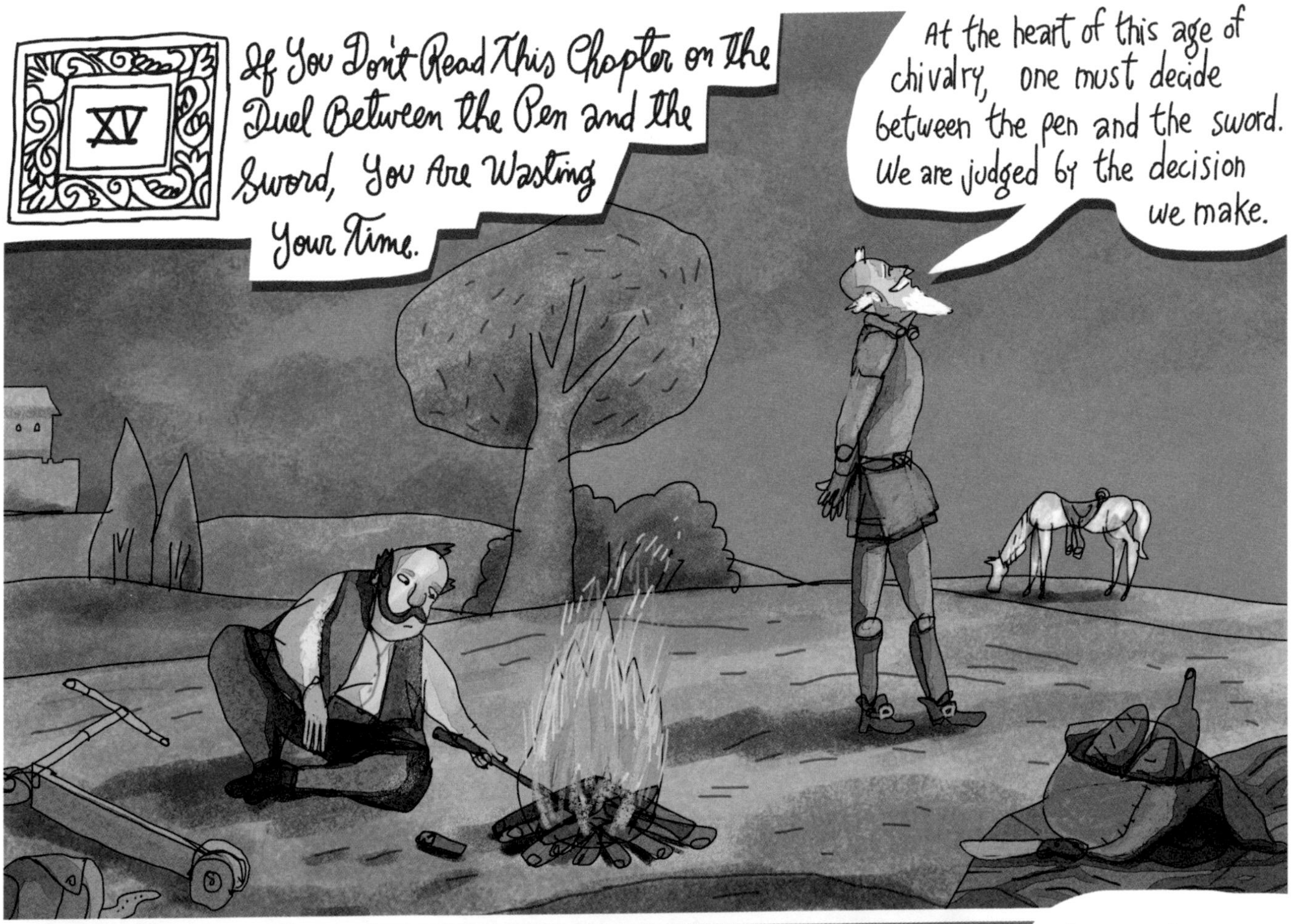
XV
If You Don't Read This Chapter on the Duel Between the Pen and the Sword, You Are Wasting Your Time.
At the heart of this age of chivalry, one must decide between the pen and the sword. We are judged by the decision we make.

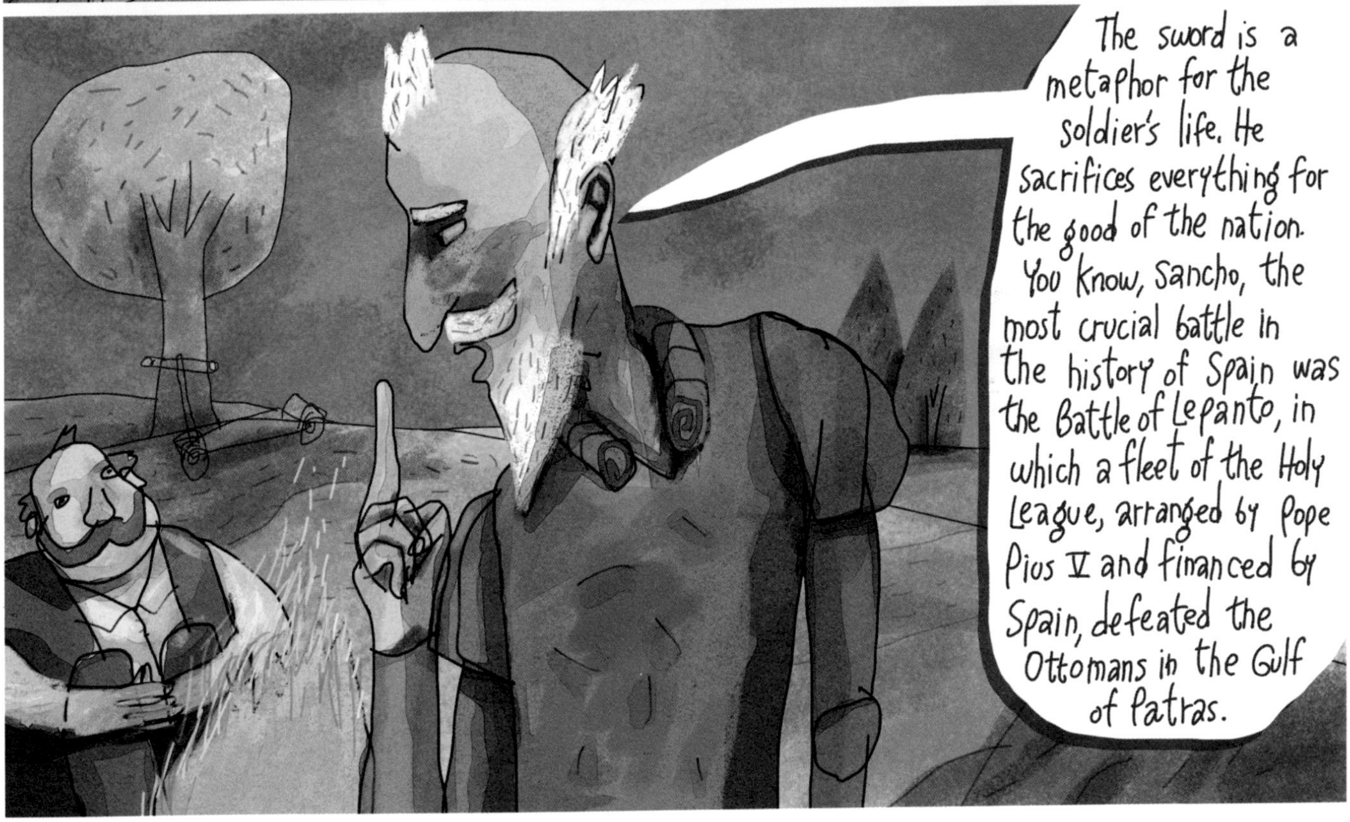
The sword is a metaphor for the soldier's life. He sacrifices everything for the good of the nation. You know, Sancho, the most crucial battle in the history of Spain was the Battle of Lepanto, in which a fleet of the Holy League, arranged by Pope Pius V and financed by Spain, defeated the Ottomans in the Gulf of Patras.

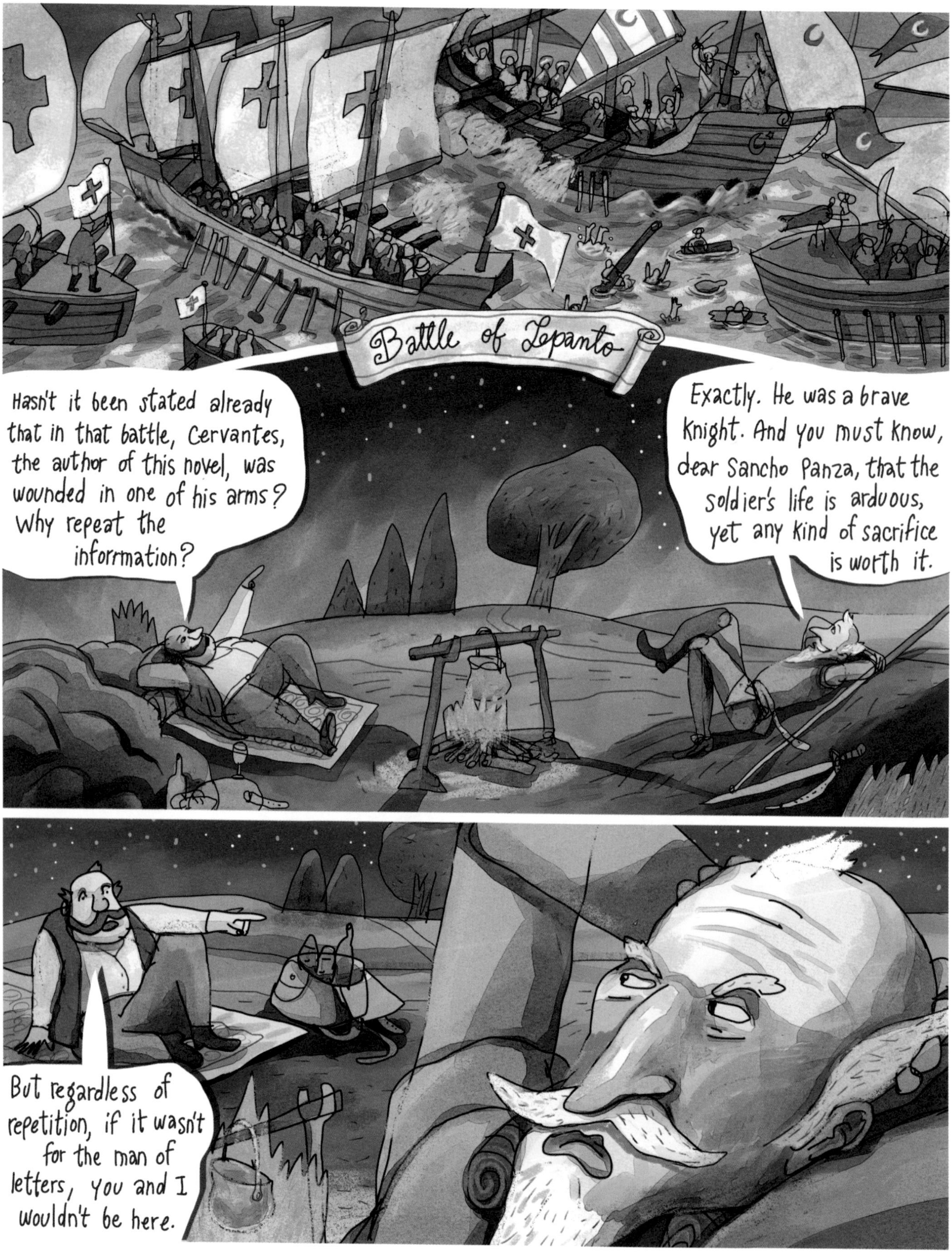
Battle of Lepanto
Hasn't it been stated already that in that battle, Cervantes, the author of this novel, was wounded in one of his arms? Why repeat the information?
Exactly. He was a brave Knight. And you must know, dear Sancho Panza, that the soldier's life is arduous, yet any kind of sacrifice is worth it.
But regardless of repetition, if it wasn't for the man of letters, you and I wouldn't be here.

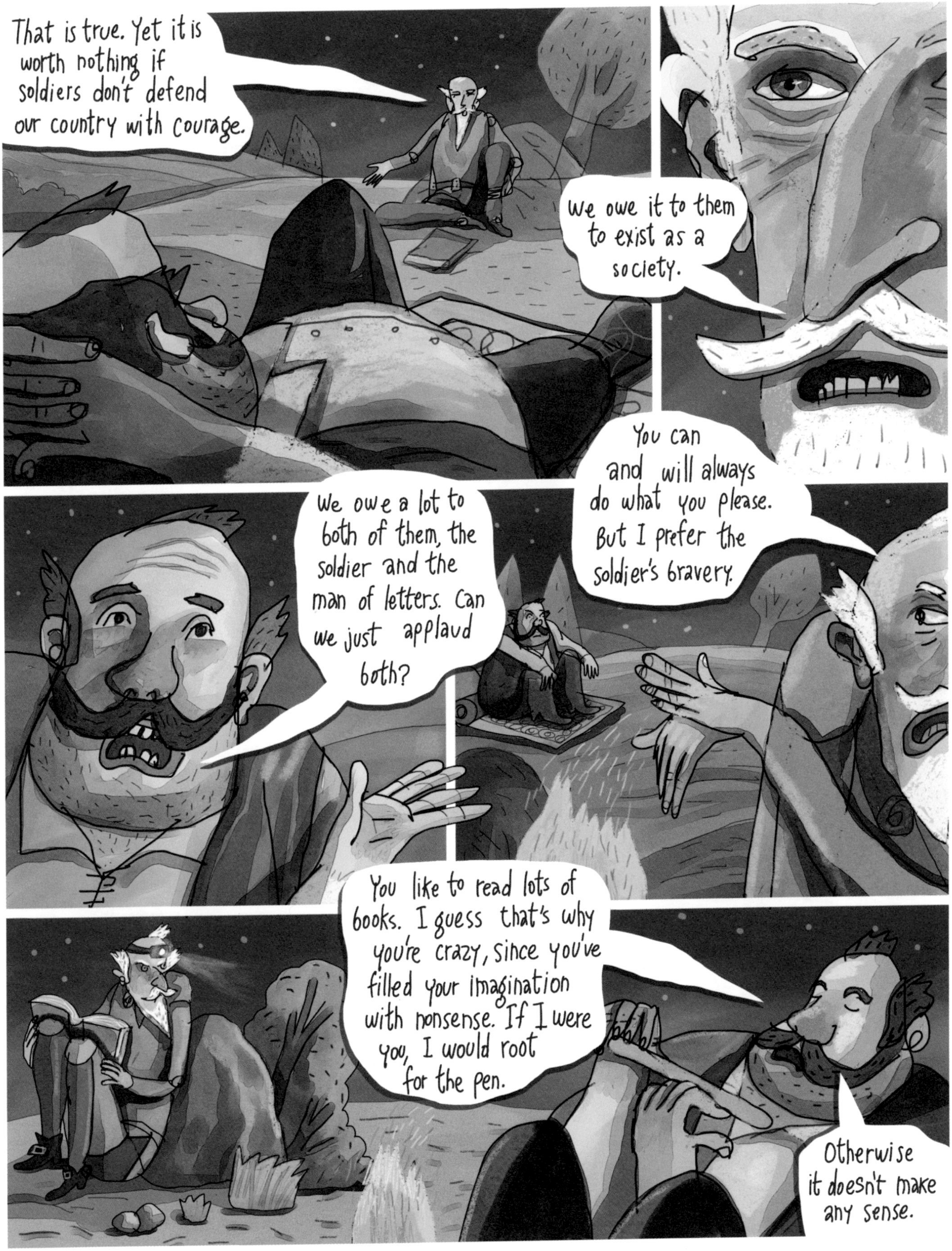
That is true. Yet it is worth nothing if soldiers don't defend our country with courage.
We owe it to them to exist as a society.
We owe a lot to both of them, the soldier and the man of letters. Can we just applaud both?
You can and will always do what you please. But I prefer the soldier's bravery.
You like to read lots of books. I guess that's why you're crazy, since you've filled your imagination with nonsense. If I were you, I would root for the pen.
Otherwise it doesn't make any sense.

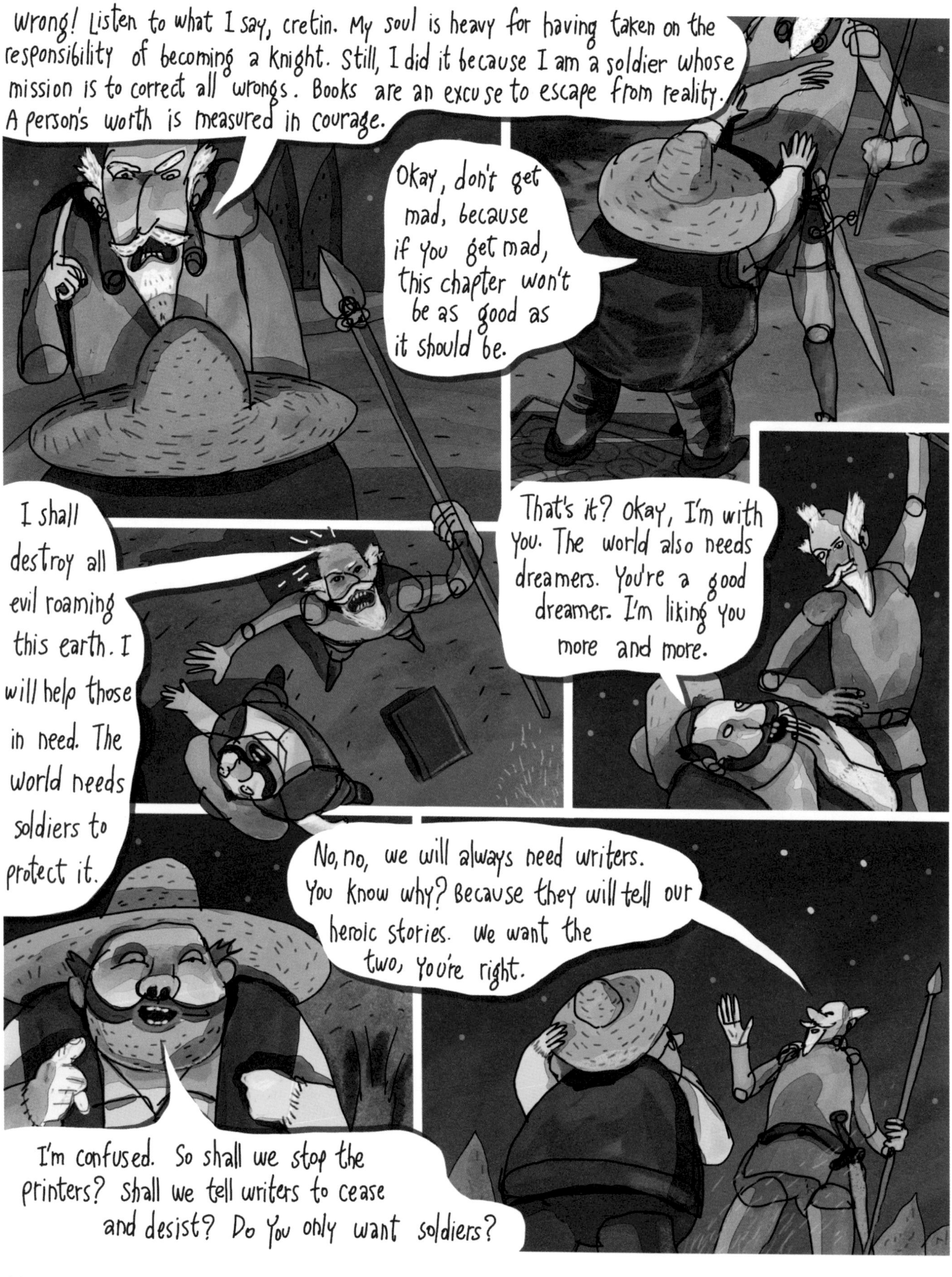

wrong! Listen to what I say, cretin. My soul is heavy for having taken on the responsibility of becoming a knight. Still, I did it because I am a soldier whose mission is to correct all wrongs. Books are an excuse to escape from reality. A person's worth is measured in courage.
Okay, don't get mad, because if you get mad, this chapter won't be as good as it should be.
I shall destroy all evil roaming this earth. I will help those in need. The world needs soldiers to protect it.
That's it? Okay, I'm with you. The world also needs dreamers. You're a good dreamer. I'm liking you more and more.
I'm confused. So shall we stop the printers? Shall we tell writers to cease and desist? Do you only want soldiers?
No, no, we will always need writers. You know why? Because they will tell our heroic stories. We want the two, you're right.

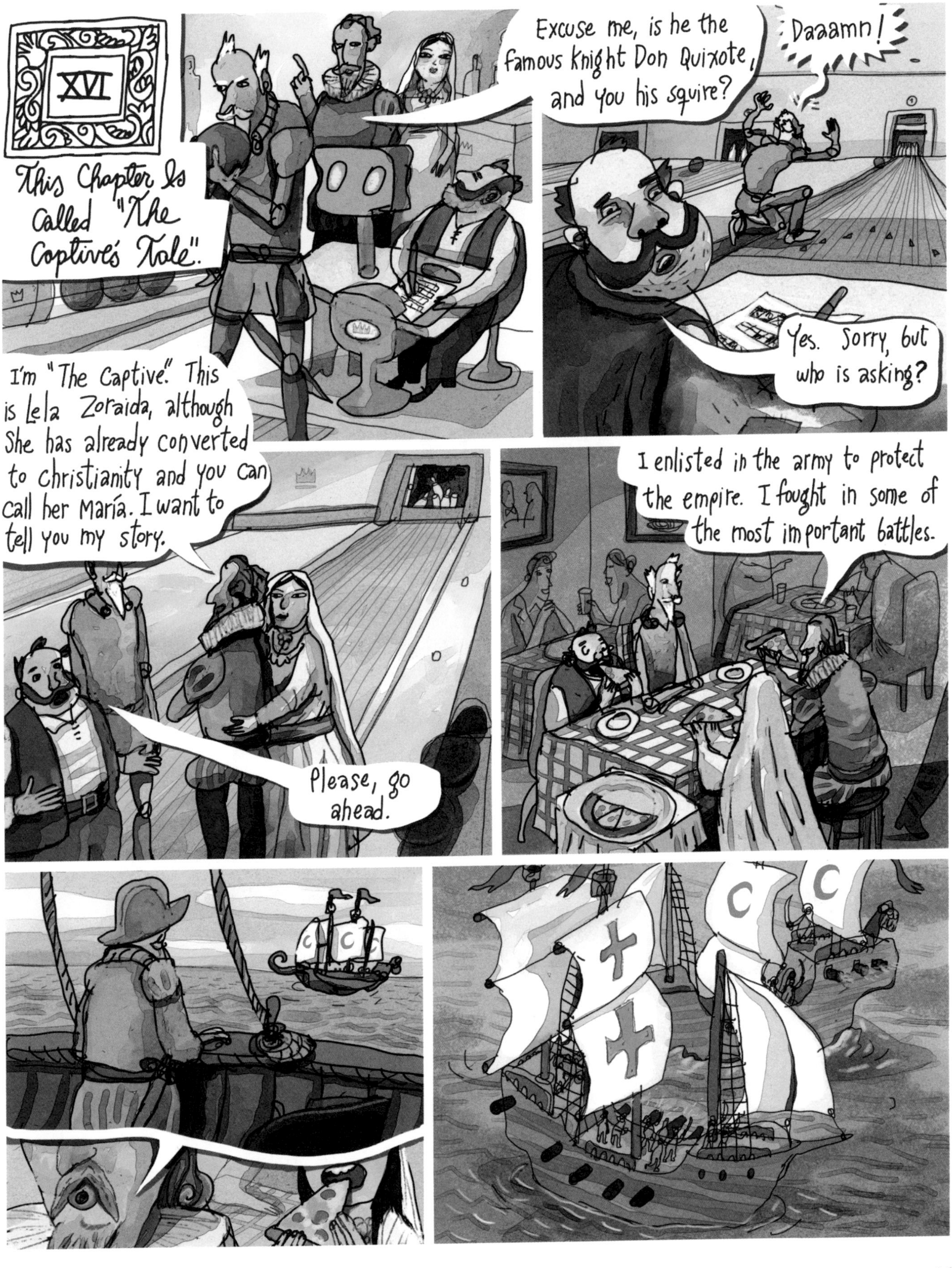
XVI
This Chapter Is Called "The Captive's Tale".
Excuse me, is he the famous Knight Don Quixote, and you his squire?
Daaamn!
Yes. Sorry, but who is asking?
I'm "The Captive." This is Lela Zoraida, although She has already converted to christianity and you can call her María. I want to tell you my story.
Please, go ahead.
I enlisted in the army to protect the empire. I fought in some of the most important battles.

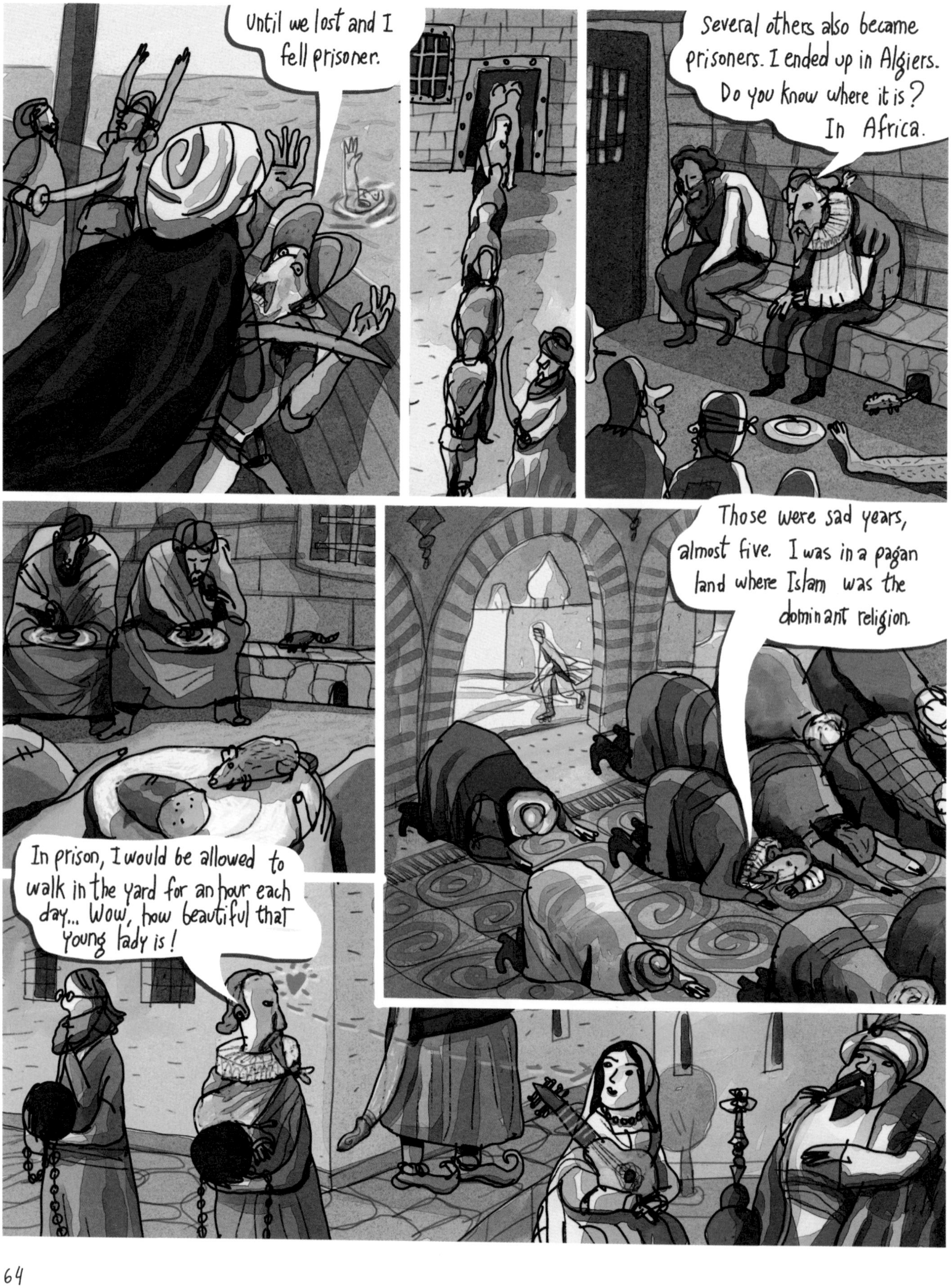
Until we lost and I fell prisoner.
Several others also became prisoners. I ended up in Algiers. Do you know where it is? In Africa.
Those were sad years, almost five. I was in a pagan land where Islam was the dominant religion.
In prison, I would be allowed to walk in the yard for an hour each day... Wow, how beautiful that young lady is!

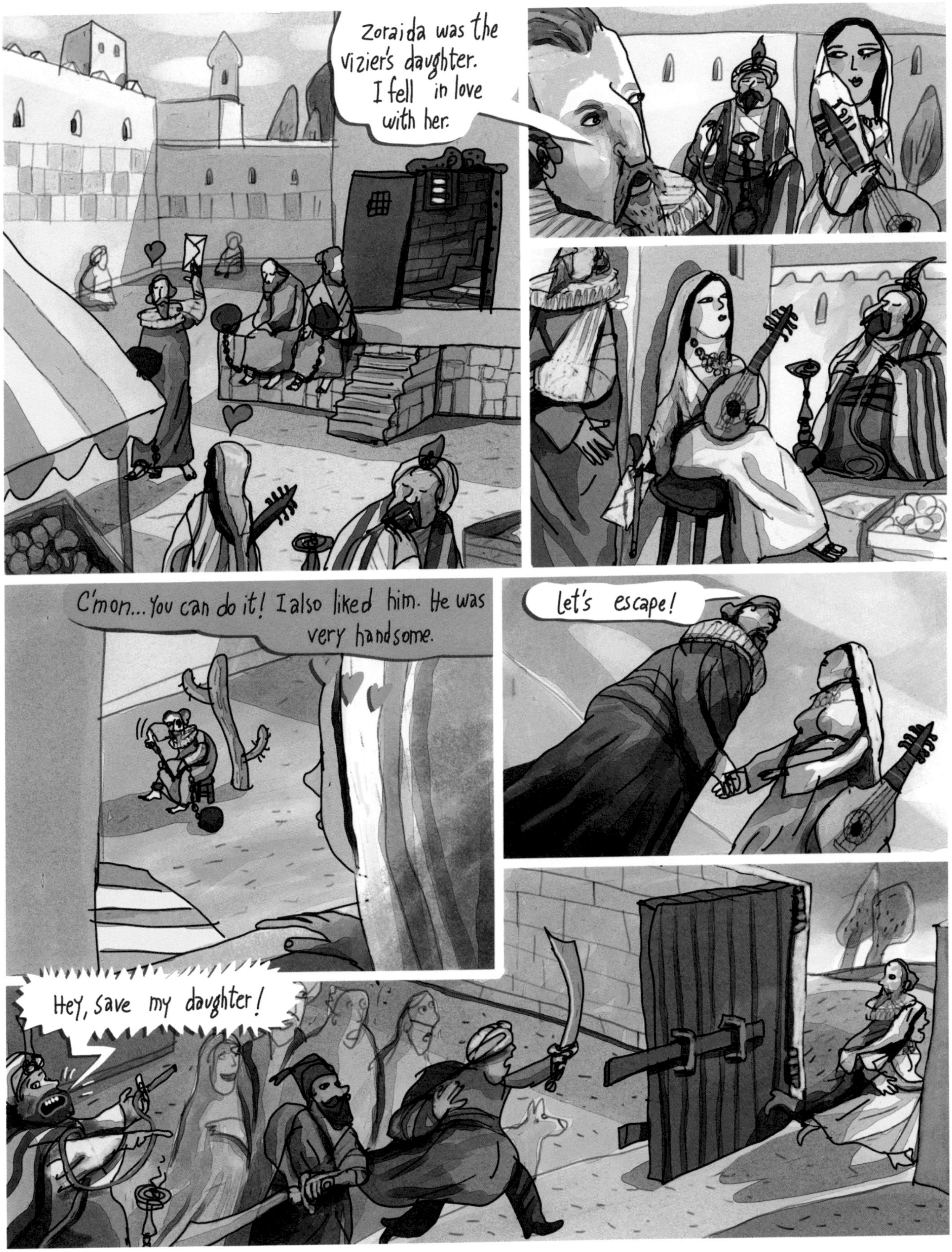
Zoraida was the vizier's daughter. I fell in love with her.
C'mon... You can do it! I also liked him. He was very handsome.
let's escape!
Hey, save my daughter!

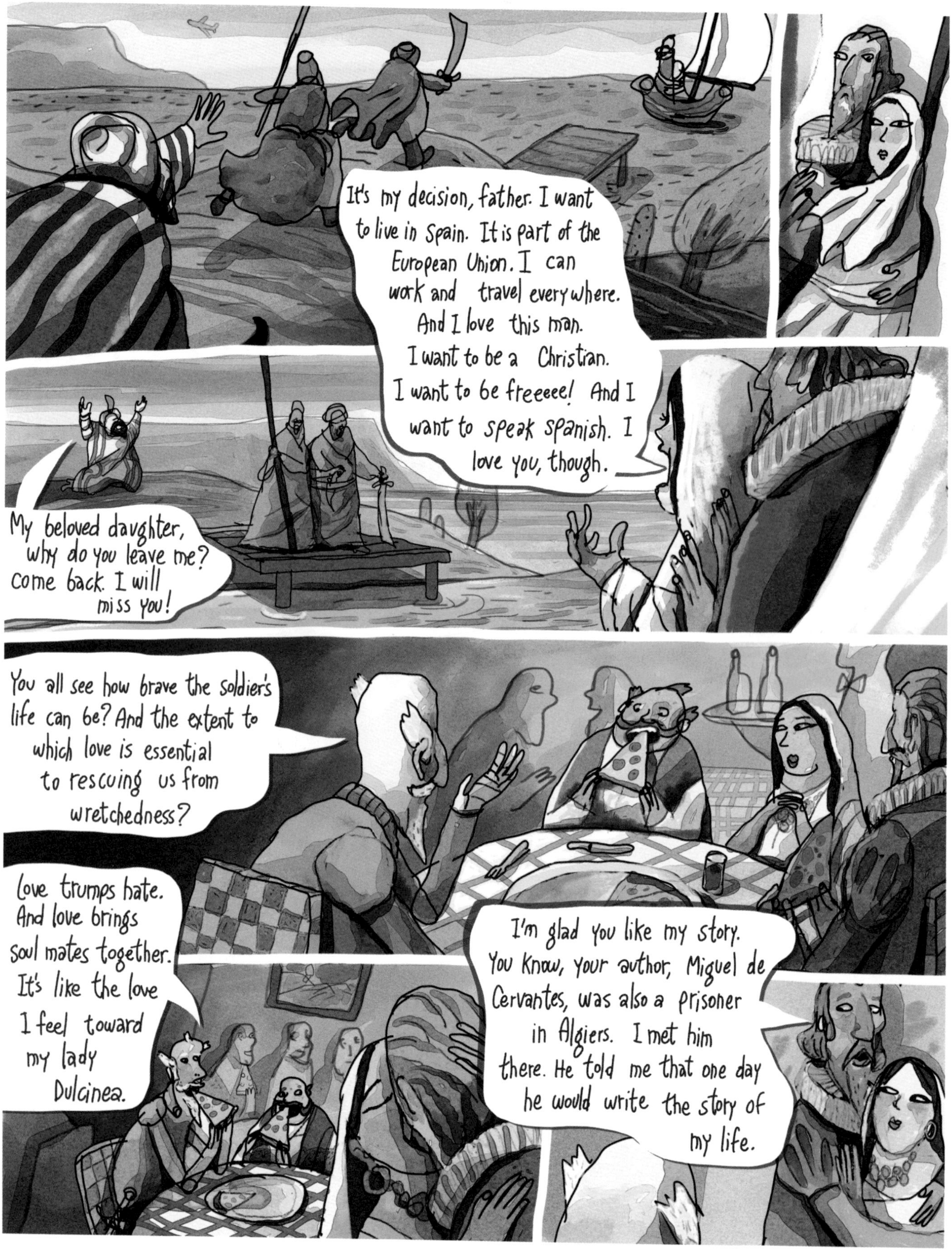
It's my decision, father. I want to live in Spain. It is part of the European Union. I can work and travel everywhere. And I love this man. I want to be a Christian. I want to be freeeee! And I want to speak spanish. I love you, though.
My beloved daughter, why do you leave me? come back. I will miss you!
You all see how brave the soldier's life can be? And the extent to which love is essential to rescuing us from wretchedness?
love trumps hate. And love brings soul mates together. It's like the love I feel toward my lady Dulcinea.
I'm glad you like my story. You know, your author, Miguel de Cervantes, was also a prisoner in Algiers. I met him there. He told me that one day he would write the story of my life.

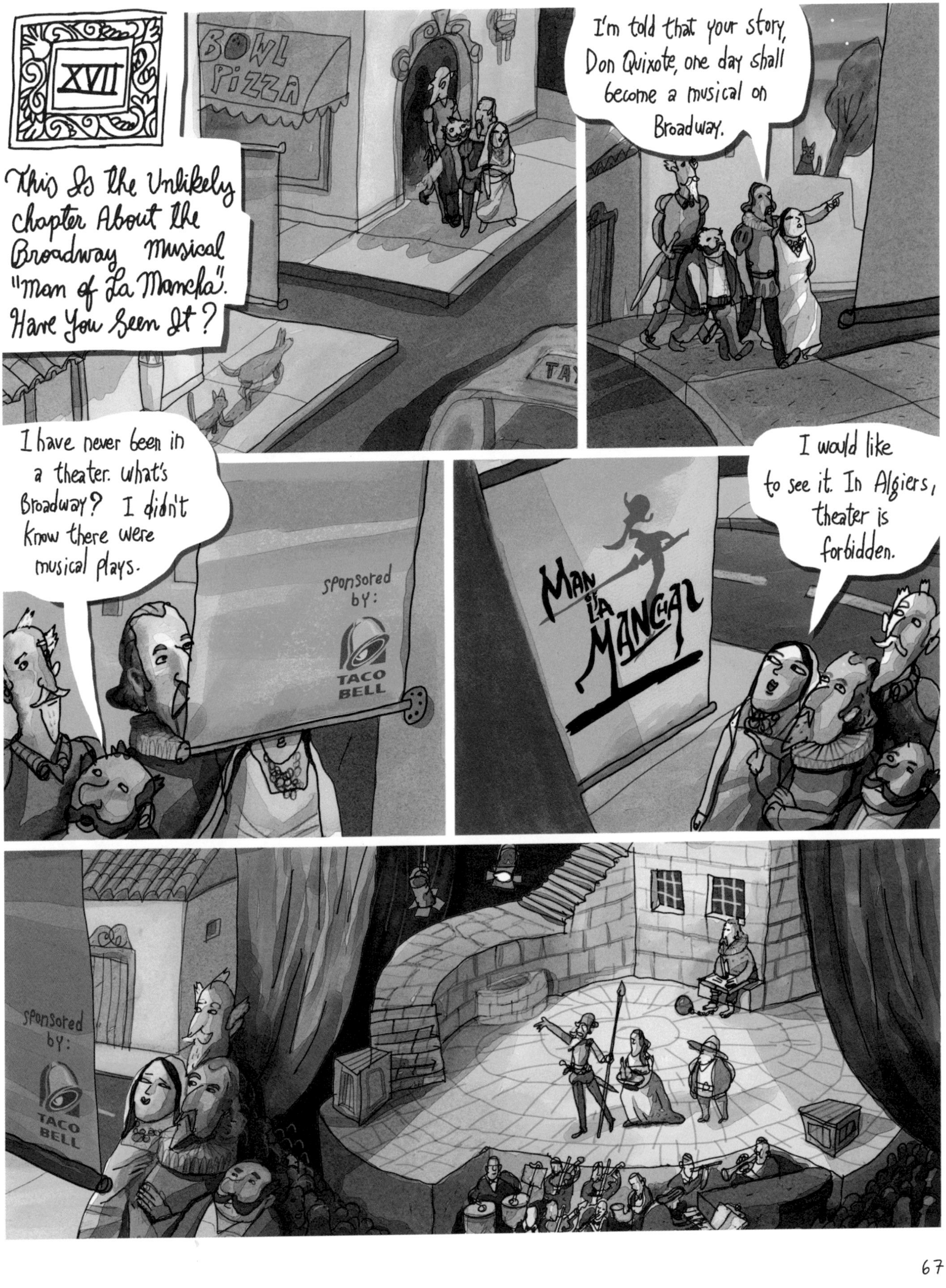
XVII
This Is the Unlikely chapter About the Broadway musical "Man of La Mancha". Have You Seen It?
BOWL PIZZA
I'm told that your story, Don Quixote, one day shall become a musical on Broadway.
I have never been in a theater. what's Broadway? I didn't know there were musical plays.
sponsored by:
TACO BELL
MAN OF LA MANCHA
I would like to see it. In Algiers, theater is forbidden.
sponsored by:
TACO BELL

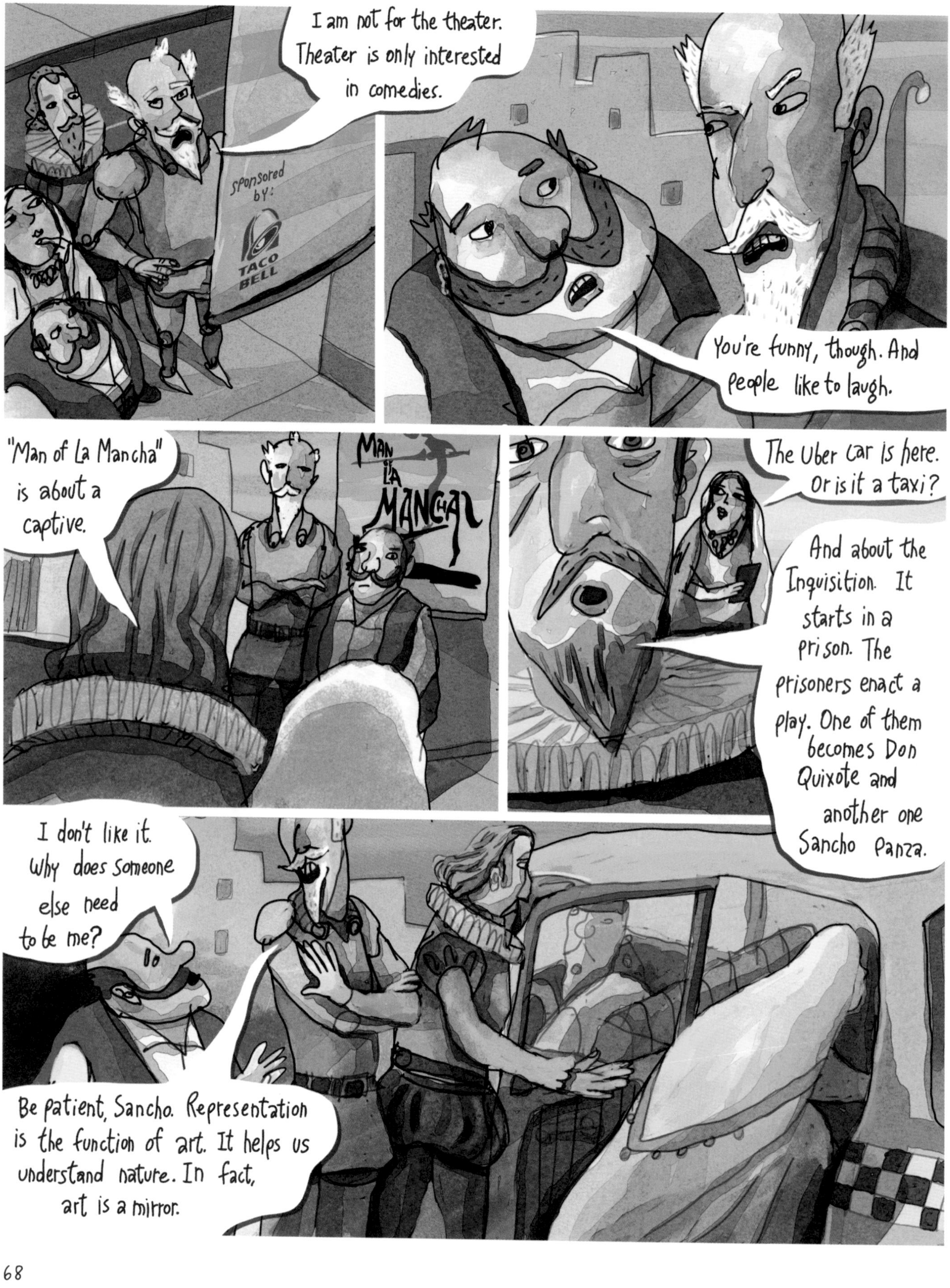

I am not for the theater. Theater is only interested in comedies.
Sponsored by:
TACO BELL
You're funny, though. And people like to laugh.
"Man of La Mancha" is about a captive.
MAN OF LA MANCHA
The Uber car is here. Or is it a taxi?
And about the Inquisition. It starts in a prison. The prisoners enact a play. One of them becomes Don Quixote and another one Sancho Panza.
I don't like it. Why does someone else need to be me?
Be patient, Sancho. Representation is the function of art. It helps us understand nature. In fact, art is a mirror.

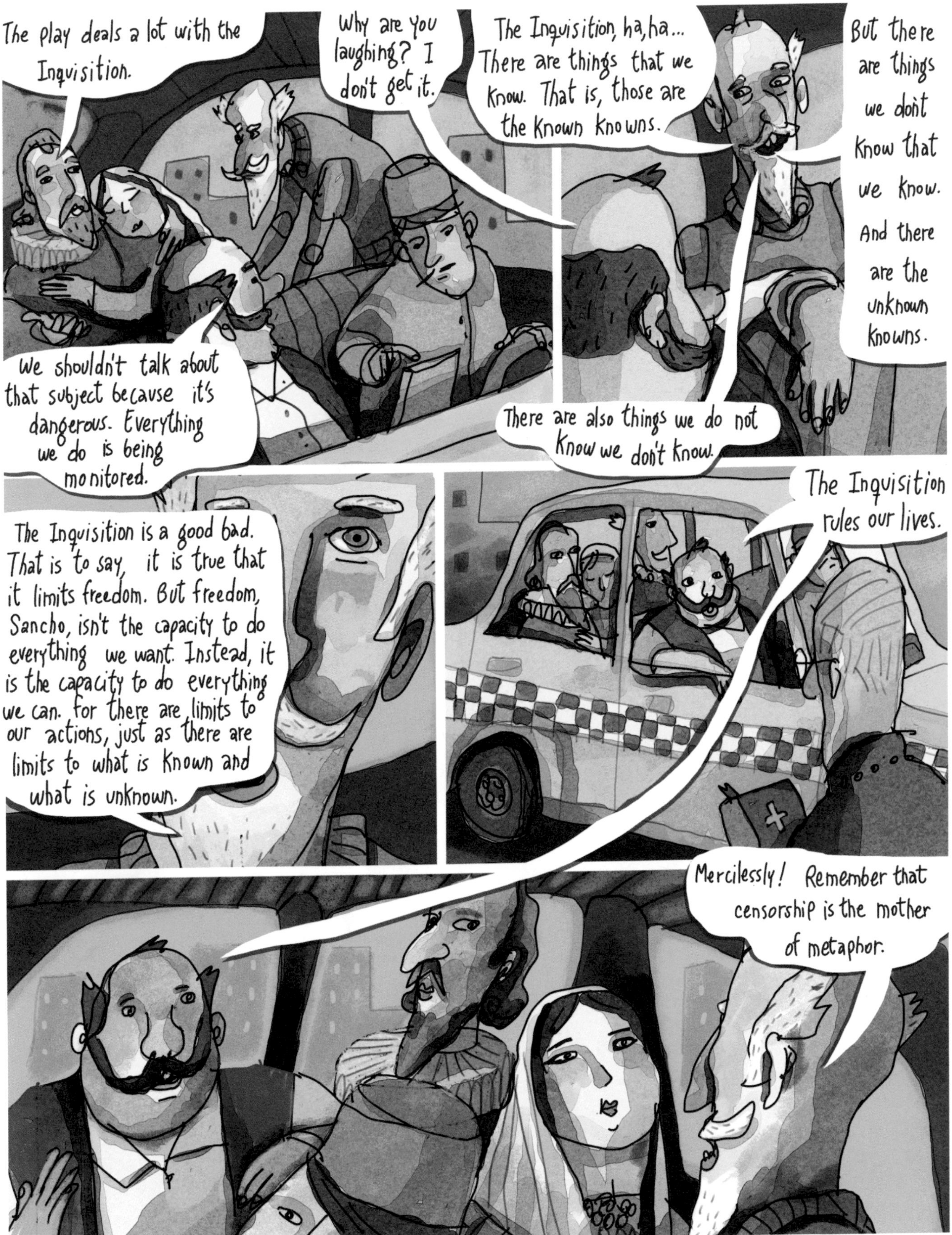

The play deals a lot with the Inquisition.
Why are you laughing? I don't get it.
The Inquisition, ha, ha... There are things that we know. That is, those are the known knowns.
But there are things we don't know that we know. And there are the unknown knowns.
We shouldn't talk about that subject because it's dangerous. Everything we do is being monitored.
There are also things we do not know we don't know.
The Inquisition is a good bad. That is to say, it is true that it limits freedom. But freedom, Sancho, isn't the capacity to do everything we want. Instead, it is the capacity to do everything we can. For there are limits to our actions, just as there are limits to what is known and what is unknown.
The Inquisition rules our lives.
Mercilessly! Remember that censorship is the mother of metaphor.

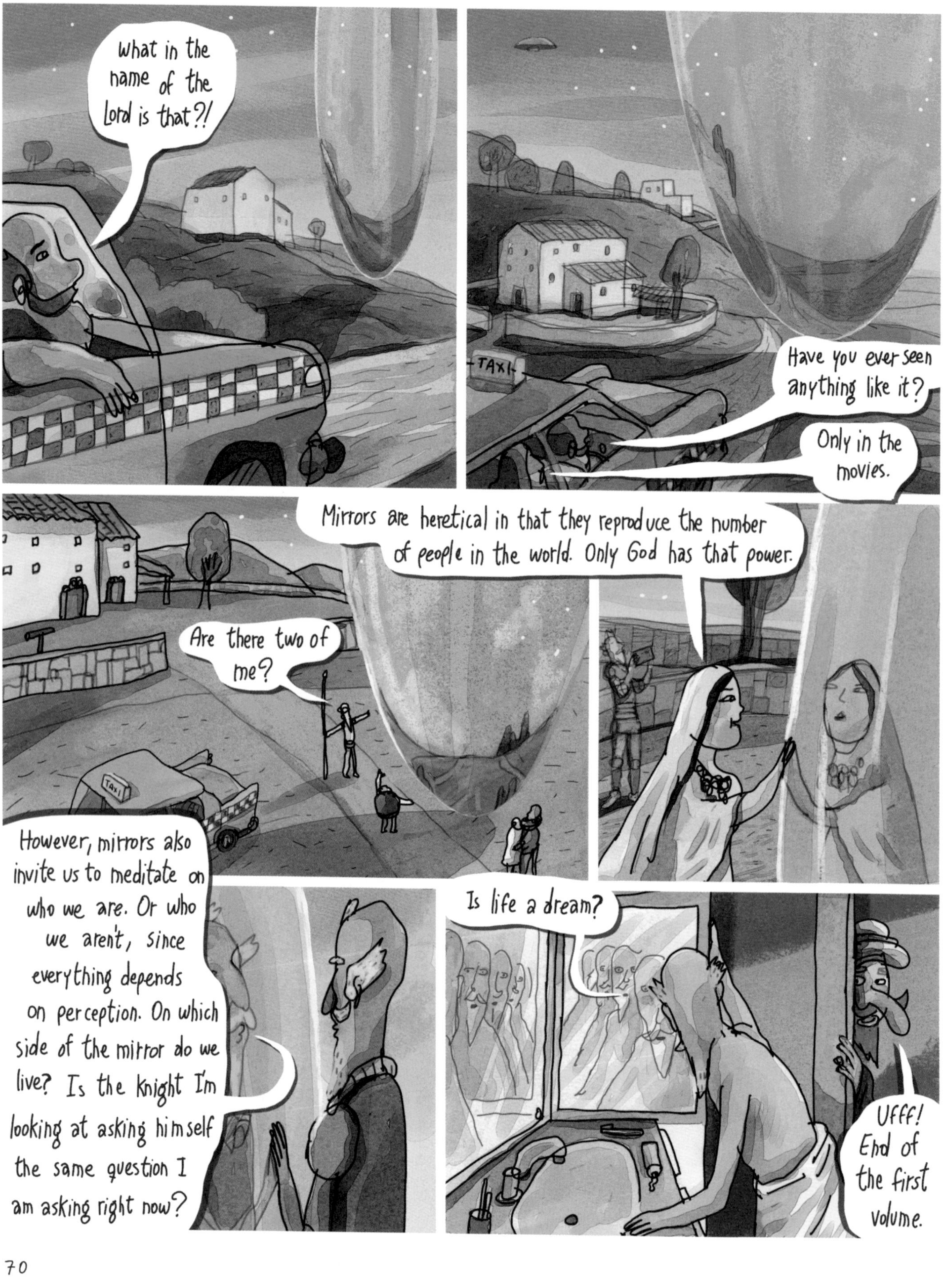
What in the name of the Lord is that?!
Have you ever seen anything like it?
Only in the movies.
Mirrors are heretical in that they reproduce the number of people in the world. Only God has that power.
Are there two of me?
However, mirrors also invite us to meditate on who we are. Or who we aren't, since everything depends on perception. On which side of the mirror do we live? Is the Knight I'm looking at asking himself the same question I am asking right now?
Is life a dream?
Ufff! End of the first volume.

Part

II

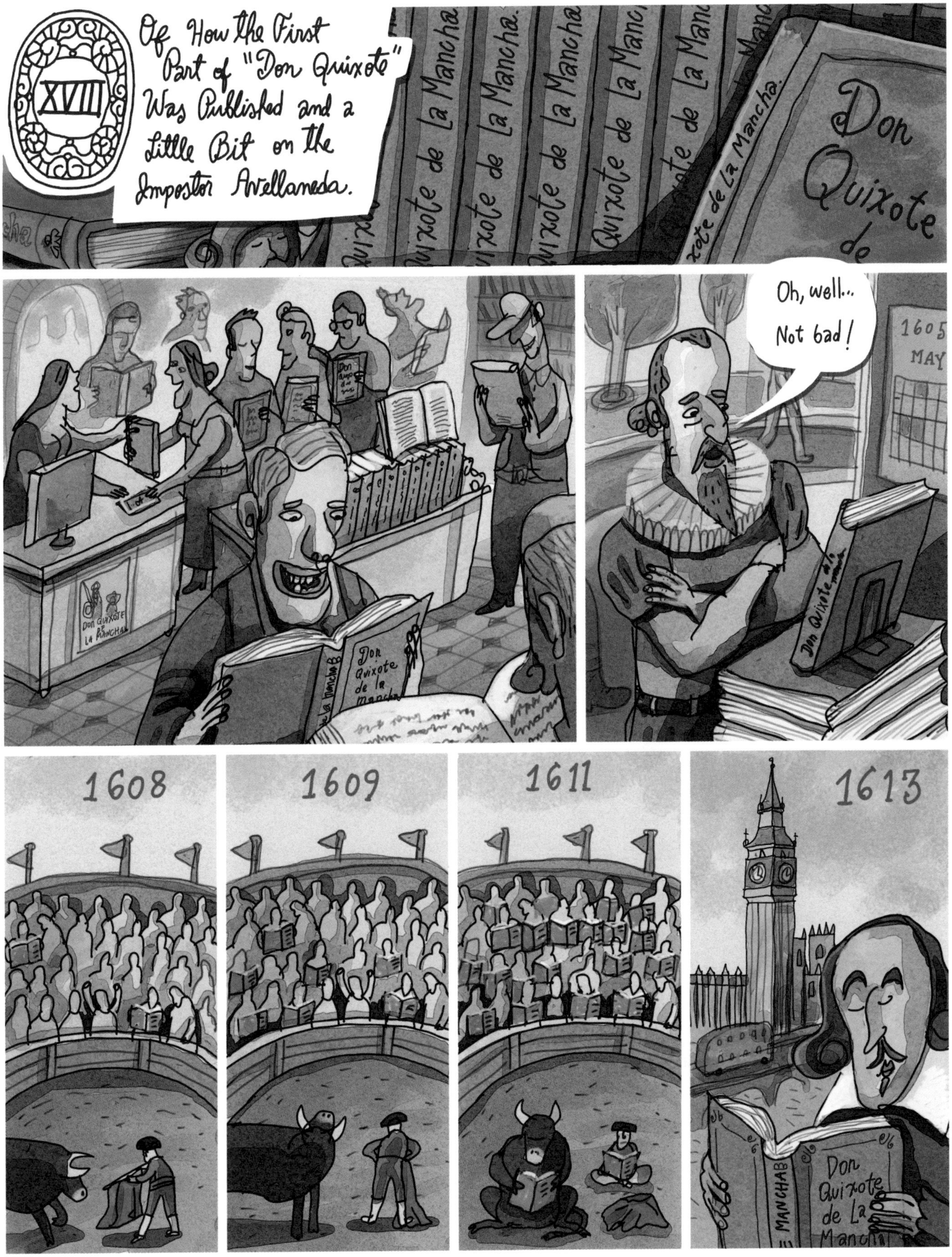
XVIII
Of How the First Part of "Don Quixote" Was Published and a Little Bit on the Impostor Avellaneda.
Don Quixote de La Mancha.
Don Quixote de
Oh, well... Not bad!
1605 MAY
Don Quixote de la Mancha
1608
1609
1611
1613
Don Quixote de La Mancha

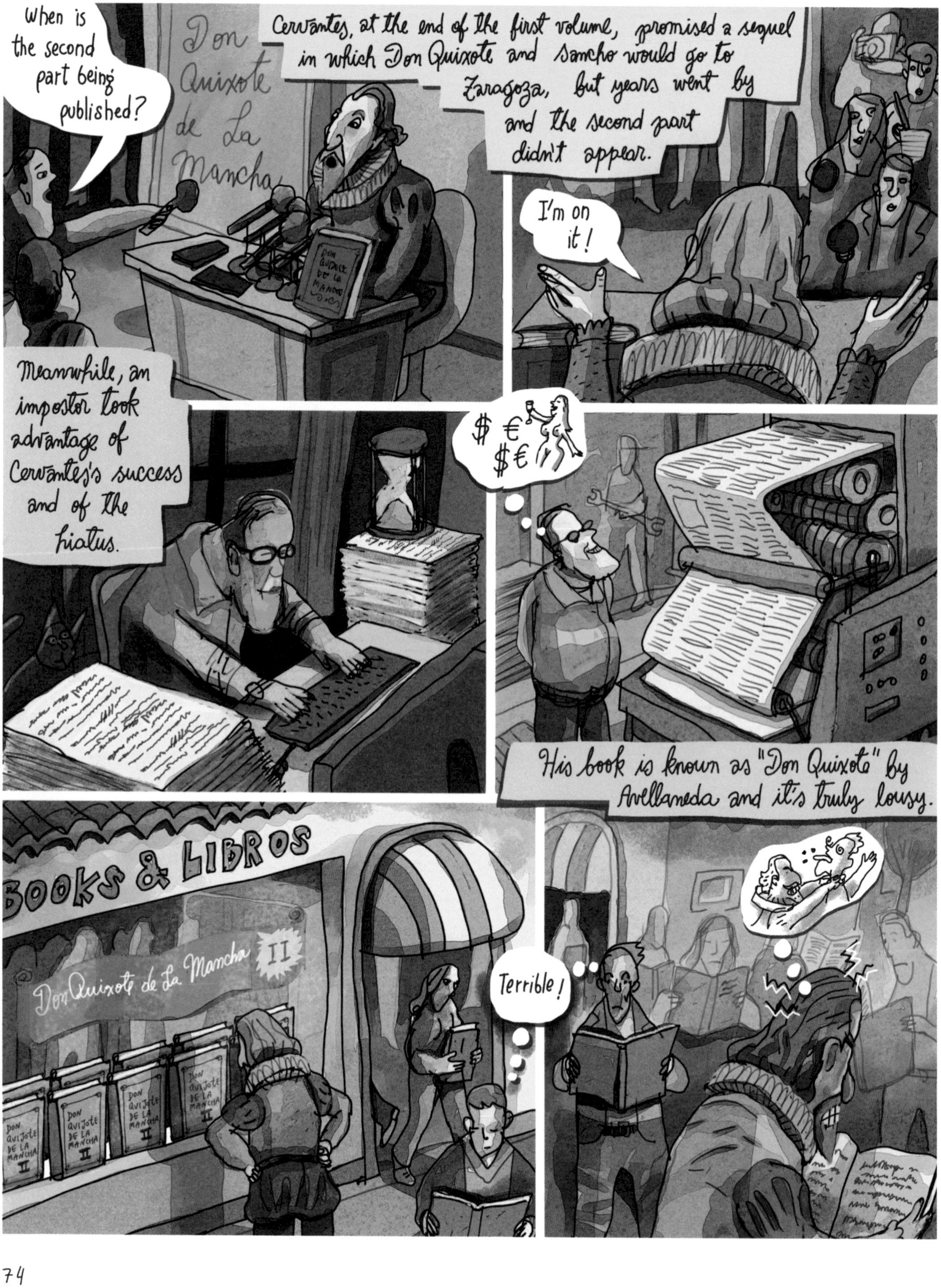
When is the second part being published?
Cervantes, at the end of the first volume, promised a sequel in which Don Quixote and Sancho would go to Zaragoza, but years went by and the second part didn't appear.
Don Quixote de La Mancha
I'm on it!
Meanwhile, an impostor took advantage of Cervantes's success and of the hiatus.
$ € $ €
His book is known as "Don Quixote" by Avellaneda and it's truly lousy.
BOOKS & LIBROS
Don Quixote de La Mancha II
DON QUIJOTE DE LA MANCHA II
Terrible!

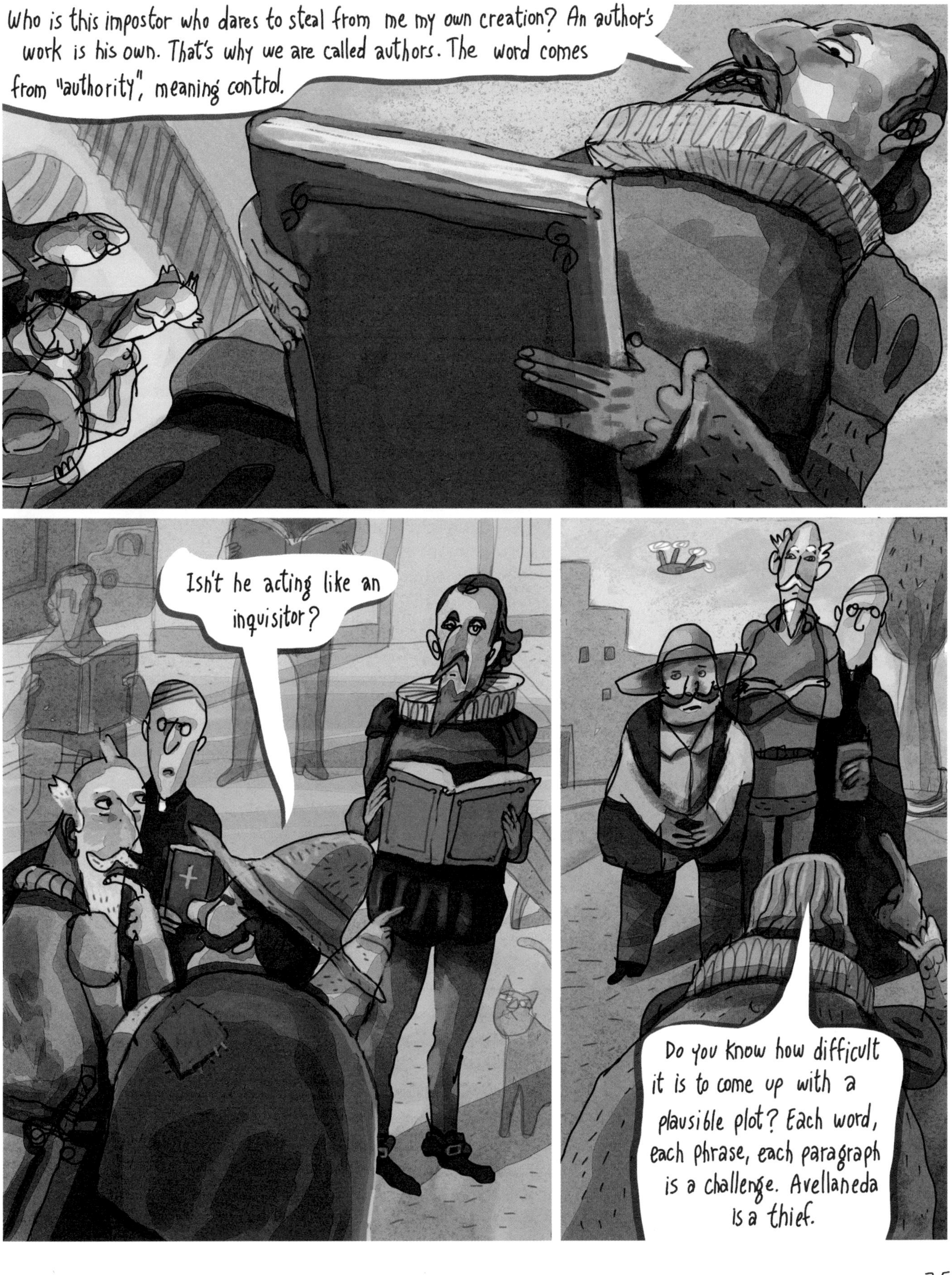

Who is this impostor who dares to steal from me my own creation? An author's work is his own. That's why we are called authors. The word comes from "authority", meaning control.
Isn't he acting like an inquisitor?
Do you know how difficult it is to come up with a plausible plot? Each word, each phrase, each paragraph is a challenge. Avellaneda is a thief.

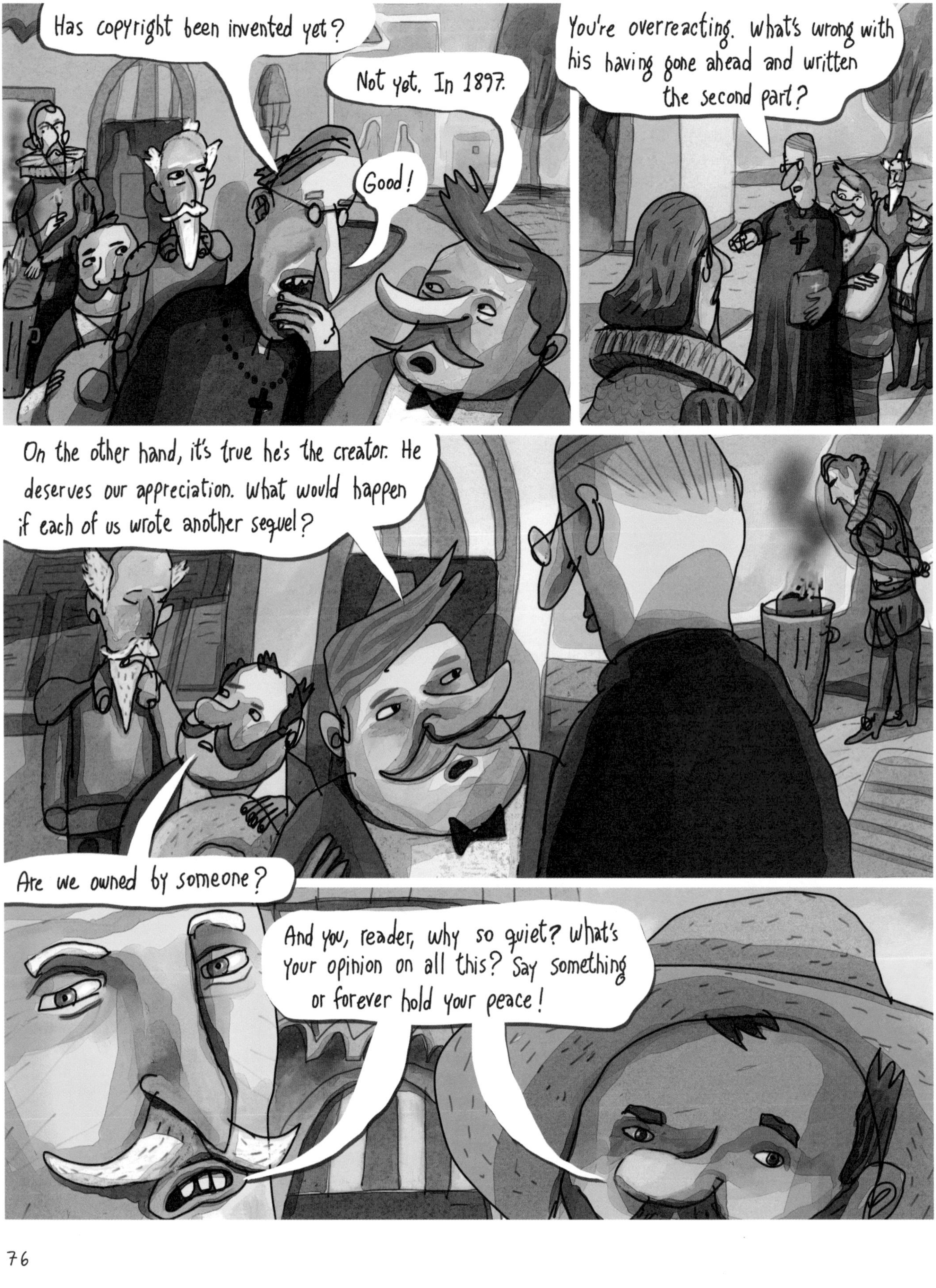
Has copyright been invented yet?
Not yet. In 1897.
Good!
You're overreacting. What's wrong with his having gone ahead and written the second part?
On the other hand, it's true he's the creator. He deserves our appreciation. What would happen if each of us wrote another sequel?
Are we owned by someone?
And you, reader, why so quiet? What's your opinion on all this? Say something or forever hold your peace!

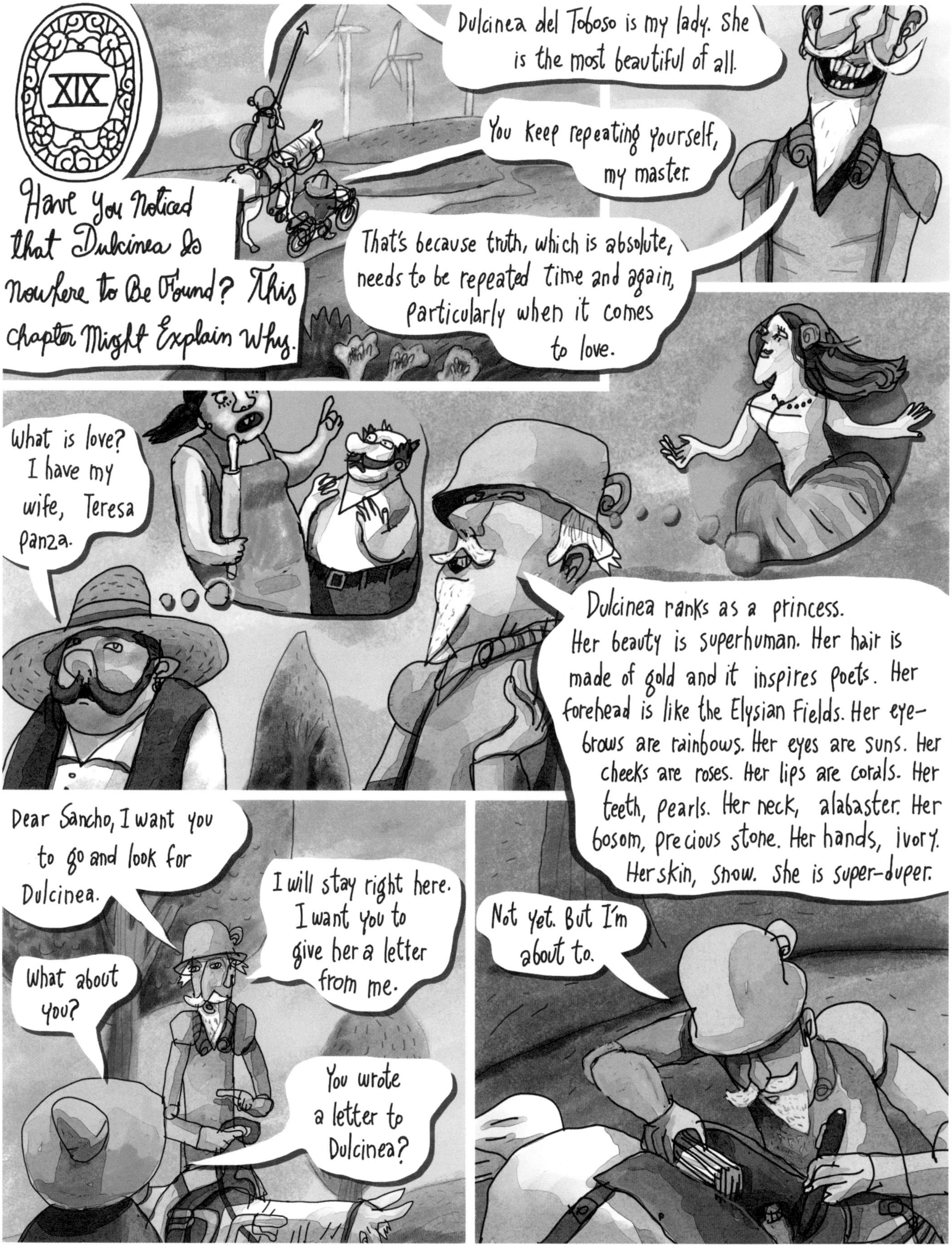

XIX
Have You Noticed that Dulcinea Is nowhere to Be Found? This chapter Might Explain Why.
Dulcinea del Toboso is my lady. She is the most beautiful of all.
You keep repeating yourself, my master.
That's because truth, which is absolute, needs to be repeated time and again, particularly when it comes to love.
What is love? I have my wife, Teresa panza.
Dulcinea ranks as a princess. Her beauty is superhuman. Her hair is made of gold and it inspires poets. Her forehead is like the Elysian Fields. Her eye-brows are rainbows. Her eyes are suns. Her cheeks are roses. Her lips are corals. Her teeth, pearls. Her neck, alabaster. Her bosom, precious stone. Her hands, ivory. Her skin, snow. she is super-duper.
Dear Sancho, I want you to go and look for Dulcinea.
What about you?
I will stay right here. I want you to give her a letter from me.
You wrote a letter to Dulcinea?
Not yet. But I'm about to.

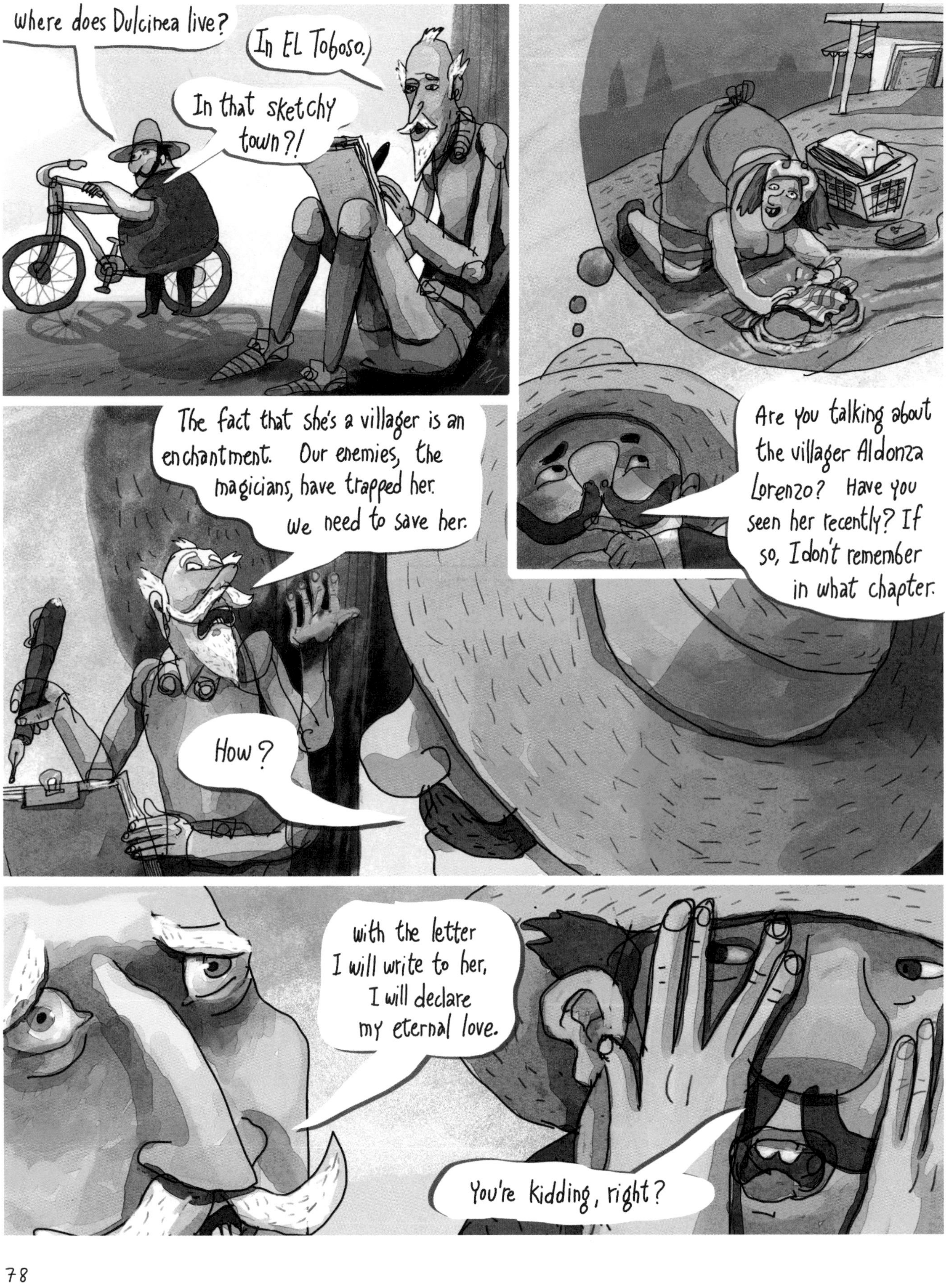
where does Dulcinea live?
In EL Toboso.
In that sketchy town?!
Are you talking about the villager Aldonza Lorenzo? Have you seen her recently? If so, I don't remember in what chapter.
The fact that she's a villager is an enchantment. Our enemies, the magicians, have trapped her. we need to save her.
How?
with the letter I will write to her, I will declare my eternal love.
You're kidding, right?

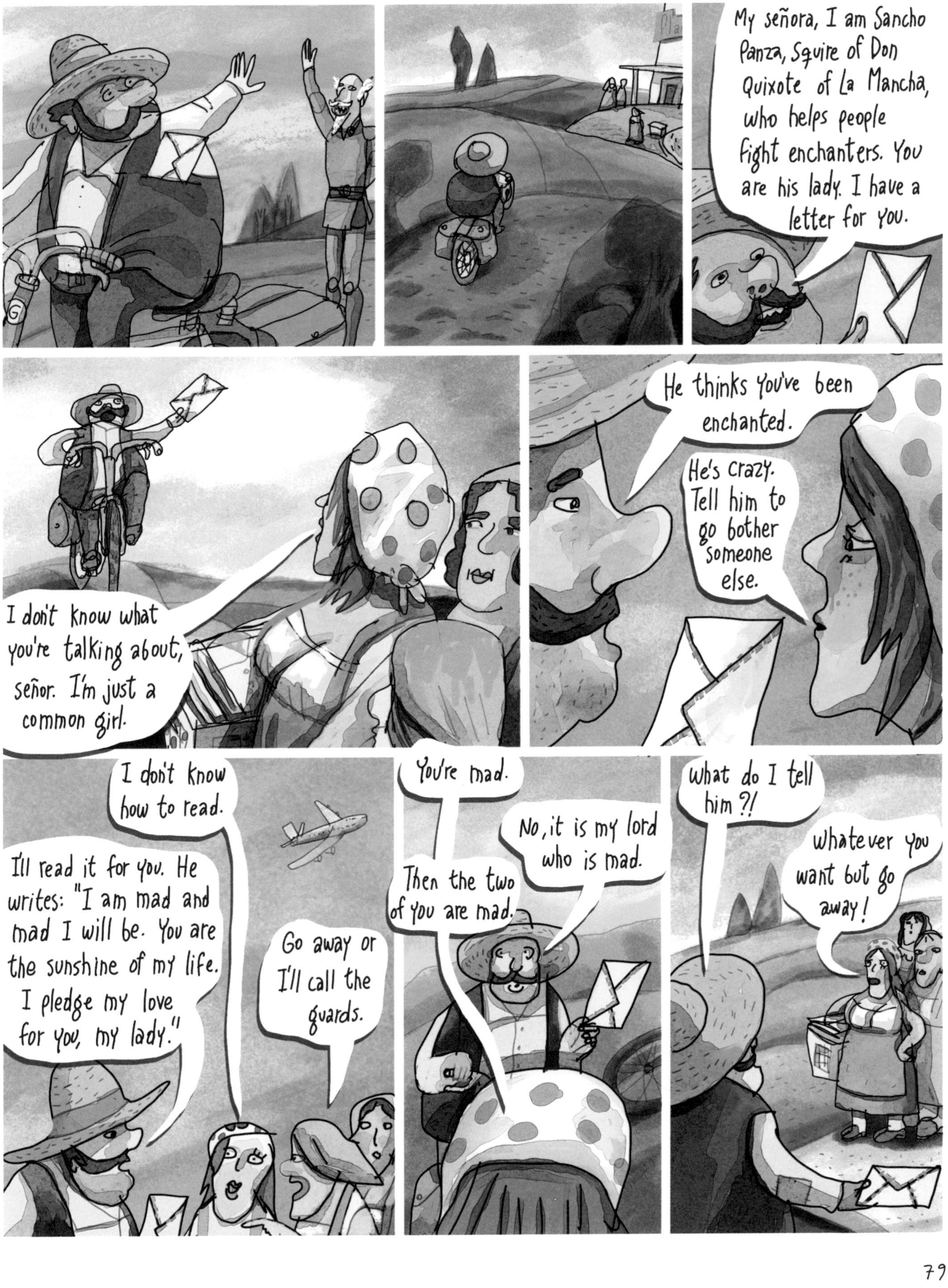
My señora, I am Sancho Panza, Squire of Don Quixote of La Mancha, who helps people fight enchanters. You are his lady. I have a letter for you.
I don't know what you're talking about, señor. I'm just a common girl.
He thinks you've been enchanted.
He's crazy. Tell him to go bother someone else.
I don't know how to read.
I'll read it for you. He writes: "I am mad and mad I will be. You are the sunshine of my life. I pledge my love for you, my lady."
Go away or I'll call the guards.
You're mad.
No, it is my lord who is mad.
Then the two of you are mad.
What do I tell him?!
Whatever you want but go away!

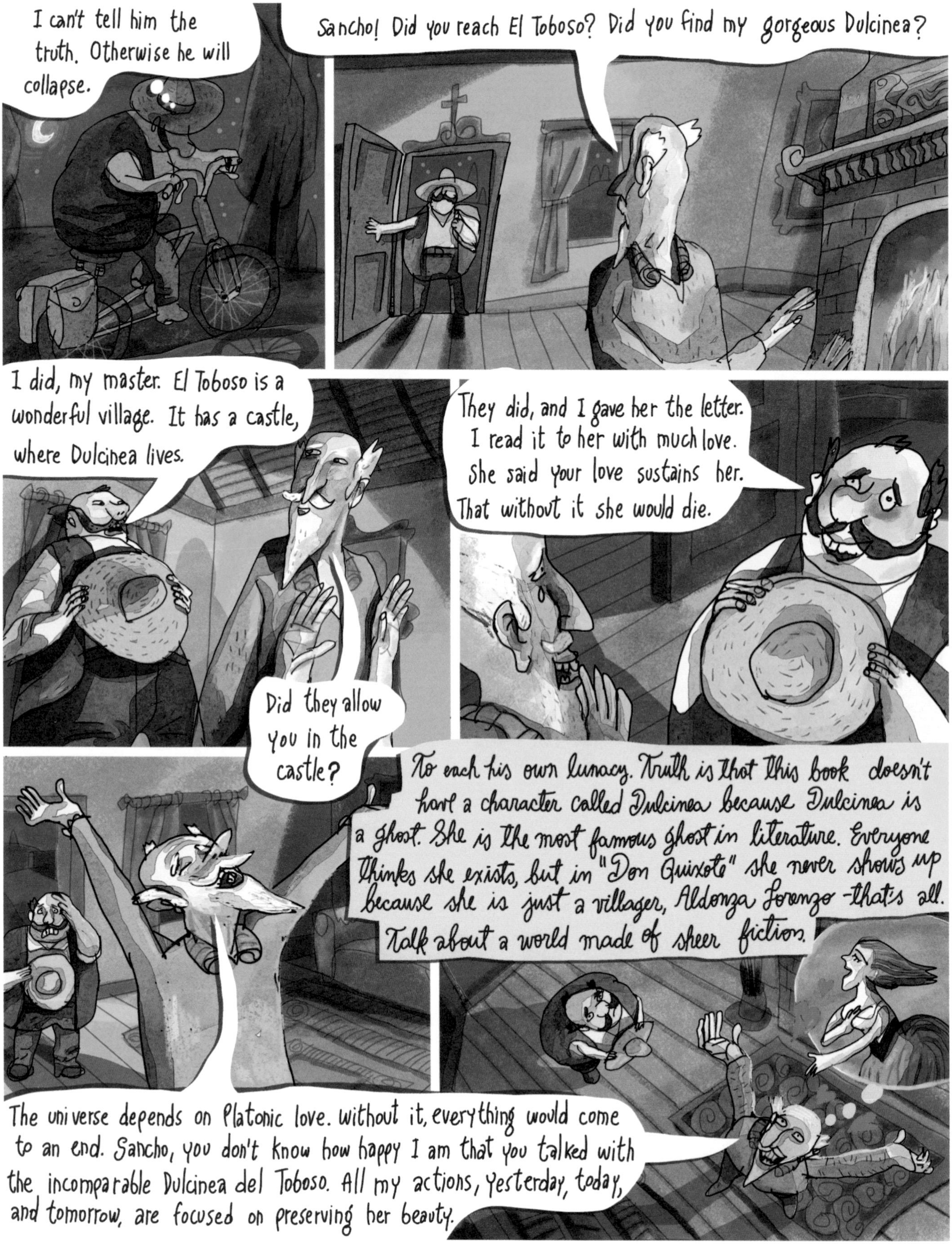

I can't tell him the truth. Otherwise he will collapse.
Sancho! Did you reach El Toboso? Did you find my gorgeous Dulcinea?
I did, my master. El Toboso is a wonderful village. It has a castle, where Dulcinea lives.
Did they allow you in the castle?
They did, and I gave her the letter. I read it to her with much love. She said your love sustains her. That without it she would die.
To each his own lunacy. Truth is that this book doesn't have a character called Dulcinea because Dulcinea is a ghost. She is the most famous ghost in literature. Everyone thinks she exists, but in "Don Quixote" she never shows up because she is just a villager, Aldonza Lorenzo - that's all. Talk about a world made of sheer fiction.
The universe depends on Platonic love. Without it, everything would come to an end. Sancho, you don't know how happy I am that you talked with the incomparable Dulcinea del Toboso. All my actions, yesterday, today, and tomorrow, are focused on preserving her beauty.

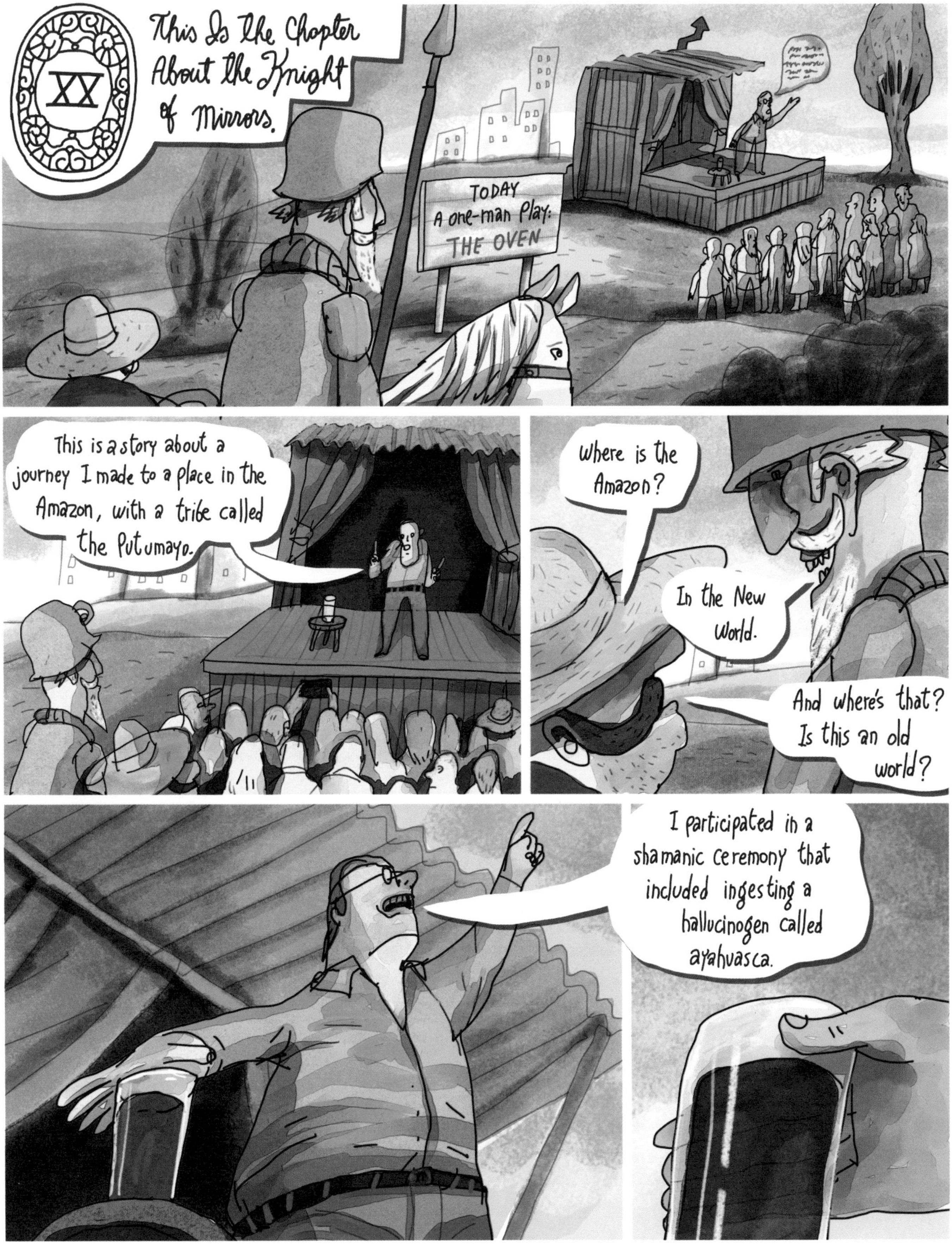
XX
This Is The Chapter About The Knight of Mirrors.
TODAY
A one-man Play:
THE OVEN
This is a story about a journey I made to a place in the Amazon, with a tribe called the Putumayo.
Where is the Amazon?
In the New World.
And where's that? Is this an old world?
I participated in a shamanic ceremony that included ingesting a hallucinogen called ayahuasca.

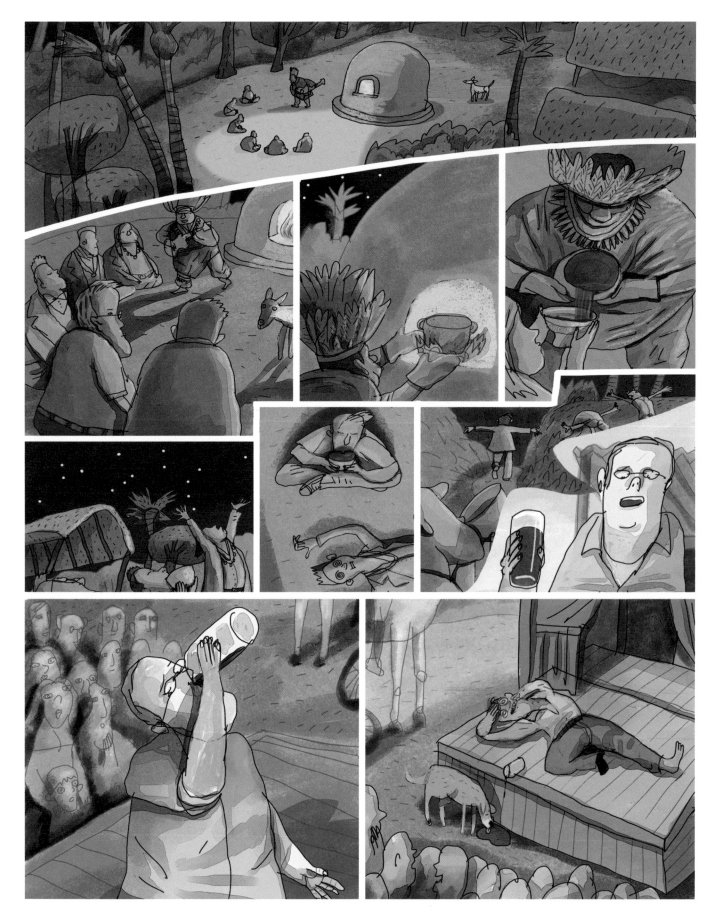

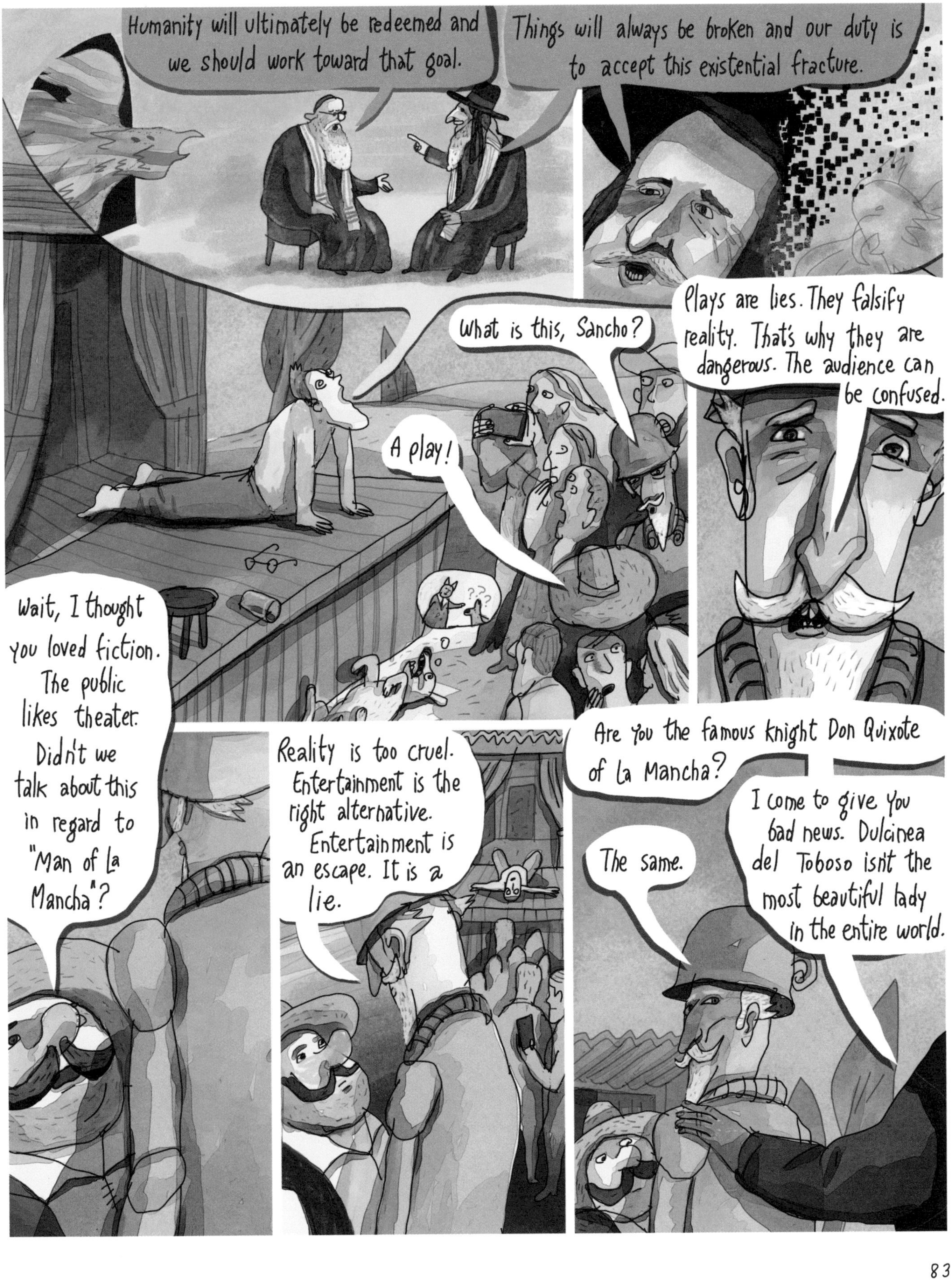
Humanity will ultimately be redeemed and we should work toward that goal.
Things will always be broken and our duty is to accept this existential fracture.
What is this, Sancho?
A play!
Plays are lies. They falsify reality. That's why they are dangerous. The audience can be confused.
Wait, I thought you loved fiction. The public likes theater. Didn't we talk about this in regard to "Man of La Mancha"?
Reality is too cruel. Entertainment is the right alternative. Entertainment is an escape. It is a lie.
Are you the famous knight Don Quixote of La Mancha?
The same.
I come to give you bad news. Dulcinea del Toboso isn't the most beautiful lady in the entire world.

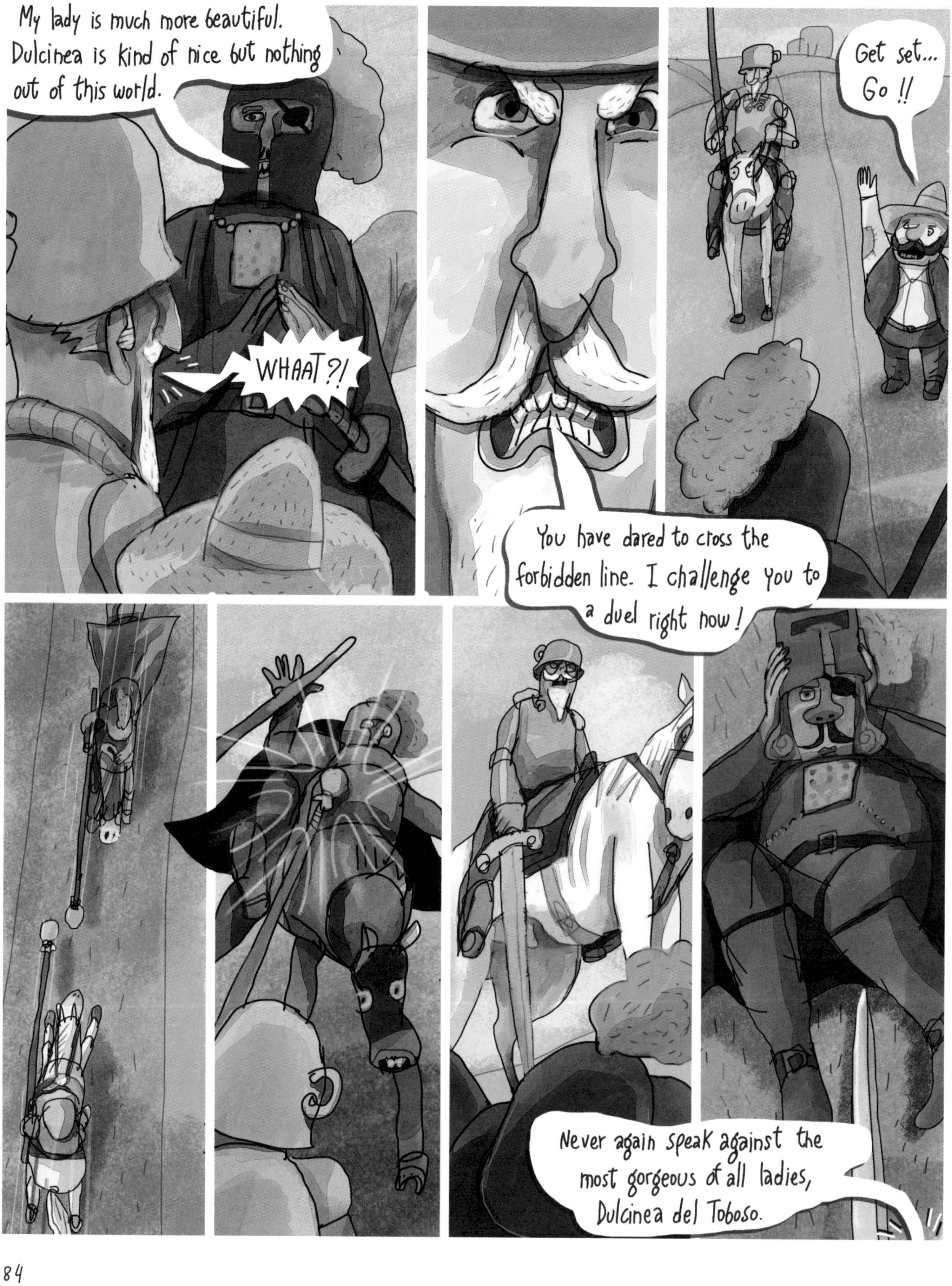

My lady is much more beautiful. Dulcinea is kind of nice but nothing out of this world.
WHAAT?!
You have dared to cross the forbidden line. I challenge you to a duel right now!
Get set... Go !!
Never again speak against the most gorgeous of all ladies, Dulcinea del Toboso.

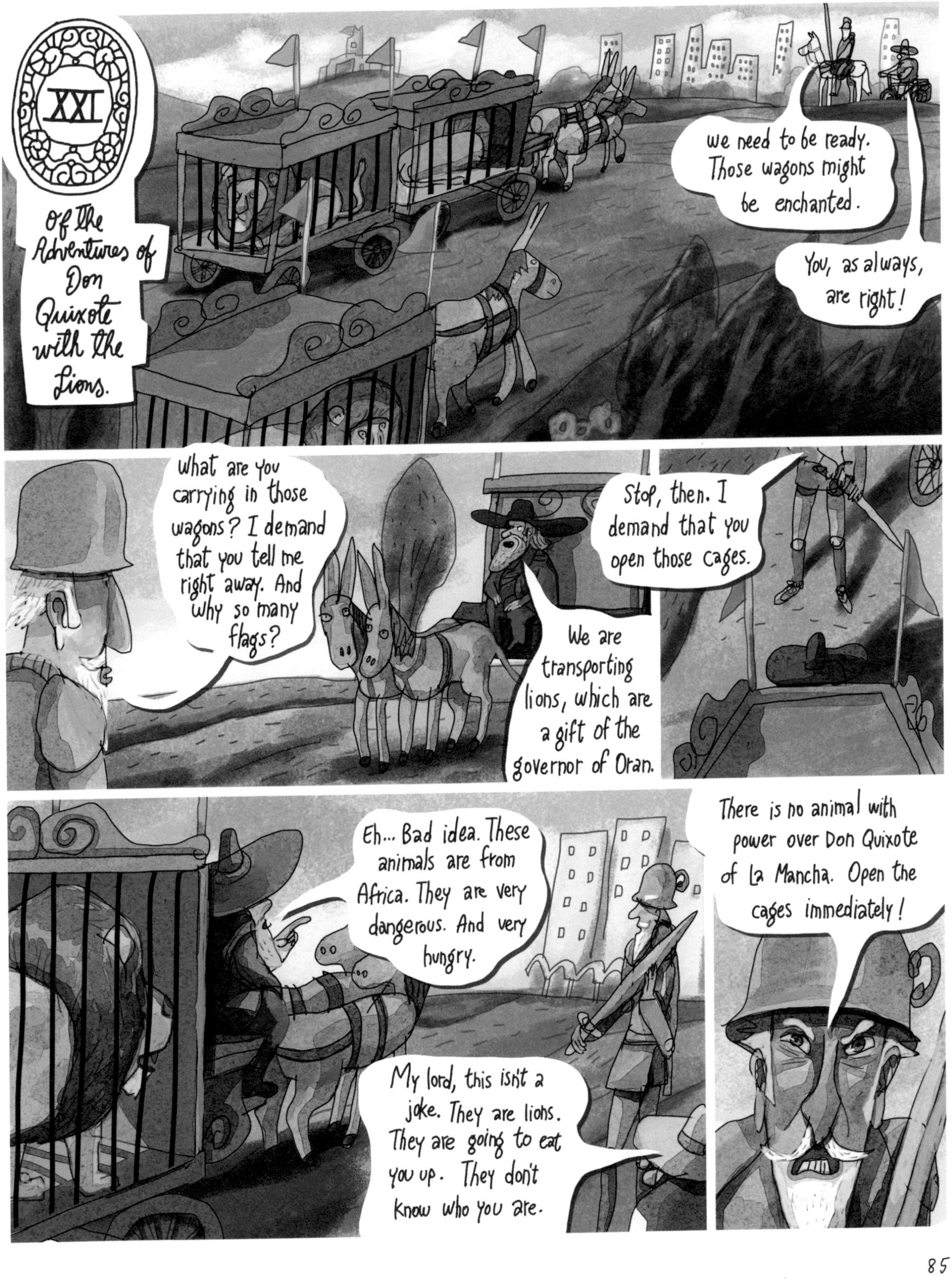
XXI
Of the Adventures of Don Quixote with the Lions.
we need to be ready. Those wagons might be enchanted.
You, as always, are right!
What are you carrying in those wagons? I demand that you tell me right away. And why so many flags?
We are transporting lions, which are a gift of the governor of Oran.
Stop, then. I demand that you open those cages.
Eh... Bad idea. These animals are from Africa. They are very dangerous. And very hungry.
My lord, this isn't a joke. They are lions. They are going to eat you up. They don't know who you are.
There is no animal with power over Don Quixote of La Mancha. Open the cages immediately!

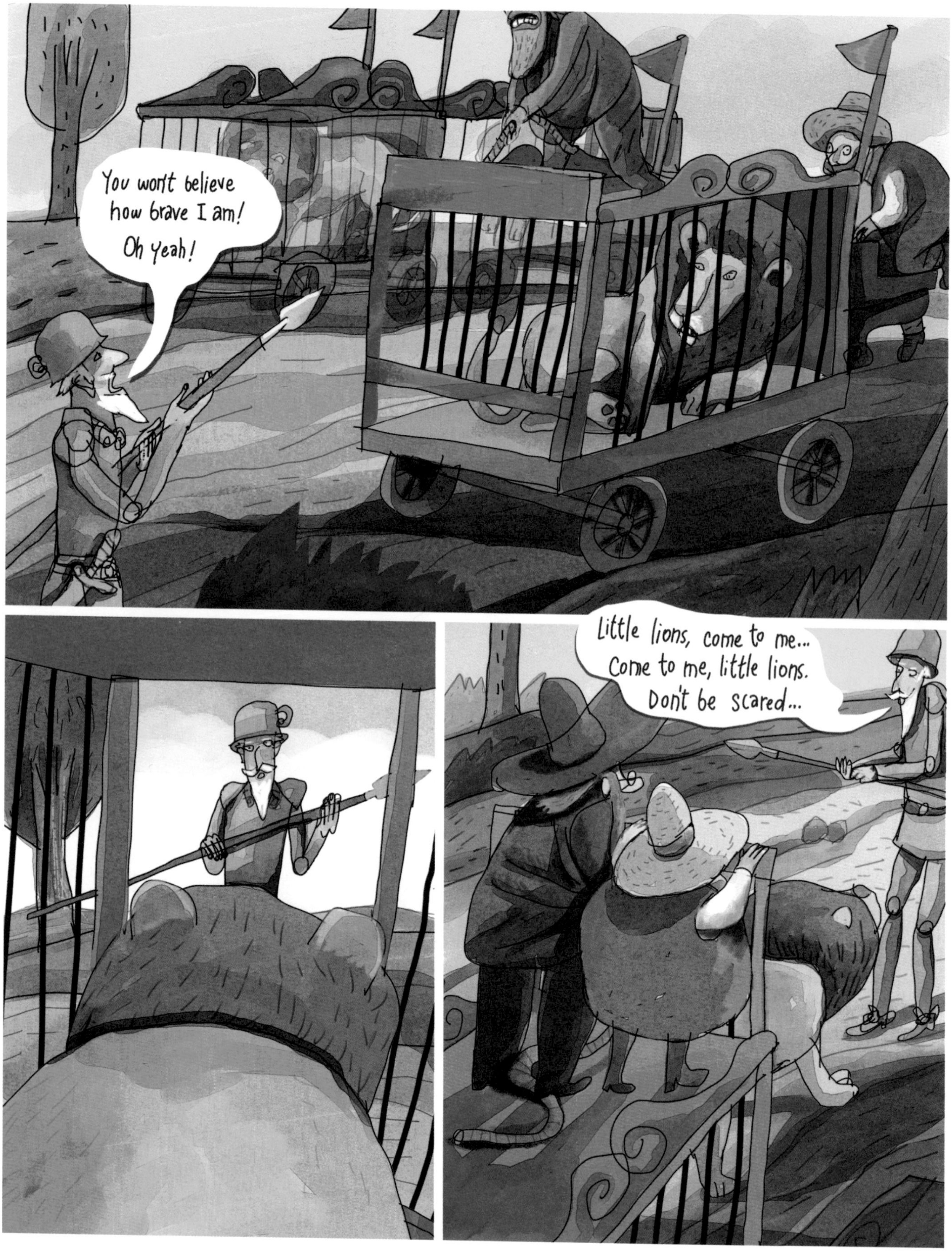
You won't believe how brave I am! Oh yeah!
Little lions, come to me... Come to me, little lions. Don't be scared...

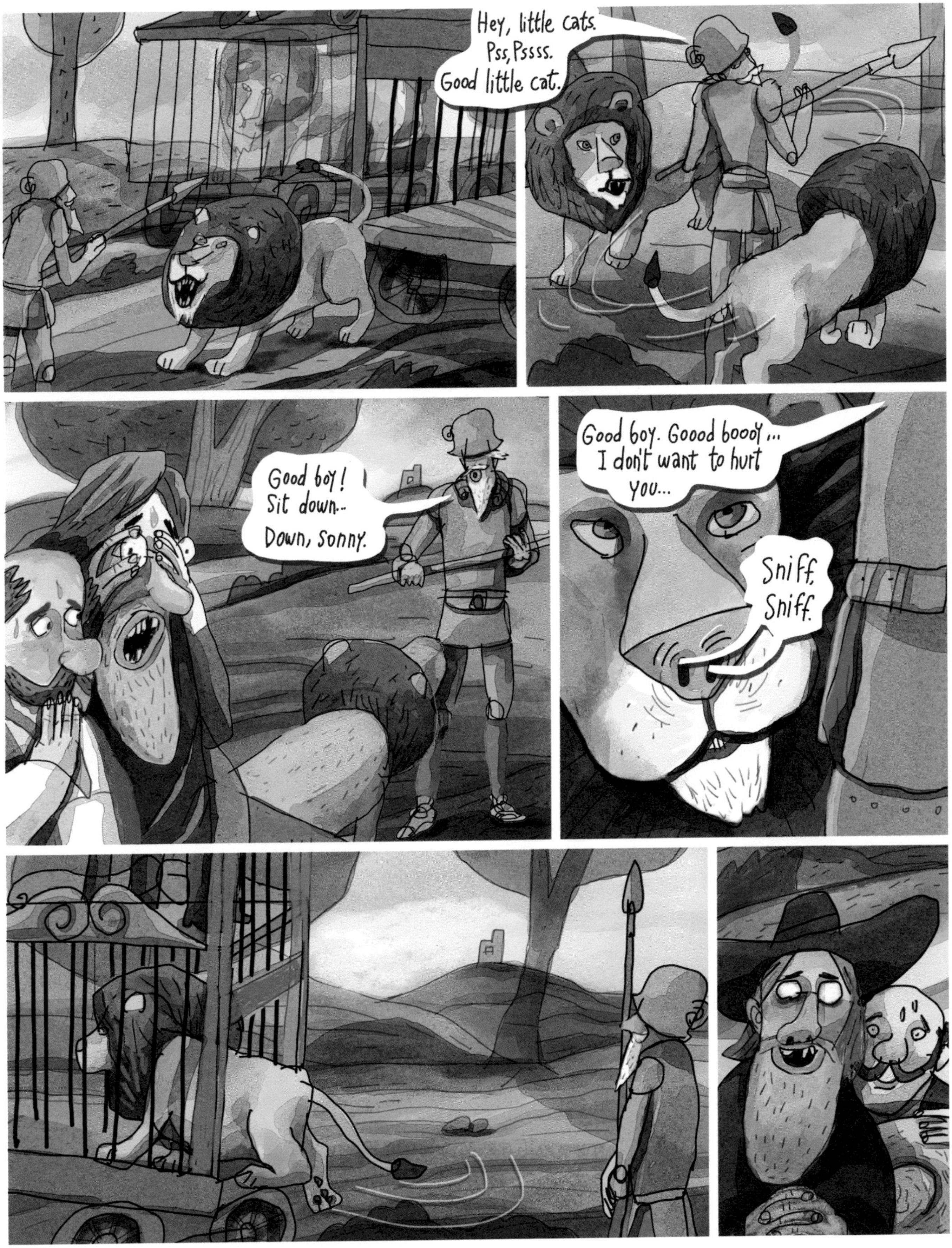
Hey, little cats.
Pss, Pssss.
Good little cat.
Good boy!
Sit down..
Down, sonny.
Good boy. Goood boooy...
I don't want to hurt you...
Sniff,
Sniff.

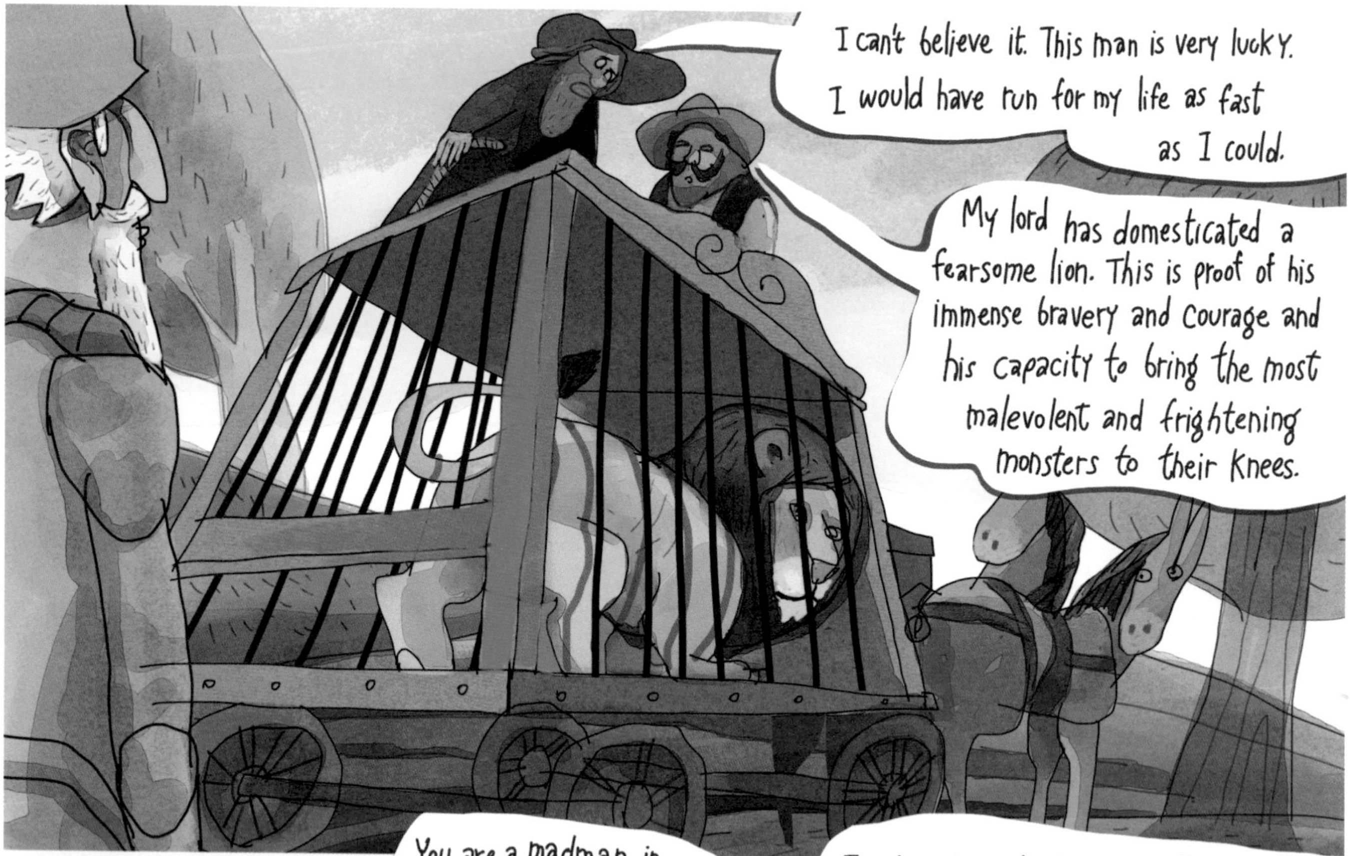
I can't believe it. This man is very lucky. I would have run for my life as fast as I could.
My lord has domesticated a fearsome lion. This is proof of his immense bravery and courage and his capacity to bring the most malevolent and frightening monsters to their knees.
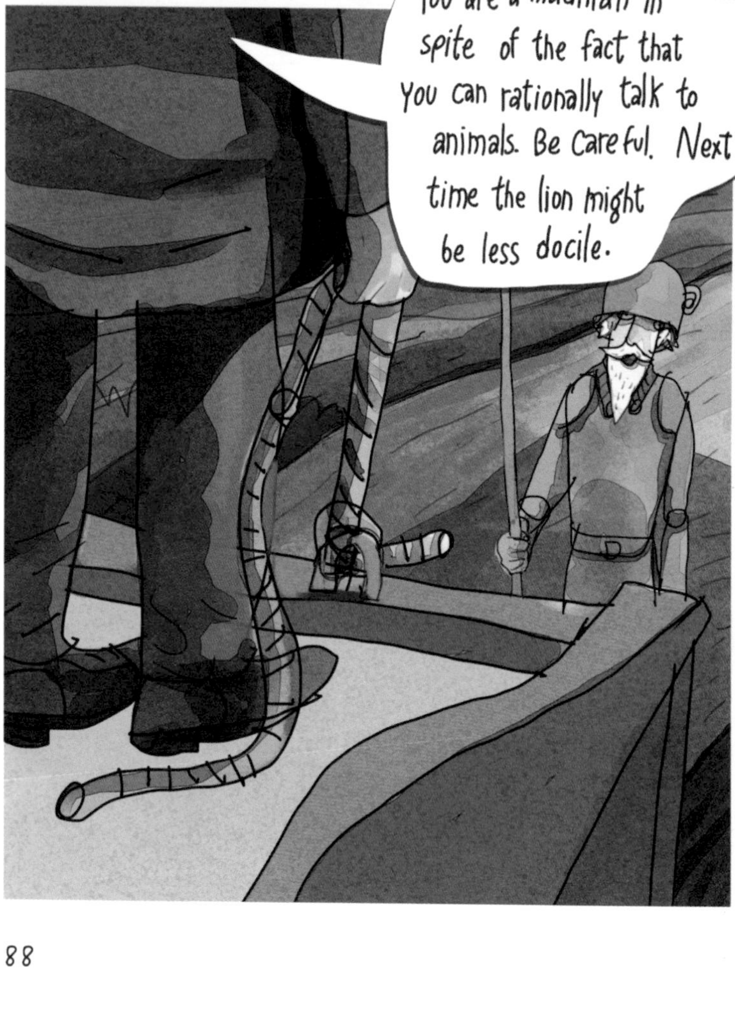
You are a madman in spite of the fact that you can rationally talk to animals. Be careful. Next time the lion might be less docile.
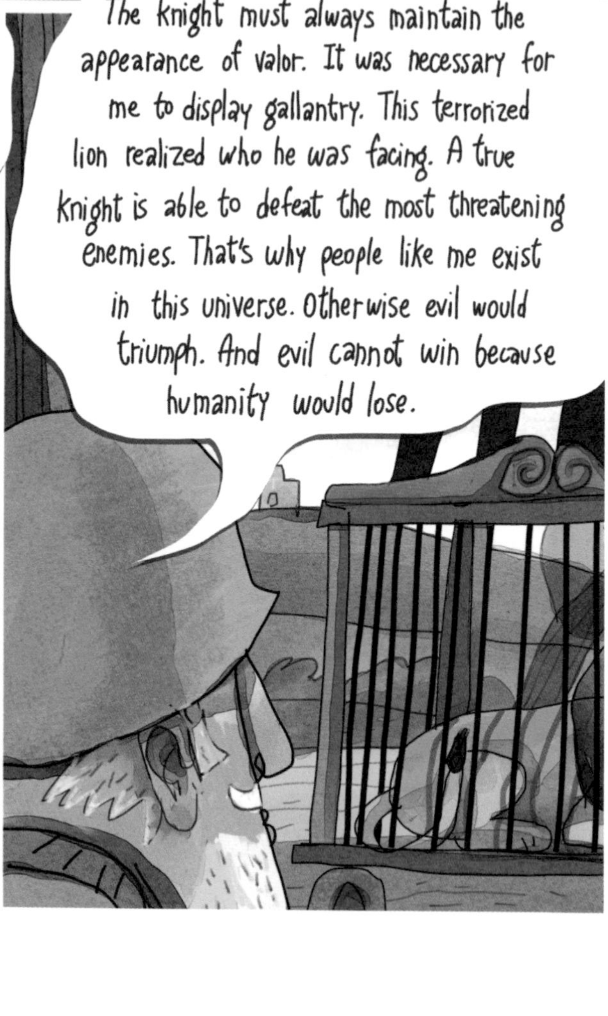
The knight must always maintain the appearance of valor. It was necessary for me to display gallantry. This terrorized lion realized who he was facing. A true knight is able to defeat the most threatening enemies. That's why people like me exist in this universe. Otherwise evil would triumph. And evil cannot win because humanity would lose.

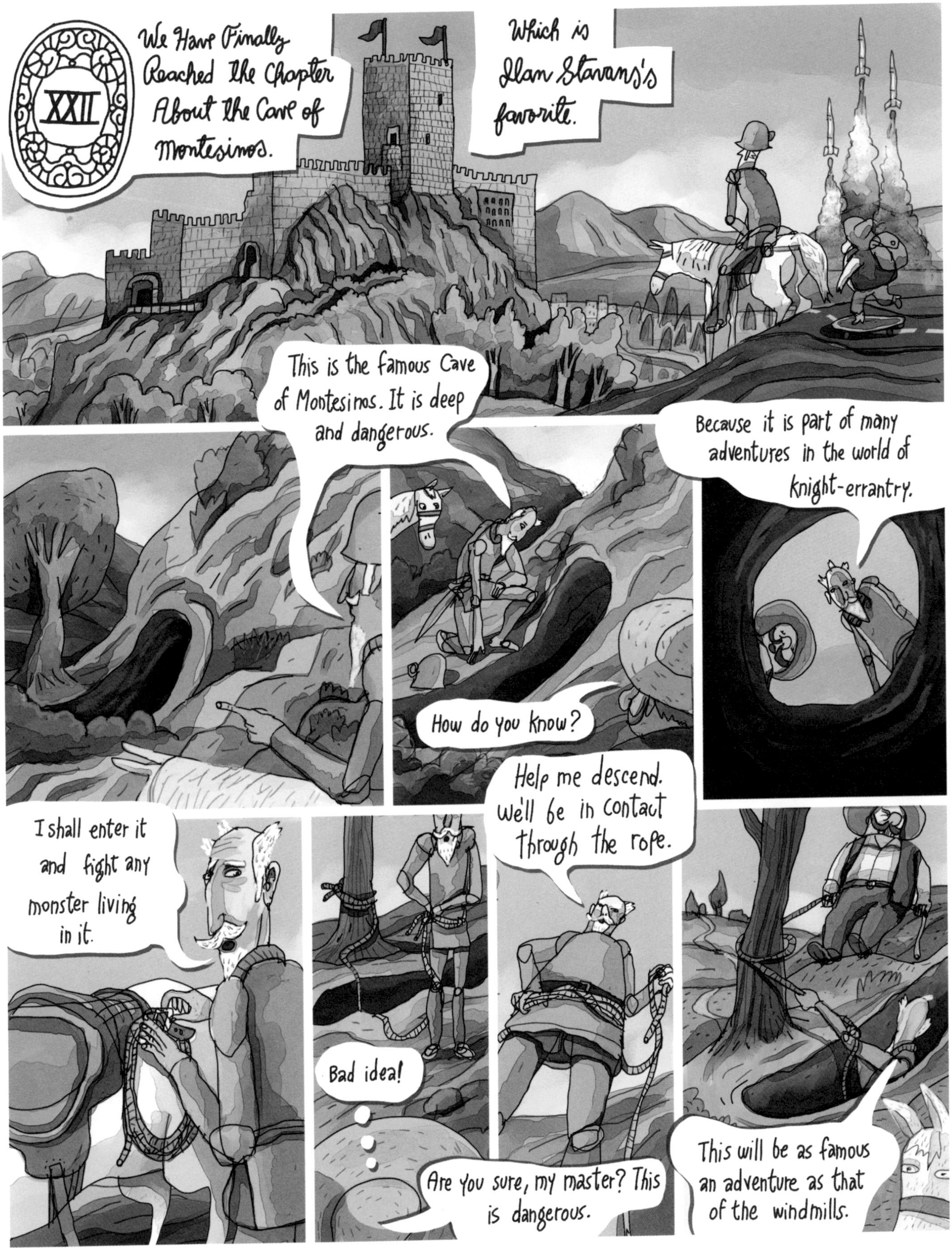
XXII
We Have Finally Reached the Chapter About the Cave of Montesinos.
Which is Ilan Stavans's favorite.
This is the famous Cave of Montesinos. It is deep and dangerous.
How do you know?
Because it is part of many adventures in the world of knight-errantry.
I shall enter it and fight any monster living in it.
Bad idea!
Help me descend. We'll be in contact through the rope.
Are you sure, my master? This is dangerous.
This will be as famous an adventure as that of the windmills.

God bless him. He'll die alone inside the cave.
Have you reached the bottom?!!
Hummm...
Okay, now I must wait...
I need a siesta.

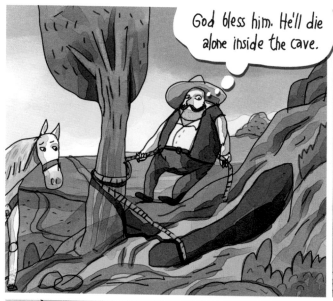

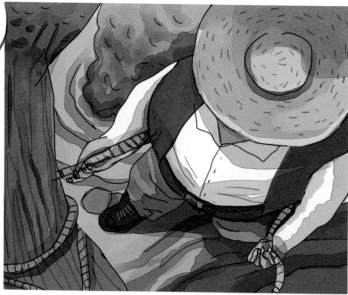

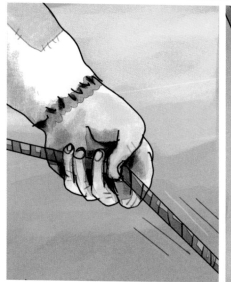

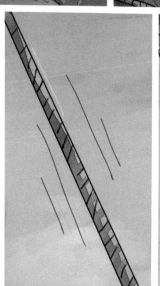

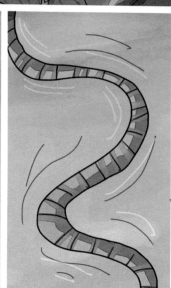

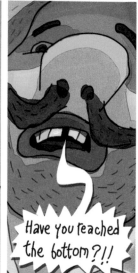

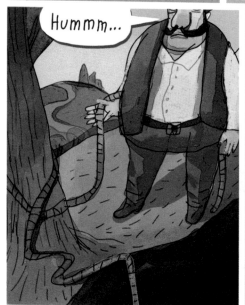

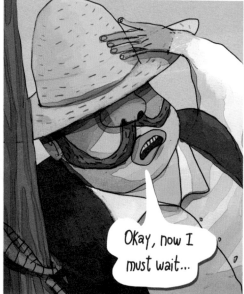

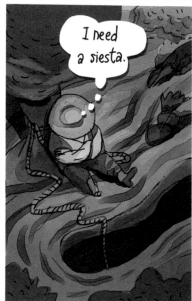

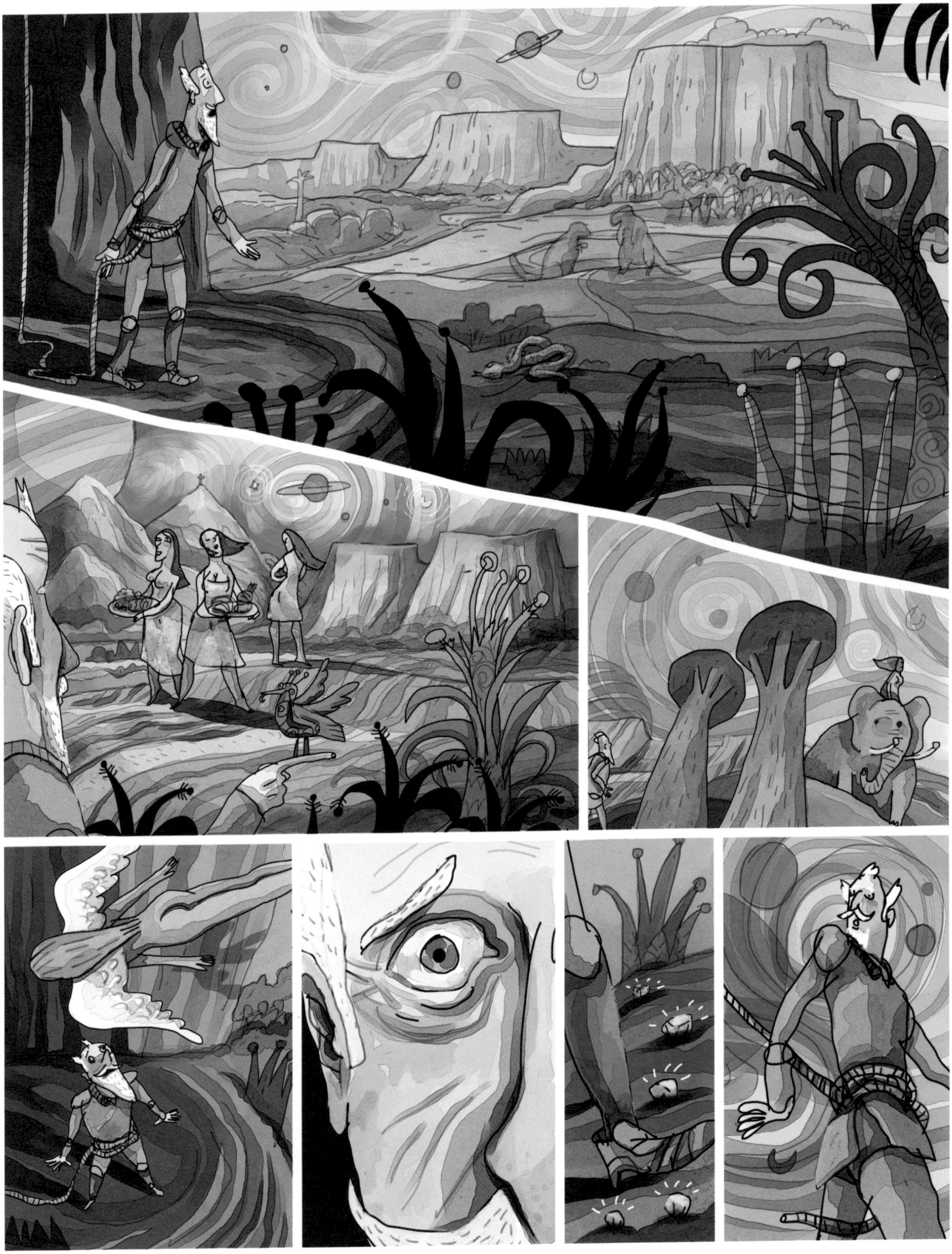

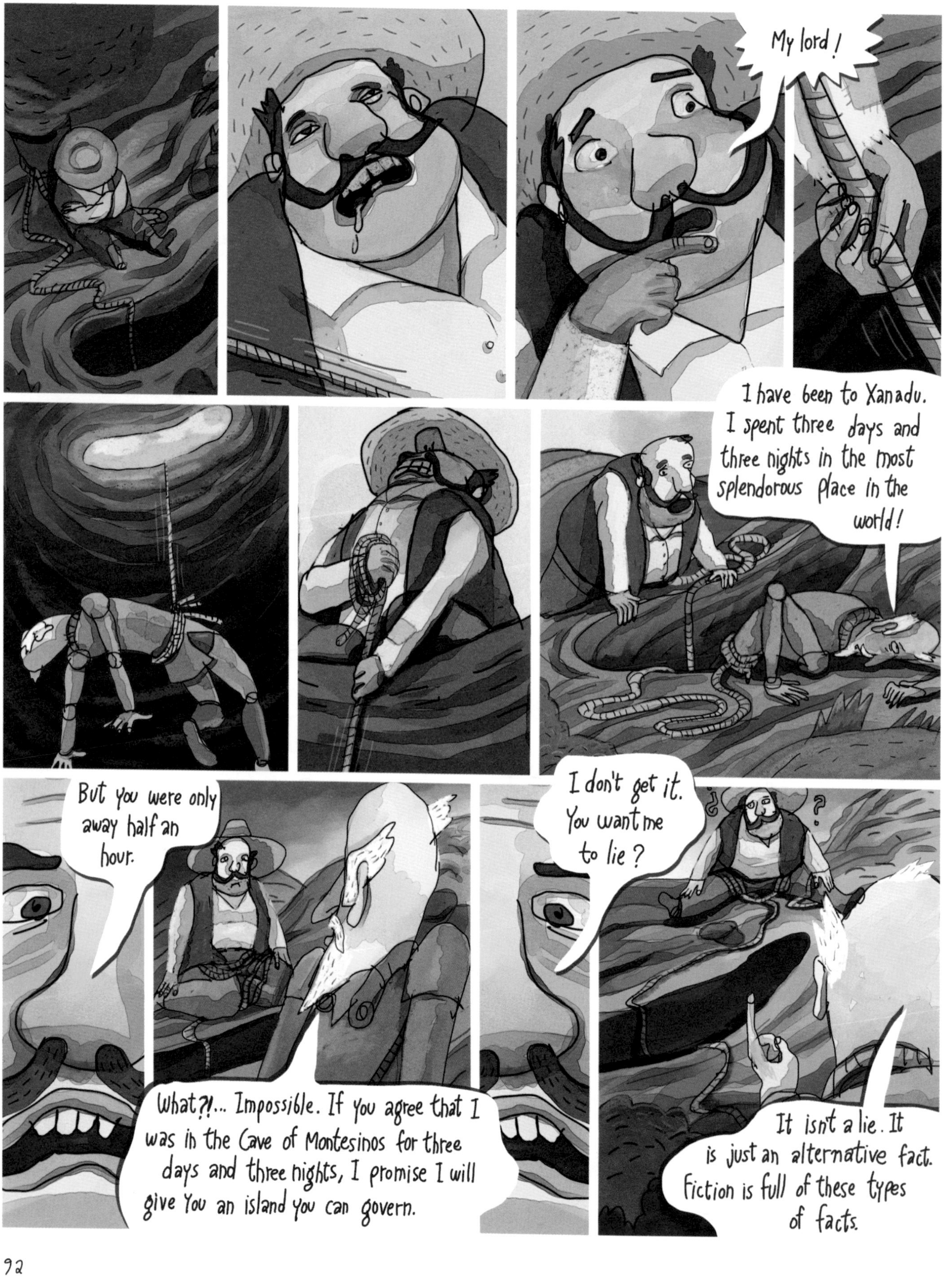
My lord!
I have been to Xanadu. I spent three days and three nights in the most splendorous place in the world!
But you were only away half an hour.
What?!... Impossible. If you agree that I was in the Cave of Montesinos for three days and three nights, I promise I will give You an island you can govern.
I don't get it. You want me to lie?
It isn't a lie. It is just an alternative fact. Fiction is full of these types of facts.

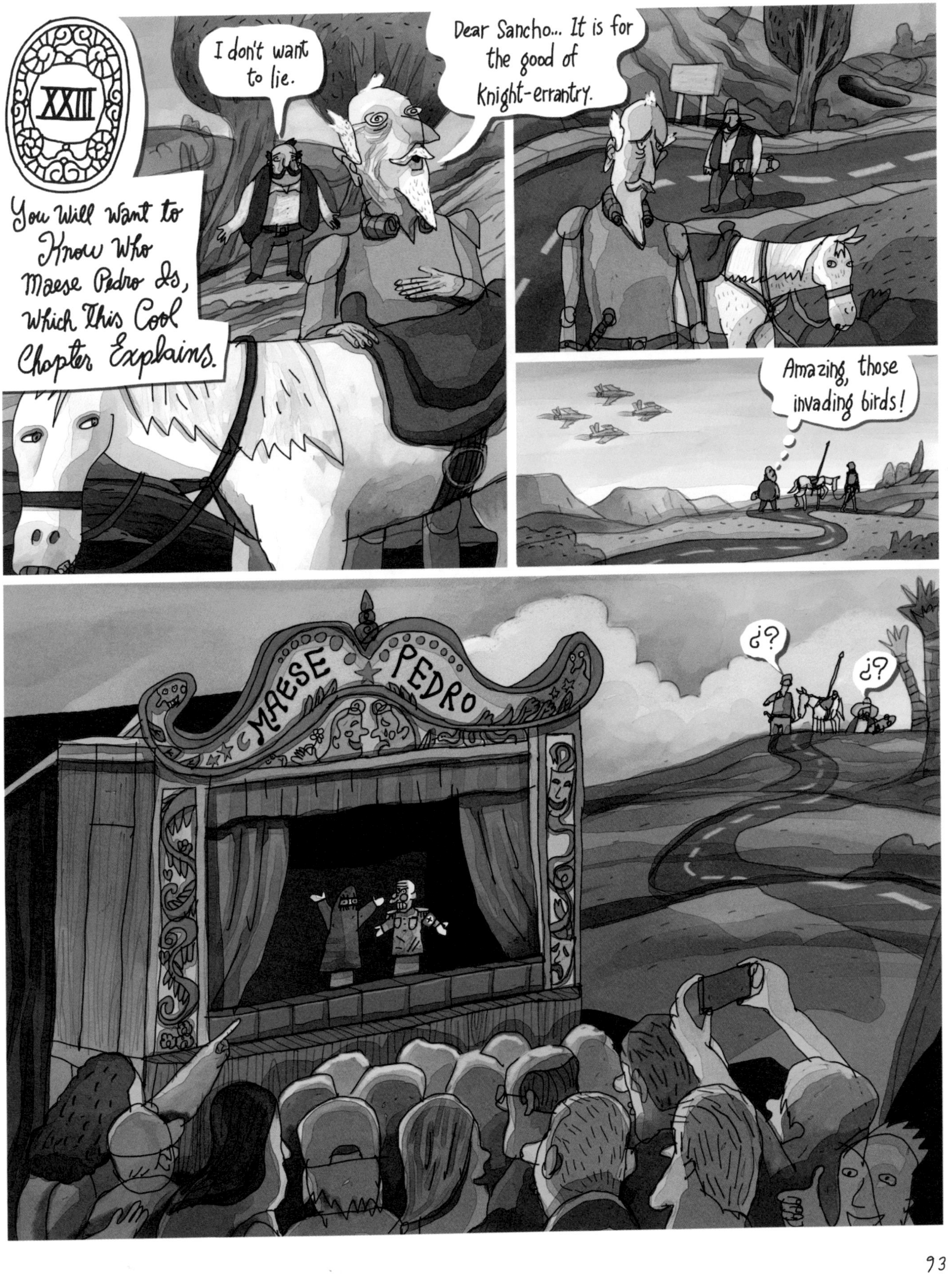
XXIII
You Will Want to Know Who Maese Pedro Is, Which This Cool Chapter Explains.
I don't want to lie.
Dear Sancho... It is for the good of Knight-errantry.
Amazing, those invading birds!
MAESE PEDRO
¿?
¿?

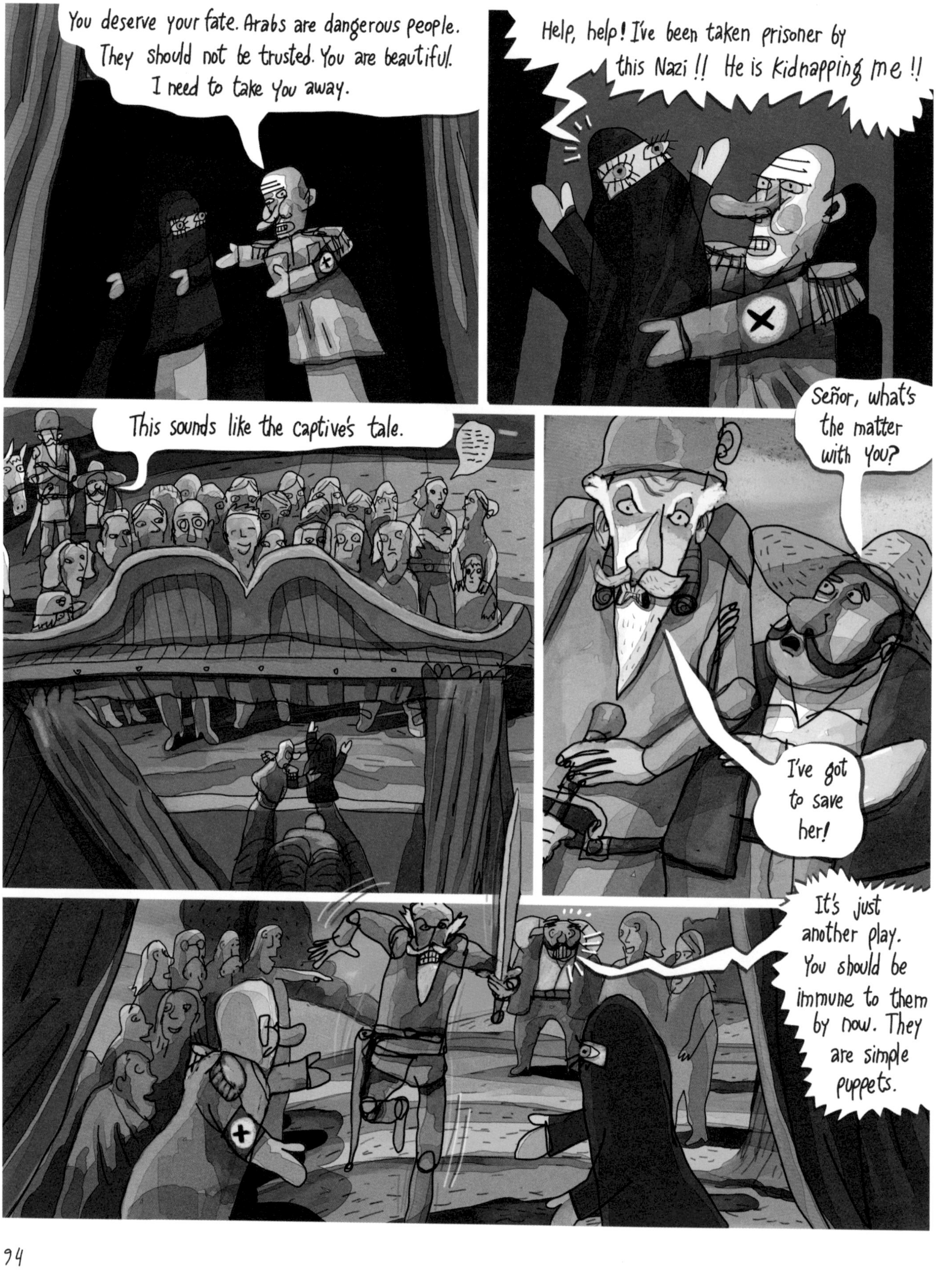
You deserve your fate. Arabs are dangerous people. They should not be trusted. You are beautiful. I need to take you away.
Help, help! I've been taken prisoner by this Nazi!! He is kidnapping me!!
This sounds like the captive's tale.
Señor, what's the matter with you?
I've got to save her!
It's just another play. You should be immune to them by now. They are simple puppets.

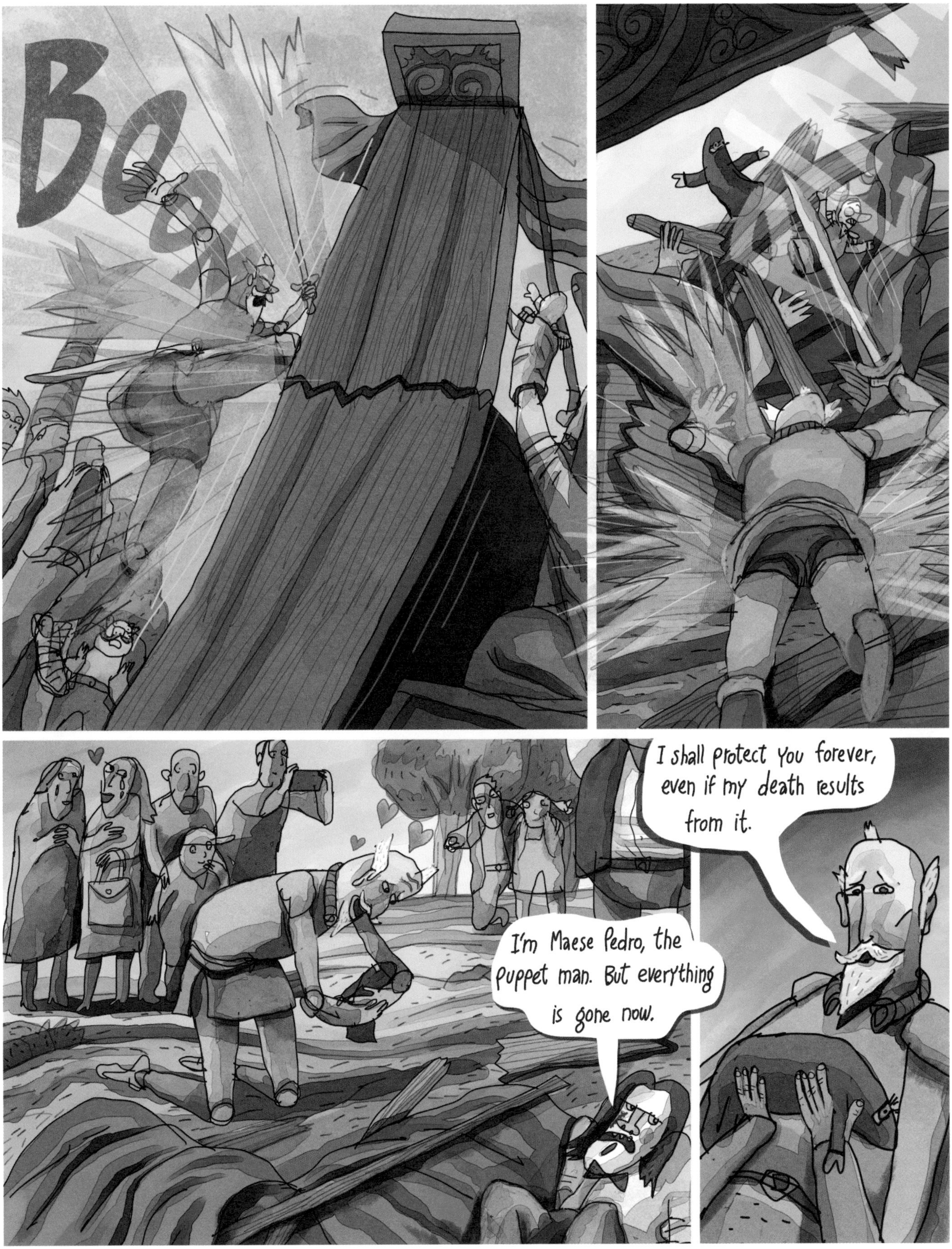
I'm Maese Pedro, the puppet man. But everything is gone now.
I shall protect you forever, even if my death results from it.

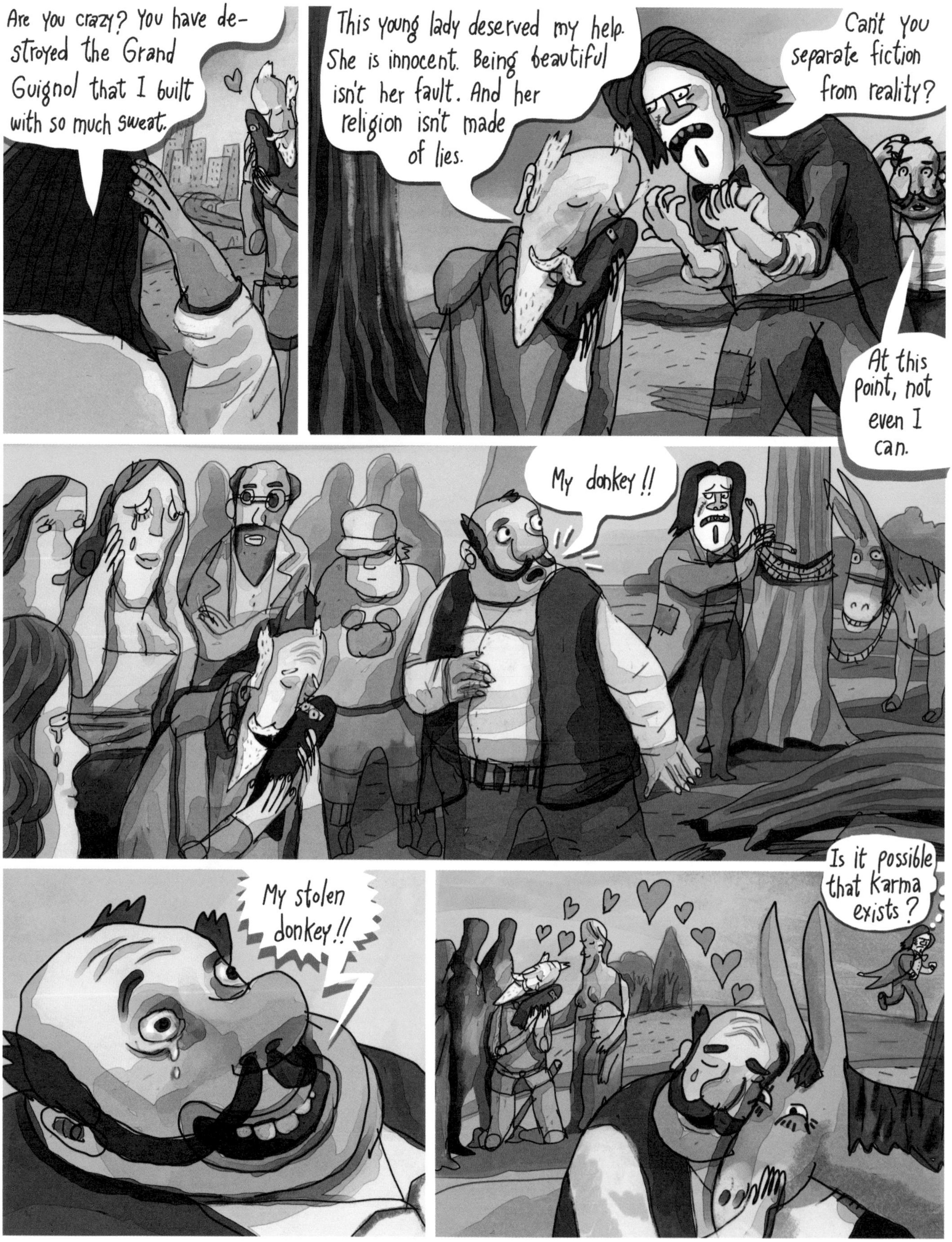

Are you crazy? You have destroyed the Grand Guignol that I built with so much sweat.
This young lady deserved my help. She is innocent. Being beautiful isn't her fault. And her religion isn't made of lies.
Can't you separate fiction from reality?
At this point, not even I can.
My donkey !!
My stolen donkey !!
Is it possible that karma exists?

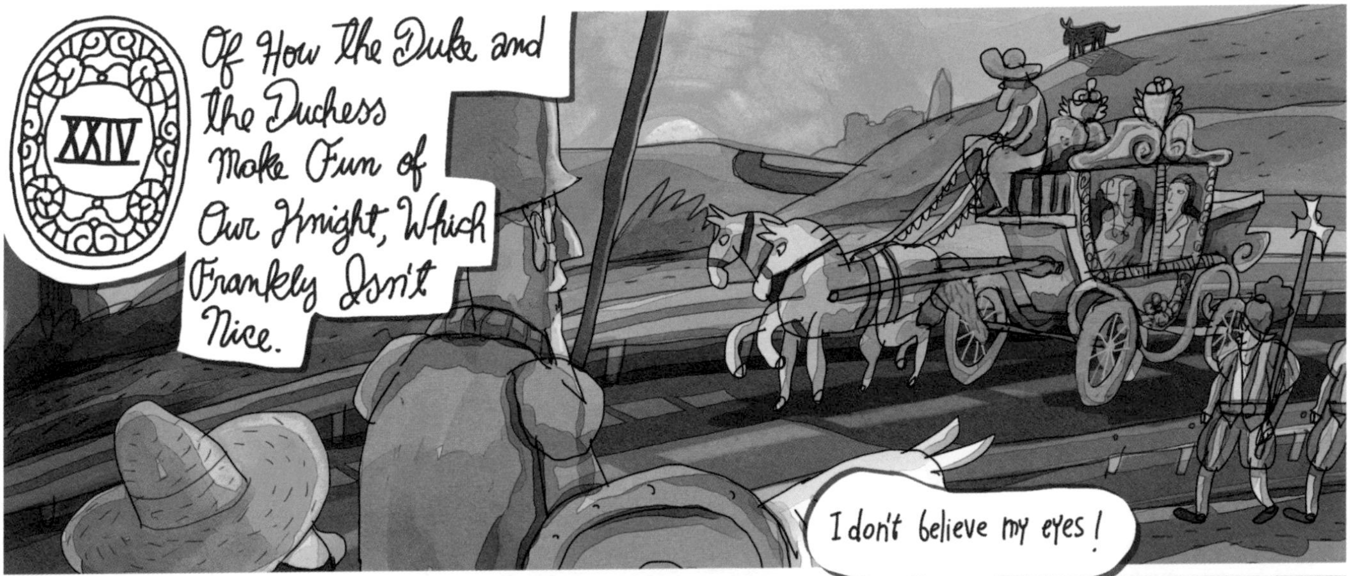
XXIV
Of How the Duke and the Duchess Make Fun of Our Knight, Which Frankly Isn't Nice.

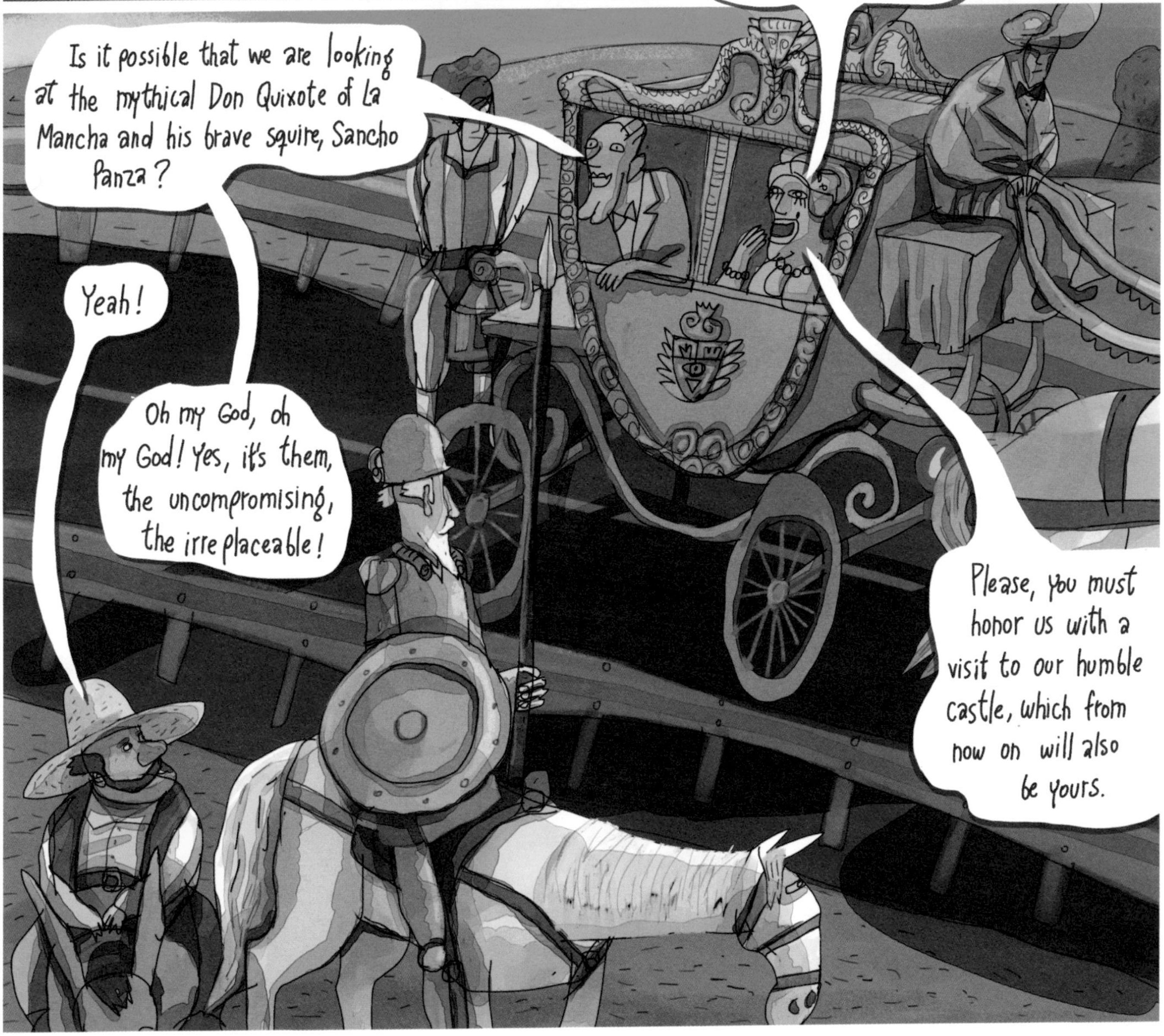
I don't believe my eyes!
Is it possible that we are looking at the mythical Don Quixote of La Mancha and his brave squire, Sancho Panza?
Yeah!
Oh my God, oh my God! Yes, it's them, the uncompromising, the irreplaceable!
Please, you must honor us with a visit to our humble castle, which from now on will also be yours.

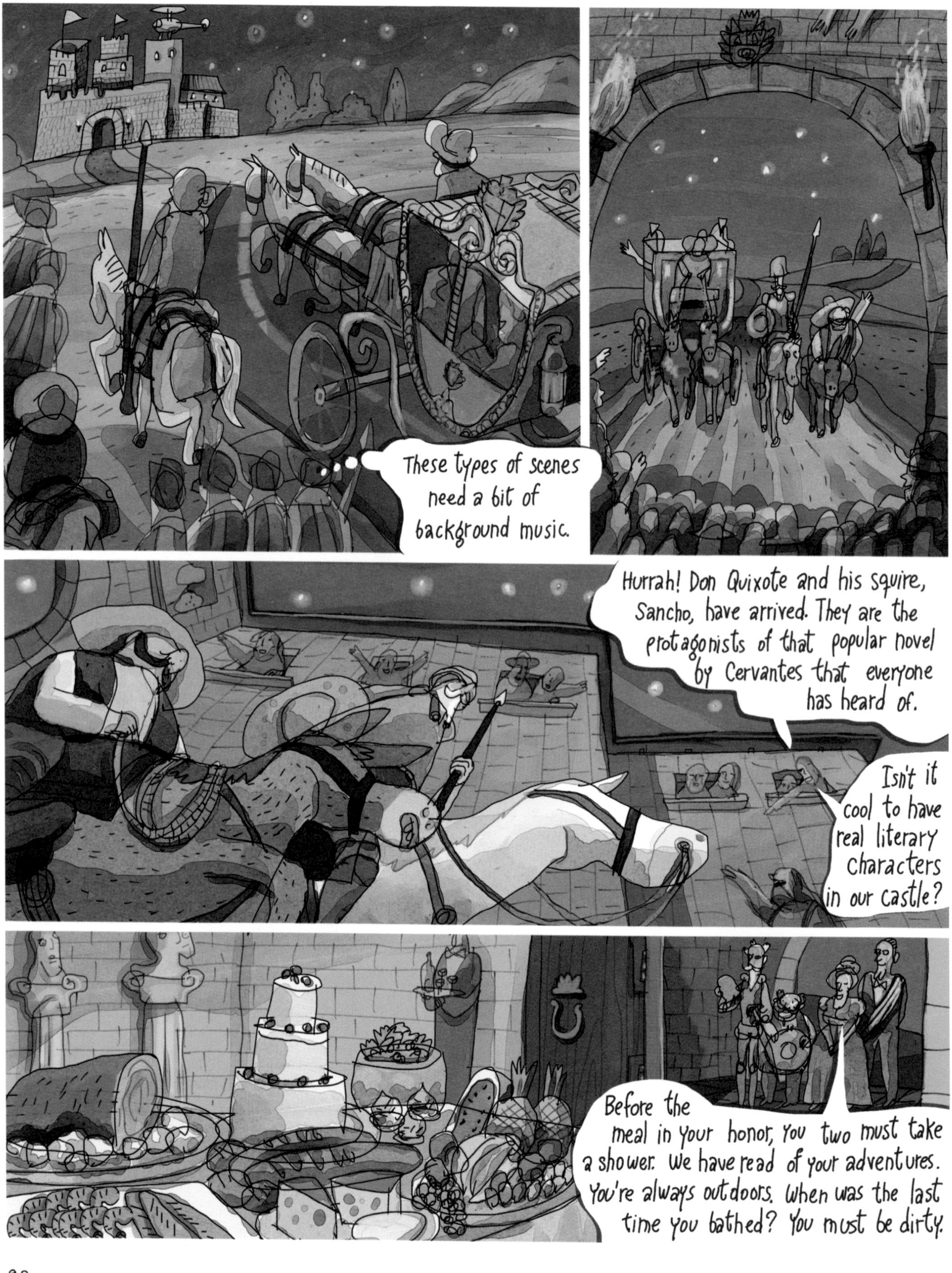
These types of scenes need a bit of background music.
Hurrah! Don Quixote and his squire, Sancho, have arrived. They are the protagonists of that popular novel by Cervantes that everyone has heard of.
Isn't it cool to have real literary characters in our castle?
Before the meal in your honor, you two must take a shower. We have read of your adventures. You're always outdoors. When was the last time you bathed? You must be dirty.

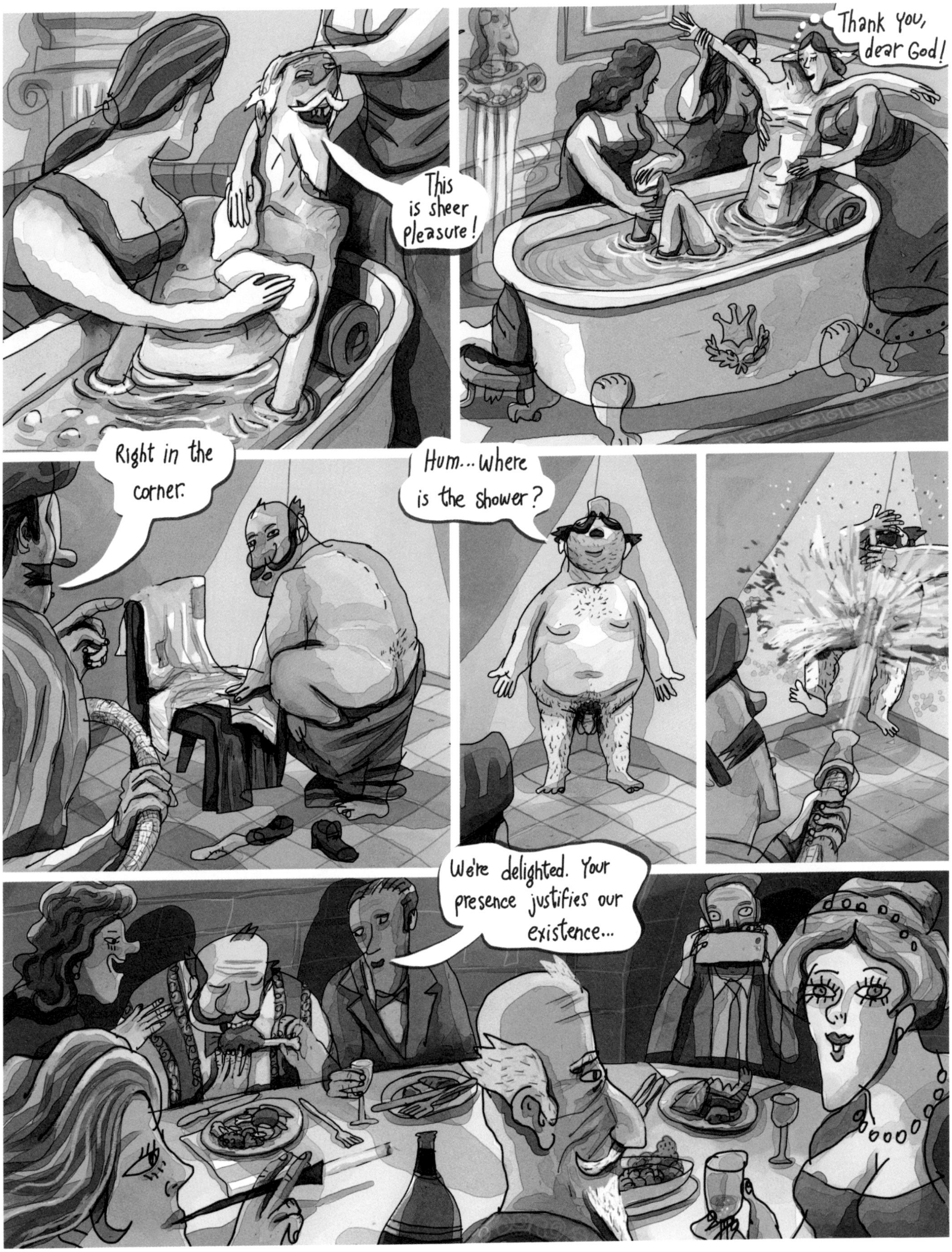
This is sheer pleasure!
Thank you, dear God!
Right in the corner.
Hum... where is the shower?
We're delighted. Your presence justifies our existence...

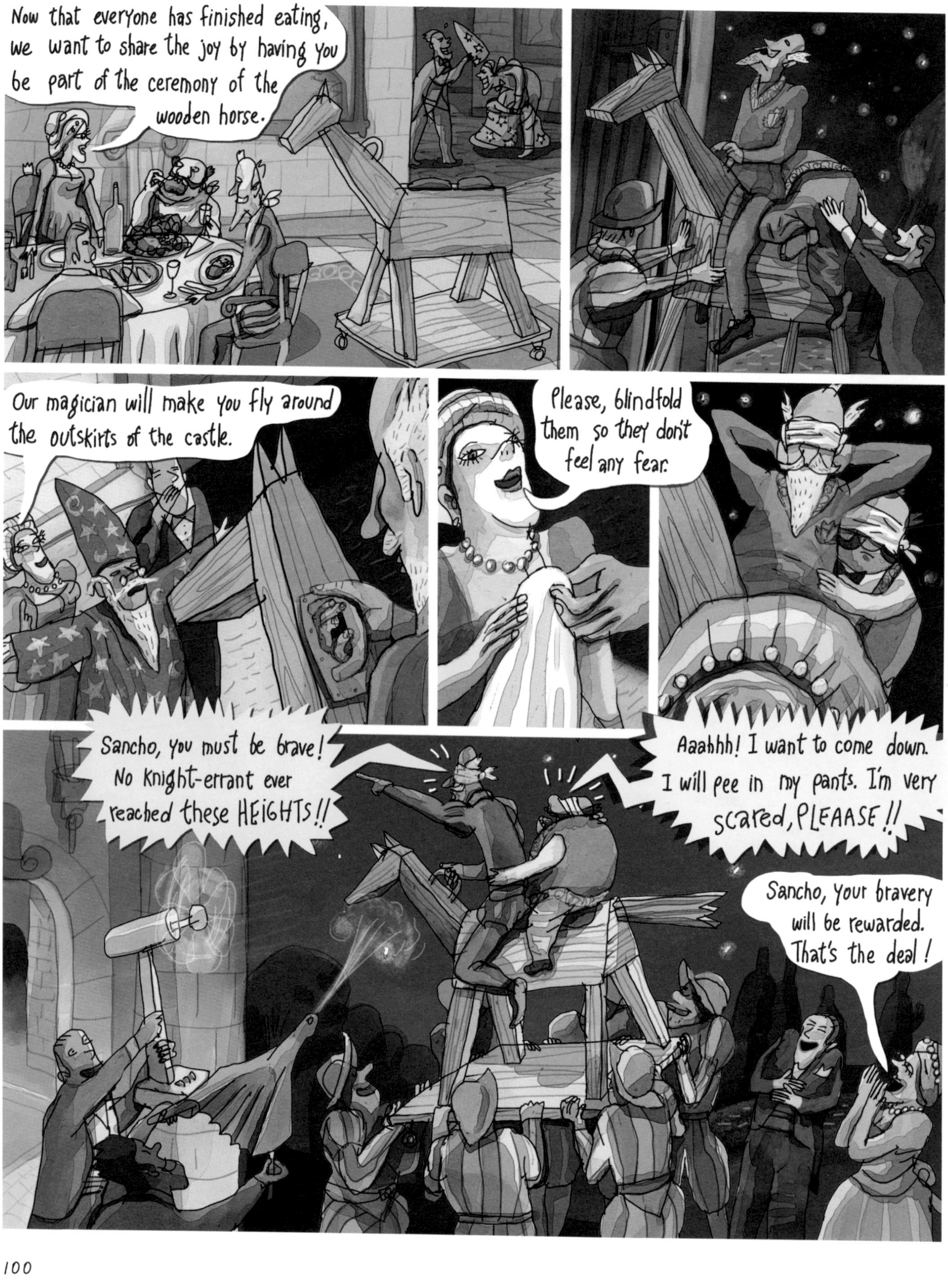

Now that everyone has finished eating, we want to share the joy by having you be part of the ceremony of the wooden horse.
Our magician will make you fly around the outskirts of the castle.
Please, blindfold them so they don't feel any fear.
Sancho, you must be brave! No Knight-errant ever reached these HEIGHTS!!
Aaahhh! I want to come down. I will pee in my pants. I'm very scared, PLEAASE!!
Sancho, your bravery will be rewarded. That's the deal!

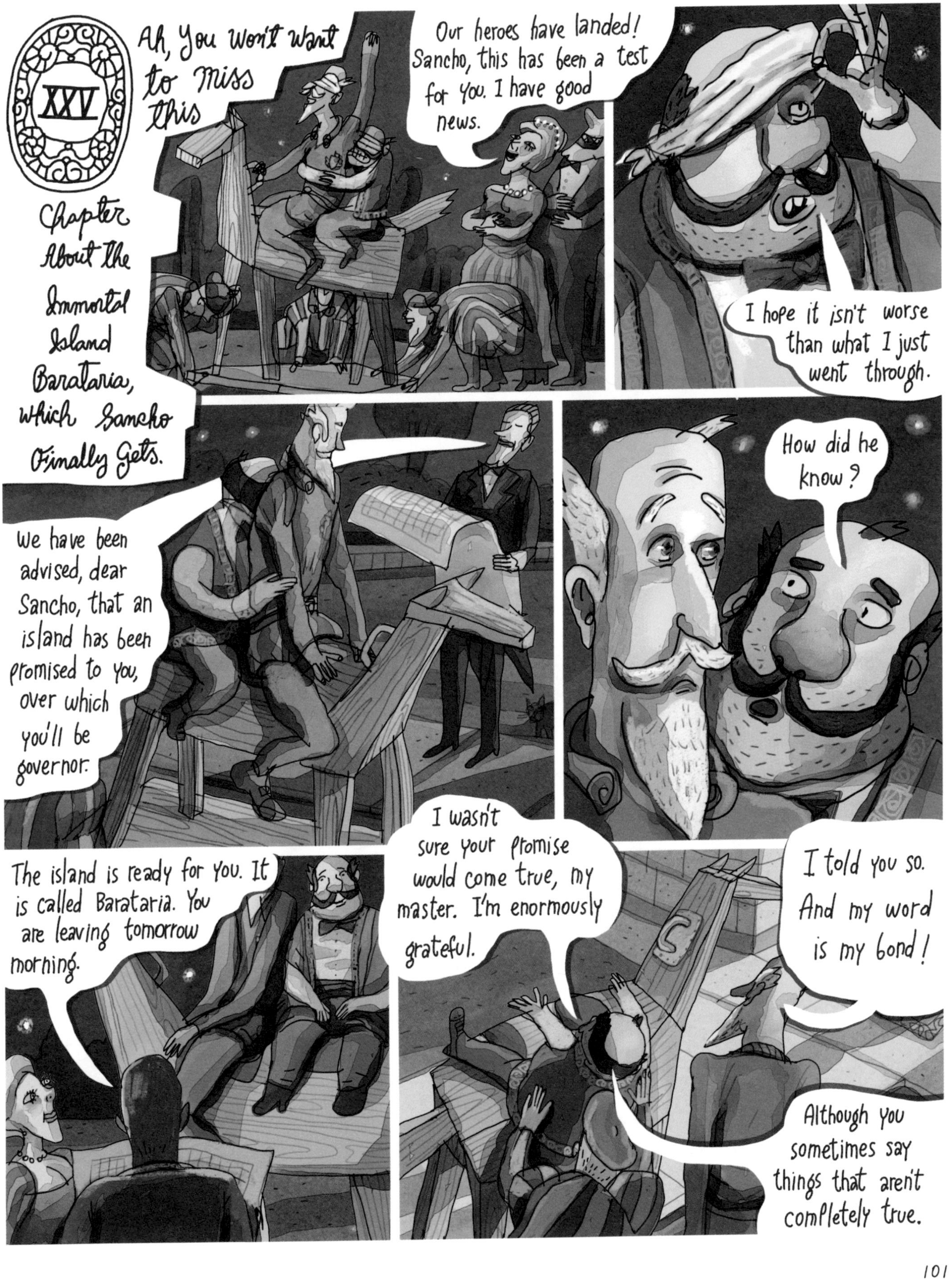
XXV
Chapter About the Immortal Island Barataria, which Sancho Finally Gets.
Ah, You Won't Want to Miss this
Our heroes have landed! Sancho, this has been a test for you. I have good news.
I hope it isn't worse than what I just went through.
We have been advised, dear Sancho, that an island has been promised to you, over which you'll be governor.
How did he know?
The island is ready for you. It is called Barataria. You are leaving tomorrow morning.
I wasn't sure your promise would come true, my master. I'm enormously grateful.
I told you so. And my word is my bond!
Although you sometimes say things that aren't completely true.

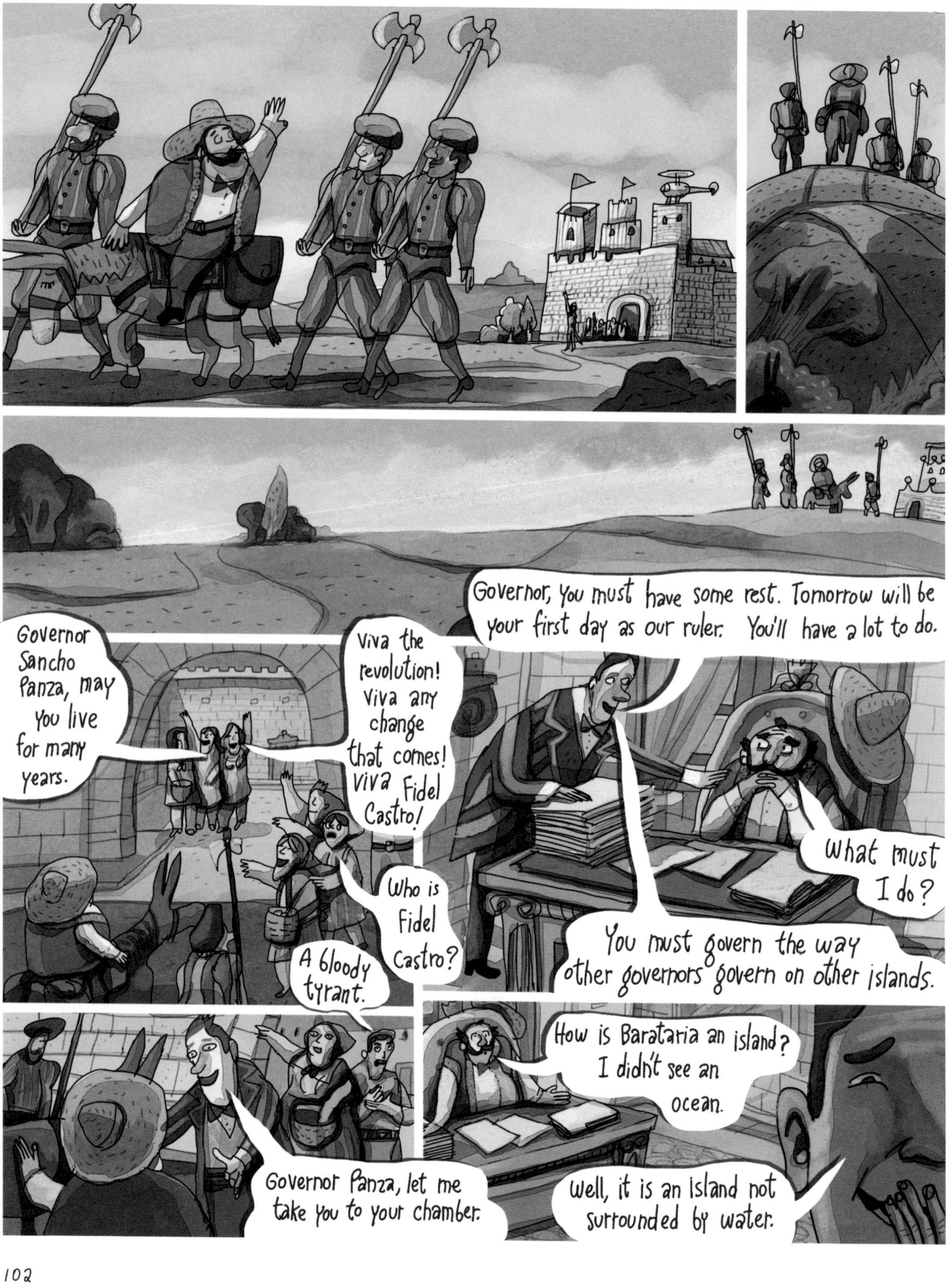
Governor, you must have some rest. Tomorrow will be your first day as our ruler. You'll have a lot to do.
Governor Sancho Panza, may you live for many years.
Viva the revolution! Viva any change that comes! Viva Fidel Castro!
Who is Fidel Castro?
A bloody tyrant.
What must I do?
You must govern the way other governors govern on other islands.
Governor Panza, let me take you to your chamber.
How is Barataria an island? I didn't see an ocean.
Well, it is an island not surrounded by water.

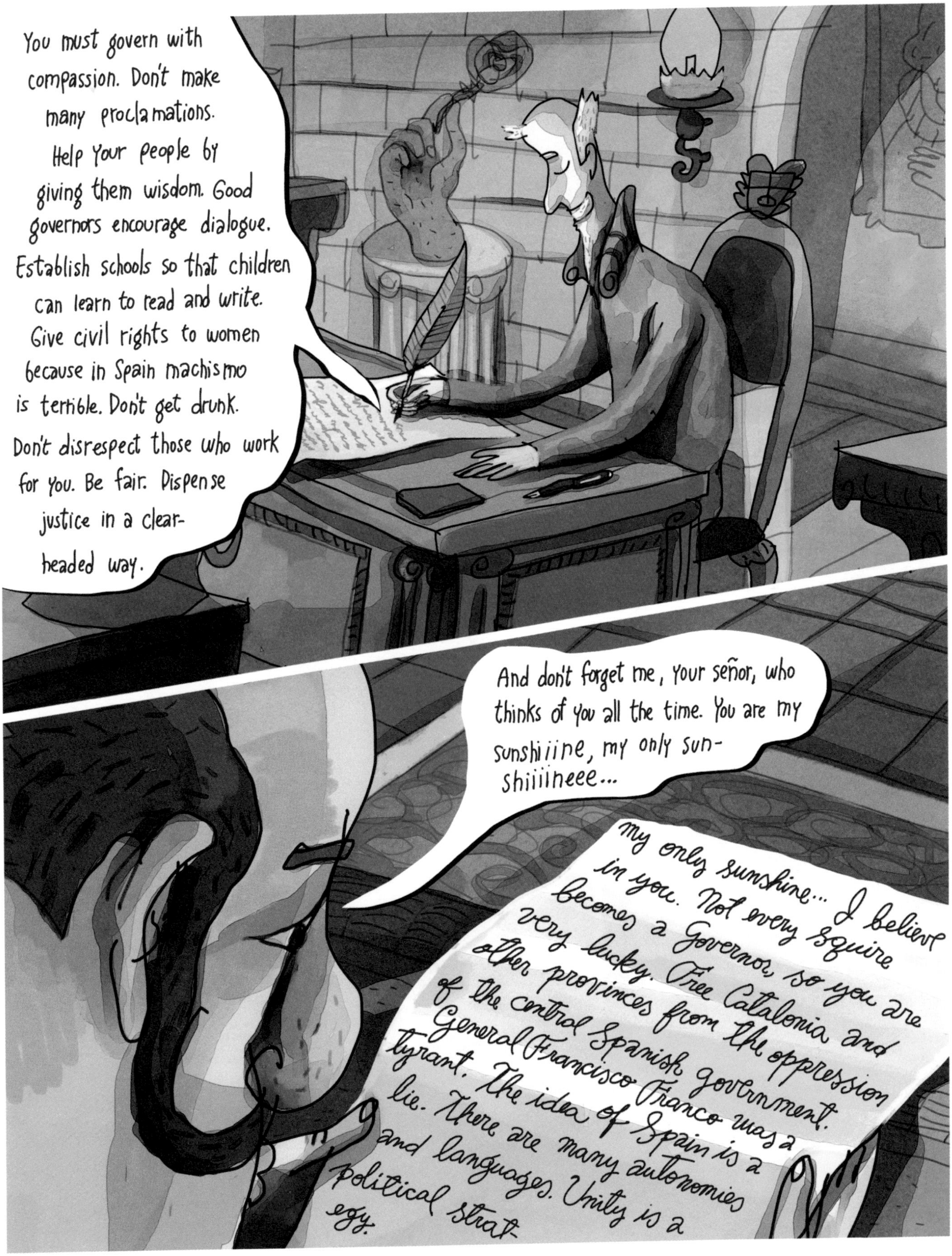
You must govern with compassion. Don't make many proclamations. Help your people by giving them wisdom. Good governors encourage dialogue. Establish schools so that children can learn to read and write. Give civil rights to women because in Spain machismo is terrible. Don't get drunk. Don't disrespect those who work for you. Be fair. Dispense justice in a clear-headed way.
And don't forget me, your señor, who thinks of you all the time. You are my sunshiiine, my only sun-shiiiineee...
my only sunshine... I believe in you. Not every squire becomes a Governor, so you are very lucky. Free Catalonia and other provinces from the oppression of the central Spanish government. General Francisco Franco was a tyrant. The idea of Spain is a lie. There are many autonomies and languages. Unity is a political strat-egy.

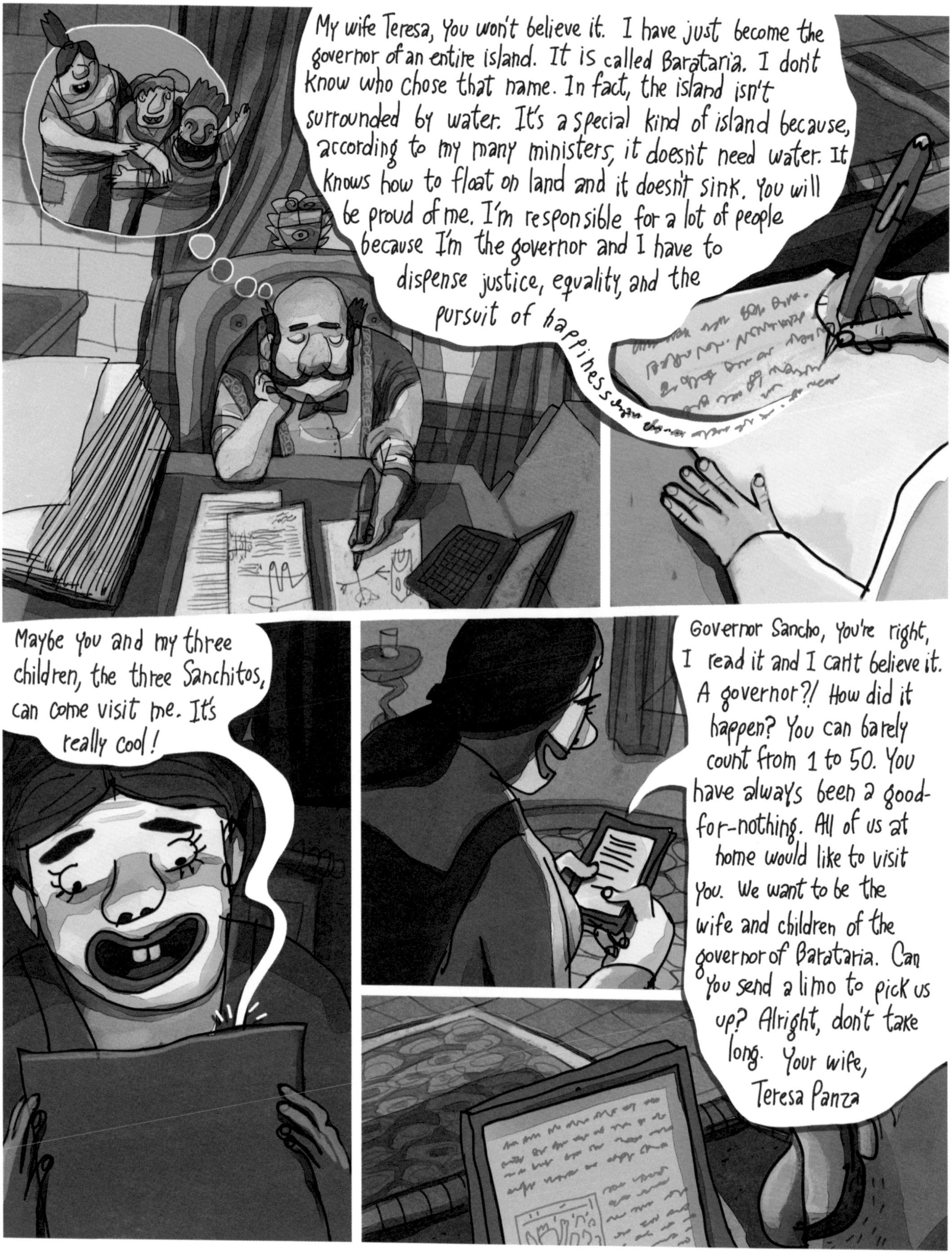
My wife Teresa, you won't believe it. I have just become the governor of an entire island. It is called Barataria. I don't know who chose that name. In fact, the island isn't surrounded by water. It's a special kind of island because, according to my many ministers, it doesn't need water. It knows how to float on land and it doesn't sink. You will be proud of me. I'm responsible for a lot of people because I'm the governor and I have to dispense justice, equality, and the pursuit of happiness
Maybe you and my three children, the three Sanchitos, can come visit me. It's really cool!
Governor Sancho, you're right, I read it and I can't believe it. A governor?! How did it happen? You can barely count from 1 to 50. You have always been a good-for-nothing. All of us at home would like to visit you. We want to be the wife and children of the governor of Barataria. Can you send a limo to pick us up? Alright, don't take long. Your wife, Teresa Panza

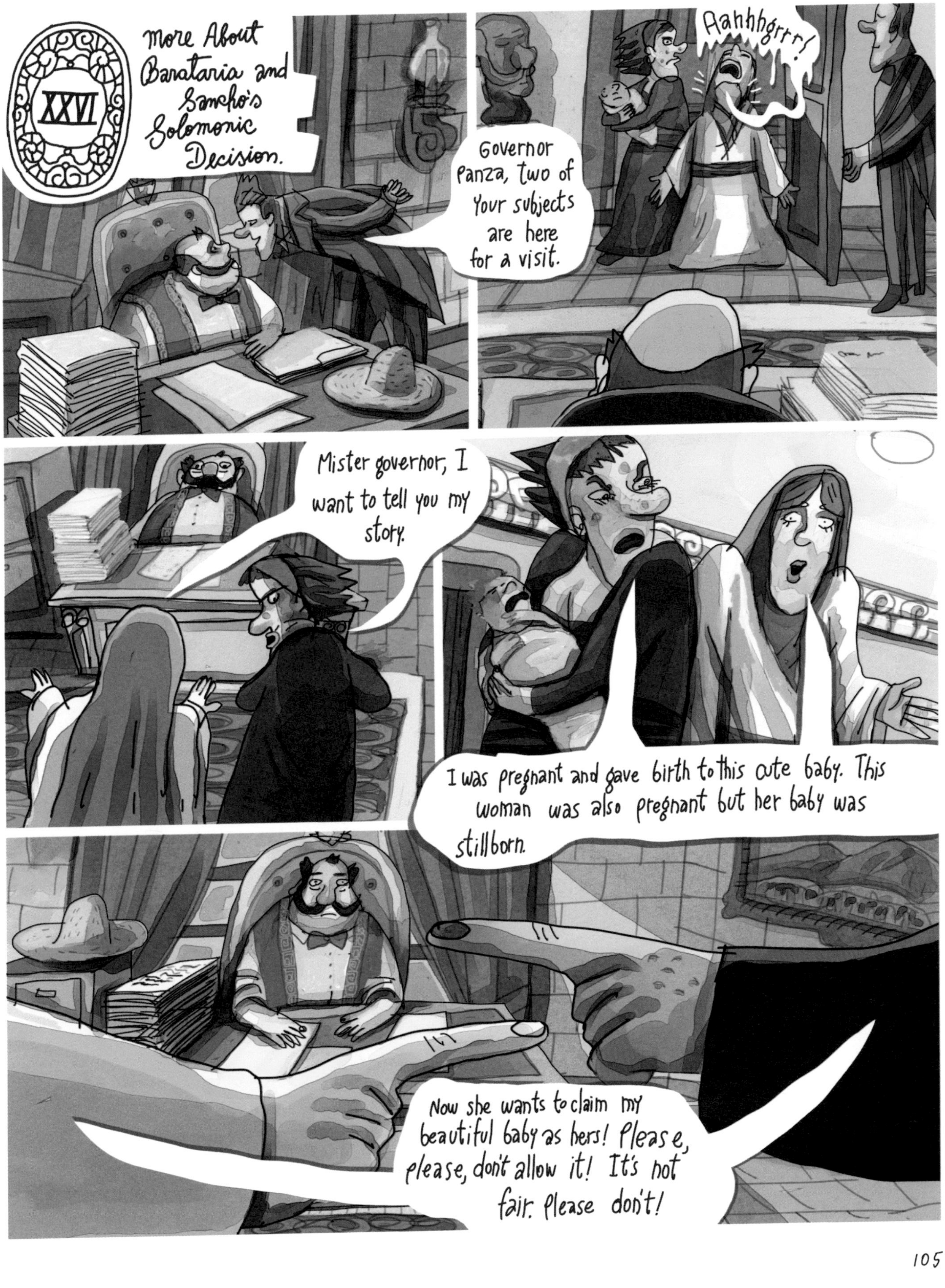
XXVI
More About Barataria and Sancho's Solomonic Decision.
Governor Panza, two of your subjects are here for a visit.
Aanhhgrrr!
Mister governor, I want to tell you my story.
I was pregnant and gave birth to this cute baby. This woman was also pregnant but her baby was stillborn.
Now she wants to claim my beautiful baby as hers! Please, please, don't allow it! It's not fair. Please don't!

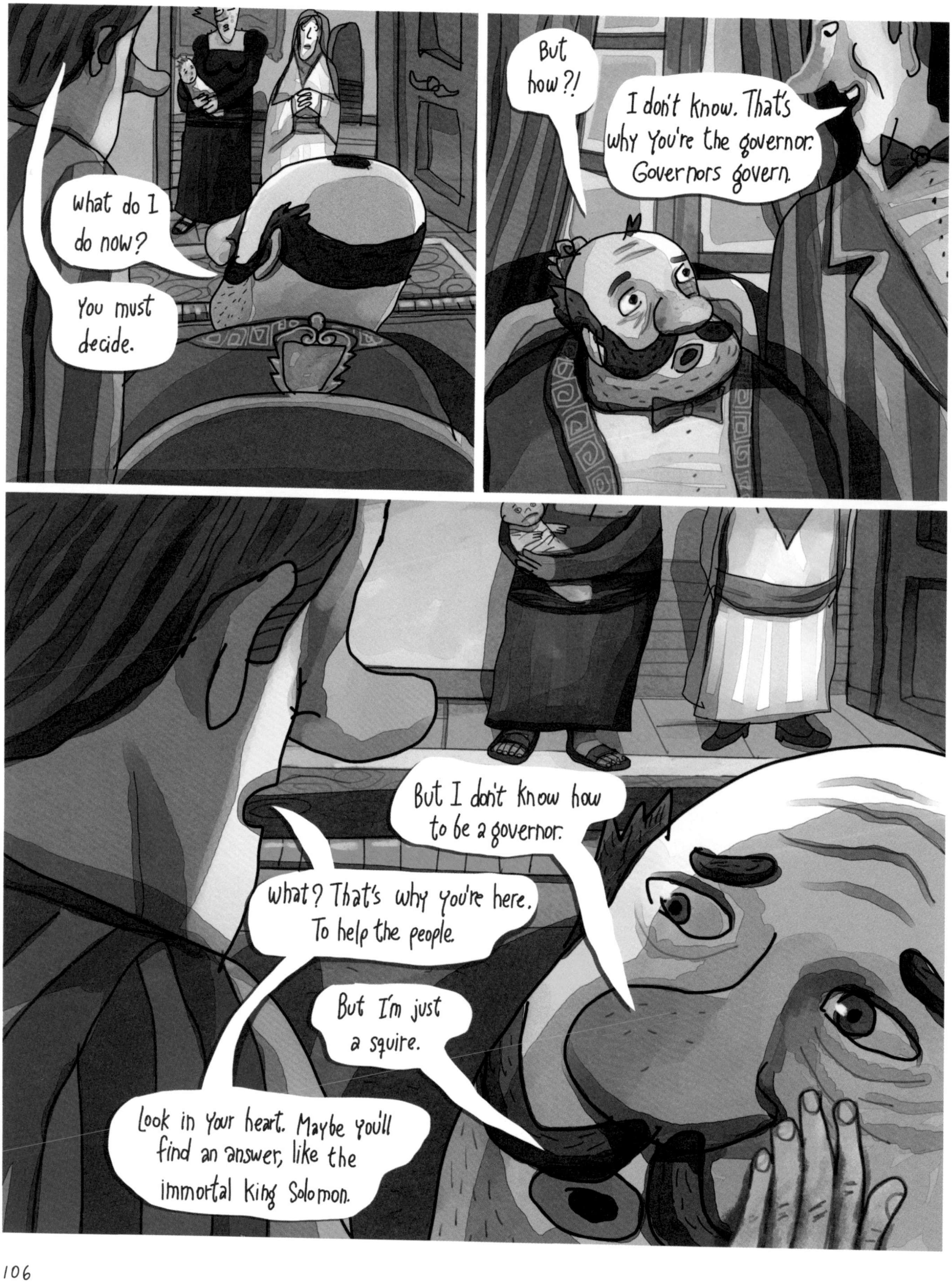
What do I do now?
You must decide.
But how?!
I don't know. That's why you're the governor. Governors govern.
But I don't know how to be a governor.
What? That's why you're here. To help the people.
But I'm just a squire.
Look in your heart. Maybe you'll find an answer, like the immortal King Solomon.

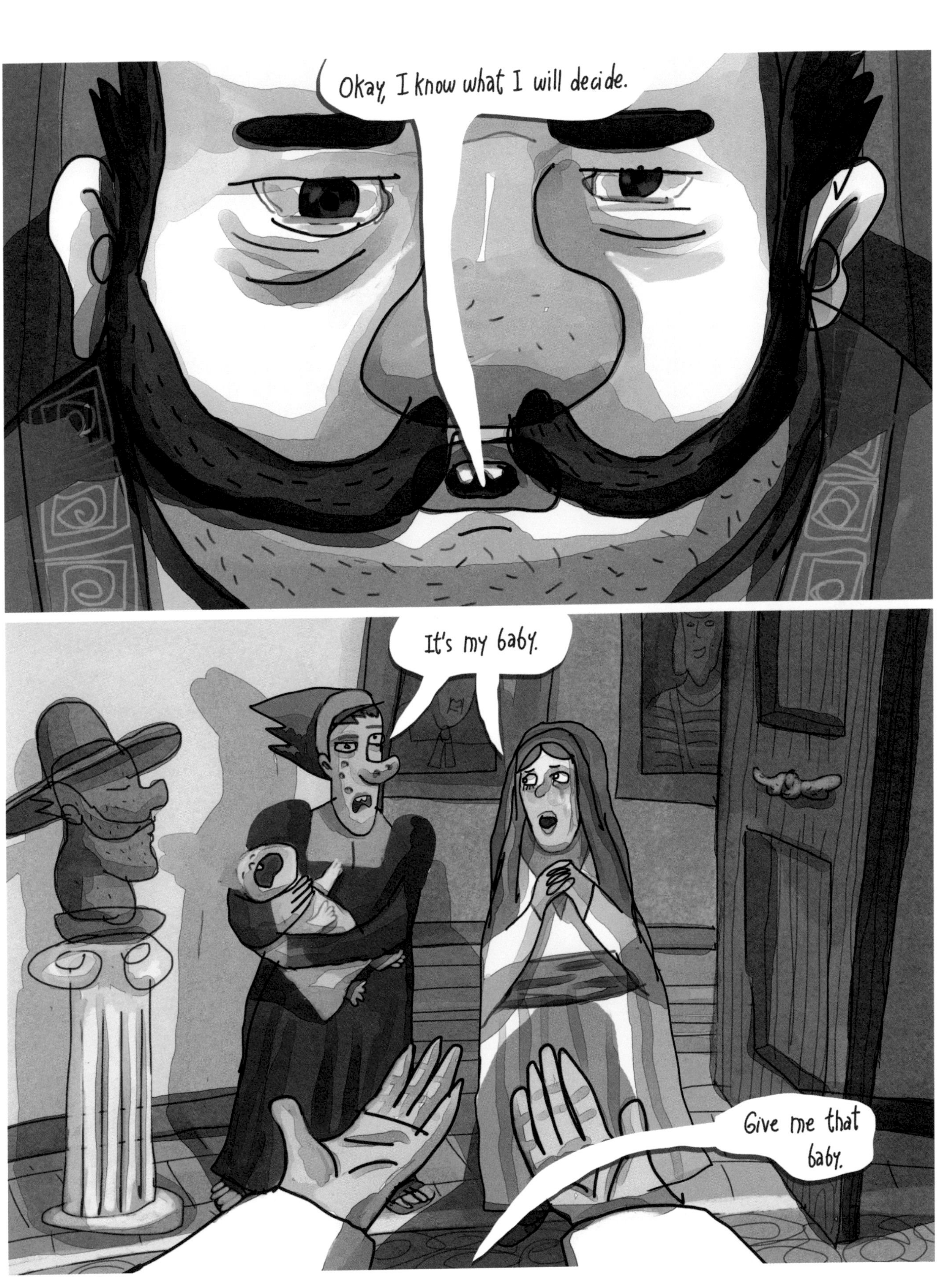

Okay, I know what I will decide.
It's my baby.
Give me that baby.

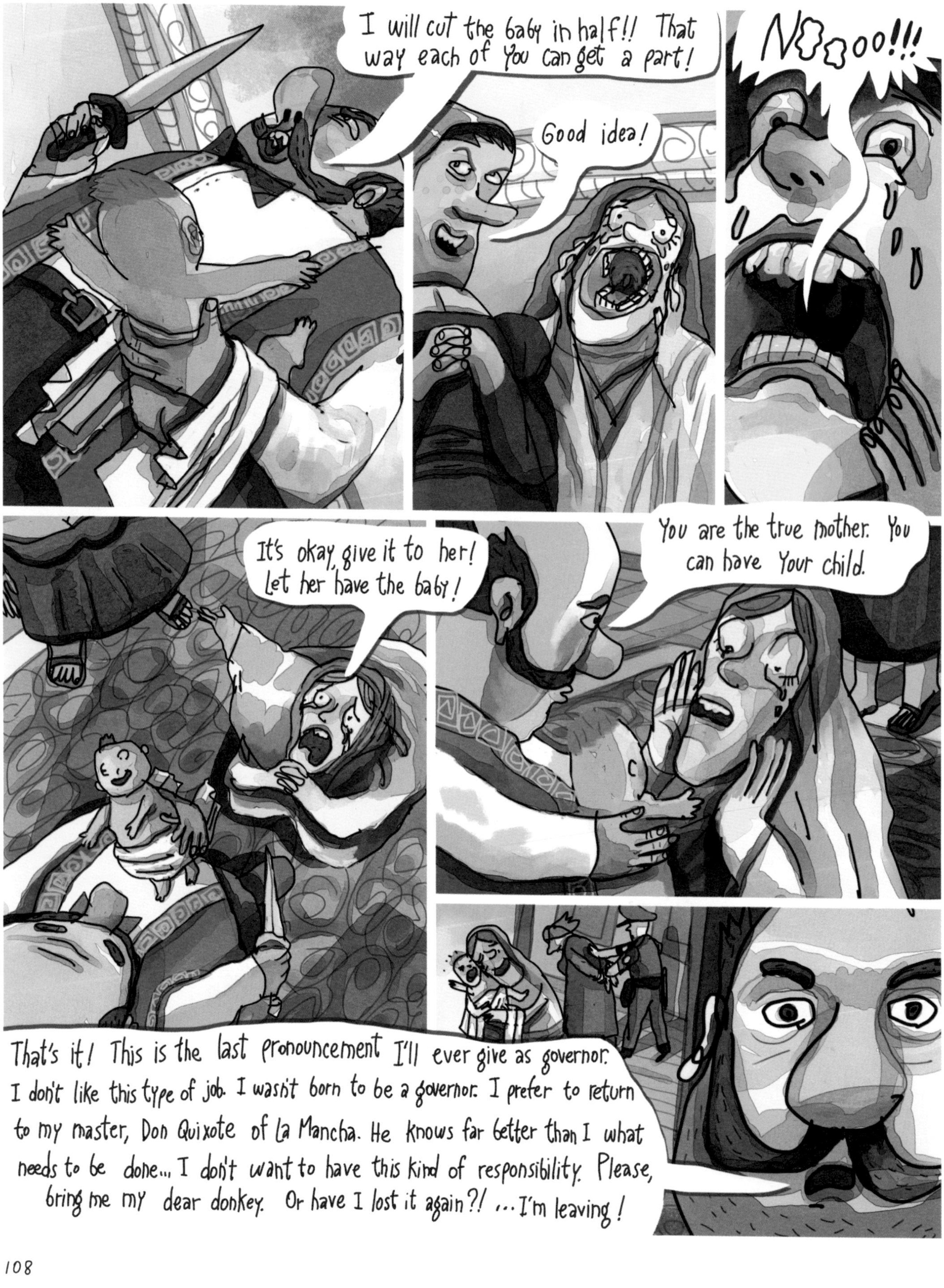
I will cut the baby in half!! That way each of you can get a part!
Good idea!
NOooo!!!
It's okay, give it to her! Let her have the baby!
You are the true mother. You can have your child.
That's it! This is the last pronouncement I'll ever give as governor. I don't like this type of job. I wasn't born to be a governor. I prefer to return to my master, Don Quixote of La Mancha. He knows far better than I what needs to be done... I don't want to have this kind of responsibility. Please, bring me my dear donkey. Or have I lost it again?! ...I'm leaving!

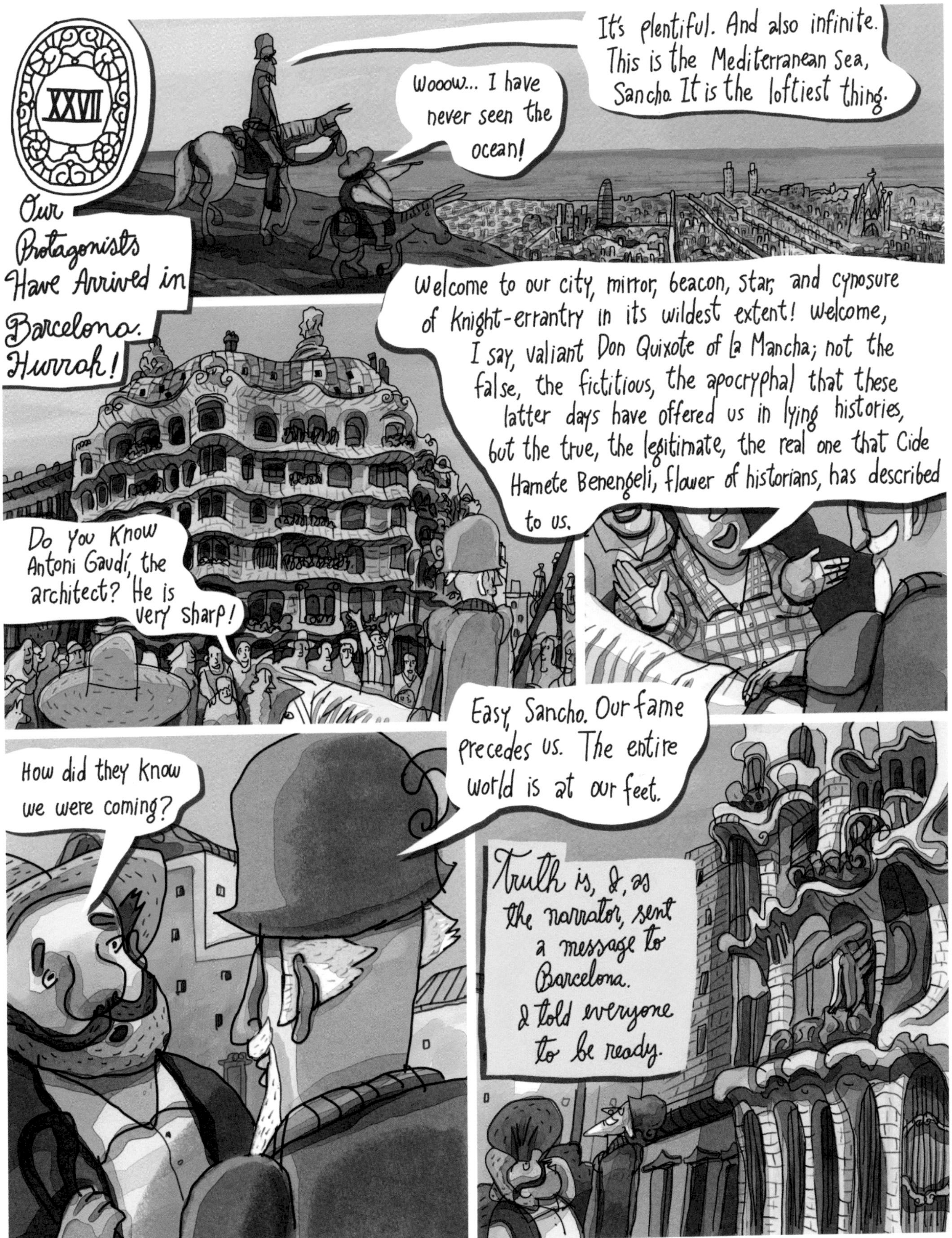
XXVII
Our Protagonists Have Arrived in Barcelona. Hurrah!
Wooow... I have never seen the ocean!
It's plentiful. And also infinite. This is the Mediterranean Sea, Sancho. It is the loftiest thing.
Welcome to our city, mirror, beacon, star, and cynosure of Knight-errantry in its wildest extent! welcome, I say, valiant Don Quixote of la Mancha; not the false, the fictitious, the apocryphal that these latter days have offered us in lying histories, but the true, the legitimate, the real one that Cide Hamete Benengeli, flower of historians, has described to us.
Do you Know Antoni Gaudí, the architect? He is very sharp!
How did they know we were coming?
Easy, Sancho. Our fame precedes us. The entire world is at our feet.
Truth is, I, as the narrator, sent a message to Barcelona. I told everyone to be ready.

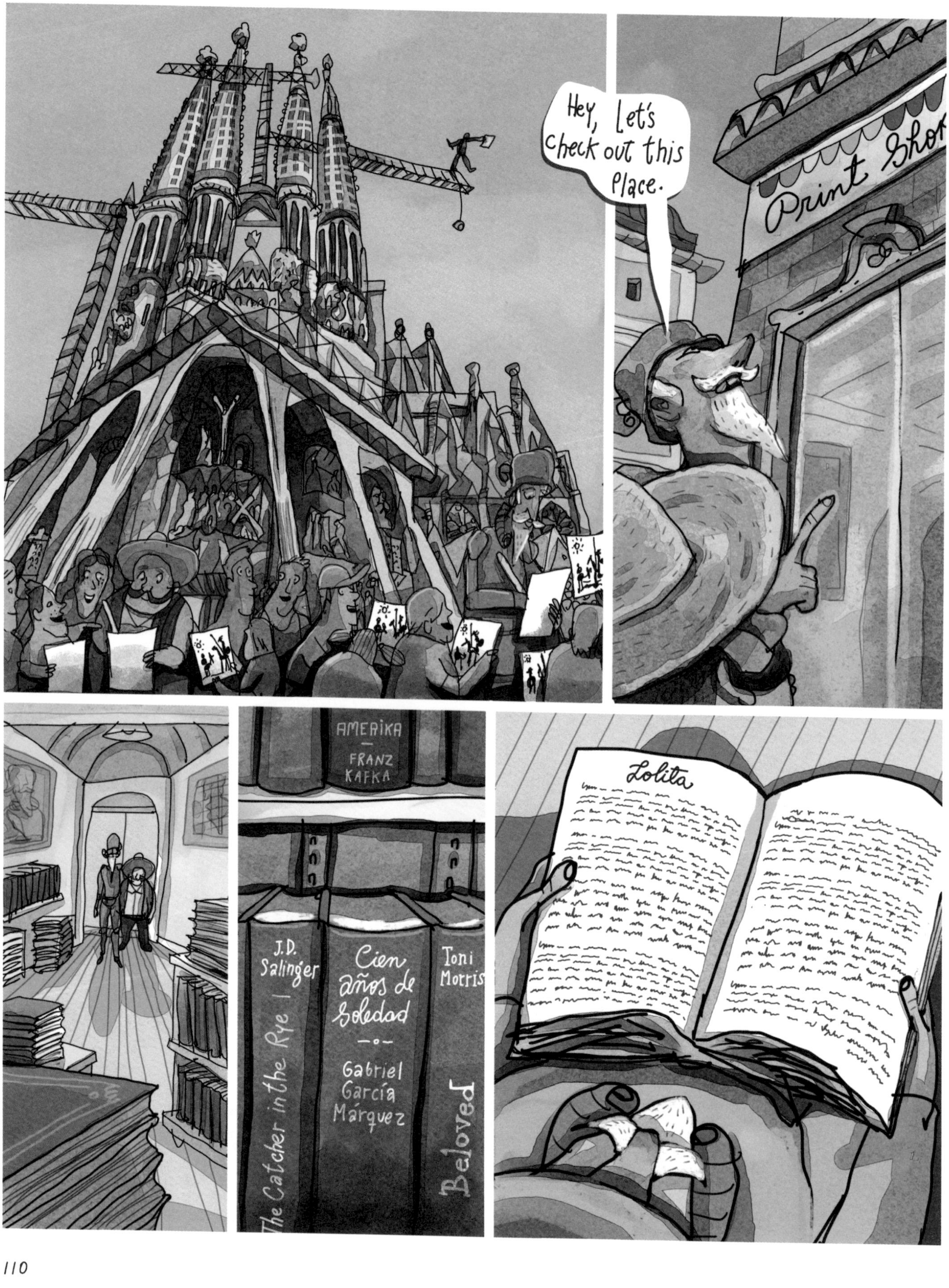
Hey, Let's check out this place.
Print Shop
AMERIKA
FRANZ KAFKA
J.D. Salinger
The Catcher in the Rye
Cien años de Soledad
Gabriel García Márquez
Toni Morris
Beloved
Lolita

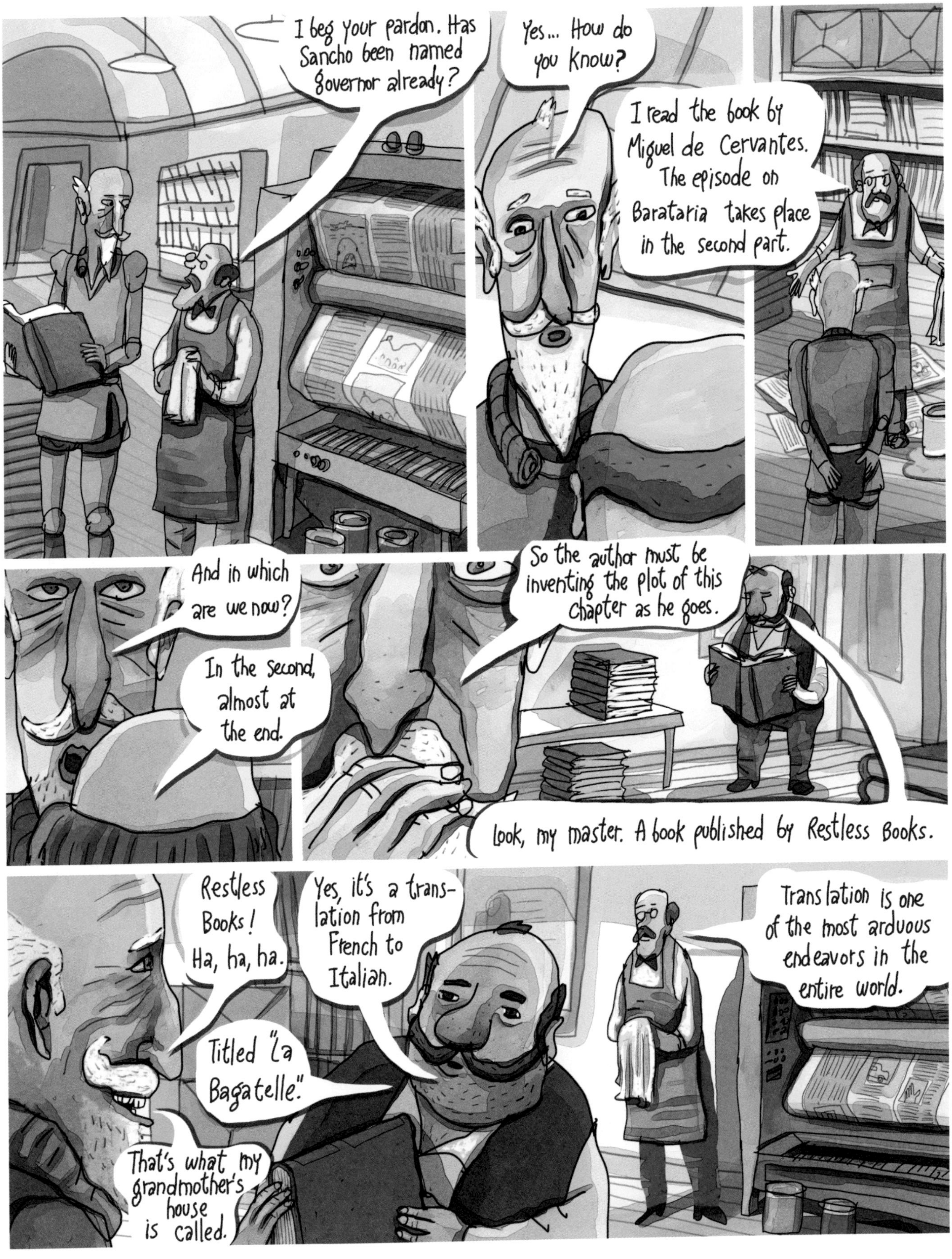
I beg your pardon. Has Sancho been named governor already?
Yes... How do you know?
I read the book by Miguel de Cervantes. The episode on Barataria takes place in the second part.
And in which are we now?
In the second, almost at the end.
So the author must be inventing the plot of this chapter as he goes.
Look, my master. A book published by Restless Books.
Restless Books! Ha, ha, ha.
Yes, it's a translation from French to Italian.
Titled "La Bagatelle."
That's what my grandmother's house is called.
Translation is one of the most arduous endeavors in the entire world.

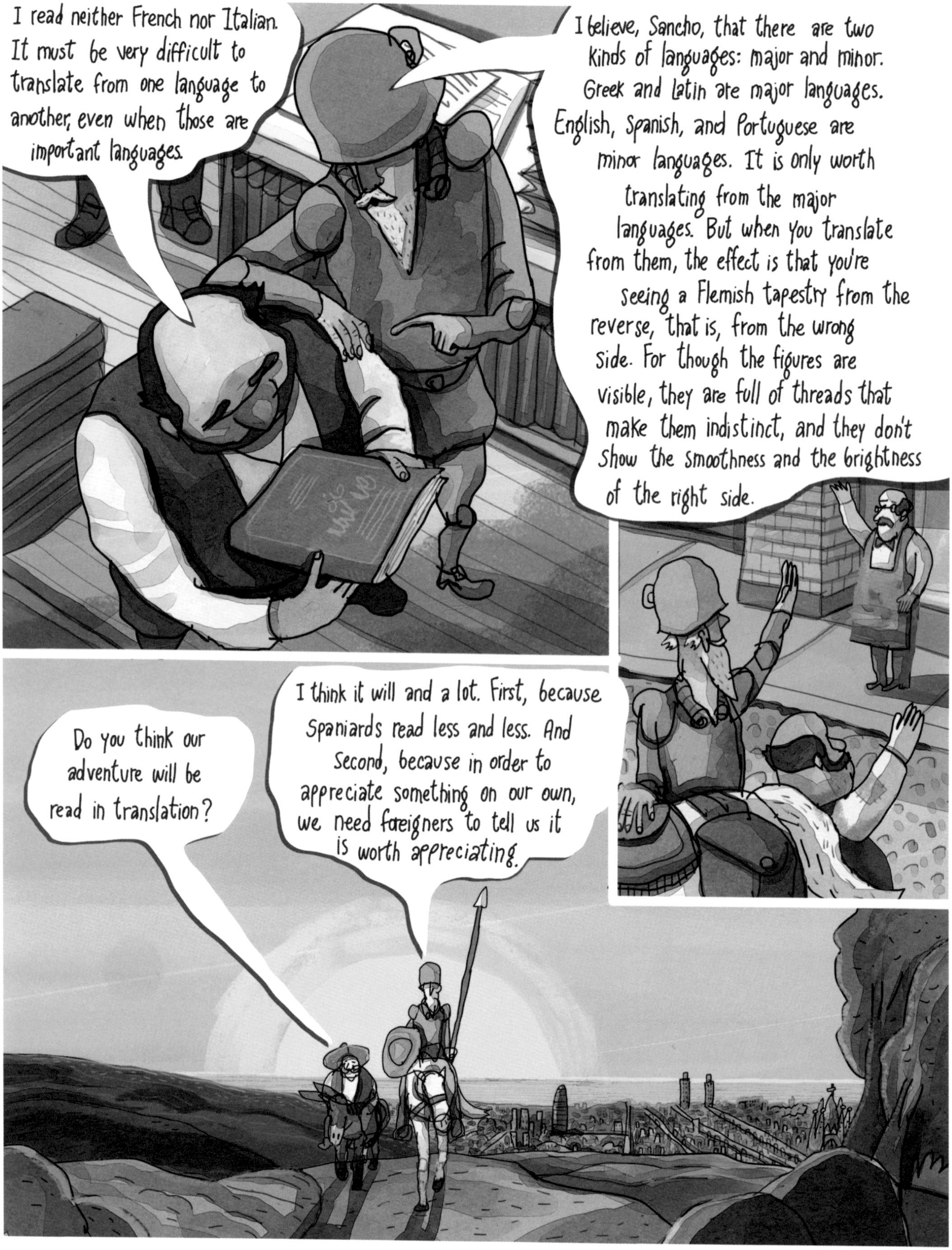
I read neither French nor Italian. It must be very difficult to translate from one language to another, even when those are important languages.
I believe, Sancho, that there are two kinds of languages: major and minor. Greek and latin are major languages. English, Spanish, and Portuguese are minor languages. It is only worth translating from the major languages. But when you translate from them, the effect is that you're seeing a Flemish tapestry from the reverse, that is, from the wrong side. For though the figures are visible, they are full of threads that make them indistinct, and they don't show the smoothness and the brightness of the right side.
Do you think our adventure will be read in translation?
I think it will and a lot. First, because Spaniards read less and less. And Second, because in order to appreciate something on our own, we need foreigners to tell us it is worth appreciating.

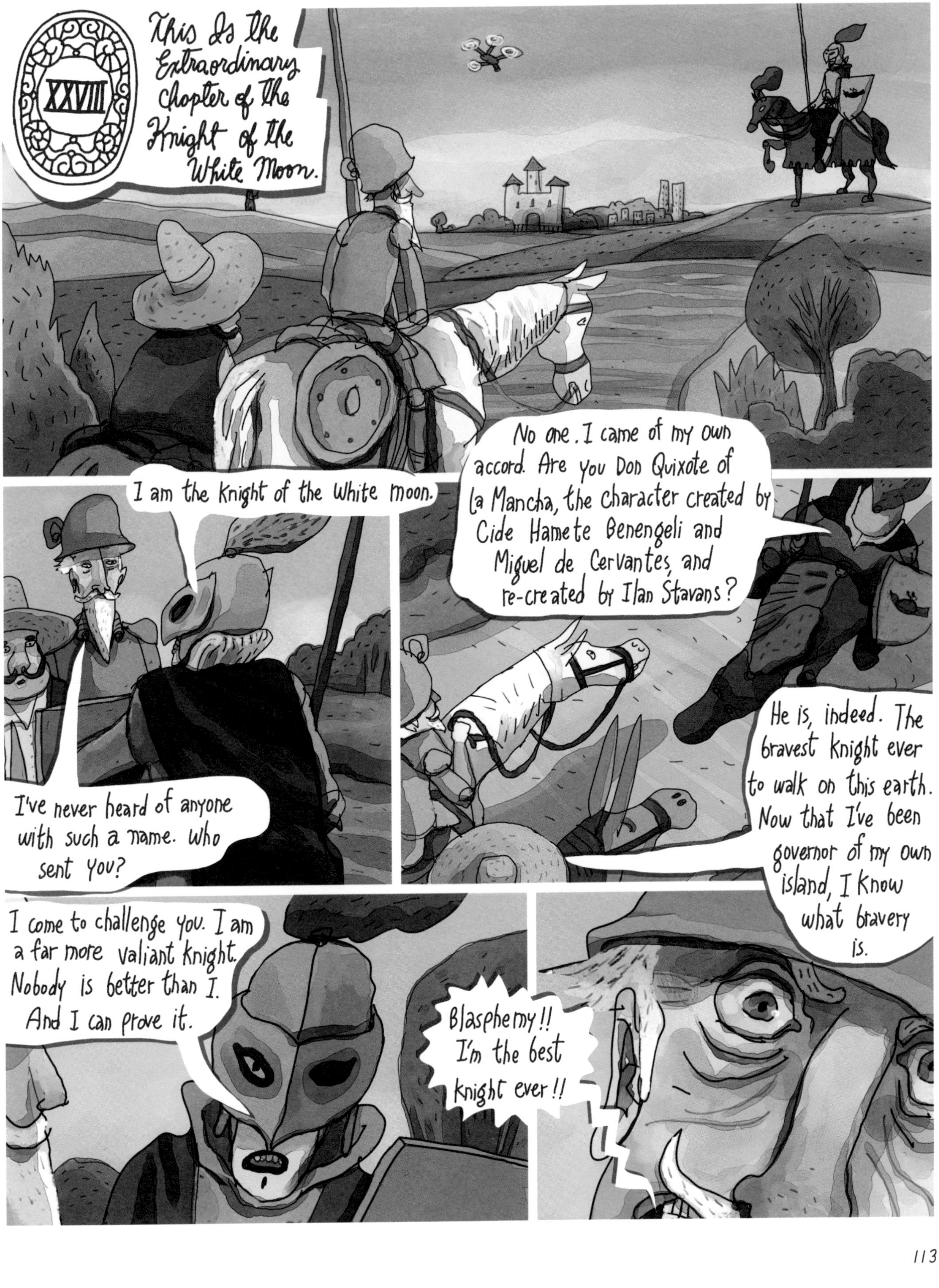
XXVIII
This Is the Extraordinary Chapter of the Knight of the White Moon.
I am the Knight of the White moon.
I've never heard of anyone with such a name. Who sent you?
No one. I came of my own accord. Are you Don Quixote of la Mancha, the character created by Cide Hamete Benengeli and Miguel de Cervantes, and re-created by Ilan Stavans?
He is, indeed. The bravest knight ever to walk on this earth. Now that I've been governor of my own island, I Know what bravery is.
I come to challenge you. I am a far more valiant knight. Nobody is better than I. And I can prove it.
Blasphemy!! I'm the best knight ever!!

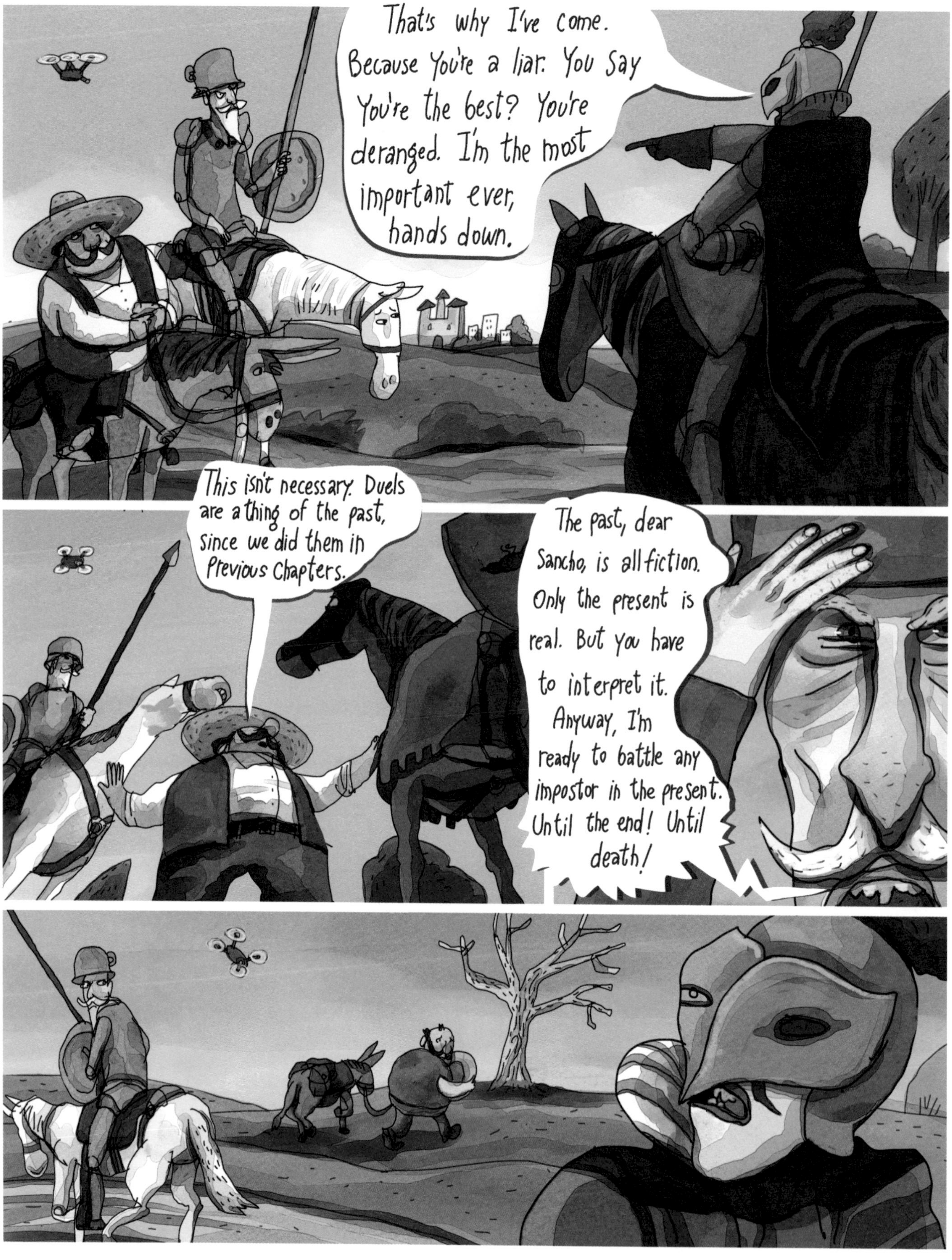
That's why I've come. Because you're a liar. You say you're the best? You're deranged. I'm the most important ever, hands down.
This isn't necessary. Duels are a thing of the past, since we did them in previous chapters.
The past, dear Sancho, is all fiction. Only the present is real. But you have to interpret it. Anyway, I'm ready to battle any impostor in the present. Until the end! Until death!

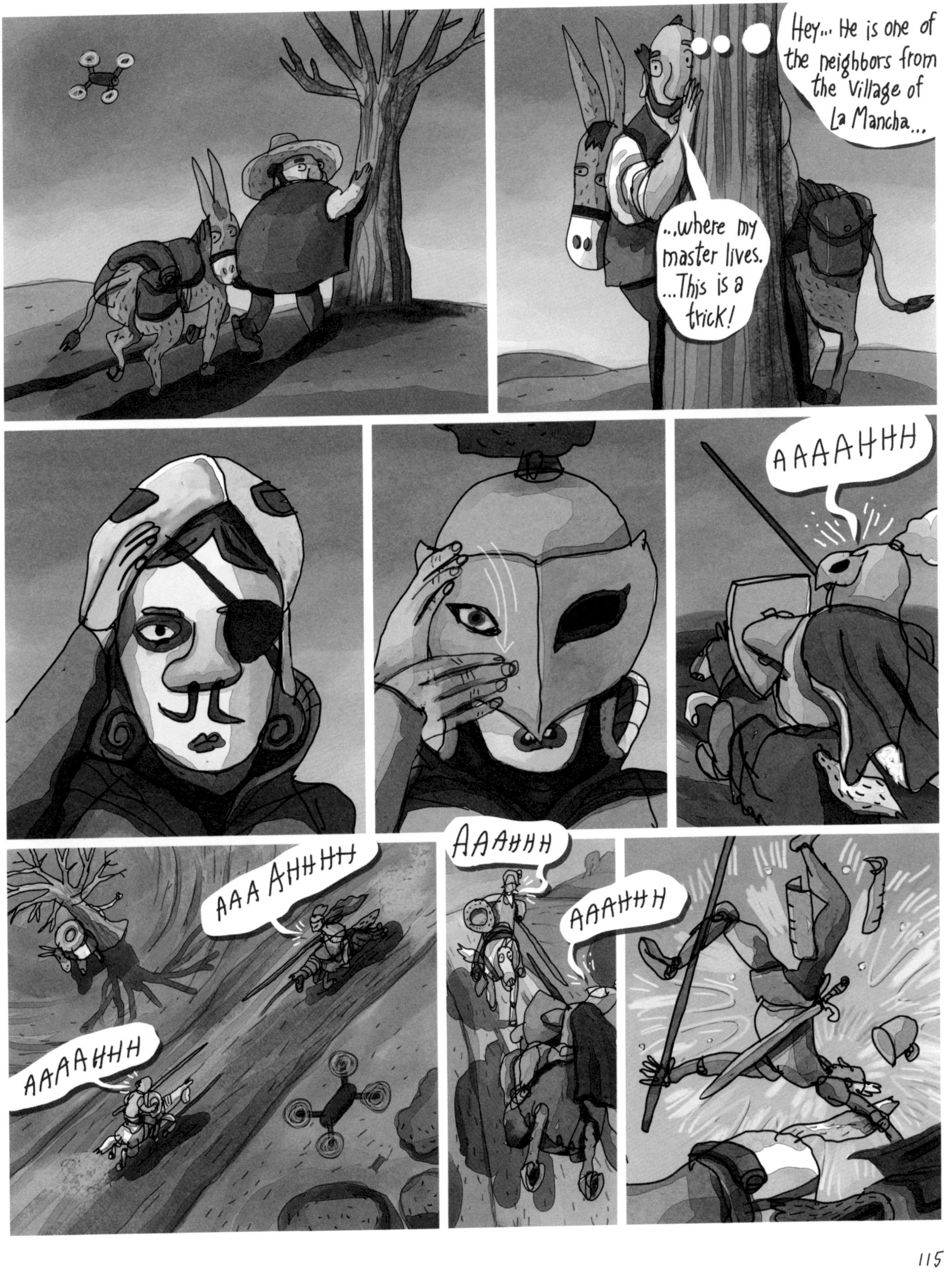
Hey... He is one of the neighbors from the Village of La Mancha...
...where my master lives. ...This is a trick!
AAAAHHH
AAA AHHHH
AAAAHHH
AAAHHH
AAAHHH

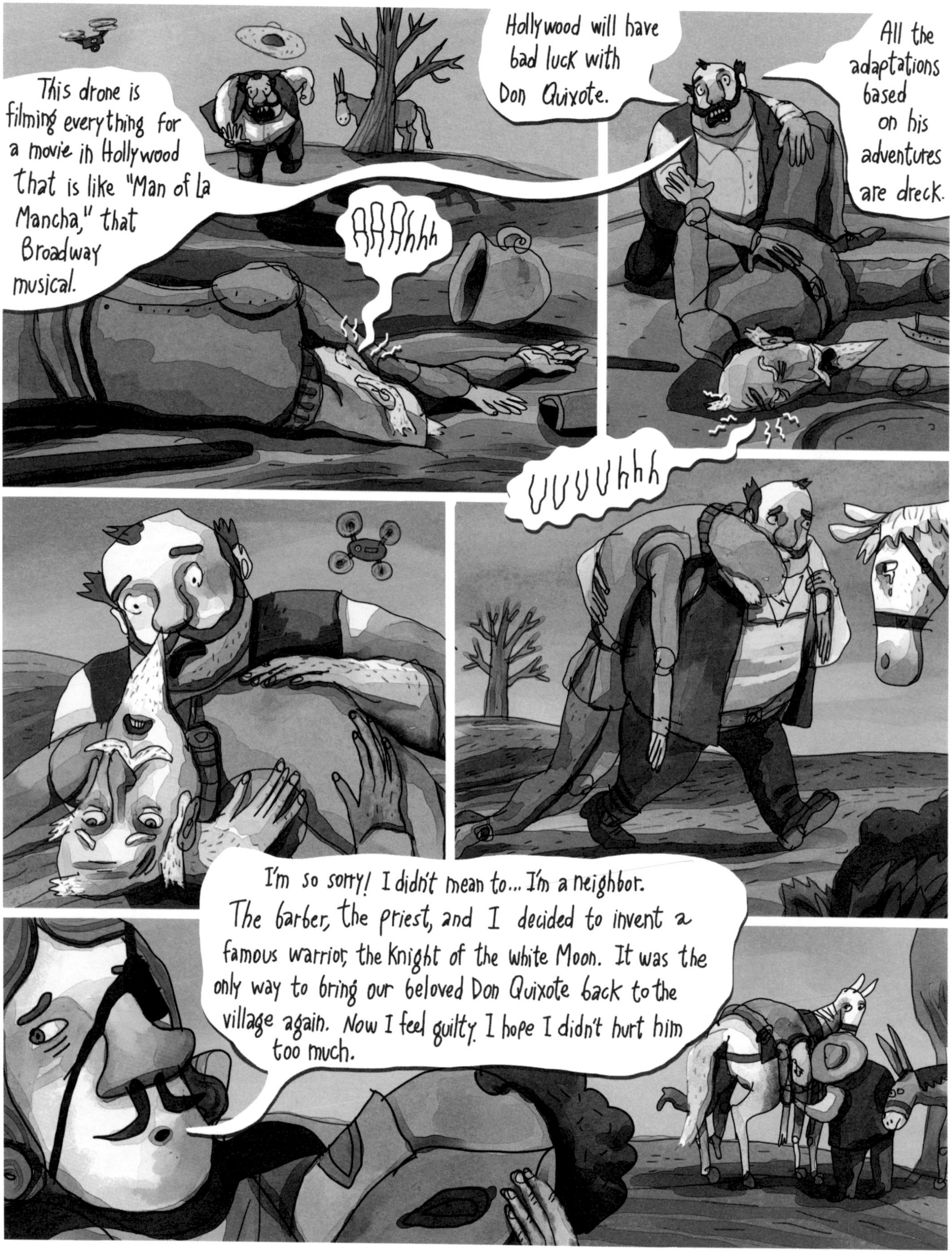

This drone is filming everything for a movie in Hollywood that is like "Man of La Mancha," that Broadway musical.
AAAhhh
Hollywood will have bad luck with Don Quixote.
All the adaptations based on his adventures are dreck.
UUUUhhh
I'm so sorry! I didn't mean to... I'm a neighbor. The barber, the priest, and I decided to invent a famous warrior, the Knight of the White Moon. It was the only way to bring our beloved Don Quixote back to the village again. Now I feel guilty. I hope I didn't hurt him too much.

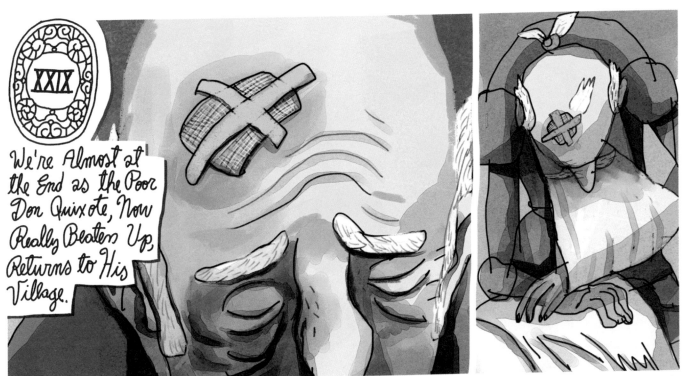

We're Almost at the End as the Poor Don Quixote, Now Really Beaten Up, Returns to His Village.

It's Don Quixote!

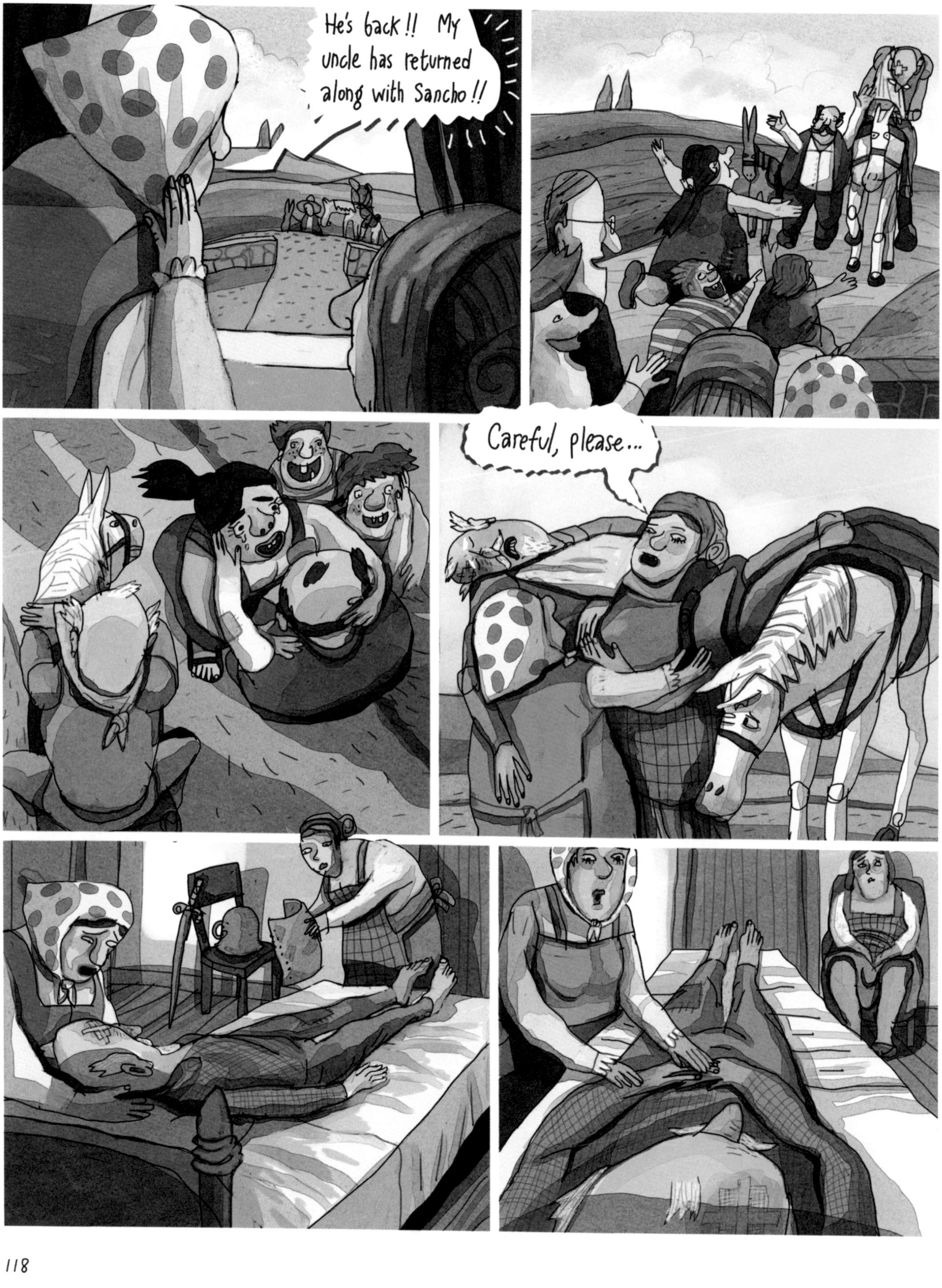
He's back!! My uncle has returned along with Sancho!!
Careful, please...

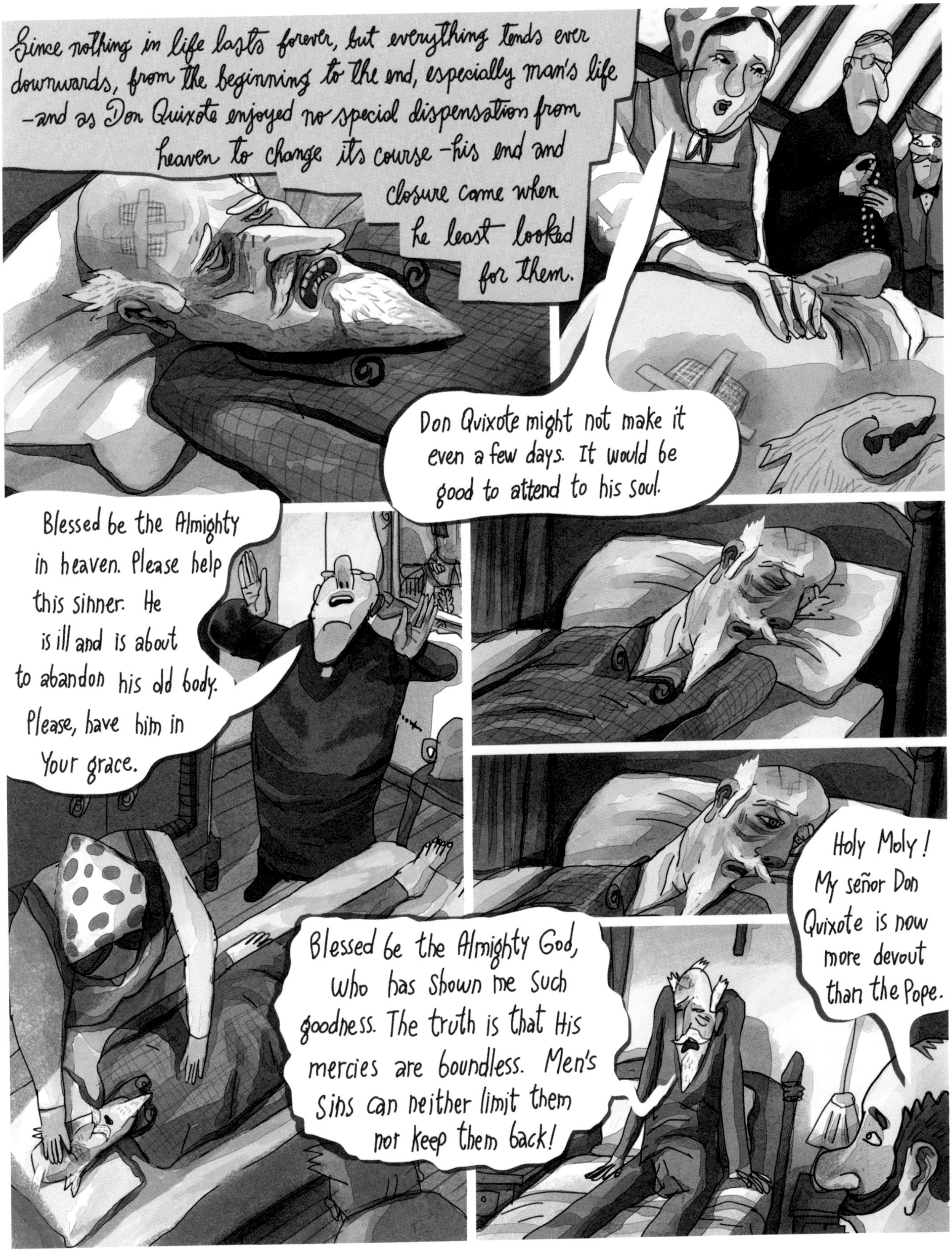
Since nothing in life lasts forever, but everything tends ever downwards, from the beginning to the end, especially man's life —and as Don Quixote enjoyed no special dispensation from heaven to change its course—his end and closure came when he least looked for them.
Don Quixote might not make it even a few days. It would be good to attend to his soul.
Blessed be the Almighty in heaven. Please help this sinner. He is ill and is about to abandon his old body. Please, have him in Your grace.
Blessed be the Almighty God, who has shown me such goodness. The truth is that His mercies are boundless. Men's sins can neither limit them nor keep them back!
Holy Moly! My señor Don Quixote is now more devout than the Pope.

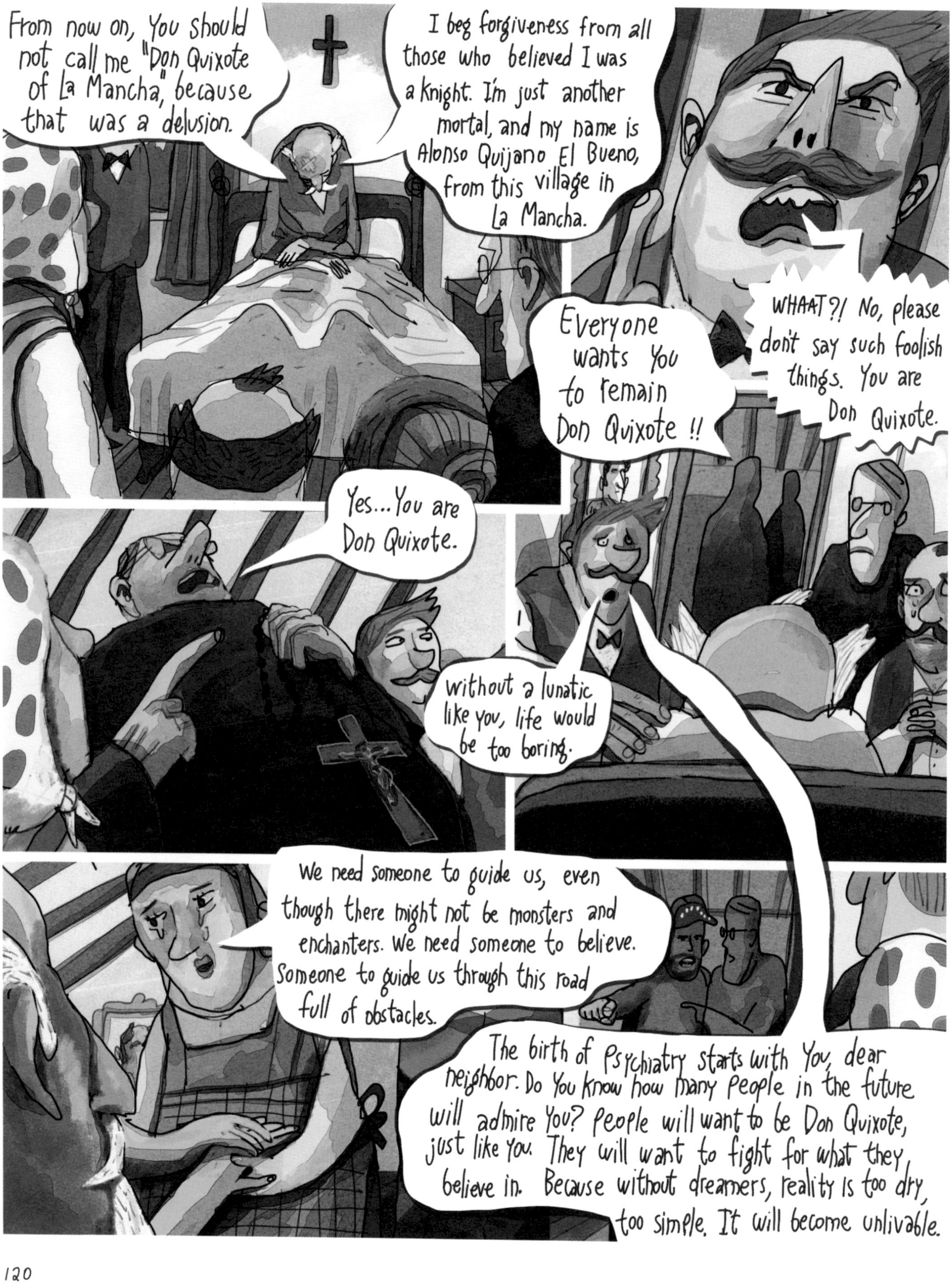
From now on, You should not call me "Don Quixote of La Mancha," because that was a delusion.
I beg forgiveness from all those who believed I was a Knight. I'm just another mortal, and my name is Alonso Quijano El Bueno, from this village in La Mancha.
WHAAT?! No, please don't say such foolish things. You are Don Quixote.
Everyone wants You to remain Don Quixote !!
Yes...You are Don Quixote.
without a lunatic like you, life would be too boring.
We need someone to guide us, even though there might not be monsters and enchanters. We need someone to believe. Someone to guide us through this road full of obstacles.
The birth of Psychiatry starts with You, dear neighbor. Do You know how many People in the future will admire You? People will want to be Don Quixote, just like You. They will want to fight for what they believe in. Because without dreamers, reality is too dry, too simple. It will become unlivable.

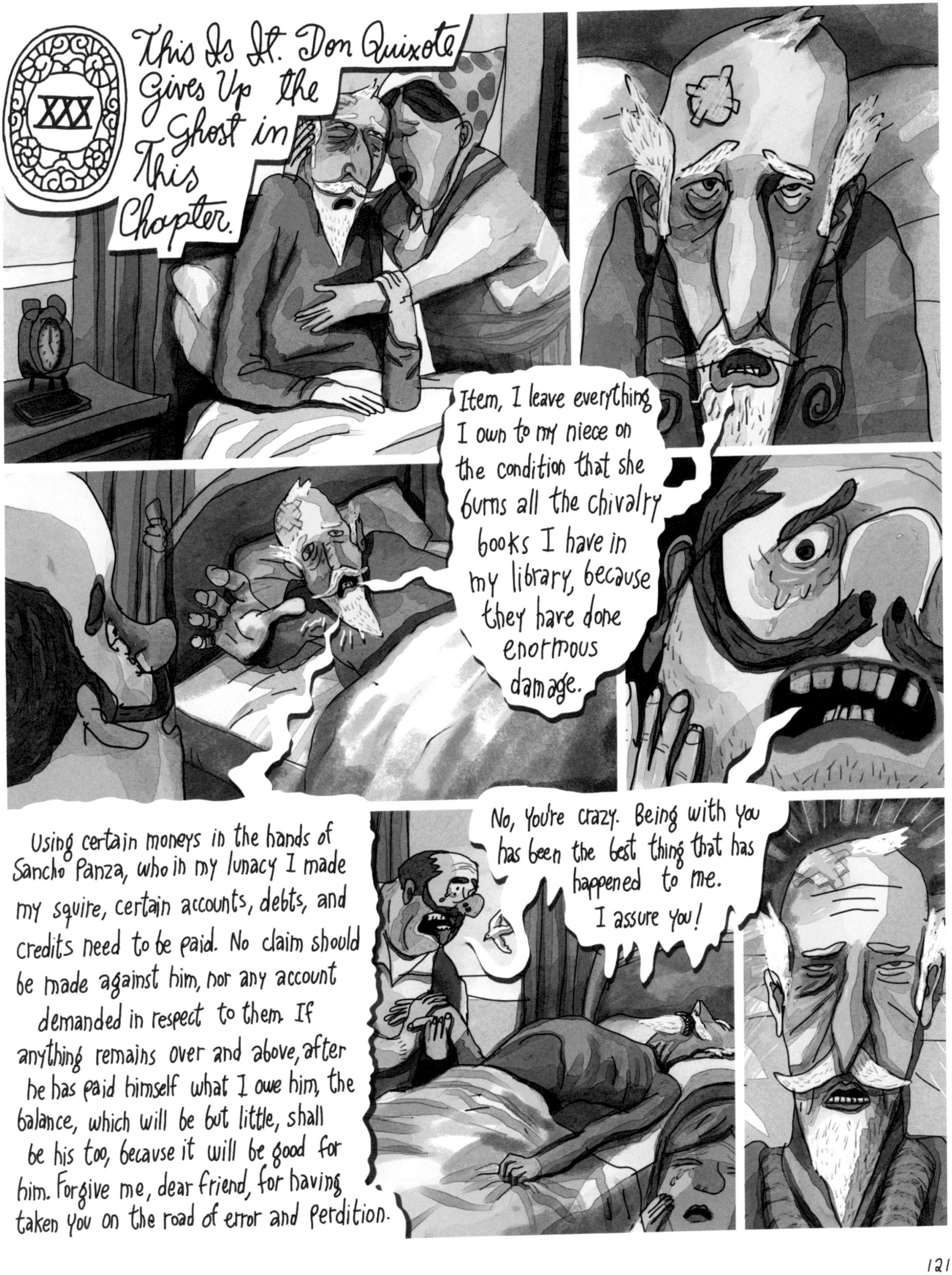
XXX
This Is It. Don Quixote Gives Up the Ghost in This Chapter.
Item, I leave everything I own to my niece on the condition that she burns all the chivalry books I have in my library, because they have done enormous damage.
Using certain moneys in the hands of Sancho Panza, who in my lunacy I made my squire, certain accounts, debts, and credits need to be paid. No claim should be made against him, nor any account demanded in respect to them. If anything remains over and above, after he has paid himself what I owe him, the balance, which will be but little, shall be his too, because it will be good for him. Forgive me, dear friend, for having taken you on the road of error and perdition.
No, You're crazy. Being with you has been the best thing that has happened to me.
I assure you!

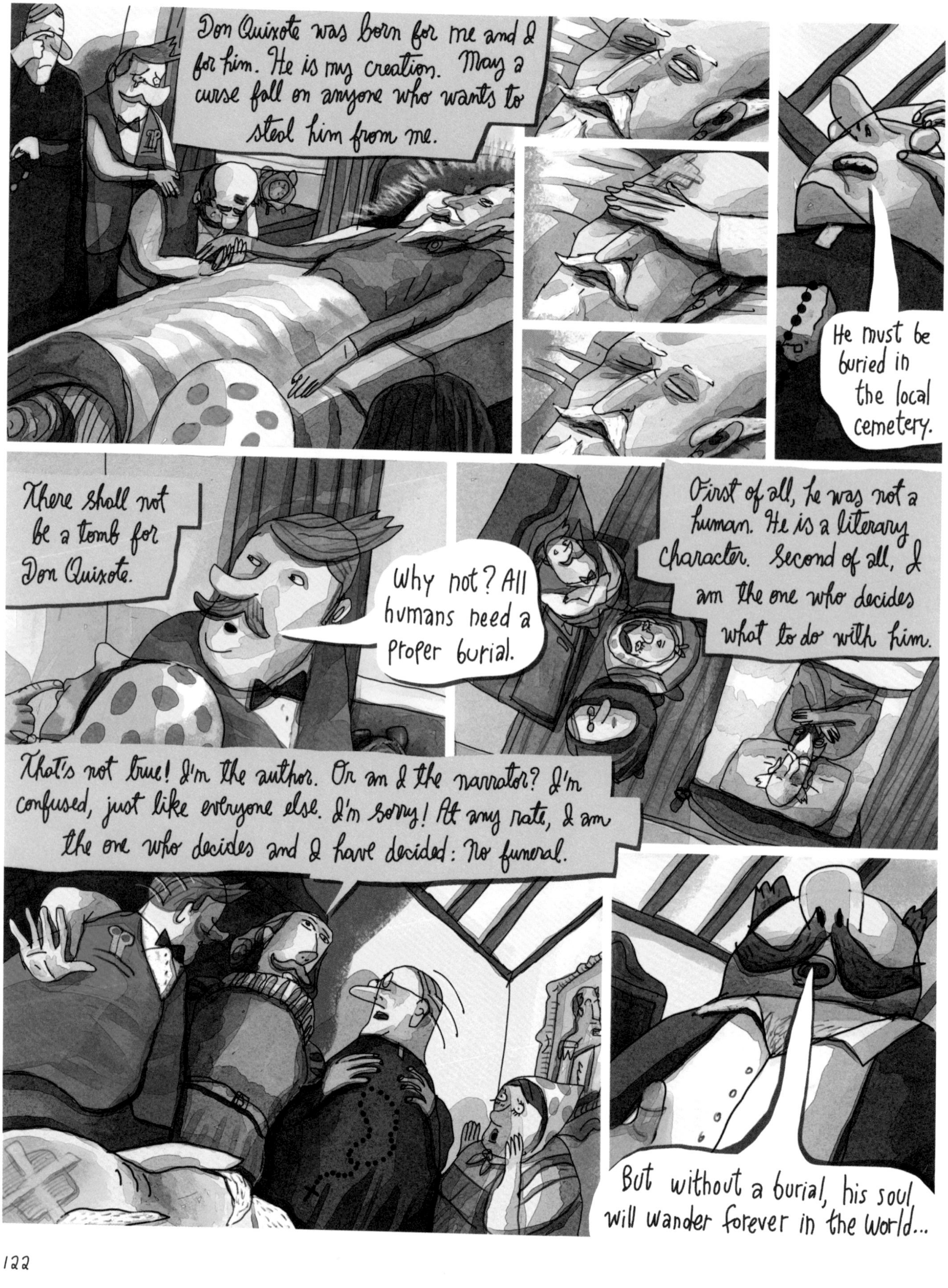
Don Quixote was born for me and I for him. He is my creation. May a curse fall on anyone who wants to steal him from me.
He must be buried in the local cemetery.
There shall not be a tomb for Don Quixote.
Why not? All humans need a proper burial.
First of all, he was not a human. He is a literary character. Second of all, I am the one who decides what to do with him.
That's not true! I'm the author. Or am I the narrator? I'm confused, just like everyone else. I'm sorry! At any rate, I am the one who decides and I have decided: No funeral.
But without a burial, his soul will wander forever in the world...

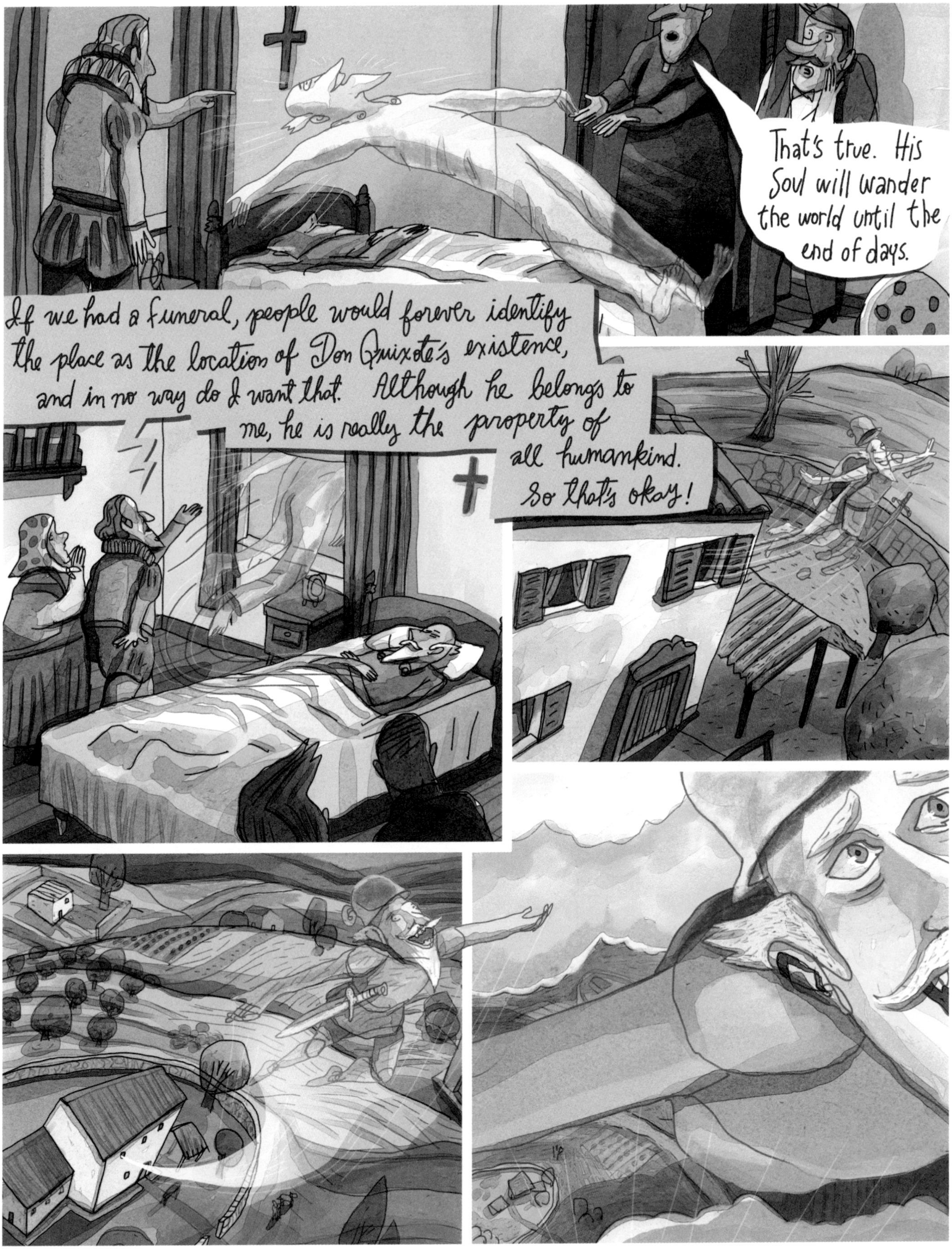

That's true. His Soul will wander the world until the end of days.
If we had a funeral, people would forever identify the place as the location of Don Quixote's existence, and in no way do I want that. Although he belongs to me, he is really the property of all humankind. So that's okay!

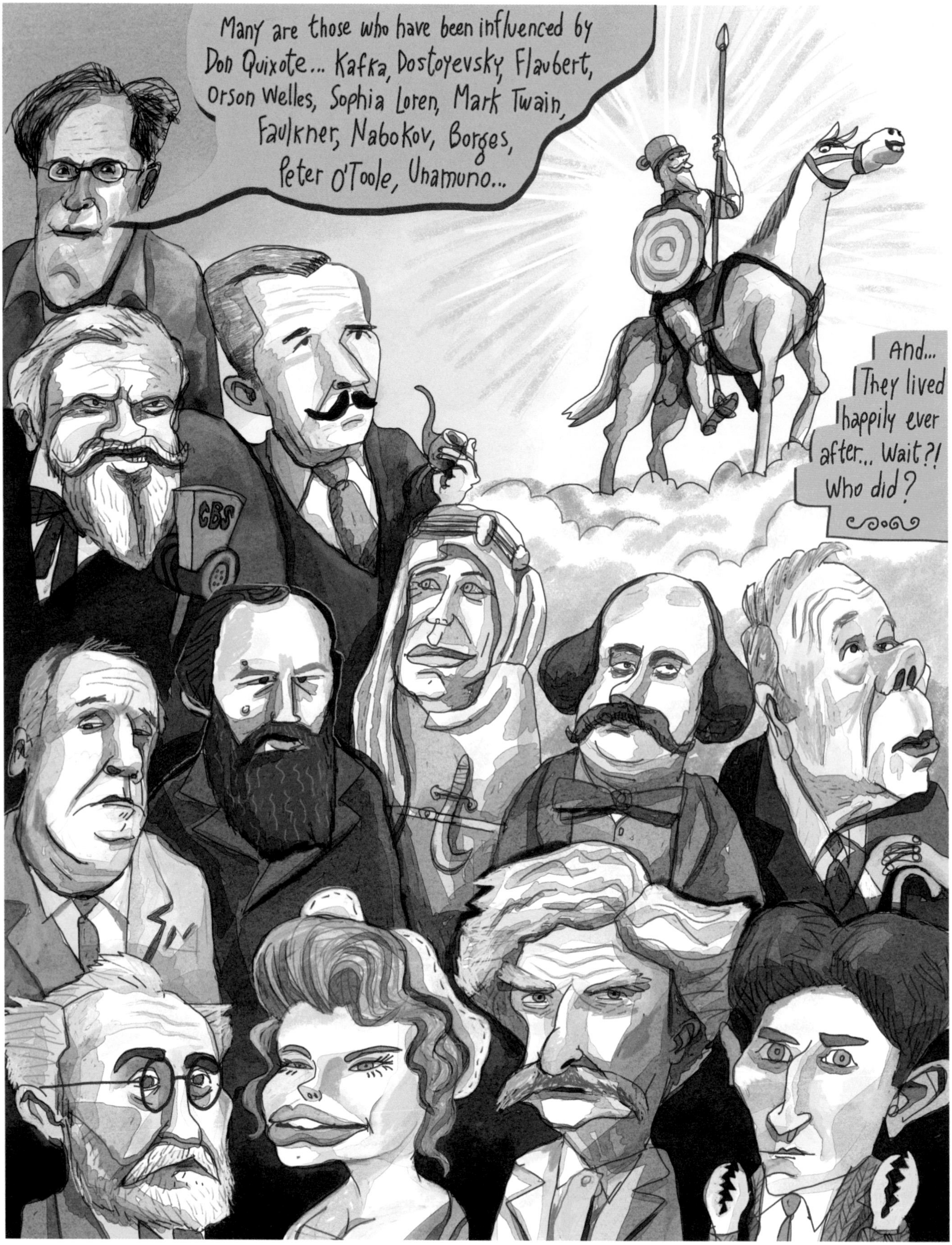
Many are those who have been influenced by Don Quixote... Kafka, Dostoyevsky, Flaubert, Orson Welles, Sophia Loren, Mark Twain, Faulkner, Nabokov, Borges, Peter O'Toole, Unamuno...
CBS
And... They lived happily ever after... Wait?! Who did?

Finis

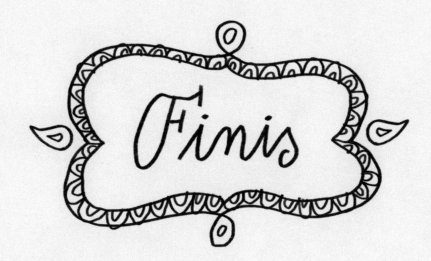